Praise for Leslie Meier and her Luc...

Silver Anniversary M...

"The frenzied pace of the city, effectively contrasted with the more tranquil atmosphere of a small town; the reappearance of familiar characters; and numerous plot twists all contribute to the appeal of this satisfying entry in a long-running series."
—*Booklist*

Turkey Trot Murder

"Timely . . . Meier's focus on racism gives this cozy a serious edge rare for this subgenre."
—*Publishers Weekly*

British Manor Murder

"Counts, countesses, and corpses highlight Lucy Stone's trip across the pond . . . A peek into British country life provides a nice break."
—*Kirkus Reviews*

Candy Corn Murder

"Meier continues to exploit the charm factor in her small-town setting, while keeping the murder plots as realistic as possible in such a cozy world." —*Booklist*

French Pastry Murder

"A delight from start to finish." —*Suspense Magazine*

Christmas Carol Murder

"Longtime Lucy Stone series readers will be happy to catch up on life in Tinker's Cove in this cozy Christmas mystery." —*Library Journal*

Easter Bunny Murder

"A fun and engaging read. It is quick and light and has enough interesting twists and turns to keep you turning the pages. If you like this type of mystery and this is your first meeting with Lucy Stone, it will probably not be your last."
—*The Barnstable Patriot*

Books by Leslie Meier

MISTLETOE MURDER
TIPPY TOE MURDER
TRICK OR TREAT MURDER
BACK TO SCHOOL MURDER
VALENTINE MURDER
CHRISTMAS COOKIE MURDER
TURKEY DAY MURDER
WEDDING DAY MURDER
BIRTHDAY PARTY MURDER
FATHER'S DAY MURDER
STAR SPANGLED MURDER
NEW YEAR'S EVE MURDER
BAKE SALE MURDER
CANDY CANE MURDER
ST. PATRICK'S DAY MURDER
MOTHER'S DAY MURDER
WICKED WITCH MURDER
GINGERBREAD COOKIE MURDER
ENGLISH TEA MURDER
CHOCOLATE COVERED MURDER
EASTER BUNNY MURDER
CHRISTMAS CAROL MURDER
FRENCH PASTRY MURDER
CANDY CORN MURDER
BRITISH MANOR MURDER
EGGNOG MURDER
TURKEY TROT MURDER
SILVER ANNIVERSARY MURDER
YULE LOG MURDER
HAUNTED HOUSE MURDER
INVITATION ONLY MURDER

Published by Kensington Publishing Corporation

'TIS THE SEASON MURDER

LESLIE MEIER

KENSINGTON BOOKS
www.kensingtonbooks.com

KENSINGTON BOOKS are published by

Kensington Publishing Corp.
119 West 40th Street
New York, NY 10018

All Kensington titles, imprints, and distributed lines are available at special quantity discounts for bulk purchases for sales promotion, premiums, fund-raising, educational, or institutional use.

Special book excerpts or customized printings can also be created to fit specific needs. For details, write or phone the office of the Kensington Sales Manager: Kensington Publishing Corp., 119 West 40th Street, New York, NY 10018. Attn. Sales Department. Phone: 1-800-221-2647.

Kensington and the K logo Reg. U.S. Pat. & TM Off.

ISBN-13: 978-1-4967-2675-9
ISBN-10: 1-4967-2675-8
Kensington Electronic Edition: November 2019

ISBN-13: 978-1-4967-2674-2
ISBN-10: 1-4967-2674-X
First Kensington Trade Paperback Printing: November 2019

10 9 8 7 6 5 4 3 2 1

Printed in the United States of America

Contents

NEW YEAR'S EVE
MURDER

Chapter One

WIN A WINTER MAKEOVER FOR YOU

AND YOUR MOM!

A solid month of baking and chasing bargains and wrapping and decorating and secret keeping and it all came down to this: a pile of torn wrapping paper under the Christmas tree, holiday plates scattered with crumbs and half-eaten cookies, punch cups filmed with egg nog, and sitting on one end table, a candy dish holding a pristine and untouched pyramid of ribbon candy. And then there was that awful letter. Why did it have to come on Christmas Eve, just in time to cast a pall over the holiday?

Lucy Stone shook out a plastic trash bag and bent down to scoop up the torn paper, only to discover the family's pet puppy, Libby, had made herself a nest of Christmas wrap and was curled up, sound asleep. No wonder. With all the excitement of opening presents, tantalizing cooking smells, and people coming and going, it had been an exhausting day for her.

Lucy stroked the little Lab's silky head and decided to leave the mess a bit longer. Best to let sleeping dogs lie, especially if the sleeping dog in question happened to be seven months old and increasingly given to bouts of manic activity, which included chewing shoes and furniture. She turned instead to the coffee table and started stacking plates and cups, then sat down on the sofa as a wave of exhaustion overtook her. It had been a long day. Zoe, her youngest at only eight years old, had awoken early and roused the rest of the house. Sara, fourteen, hadn't minded, but their older sister, Elizabeth, protested the early hour. She was home for Christmas break from Chamberlain College in Boston, where she was a sophomore, and had stayed out late on Christmas Eve catching up with her old high school friends.

She had finally given in and gotten out of bed after a half-hour of coaxing, and the Christmas morning orgy of exchanging presents had begun. What had they been thinking, wondered Lucy, dreading the credit card bills that would arrive as certainly as snow in January. She and Bill had really gone overboard this year, buying skis for Elizabeth and high-tech ice skates for Sara and Zoe. When their oldest child, Toby, arrived later in the day with his fiancée, Molly, they had presented him with a snowboard and her with a luxurious cashmere sweater. And those were only the big presents. There had been all the budget-busting books, CDs, video games, sweaters, and pajamas, right on down to the chocolate oranges and lip balm tucked in the toe of each bulging Christmas stocking.

It all must have cost a fortune, guessed Lucy, who had lost track of the actual total sometime around December 18. Oh, sure, it had been great fun for the hour or two it took to open all the presents, but those credit card balances would linger for months. And what was she going to do about the letter? It was from the financial aid office at Chamberlain College advising her that they had reviewed the family's finances and had cut Elizabeth's aid package by ten thousand dollars. That meant they had to come up with the money or Elizabeth would have to leave school.

She guiltily fingered the diamond studs Bill had surprised her with, saying they were a reward for all the Christmases he was only able to give her a handmade coupon book of promises after they finished buying presents for the kids. It was a lovely gesture, but she knew they couldn't really afford it. She wasn't even sure he had work lined up for the winter. The economy was supposed to be recovering, but like many in the little town of Tinker's Cove, Maine, Bill was self-employed. Over the years he had built a solid reputation as a restoration carpenter, renovating rundown older homes for city folks who wanted a vacation home by the shore. Last year, when the stock market was soaring he had made plenty of money, which was probably why the financial aid office had decided they could afford to pay more. But even last year, Bill's best year ever, they had struggled to meet Elizabeth's college expenses. Now that the Dow was hovering well below its former dizzying heights, Bill's earnings had dropped dramatically. The economists called it a "correction" but it had been a disaster for vacation communities like Tinker's Cove, as the big city lawyers and bankers and stockbrokers who were the mainstay of the second home market found themselves without the fat bonus checks they were counting on.

The sensible course would be to return the earrings to the store for a refund, but that was out of the question. She remembered how excited Bill had been when he gave her the little box and how pleased he'd been at her surprised reaction when she opened it and found the sparkling earrings. All she'd hoped for, really, was a new flannel nightgown. But now she had diamond earrings. He'd also written a private note, apologizing for all the years he'd taken her for granted, like one of the kids. But they had surprised her, too, with their presents. Toby and Molly had given her a pair of buttery soft kid gloves, Elizabeth had presented her with a jar of luxurious lavender body lotion from a trendy Newbury Street shop, Sara had put together a tape of her favorite songs to play in the car and Zoe had found a calendar with photos of Labrador puppies—all presents that had delighted her because they showed a lot of thought.

So how was she repaying them for all their love and thoughtfulness? In just a short while she was going off to New York City with Elizabeth and leaving the rest of the family to fend for themselves. Really abandoning them for most of their Christmas vacation. The bags were packed and standing ready in the hallway; they would leave as soon as Elizabeth returned from saying goodbye to her friends.

She had been thrilled when Elizabeth announced she had entered a *Jolie* magazine contest and won winter makeovers for herself and her mother. Not only was she enormously proud of her clever daughter but at first she was excited at the prospect of the makeover itself. What working mother wouldn't enjoy a few days of luxurious pampering? But now she wished she could convert the prize into cash. Besides, how would Bill manage without her? What would Zoe and Sara do all day? Watch TV? That was no way to spend a week-long holiday from school.

Also, worried Lucy, checking to make sure the earrings were still firmly in place, what if the supposedly "all-expense paid" makeover wasn't quite as "all-expense paid" as promised? Traveling was expensive—there were always those little incidentals, like tips and magazines and mints and even airplane meals, now that you had to buy them, that added up. What if it turned out to be like those "free" facials at the make-up counter where the sales associates pressured you to buy a lot of expensive products that you would never use again?

Lucy sighed. To tell the truth, she was a little uneasy about the whole concept of being made over. There was nothing the matter with her. She stood up and looked at her reflection in the mirror that hung over the couch. She looked fine. Not perfect, of course. She was getting a few crow's feet, there were a few gray hairs and that stubborn five pounds she couldn't seem to lose, but she was neat and trim and could still fit in the sparkly Christmas sweatshirt the kids had given her years ago. And since she only wore it a few times a year it still looked as festive as ever.

Now that she was actually giving it a critical eye, she could understand why her friend Sue always teased her about the sweatshirt. It was boxy and didn't do a thing for her figure. Furthermore, it was the height of kitsch, featuring a bright green Christmas tree decorated with sequins, beads, and bows. Not the least bit sophisticated.

She sighed. She hadn't always been a country mouse; she'd grown up in a suburb of the city and had made frequent forays with her mother, and later with her friends, to shop, see a show, or visit a museum. It would be fun to go back to New York, especially since she hadn't been in years. And she was looking forward to a reunion with her old college buddy, Samantha Blackwell. They had been faithful correspondents through the years, apparently both stuck in the days when people wrote letters, but had never gotten in the habit of telephoning each other. Caught in busy lives with numerous responsibilities, they'd never been able to visit each other, despite numerous attempts. Lucy had married right out of college and moved to Maine, where she started a family and worked as a part-time reporter for the local weekly newspaper. Sam had been one of a handful of pioneering women accepted to study for the ministry at Union Theological Seminary and had promptly fulfilled the reluctant admission officer's misgivings by dropping out when she met her lawyer husband, Brad. She now worked for the International AIDS Foundation, and Lucy couldn't wait to see her and renew their friendship.

Which reminded her, she hadn't had a chance yet today to call her friends to wish them a Merry Christmas. That was one holiday tradition she really enjoyed. She sat back down on the couch and reached for the phone, dialing Sue Finch's number.

"Are you all ready for the trip?" asked Sue, after they'd gotten the formalities out of the way.

"All packed and ready to go."

"I hope you left room in your suitcase so you can take advantage of the after-Christmas sales. Sidra says they're fabulous."

Sidra, Sue's daughter, lived in New York with her husband, Geoff Rumford, and was an assistant producer of the *Norah!* TV show.

"No sales for me." Lucy didn't want the whole town to know about the family's finances, so she prevaricated. "I think I'll be too busy."

"They can't keep you busy every minute."

"I think they intend to. We're catching the ten o'clock flight out of Portland tonight so we can make a fashion show breakfast first thing tomorrow morning, then there are numerous expert consultations, a spa afternoon, photo sessions, and interviews. I'm worried I won't even have time to see Sam." She paused. "And if I do have some free time, I'm planning to visit some museums like the Met and MoMA. . . ."

Sue, who lived to shop, couldn't believe this heresy. "But what about Bloomingdale's?"

"I've spent quite enough on Christmas as it is," said Lucy. "I've got to economize."

"Sure," acknowledged Sue, "but you have to spend money to save it."

It was exactly this sort of logic that had led her into spending too much on Christmas in the first place, thought Lucy, but she wasn't about to argue. "If you say so," she laughed. "I've got to go. Someone's on call waiting."

It was Rachel Goodman, another member of the group of four that met for breakfast each week at Jake's Donut Shack.

"Did Santa bring you anything special?" asked Rachel.

Something in her tone made Lucy suspicious. "How did you know?"

"Bill asked me to help pick them out. Do you like them?"

"I love them, but he shouldn't have spent so much."

"I told him you'd be happy with pearls," said Rachel, "but he insisted on the diamonds. He was really cute about it. He said he wanted you to wear them in New York."

This was a whole new side of Bill that Lucy wasn't familiar with. She wasn't sure she could get used to this sensitive, considerate Bill. She wondered fleetingly if he was having some sort of midlife crisis.

"Aw, gee, you know I'm really having second thoughts about this trip."

"Of course you are."

Lucy wondered if Rachel knew more than she was letting on. "What do you mean?"

"Haven't you heard? There's this awful flu going around."

"What flu?"

"It's an epidemic. I read about it in the *New York Times*. They're advising everyone to avoid crowds and wash their hands frequently."

"How do you avoid crowds in a city?"

"I don't know, but I think you should try. Flu can be serious. It kills thousands of people every year."

"That was 1918," scoffed Lucy.

"Laugh if you want. I'm only trying to help."

Lucy immediately felt terrible for hurting Rachel's feelings. "I know, and I appreciate it. I really do."

"Promise you'll take precautions?"

"Sure. And thanks for the warning."

She was wondering whether she should buy some disinfectant wipes as she dialed Pam's number. Pam, also a member of the breakfast group, was married to Lucy's boss at the newspaper, Ted Stillings, and was a great believer in natural remedies.

"Disinfectant wipes? Are you crazy? That sort of thing just weakens your immune system."

"Rachel says there's a flu epidemic and I have to watch out for germs."

"How are you supposed to do that? The world is full of millions, billions, zillions of germs that are invisible to the human eye. If Mother Nature intended us to watch out for them, don't you think she would have made them bigger, like mosquitoes or spiders?"

It was a frightening picture. "I never thought of that."

"Well, trust me, Mother Nature did. She gave you a fabulous immune system to protect the Good Body." That's how Pam pronounced it, with capital letter emphasis. "Your immune system worries about the germs so you don't have to."

"If that's true, how come so many people get sick?"

"People get sick because they abuse their bodies. They pollute their Good Bodies with empty calories and preservatives instead of natural whole foods, they don't get enough sleep, they don't take care of themselves." Pam huffed. "You have to help Mother Nature. She can't do it all, you know."

"Okay. How do I help her?"

"One thing you can do is take vitamin C. It gives the immune system a boost. That's what I'd do if I were you, especially since you're going into a new environment that might stress your organic equilibrium."

Lucy was picturing a dusty brown bottle in the back of the medicine cabinet. "You know, I think I've got some. Now I just have to remember to take it. It looks like we're going to be pretty busy with this makeover."

"Don't let them go crazy with eye shadow and stuff," advised Pam.

"Is it bad for you?"

"It's probably a germ farm, especially if they use it on more than one person, but that isn't what I was thinking about." She paused, choosing her words. "You're beautiful already. You don't need that stuff."

"Why, thanks, Pam," said Lucy, surprised at the compliment.

"I mean it. Beauty comes from inside. It doesn't come from lipstick and stuff."

"That's the way it ought to be," said Lucy, "but lately I've been noticing some wrinkles and gray hairs, and I don't like them. Maybe they'll have some ideas that can help."

"Those things are signs of character. You've earned those wrinkles and gray hairs!"

"And the mommy tummy, too, but I'm not crazy about it."

"Don't even think about liposuction," warned Pam, horrified. "Promise?"

"Believe me, it's not an option," said Lucy, hearing Bill's footsteps in the kitchen. "I've got to go."

When she looked up he was standing in the doorway, dressed in his Christmas red plaid flannel shirt and new corduroy pants. He was holding a small box wrapped with a red bow, and her heart sank. "Not another present!"

"It's something special I picked up for you."

Lucy couldn't hide her dismay. "But we've spent so much already. We'll be lucky to get this year's bills paid off before next Christmas!" She paused, considering. There was no sense in putting it off any longer. "And Elizabeth's tuition bill came yesterday. Chamberlain College wants sixteen thousand dollars by January 6. That's ten thousand more than we were expecting to pay. Ten thousand more than we have."

He sat down next to her on the couch. "It's not the end of the world, Lucy. She can take a year off and work."

"At what? There are no good jobs around here."

"She could work in Boston."

"She'd be lucky to earn enough to cover her rent! She'd never be able to save."

Bill sighed. "I know giving the kids college educations is important to you, Lucy, but I don't see what it did for us. I'm not convinced it really is a good investment—not at these prices."

Lucy had heard him say the same thing many times, and it always made her angry.

"That's a cop-out, and you know it. It's our responsibility as parents to give our kids every opportunity we can." She sighed. "I admit it doesn't always work out. Toby hated college; it wasn't for him. And that's okay. But Elizabeth's been doing so well. It makes me sick to think she'll have to drop out."

Bill put his arm around her shoulder. "We'll figure something out . . . or we won't. There's nothing we can do about it right now. Open your present."

Lucy's eyes met his, and something inside her began to melt. She reached up and stroked his beard. "You've given me too much already."

"It's all right, really," said Bill, placing the little box in her hand. "Trust me."

"Okay." Lucy prepared herself to accept another lavish gift, promising herself that she would quietly return it for a refund when she got back from New York. What could it be? A diamond pendant to match the earrings? A gold bangle? What had he gone and done? She set the box in her lap and pulled the ends of the red satin bow. She took a deep breath and lifted the top, then pushed the cotton batting aside.

"Oh my goodness," she said, discovering a bright red plastic watch wrapped in cellophane. "It's got lobster hands."

"That's because it's a lobster watch," said Bill. "They gave them out at the hardware store. Do you like it?"

"Like it? I love it," she said. "I think it makes quite a fashion statement."

"And it tells time," said Bill, pulling her close.

Lucy took a second look at the watch. "Was it really free?"

"Absolutely. Positively. Completely."

"I'll wear it the whole time I'm away," said Lucy. "I'll be counting the minutes until I get home."

"That's the idea," said Bill, nuzzling her neck.

The wrapping paper underneath the tree crinkled and rustled as Libby rolled over. Instinctively, just as they had when they'd briefly shared their bedroom with the newest baby, they held their breaths, afraid she would wake up. They waited until she let out a big doggy sigh and her breathing became deep and regular, then they tiptoed out of the living room.

As they joined Sara and Zoe in the family room, where they were watching *A Christmas Story,* Lucy resolved to enjoy the few remaining hours of Christmas. She'd have plenty of time on the plane to break the news to Elizabeth and to try to come up with a solution. A ten-thousand-dollar solution.

Chapter Two

THE ONE BEAUTY AID YOU CAN'T LEAVE
HOME WITHOUT!

"Mom, we have to turn back. I forgot something."

Lucy and Elizabeth were driving through the prime-time darkness, approaching the on ramp to the interstate. They were running late because Elizabeth's round of farewells had taken longer than expected. When she'd finally arrived home she decided the clothes she'd packed were all wrong for New York City. The result was a frantic rush to get organized at the last minute.

"What did you forget?" demanded Lucy, slamming on the brakes and pulling to the side of the road. "Your asthma medicine? Your contacts?"

"Water."

Lucy couldn't believe her ears. "Water?"

"Yeah. In the last issue of *Jolie* they said you should take it along whenever you fly. Flying is very dehydrating and you need to drink lots of water." Elizabeth flipped down the visor and checked her reflection in the mirror. "Especially if you're older, Mom."

Lucy signaled and eased the Subaru back onto the road.

"We're not going back for water. You can get some at the airport." She turned onto the ramp.

Elizabeth's eyebrows shot up and her voice became shrill. "But I bought a gigantic bottle of Evian. That's what the models drink, you know. It cost a fortune, and those weasely little worms will drink it."

"Please don't refer to your sisters as worms." Lucy checked her mirrors: not a headlight in sight. The road was clear and she accelerated, speeding down the empty highway as fast as she dared. "And why would they drink your water when there's perfectly good tap water?"

"Just to spite me."

"It would serve you right for wasting money like that. Our water comes from our own well, you know. It's perfectly pure and good."

"It's not Evian."

"It's probably better." Lucy sighed. "Besides, I've heard they won't let you carry liquids onto the plane. There are all these new security rules, you know."

"That's ridiculous! Water's harmless."

"So are nail clippers and tweezers, but you can't have them, either. And how are they supposed to know it's really water? It could be some explosive or poison, cleverly disguised in a water bottle."

Elizabeth yawned. "You're getting paranoid."

Lucy checked the speedometer and slowed to a speed ten miles above the legal limit.

"I'll tell you what I'm paranoid about," she said, lowering her voice. "I've heard they actually have machines that can see through your clothes. And sometimes they do strip searches."

Elizabeth rolled her eyes. "Mom, nobody is going to strip search *you.*" Lucy was wondering what exactly she meant by that when Elizabeth chuckled. "But they probably will confiscate that lobster watch. They'll call the fashion police."

"Very funny," said Lucy, flipping on the windshield wipers. "Do you believe it? It's snowing. Again."

When they arrived at the airport they discovered all flights were delayed due to the weather. The snow was accumulating fast, and the runways had to be plowed and the wings de-iced before any planes could take off.

"How long is this going to take?" fumed Elizabeth.

"As long as it takes," said Lucy. "It's never the thing you're worried about, is it? I was worried about getting through security but that was a breeze. I never gave a thought to the weather."

"How come they can send robots to Mars, but they can't get our plane in the air?"

"Dunno," said Lucy, propping her feet on her carry-on suitcase and opening her book. "There's nothing we can do about it so we might as well relax."

For once, Elizabeth was taking her advice. She was already slumped down in the seat beside Lucy, resting her head on her mother's shoulder. Lucy decided it was as good a time as any to break the news about the increased tuition.

"Chamberlain sent a revised financial aid statement along with the tuition bill," she said, getting straight to the point. "It came Christmas Eve."

Elizabeth sat up straight. "What did it say?"

"That we have to pay sixteen thousand dollars for next semester."

"That's crazy!"

"You don't have to tell me," said Lucy, checking the flight status monitor hanging above them. Their flight was still delayed. "I'm going to call the financial aid office and beg for more help, but there's a real possibility we can't afford to send you back. They cut your aid by ten thousand dollars, and we just don't have it. To tell the truth, the six thousand I was expecting to pay will pretty much wipe out our savings."

Elizabeth was frowning, concentrating on her Ugg boots. "You might as well not bother calling. People always try, but they never get anywhere."

This was heresy to Lucy. "Of course I'll try. A lot of it depends on federal guidelines and stuff. Now that your father's not working we probably qualify for a Pell grant or something."

"Trust me, the most you'll get is a loan application."

"That might be doable," said Lucy, eager to seize the slimmest excuse for hope. In her heart she knew it was unlikely that the family would be able to afford a college loan, and Elizabeth was already saddled with thousands in student loans.

Elizabeth continued studying her boots. "How much do we need?" she asked.

"Ten thousand."

"That's weird." Elizabeth was sitting up straighter. "That's really weird. I didn't tell you before, but this makeover thing is also a contest." The usually sullen Elizabeth was practically bubbling with excitement. "The best mother and daughter makeover team wins ten thousand dollars."

The view through the plate glass windows of the terminal was dark and snowy, but Lucy felt as if it was morning and the sun was shining. "Really? That's fabulous. It's like fate or something."

Elizabeth was actually smiling. "I know. Like it's meant to be."

"All we have to do is be the best makeover?"

"Yeah."

Lucy felt her optimism dim slightly. "How do we do that?"

"I don't know. I think the editors vote or something."

"They're probably looking for the most dramatic change," said Lucy. "We might be at a disadvantage, I mean, we're pretty cute to start with."

Elizabeth turned and gave her mother a withering glance. "Mom, you're wearing duck boots, a plaid coat and a green fake fur hat—I think we've got a pretty good chance."

Lucy couldn't believe what she was hearing. She'd chosen her outfit carefully and thought she looked fabulous. It was her best coat, after all, and only six years old. The hat had been an impulse purchase and the boots, well, come winter in Maine you didn't leave the house in anything else. "Well then," she finally said, "that's good, isn't it?"

It was well into the wee hours of the morning when the plane landed at New York's La Guardia Airport and Lucy was congratulating herself on her decision not to check their luggage. She was bone tired and didn't want to waste precious sleep time standing around a balky carousel trying to decide which black suitcase was hers. Fortunately, however, they were supposed to be met by a limousine that would, in the words of the official makeover itinerary, "whisk them into the world's most glamorous city for a magical three days of luxurious pampering and personal consultations with top fashion and beauty experts."

Disembarking from the crowded plane seemed to take forever as passengers wrestled with the maximum number of bags allowable, all of which seemed much larger than the prescribed dimensions. Lucy and Elizabeth finally broke free from the shuffling herd and ran through the jet way, towing their neat little rolling suitcases. There were a handful of people waiting in the arrivals hall, holding placards with names, but none of the names was "Stone."

"The limo must have left without us," said Lucy.

"No wonder. We're late," said Elizabeth. "What do we do now?"

Lucy weighed her options and decided this was no time to pinch pennies by searching for a shuttle bus—if they were even running at this hour. You had to spend money to save it, or in this case, win it. "Taxi," she said.

The ride on the expressway was disorienting, as they sped along in a whirl of red and white automobile lights. The stretches of road that were illuminated by streetlamps gave only depressing views of the filthy slush and ice that lined the roadway, but their spirits brightened when they rounded a curve and there, right in front of them, was the glittering New York skyline.

"Wow," breathed Elizabeth. "It's really like the pictures."

Lucy studied the ranks of tall buildings and looked for the familiar outlines of the Empire State Building and the Chrysler Building, the only two she could identify with certainty. Those and the twin towers of the World Trade Center, but there was only an empty gap where they had stood. The thought made her heart lurch and she was surprised at her reaction; she didn't trust herself to speak about it for fear she would start crying. Instead, she firmly turned her thoughts to the promised "three days of luxury at New York's fabulous Melrose Hotel."

New York must indeed be "the city that never sleeps," thought Lucy, as the taxi pulled up to the hotel and the doorman rushed for-

ward to greet them. "Welcome to the Melrose," he said, opening
the door and extending a hand to help them alight from the car.

In no time at all they were checked in and whisked through the
marble lobby to the elevators and taken to their room, which Lucy
was delighted to discover was decorated in a French-inspired style
with wrought iron filigree headboards and wooden shutters at the
windows. It was also very tiny and she had to maneuver carefully
around Elizabeth before she could collapse on her bed.

"Did you know this used to be the Barbizon?" she asked,
quickly leafing through the leather-bound book listing the hotel's
amenities.

"Is that supposed to mean something to me?" demanded Elizabeth.

"I guess not," admitted Lucy, reminded yet again of the knowledge gap between generations. "It was a famous hotel for women."

"Like for lesbians or something?"

"No. Girls who were coming to the city for careers would stay
here until they got married. It was a safe, respectable address."

Elizabeth was regarding her as if she was speaking in tongues.

"Times were different then," she said, with a sigh. She'd hoped
this trip would be an opportunity to spend some quality time with
her oldest daughter but now she was beginning to think that three
days with Elizabeth might be too much of a good thing.

"We might as well unpack," she said, getting to her feet and
lifting her suitcase onto the bed. "Then we can sleep a little later
tomorrow morning."

"This morning," corrected Elizabeth, reluctantly dragging herself off the bed and pulling her nightgown out of her suitcase.

They soon discovered, however, that the bank of louvered
doors along one wall concealed heating ducts and other parapher-
nalia, offering only limited closet space that was quickly filled
with their coats and boots. A chest of drawers was also a cheat—
the drawers weren't drawers at all but a trompe l'oeil door concealing the minibar.

"Where am I supposed to put my stuff?" demanded Elizabeth.

"We'll keep our clothes in the suitcases and slide them under
the bed." Lucy's cheery tone belied her displeasure. She hated liv-

ing out of a suitcase. But when she dropped to her knees to investigate she discovered the bed was too low for the suitcases to fit. She sat back on her heels and sighed. "I'm getting the feeling that *Jolie* must have gotten the cheapest rooms in this joint."

Elizabeth was in bed, reading the breakfast menu conveniently printed on a cardboard tag you could hang on the outside doorknob. "I don't think anything's cheap about this place," she said. "The continental breakfast is twenty bucks."

"Well, I don't think we'll be getting room service," said Lucy, stacking the suitcases in a corner. "There's no place to put the tray."

All too soon they were awakened by the shrill ringing of the phone. Lucy immediately panicked, thinking something terrible must have happened at home, but when she held the receiver to her ear and heard the automated voice, she realized it was only the wake-up call she'd ordered.

"Up and at 'em," she said, shaking Elizabeth's shoulder, and heading directly for the bathroom. "Today's our first day of beauty."

Lucy's eyes were bleary from sleep, but from what she could see of her reflection in the bathroom mirror she was pretty sure the beauty experts had their work cut out for them. She quickly brushed her teeth, splashed some water on her face, added a dab of moisturizer, and grabbed her hairbrush. There was no time to spare; they were supposed to meet the other makeover winners in the hotel lobby at eight o'clock and it was already a quarter to.

"C'mon, Elizabeth. We've got to hurry."

Elizabeth pulled the pillow over her head and rolled over.

Lucy picked up the pillow, and Elizabeth pulled the sheet over her face. Lucy threw the pillow at her, but she didn't budge.

Lucy sighed and began brushing her hair. A hundred strokes later, Elizabeth's breaths were regular and she'd settled into a deep sleep. Lucy sat down on the bed and dialed room service, ordering a pot of coffee for two at twelve dollars.

The caffeine did the trick and they were on their way by eight-thirty. They'd missed the rest of the group and the limo, but the doorman hailed a taxi for them.

"Better late than never," said Lucy, looking on the bright side as they settled in for the short ride. "You'll love Tavern on the Green. It's beautiful."

And indeed it was, when the taxi turned into Central Park and pulled up at the landmark restaurant. A light snow had started to fall, transforming the park into a magical fairyland, and the trees around the restaurant were outlined in tiny white lights. The inside was warm and welcoming, and they could hear the hum of voices as they checked their bags and coats and hurried off to the ladies' room. Lucy wasn't about to appear before this crowd without checking her hair and lipstick.

"Look," said Elizabeth, pointing to a tray filled with bottles next to the sink. "It's fancy perfume."

Lucy recognized the distinctive bottle of her favorite, Pleasures, and gave herself a generous spritz, then they hurried out to claim their empty places. Lucy squared her shoulders, prepared to do battle for the ten thousand dollars, and followed the hostess to their table. Polite smiles were exchanged as Lucy and Elizabeth sat down and unfolded their cloth napkins, but all attention was on the speaker standing at the podium.

"That's Camilla Keith, the editor," whispered the woman next to Lucy, speaking with a Southern accent. "She's just started speaking."

Even Lucy had heard of Camilla; she was a legend in the magazine business, and her name was always popping up on tabloid-style TV shows, usually in connection with a lawsuit filed by a disgruntled household employee claiming verbal abuse or unpaid wages. Lucy studied her with interest; as editor-in-chief of the magazine her opinion would probably be decisive in choosing who would win the ten thousand dollars. Camilla was a very petite woman with dark hair pulled tightly back from her face, emphasizing her sharply defined cheekbones and chin. She was wearing a white tweed suit that Lucy suspected was a genuine Chanel, and her lips and fingernails were painted bright scarlet. Lucy knew that imitation was the sincerest form of flattery, but she couldn't for the life of her see how she could ever manage to look anything like the sleek and sophisticated Camilla.

"As editor of *Jolie* magazine, it is my pleasure to welcome our twelve winners to our fabulous Mother–Daughter Winter Makeover," she said, giving the group at Lucy's table a nod. "This is a very accomplished group—they had to be to attract the attention of our judges who chose them from more than forty thousand entries."

A collective gasp arose from the crowd assembled in the restaurant, and Lucy wondered who all the people at the other tables were. Her question was answered as Camilla continued speaking.

"I would also like to welcome all of you who got up bright and early to join our winners today at our annual breakfast and fashion show supporting the Jolie Foundation, which you all know is a major contributor to the fight against AIDS and breast cancer."

Lucy checked out the well-dressed ladies and wondered how much they had spent for tickets to the breakfast. These must be the "ladies who lunch" that she'd read about, she realized with surprise. Many of them were much younger than she expected, and she wondered what they did when they weren't eating out at one benefit or another. She suspected their lives must be very different from hers. There was no going out in jeans and sweaters and duck boots for them—they had to keep up with fashion, and that would require lots of shopping. While Lucy could get away with splashing some water on her face and running a comb through her hair, these ladies' polished appearances required hours in the salon, not to mention facials and exercise and waxing sessions. Probably even plastic surgery, she guessed, noticing several extremely tight faces.

Recalled from her reverie by a burst of polite laughter, she turned her attention back to Camilla. "Without further ado," she was saying, "I would like to introduce our winners who have come from all over the country to be with us today."

Lucy smiled at the others at the table, eager to learn more about them. She wondered if they were all as desperate to win the ten thousand dollars as she was.

"I'll begin with our California girls, Ocean Blaustein and her mother, Serena Blaustein, from La Jolla," said Camilla.

There was applause as the two stood. Ocean fulfilled the stereotype Lucy had come to expect from TV, with long blond hair and a tan, dressed in a tummy-baring top and hip-hugging jeans. Serena was a shorter, plumper version of her daughter, with curly red hair and wearing a colorful Mexican-inspired blouse and gathered skirt.

"Moving east, we come to the Great Plains and our winners from Omaha, Nebraska: Amanda McKee and her mother, Ginny McKee."

Lucy smiled and joined in the applause as Amanda and Ginny got to their feet. Amanda was tall and willowy, dressed in a simple turtleneck sweater and skirt. Her mother was also tall and slim, and her red wool suit complemented her dark hair.

"We couldn't ignore a state the size of Texas, so we have Tiffany Montgomery and her stepmom, Cathy Montgomery, from Dallas."

Even if she hadn't been told, Lucy would have guessed Tiffany and Cathy, who was sitting next to her, were from Texas. They were both wearing expensive-looking tweed jackets, they both had big hair, and they were wearing matching coral lipstick on their collagen-boosted lips. They also both appeared to be about the same age.

"The South is famous for its belles, and we have two lovely ladies from Wilmington, North Carolina: Faith Edwards and her mother, Lurleen Edwards."

Lucy guessed that Faith took her religion seriously; she was wearing a gold cross on a chain over her flower-patterned dress. So was her mother, also in a loose-fitting number trimmed with lace. Their faces were devoid of make-up, and their hair was combed back and held by plastic headbands.

"New England is known for its independent, strong-minded women and we have two of those hardy souls with us today: Elizabeth Stone and her mother, Lucy Stone."

Suddenly self-conscious in her best sweater and wool slacks, Lucy discovered there's nothing like a pair of diamond earrings to give a woman confidence. She got to her feet and smiled at everyone, including Elizabeth, who was the very picture of urban so-phistication with her shaggy haircut and black turtleneck dress.

"And last but not least we have two uptown girls from New York City: Carmela Rodriguez and her mother, Maria Rodriguez."

The applause was loudest for Carmela and Maria, and Lucy felt a little surge of competitive spirit as she studied the two with their matching heads of thick, curly black hair. Carmela was dressed in a simple black pantsuit, with subtle make-up, but her mother was dressed in a form-fitting orange suit with a very short skirt and matching lipstick and nail polish.

Surveying the assembled group of makeover winners, Lucy wondered if they had really been chosen on the basis of the girls' essays. She doubted that the staff had time to read forty thousand entries, and it seemed suspicious that each of the six mother–daughter pairs came from a different part of the country. As a re-porter for the weekly newspaper in Tinker's Cove, the *Pennysaver*, she knew that so-called contests were sometimes shams. Every year Ted, the editor and publisher, asked readers to vote for their favorite businesses in the "Best of Tinker's Cove" contest, but the truth was that few people bothered to fill out the form and mail it in. The last "best pizza" winner received five votes, and the provider of the "best massage" only got one vote, from her mother. Neverthe-less, all the winners got official certificates, which they proudly dis-played in their places of business.

A sudden burst of laughter drew her attention back to the speaker, who was concluding her talk. "And now, I promise you, no more speeches," said Camilla. "Breakfast will be served, and then we'll show you fabulous fashions from the new spring collec-tions."

Camilla had no sooner left the podium than Lucy found a fruit cup set on her plate. "I hadn't realized I was so hungry," she said, picking up her spoon and surveying the competition.

Ginny McKee was the first to respond, speaking with a mid-western twang. "I noticed you were late—did you have a rough trip?"

"The snow was heavier in Maine," said Lucy. "They had to clear the runway before we could take off."

"You never know what will happen when you fly these days, do you?" offered Lurleen, taking her daughter's hand. "We were praying the whole time we were in the air."

Lurleen and Faith could be trouble, thought Lucy. She was itching to give them some fashion tips herself and she was sure the editors would relish the opportunity to transform these country bumpkins.

"I find a couple of those cute little bottles of scotch quite helpful myself," said Cathy, with a throaty chuckle.

She had a breezy Texan confidence that Lucy found appealing, but she wondered how it would play with the editors. First impressions could be deceiving, but she had a feeling Cathy did exactly what she wanted. The giant diamond on her finger gave Lucy reason to hope she wasn't particularly interested in competing for ten thousand dollars.

"None of that poison for me," said Serena. "I always bring along a vitamin-packed wheat grass smoothie. I can give you the recipe if you want."

"I'll stick to scotch, thanks." Cathy laughed, turning to Maria and Carmela. "You guys didn't have to fly. How did you get here?"

Lucy studied the Rodriguezes with interest, trying to determine how much of a hometown advantage they had. Plenty, she decided, taking in Maria's curves and Carmela's dimples.

"The magazine sent a limo," said Maria. "And I can tell you, it sure beats the subway!"

"The subway!" Lurleen was horrified. "You won't get me down there, that's for sure."

"You're so lucky to live in the city," continued Cathy, ignoring Lurleen. "I come twice a year, but it's not enough."

"Do you come for the shopping or the shows?" asked Ginny, as the waiter refilled her coffee cup.

"Mostly the shopping," offered Tiffany.

Cathy turned to her stepdaughter. "We love it all, don't we, honey?"

"East or west, home is best, that's what I always say," said Lurleen, who was suspiciously poking at her salad with a fork. "What is this red stuff?"

"Pomegranate. It's delicious," said Cathy, rolling her eyes and turning to Maria. "Is it true the really hot new boutiques are all uptown? I've heard Soho's over and Harlem's where the action is these days."

Lurleen began to choke, and Faith offered her a glass of water and patted her back.

"I know a few places," said Maria, smiling broadly. "I could show you."

"Deal," said Cathy.

"Amanda didn't tell me she'd entered this contest," said Ginny. "I didn't know a thing about it until the letter arrived. I almost threw it out; I thought it was a subscription offer."

"Aren't you glad you didn't?" asked Amanda. "This is going to be fun."

"And there's the possibility of winning ten thousand dollars," said Ocean. "If we win, Mom says I can buy a car."

"If we win we're going to donate the ten thousand dollars to our church," said Lurleen. "That's the main reason I came. I mean, if the good Lord presents you with an opportunity you can't turn it down, can you? I just hope they don't change my hair color; that's something I don't approve of. The good Lord knew what he was doing when he gave us our hair, and everything else, too. Like my mama used to tell me, 'Just keep your face clean and your soul pure and your beauty will shine through.'"

Cathy shook her head in disbelief. "You're in the wrong place then, honey. You should've stayed in South Carolina."

"North Carolina."

"Well, wherever you're from, you're in Camilla's hands now. Around here she's the boss, and you better do what she says. Her temper is a legend in the industry, believe me, I know. Back in the days before I met Tiffany's wonderful father, Mr. Montgomery, I was a marketing executive at Neiman Marcus. I dealt with her quite a bit, and I soon learned that there was Camilla's way or the highway. It didn't matter that I was the customer, that I was putting up the money and buying the ads. Being the customer didn't make me right, not with her anyway."

Lurleen looked worried, and Lucy wondered if she'd only consented to the makeover to win the prize money for her church.

Lucy understood her anxiety; she hoped the magazine's experts wouldn't make them look ridiculous. Not that she had any complaints so far. The fruit cup had been tasty, and the eggs Benedict was a delicious treat. She realized with a shock that she was enjoying herself, in the heart of New York City. Tinker's Cove seemed very far away.

The waiters were clearing away the last of the dishes when the lights suddenly dimmed and strobe lights began flashing in time to loud techno music. It was the promised fashion show, but Lucy thought the parade of excruciatingly thin models dressed in skimpy outfits was more suited to a Save the Children campaign than daily life. Thigh-high buccaneer boots with pointy toes and stiletto heels, belt-sized miniskirts, and bondage-inspired bustiers were hardly the sort of thing she would wear. Neither were the flowing and fluttering evening dresses constructed of torn bits of fabric and ribbon. None of the moms at her table seemed to know what to make of the molded foam dress with an additional pair of buttocks stitched onto the backside, a detail the announcer described as "humorous whimsy."

"Like I need a second one of those," said Cathy.

"That poor model doesn't even have a first bottom," said Ginny, giggling.

But when the fashion show was over and they were ensconced in a limo with Ginny and Amanda en route to the hotel, Lucy discovered that Elizabeth had a very different reaction.

"I'm too fat, Mom," she said, sighing. "I should never have eaten all those Christmas cookies and stuff."

"Me, too," said Amanda.

"You look great," said Lucy, firmly. "You both look great. You're normal. Those models are freaks, and whether you believe it or not they're putting their health at risk."

"That's not true, Mom. Now they're saying people who stress their systems by skipping meals actually add years to their lives."

"You can't believe everything you read," said Ginny.

"That's for sure," said Lucy. "Besides, they do more than skip lunch to stay that thin. I wouldn't be surprised if they smoke cigarettes and take amphetamines and diet pills."

"Mom, you don't know that. You read it somewhere. So now who's the one who needs to remember you can't believe everything you read."

Lucy was tempted to retort but didn't want to fight in front of Ginny and Amanda. Instead, she held her tongue as they pulled up to the gleaming steel and glass office tower. Looking up, she was suddenly thrilled and excited about the adventure ahead. She could hardly contain herself as she sat waiting for the chauffeur to open the door.

Chapter Three

THE YEAR'S *BEST* AND *WORST* LOOKS

L ucy was standing with the other winners in the black-marble lobby, waiting for Camilla and the other editors who would escort them to the *Jolie* offices, which occupied the eighteenth through twenty-first floors, when her cell phone rang.

"How was the trip?" asked Bill.

Just the sound of his voice made her feel homesick and she stepped apart from the others so she could have a private conversation. "Okay," she said, staring out the window at the busy street. It was still snowing, producing a slippery gray slush on the sidewalk and roadway. "New York is a lot different from Tinker's Cove. How's everything at home?"

"Everything's fine. We're all great. The girls went ice skating on the pond. They say the new skates are terrific." He paused. "Did you talk to Elizabeth about taking some time off from school?"

"She might not have to. It turns out the magazine is giving ten thousand dollars to the best makeover team. It's a contest."

"No way!"

"Way," said Lucy, watching a fashionably dressed woman striding along in impossibly high heels despite the slippery sidewalk. "and after seeing the others I think Elizabeth and I have a pretty good chance of winning."

"How come?"

"I don't think the others are as desperate for the money as we are.

Take the pair from California, for example. The daughter wants a new car, but the mom is pretty laid back and relaxed. The only others who expressed any serious interest in the money are from North Carolina, and they say they'll give it to their church if they win."

"The others aren't interested?" Bill sounded doubtful.

"I honestly don't think the girls from Texas are. They already seem to have more money than they know what to do with. That leaves the New Yorkers, Maria and Carmela. I don't know much about them yet so I'm keeping an eye on them, and the midwest-erners." Lucy paused, thinking about Ginny and Amanda. "They're very polite, and polite doesn't win contests."

Bill chuckled. "I didn't know you were such a cutthroat com-petitor yourself."

"I'm desperate. I'll do anything to win."

"If you're really serious about this, I've got some advice for you. You know that TV show, *Survivor*? The winners often form alliances with other players to gain an advantage. They help each other wipe out the competition."

"But there's only one prize. Why would you help somebody else win?"

"Because they'll help you in return. Two are better than one."

"And three's a crowd," said Lucy. "That's what my mother used to say." She lowered her voice. "I'm worried about Eliza-beth," she whispered. "She hardly ate a bite of breakfast."

"Maybe she wasn't hungry."

"She thinks she's fat."

"That's crazy. She's skin and bones."

"I know, but they had this fashion show today and the models were even skinnier than she is so she's decided she needs to lose weight."

"It's probably just a phase," he said, sounding distracted. In the distance she heard muffled shouts. "Sorry, honey, I've got to go. The girls say the dog knocked over a lamp."

Lucy closed the phone and replaced it in her purse, thinking over Bill's advice. The editors had finally arrived and were shep-herding the group through the security checkpoint, where a guard was peering into each woman's purse with a flashlight. Who would make the best accomplice, she wondered, hurrying to join them.

Boarding the elevator, she gave Elizabeth a nudge. "Look, I found this protein bar in my bag. Why don't you have a bite or two, just to keep up your strength."

Elizabeth glared at her. "You're embarrassing me, Mom," she hissed. "It's bad enough you're wearing those duck boots, but now you're fussing at me."

"These boots are practical," muttered Lucy, heading for the revolving door.

"Will you shut up if I take the bar?" asked Elizabeth, when they'd exited onto the eighteenth floor into the magazine's reception area.

"You have to eat half of it," insisted Lucy, trying to hide her disappointment. She'd expected the *Jolie* office to look like something out of the movie *Funny Face* but instead of glamorous chic pink décor there was only utilitarian, understated beige. The receptionist, a mousy little thing who seemed to physically quail under Camilla's gaze, gave them a lukewarm smile as they all filed past.

Camilla stopped suddenly and held up a hand, causing a bit of awkward bumping as the women in back came to a halt.

"Okay." Elizabeth carefully unwrapped the bar and took a bite, chewed slowly, and finally swallowed.

Lucy let out the breath she had been holding and turned her attention to Camilla, who was standing in front of a wall decorated with framed cover photos.

"Ladies, ladies!"

The group fell silent.

"Welcome to the world of *Jolie* magazine," she said, waving her arm expansively. "This is where your transformations will take place." She paused dramatically. "Are you ready?"

"You betcha," declared Serena. "Make me into Kate Moss."

"That may not be possi . . ." began Camilla, giving Serena a quick up and down. Then, realizing it was a joke, she trilled, "We'll do our best."

The women all laughed.

"But first on our agenda," she continued, holding up a finger, "is the infamous *before* picture. And for that, I'm putting you in the capable hands of our art director, Nancy Glass." She indicated a tiny woman in oversized tortoise-shell glasses, who was wearing a tight gray pencil skirt, a black blazer, and a shiny pink silk blouse along with high-heeled sandals.

"Follow me, ladies. The photo studio is this way," she said, pointing towards a long, beige-carpeted hallway lined with doors.

Once again, they were off and running and Lucy was beginning to understand how city people managed to stay so thin. At home, she drove to the *Pennysaver* office, parked outside the back door, walked twenty feet to her desk, sat down, and, often as not, reached for one of the donuts Phyllis had taken to bringing to work every morning.

"Here we are," announced Nancy, dramatically opening the studio door.

Lucy wasn't quite sure what she expected, but it wasn't this large, windowless room with a raised platform at one end. Several contraptions resembling the screens people used to have for showing slides and home movies dangled from the ceiling behind the platform, along with a silvery umbrella. A cluster of tripods was stacked in one corner, a table held a coffee carafe and a stack of cups but no donuts, and a few mismatched chairs were scattered about. There was no sign of the photographer.

"I see Pablo's not here yet," said Nancy, drumming her nails, polished in a shade of pink that matched her blouse, against her pointy hip bone. "I'll have to go find him."

Figuring they might have a bit of a wait, Lucy and Elizabeth joined Ginny and Amanda. Across the room, Maria and Carmela were having an animated conversation with the Blausteins and the Montgomerys, fueled perhaps by the Styrofoam cups of coffee they were sipping. Lurleen and Faith Edwards formed a little island, standing by themselves. It was Ginny who broke the ice. "So what do you think of the competition?" she asked.

Lucy turned to her with interest. "What about you? Are you trying to win the prize?"

"You bet," volunteered Amanda. "Mom and Dad went into business for themselves last year."

"We do upholstery and slipcovers," added Ginny.

"It's been very successful."

"Beyond our wildest dreams," said Ginny. "Unfortunately, we knew a lot more about slipcovers than the tax code. Our accountant tells us we have to pay the IRS a quarterly payment on January 15 that's almost ten thousand more than we budgeted for."

"We're in a similar bind," confessed Lucy, explaining the financial aid dilemma. "I guess I was kidding myself. I didn't think anybody else was very interested, except for Faith and Lurleen."

"They're definitely motivated," agreed Ginny. "Driven by religious fervor."

"But the gals from Texas certainly don't need the money."

"No, but Cathy had a successful career before she married; she even won a few beauty pageants. She might not be able to resist the challenge."

"I never thought of that," said Lucy, gaining new respect for Ginny. "What about Carmela and Maria?"

"Maria was an abused wife who went to law school after getting her husband sent to jail. She's now one of New York's top divorce attorneys. They call her Merciless Maria."

Lucy didn't say anything but swallowed hard. This was going to be much more challenging than she thought. She was almost ready to give up and go home.

"Serena and Ocean?" asked Elizabeth, her voice practically a squeak.

"Don't be fooled by Serena's California cool. She lets that girl get away with anything—just look at how she goes around with her stomach hanging out in the middle of winter! Trust me, that woman will do anything for that girl, and we already know that Ocean wants a new car." Ginny narrowed her eyes. "The only way we stand a chance is if we team up and help each other."

"That would be great!" exclaimed Lucy, wondering what she could contribute to their partnership. "Tell you what, I'll try to find out the rules for this contest. So far, they've been pretty vague."

"Deal," said Ginny, extending her hand.

Lucy took it and gave a firm shake, just as Nancy returned with Pablo in tow.

"We're good to go," trilled Nancy. "This is our photo editor and I'm sure he's going to get some great photos of you ladies."

Pablo, a muscular man dressed in a black silk T-shirt and pleated-front slacks, gave them a nod. He looked as if he hadn't shaved his chin in a day or two but Lucy decided the look must be intentional since he'd certainly shaved his head that morning: it was perfectly smooth and shiny. He stood silently, arms crossed, and studied them. Then, coming to a decision he snapped his fingers and an assistant magically appeared with a camera. Pablo took it and began snapping photos of the women, just as they were, scattered around the room in groups.

"What are you doing? This isn't what we talked about," protested Nancy.

"That was no good. This is better. Natural, unstudied. Like Degas backstage at the ballet, no?"

"I see," said Nancy, with a shrug. "That's why he's a genius. Stay as you are, ladies; it seems Pablo's having one of his creative moments."

The camera flashed in Lucy's face, then Pablo was gone, making his way around the room followed by Nancy and the assistant. Nancy kept up a steady stream of chatter while Pablo snapped photos, pausing only to toss his camera to the helper when the film ran out and to snatch a loaded one.

Eventually his energy, or inspiration, seemed to flag and he collapsed into a chair. The assistant vanished with the cameras while another rushed up with a towel and a bottle of water. Pablo wiped his face with a towel, as if he'd just completed the Boston Marathon, and chugged a pint or two of water.

While he rested Nancy gathered the group together on the platform and began arranging them according to height. Lucy cleared her throat and raised her hand.

"Yes?" asked Nancy. "Is there a problem?"

It was then that Camilla arrived, and stood by the door, watching, her arms folded across her chest. She had changed out of the white Chanel suit and into more practical working clothes, a black jersey dress, black tights and knee-high black boots with stiletto heels and extremely pointed toes. She was a perfect, self-contained package.

"No, not a problem," said Lucy. "But I do have a question. I think we're all interested in the contest for the ten thousand dollars."

This was greeted with a murmur of approval from the others.

"It would be helpful to know on what basis the winning mother and daughter will be chosen."

Camilla's eyes widened, giving her a doll-like appearance. "That decision will be made by the editors," she said.

"Of course," persisted Lucy. "But how will the editors decide? What are the rules?"

Camilla became rigid as a poker, except for one foot, which tapped a rapid beat on the tile floor. "That's for us to know and you to find out," she said, as a tight little smile flitted across her lips and disappeared. "Otherwise it wouldn't be much of a contest, would it?"

"I'd like to get her into my stress-reduction class," whispered Serena. "People really relax after a session or two of genital breathing. Give me a week and I'll have her loose as a goose."

"Genital breathing?" Lucy was intrigued.

"Not in front of the girls," whispered Lurleen, prompting embarrassed giggles from Faith.

"It's just a relaxation technique; there's nothing sexual about it," said Ocean, defending her mother.

"Well, I never," began Lurleen, only to fall silent as Camilla approached the group for a closer look. The winners shifted uncomfortably under her gaze.

"This is no good," she finally said.

Pablo was on his feet, eyes glaring. "No good? What you mean?"

Nancy was quick to intervene. "If you don't like the group photo we can use individual shots. Pablo took some really nice, creative informals."

"No, that's not the problem," said Camilla, tapping her fingers on her hip. "The problem is . . ."

Nancy leaned forward, as if to catch the words as they fell from her lips. Pablo stood, arms crossed, waiting warily.

"They look too good!"

Pablo threw up his arms and stalked out of the studio.

Nancy was puzzled. "They look too good?"

"This is supposed to be a *before* photo, but they don't look *before* enough."

"Oh," said Nancy. "I understand. Maybe they could take off their make-up. We could change their hair a little bit, give them some ugly clothes. . . ."

Camilla wasn't listening. She rushed forward and pointed a scarlet-tipped finger at Lucy's feet. "What are those?"

Elizabeth looked upward, rolling her eyes in mortification.

"I think they're called duck boots," said Lucy, lifting her slacks to reveal the brown rubber bottoms and tan leather uppers of her footwear. "Everyone wears them at home."

Camilla was examining the rest of Lucy's ensemble with an eagle eye. "What's that?" she asked, pointing at the watch.

"Oh," said Lucy, with a little giggle, "that's my lobster watch. It was a joke present from my husband."

Camilla pulled Lucy out of the group and she blushed, uncomfortably aware that she was about to be an example. She was pretty sure this was not the way to win the ten thousand dollars.

"Get Deb up here," she told Nancy, who scurried over to the phone on the wall.

Ginny's eyes met Lucy's, and she smiled sympathetically. Serena gazed into the distance, apparently meditating. The others looked down at their feet while Lucy stood awkwardly, waiting for Deb's arrival, whoever she was. Fortunately, they didn't have to wait long.

"Deb Shertzer is our accessories editor," said Nancy, as a woman with short hair burst into the studio. She was dressed in a rosy twin set to which she had added a colorful scarf and small gold hoop earrings, and she was quite breathless. She'd wasted no time in obeying Camilla's order to appear.

"This is interesting," said Camilla, pointing Lucy out. "You can tell this woman isn't from New York just by looking at her boots."

"I brought heels," said Lucy, bristling, "but the streets are slushy and I didn't want to ruin them so I wore my boots. I can get the shoes, if you want."

"No! Don't change," said Camilla, turning to Deb. "Look at her watch."

Lucy obediently held out her arm, and Deb's eyes widened as she took in the red plastic watch.

"The hands are little lobster claws," said Camilla.

"So I see," said Deb.

"I want this for everyone."

"Duck boots? Lobster watches?"

"No." Camilla tapped her foot impatiently. "Regional accessories. Stuff that tells a story. Like the pair from Iowa. . . ."

"Omaha," said Ginny, with a little edge in her voice. "Omaha, Nebraska."

"Whatever." Camilla waved her hand. "She and her kid can wear overalls and hold a pitchfork, like that painting."

"Grant Wood," said Nancy, nodding enthusiastically.

"Whatever. And the ones from California?"

Serena hesitated a moment before raising her hand. "That's me," she finally said, sounding as if Camilla was taxing even her patience.

"What about a surfboard and swimsuits?" suggested Deb, eager to show her boss that she'd got the idea.

"Cool," said Ocean. "I can show off my tan."

"Hold on a minute," said Cathy, pulling herself up to her almost six-foot height. "I protest. This is tacky. I'm not going to wear a cowboy hat just because I'm from Texas."

"Don't worry, honey," crooned Camilla, "we wouldn't dream of changing a thing." Her voice hardened and her eyes flashed. "With that hair and jewelry you look exactly like the Texas trophy wife you are."

There was a shocked silence, and everyone watched as Camilla turned on her heel and marched out of the studio. When she was gone everyone seemed to let out a big sigh of relief.

"Well now, ladies," said Nancy, stepping forward briskly, "we have work to do."

"You're not kidding," said Deb. "Where am I going to get a surfboard in New York City in December?"

Nancy turned and looked around the studio. "Where's Pablo? Has anyone seen Pablo?"

She rushed out to look for him, and the women, who had been standing shoulder to shoulder on the platform, began to pull apart; Lucy felt suddenly chilly. Her eyes met Ginny's in a mute apology. Ginny shrugged in return, as if to say it didn't matter, but Lucy knew she had handled things badly and hadn't kept her half of the bargain. She had a feeling the alliance had broken down.

Chapter Four

PLUCK OR WAX?

OUR BROW EXPERTS HAVE THE ANSWERS

When the photo session was finally over, the women were divided into three groups and sent to consult with the magazine's experts. Lucy and Elizabeth found themselves paired with Lurleen and Faith Edwards for make-up advice, the Montgomerys and Blausteins went off to a spa, and the McKees and Rodriguezes were sent to the fashion department. As Lucy watched Ginny and Maria walking down the hall with their heads together she wondered if Ginny's offer to team up had simply been a ploy to trick her into making a foolish mistake. If so, it had certainly worked. The editors probably thought she was a troublemaker now, and the other contestants didn't seem to want anything to do with her. Even Lurleen seemed unwilling to "turn the other cheek" and forgive her and was keeping her distance as they followed the directions to the beauty department. It wasn't until they were in the elevator that she broke her silence.

"I'm of half a mind to pack up and go home," said Lurleen, as the doors slid shut. "This isn't at all what I expected. I feel as if I've been put through the wringer."

"Mom was looking forward to some pampering and relaxation," explained Faith.

"You can say that again. Faith here is my oldest, you see. I've got six more at home."

"Seven children?" Lucy's eyebrows shot up as the elevator landed with a thud.

"And another on the way," she sighed, stepping into the hallway. "I'm really looking forward to that massage they promised us, but I don't think there's time today since we're all going to that TV show."

Lucy was consulting the agenda, wondering which TV show they were going to see, but the notation didn't specify. "Maybe it's the *Norah!* show," she said, giving Elizabeth a nudge.

"Doesn't mean a thing to me," said Lurleen. "I can't tell one show from another."

"We don't watch TV except for inspirational videos and Bible stories," said Faith.

Lucy glanced at Elizabeth, who was rolling her eyes as she pushed open the door to the beauty department. Inside they found three desks—small, medium, and large like the chairs and beds in the three bears' house, only Baby Bear was occupying her desk.

"Hi, I'm Fiona. Fiona Gray," she said, jumping up and extending her hand.

Lucy took it, finding it impossible not to smile at this bright young thing. Fiona had short, dark hair in a style similar to Elizabeth's and enormous blue eyes, and she was dressed in a very short teal dress topped with a wide leather belt with oversized chrome grommets and buckle.

"Welcome to the beauty department," she continued, speaking in a crisp British accent. "According to the schedule . . ."

Lucy was enchanted. Fiona actually pronounced it *shed-yule.*

". . . you must be the Edwards and the Stones and you're here for make-up. Though I must say, you all look positively brilliant, and I can't imagine what old Nadine, that's Nadine Nelson, our beauty editor, can possibly do to improve you."

"Now, now," clucked an older woman, entering through a door at the rear of the office, "there's always something we can do." She paused. "I'm Phyllis Jackson, the assistant beauty editor. Nadine left instructions for me to get you settled. She'll be in shortly to supervise. Follow me."

As they trooped after her, Lucy noticed that Phyllis had a rather harried and disheveled air about her. Although to be honest, thought

Lucy, she certainly looked better than the average woman in Tinker's Cove, even with her smudged lipstick and worn shoes. It was only in the rarefied atmosphere of the magazine that you noticed that her olive green blouse didn't perfectly match the acid green flecks in her tweed skirt.

The studio looked like a beauty shop with mirrors, raised chairs, and a counter filled with every imaginable make-up product. Fiona flipped a switch and they were suddenly all bathed in bright light as they seated themselves. Elizabeth was goggle-eyed at the array of cosmetics, but there was no chance for her to get her hands on them as Phyllis tilted the chair back and started sponging her face.

"Fiona, heat up the wax for the brows, and then you can start cleansing Lucy's face," she said.

"Brows?" squeaked Lucy. "Wax?"

"Trust her," advised Fiona, raising one of her own delicately arched brows. "She's a genius at shaping."

"It makes all the difference in the world," said Phyllis. "Really opens up your face and makes your eyes look bigger."

"Does it hurt?" asked Elizabeth.

"Like hell," said Fiona.

When they were through cleansing and waxing and plucking, Lucy had to admit they all looked improved, at least in the brow department. The rest of their faces were a bit like blank slates, however, awaiting the master's touch.

"She's running late this morning," said Fiona, speaking to Phyllis in a whisper. "I think we should start with the foundation."

"We better wait," replied Phyllis, looking worried. "You know how Nadine is."

"I know," agreed Fiona, "but the next group is due in less than half an hour."

Phyllis pursed her lips anxiously but was spared the agony of making a decision by the arrival of the beauty editor herself. Nadine Nelson thumped into the studio, trailing numerous scarves and carrying an assortment of bags including a purse (Louis Vuitton), brief case (Coach) and crumpled brown paper shopping bags (Bloomingdale's and Schlagel's Bagels).

"I'm exhausted," she said, dropping the bags on the floor and shrugging out of her mink coat. It would have fallen on the floor, too, except for Phyllis, who lunged forward and snatched it in the nick of time.

"Still feeling poorly?" inquired Phyllis, draping the coat on a padded satin hanger.

Nadine replied with a burst of coughing, and Phyllis proffered a box of tissues, which she waved away. Instead, she scrabbled around in her enormous purse, finally extracting an eye-catching gold compact lavishly decorated with colorful enamel in a pansy design.

"Ghastly," she said, flipping the compact open and peering into the mirror. She got to work rubbing the puff all over her face, and it wasn't until she'd shut it with a click that she noticed the four makeover winners. "Cripes!" she exclaimed. "That damn makeover. We have them all day, don't we?"

Phyllis's face reddened, embarrassed by her boss's rudeness. "Let me introduce Lucy and Elizabeth Stone and Lurleen and Faith Edwards. We've cleansed their faces and shaped their brows, but we didn't want to go any further without you. . . ."

"I've got to sit down," said Nadine, abruptly interrupting her. "I've got to catch my breath."

Fiona grabbed a nearby chair and shoved it under her, with hardly a moment to spare. The beauty editor sat, knees splayed out, amidst her pile of bags. She looked like an upscale bag lady, despite her expensive designer pants and elaborately beaded sweater. She bore a strong resemblance to the homeless woman Lucy had spotted sheltering in a doorway a few feet from the hotel.

"Shall I start?" asked Phyllis, with a little bob of her head. "I mean, for Lucy here, I was thinking of that Bobbi Brown gloss, some mascara, but I think we should stick with a natural look she can maintain. . . ."

"Did you see the Dior show? They used a lot of color," said Nadine.

"Actually, I didn't. You went but I couldn't get away. It was too close to deadline."

"It was war paint," said Fiona, with a mischievous gleam in her eye. "Big jags of pink and green and yellow, smeared right across the models' noses."

"I certainly don't want that," began Lucy, until she thought of the ten thousand dollars. "But, of course, I trust your judgment."

Lurleen, on the other hand, was determined to stick to her guns. "I'm for the natural look," she said.

"I don't want a green nose, but I wouldn't mind some eye shadow," said Elizabeth.

"Pink's big this season," observed Nadine, opening the compact again.

"As eye shadow?" This was a new one to Lucy.

"It would make you look like you've got conjunctivitis," said Lurleen. "My three-year-old had it last week but, praise the Lord, I got it treated before it spread to the others."

"It was a miracle, that's what Mama said," added Faith, nodding piously.

Lucy thought it would be more miraculous if the child hadn't got conjunctivitis in the first place, but she was determined to be Miss Congeniality and held her tongue.

"Glitter," declared Nadine, patting yet more powder on her nose. "Glitter everywhere." She stopped, powder puff in midair, and sneezed. The compact flew across the room and landed at Elizabeth's feet, releasing a fine dust of powder that settled around it on the floor.

Elizabeth hopped out of the chair and retrieved it, politely returning it to Nadine.

Nadine didn't thank her but instead examined the compact for damage while continuing to throw out extreme suggestions. "Very, very dark lips. Almost black."

"Sounds great," said Elizabeth, brushing a bit of spilled powder off her hands and settling back in her chair. "Bring it on."

"Me, too," said Lucy, determined to play along.

"Trust me," said Fiona, spinning the chair so Lucy's back was to the mirror and reaching for a brush.

When they were finally allowed to see their reflections, Lucy was pleased to discover she still recognized herself. She even looked, she had to admit, improved in a subtle way, and she resolved to take a few minutes every morning to apply a bit of foundation and a touch of mascara. She always wore lipstick but she now realized she hadn't been using the right color. The natural brownish gloss Fiona had applied was a lot more flattering than the bright pink she had been wearing.

Fiona and Phyllis had released them from the chairs and were distributing pink-and-white–striped gift bags when they heard the voices of the next group in the outer office. Nadine ignored it, interested only in the contents of the bags.

"What are you giving them?" she asked, pouting.

"A nice assortment of basic cosmetics," said Phyllis, practically cringing with fear. "It was all donated. Mostly Urban Decay for the girls and Lancôme for the moms."

"How come I didn't know about this?"

"You'd have to ask Camilla. She sent them down."

"Oh, all right then." Nadine dismissed them with a wave of the arm, and they left the studio, but as the door closed behind them they could hear Nadine coughing.

Ginny and Amanda were standing in the office, waiting their turn in the studio along with Maria and Carmela. If Lucy had any doubts that the make-up was a success they were erased when she saw Maria and Ginny's reaction. Both of them looked as if they'd like to kill her.

"You look fabulous, all of you," cooed Carmela. "I hope they do the same for us."

"I was pretty worried for a while there," said Lurleen, who looked years younger now that the dark circles under her eyes were hidden and her cheeks were rosy. "They were talking about giving us war paint."

Both Ginny and Maria seemed more than willing to don war paint, but before they could launch an offensive Lucy offered an olive branch. "They gave us gift bags," she said, holding hers up.

Lurleen also offered her gift bag for inspection, but the newcomers were quickly shooed into the studio.

"Where to now?" wondered Lucy, pulling the schedule out of her bag.

"Photo, again," said Faith. "For *after* photos."

"Lord, give me strength," prayed Lurleen.

"Amen," said Lucy.

Chapter Five

FOODS THAT ACTUALLY TAKE OFF POUNDS!

When Pablo finally finished photographing their newly made-up faces, Lucy was tired and hungry. She never would have guessed that posing was such hard work and had new respect for the models whose pictures filled the fashion magazines every month. She also wondered how they managed to stay so thin since she had worked up quite an appetite.

So far, she decided, the makeover had been surprisingly stressful. Like Lurleen, she had expected to be petted and pampered, but instead she'd spent the morning enduring Pablo's egotism, Camilla's abusive temper, and Nadine's rudeness. Add to that Elizabeth's determination to starve herself and the competitive atmosphere created by the ten-thousand-dollar prize and she was more than ready for a break. Fortunately, she'd arranged to meet Samantha Blackwell for lunch and was looking forward to spending a relaxing hour or two reminiscing about college.

"It's a working lunch," said Elizabeth, reading from the well-worn Xerox schedule. "Deli sandwiches and a motivational speaker in the boardroom."

Lucy stopped in her tracks. "But I have a lunch date with Sam," protested Lucy. The true horror of her situation was slowly dawning. "She promised to make her fabulous brownies for me, the ones with chocolate chunks, pecans, *and* icing."

"No way," said Elizabeth, shaking her head. "It's pastrami on rye with a big helping of team spirit."

"They'll never miss me."

Elizabeth stamped her foot. "Mom! What about the contest? You can't sneak away. You've got to participate to win. That's what you're always telling me. 'Showing up is ninety percent of success.' Right?"

Lucy hated it when her kids quoted her own words back at her, but she knew Elizabeth was right. She pulled out her cell phone and called Sam.

"I'm not surprised," said Sam, when Lucy told her she couldn't make it. "I figured they'd keep you busy. We'll do it another time."

"When?" wailed Lucy. "It's been more than twenty years."

"I know. It's pathetic. But I have an idea."

"Tell me."

"Nope. It's a surprise," said Sam. "Enjoy your lunch."

Nobody enjoyed the lunch. Lucy and Maria were the only ones who actually ate the oversized deli sandwiches which contained at least a pound of salty, highly seasoned meat. Lurleen regarded hers with suspicion, declaring she preferred white bread and mayonnaise to rye and mustard. Cathy followed the Atkins diet, eating all of the meat and none of the bread, and the others ignored the sandwiches entirely and nibbled on the pickles instead. The motivational speaker was a disappointment, too, offering a single message: You can choose to be happy or sad, so why not choose to be happy? She said it various ways, of course, but each rephrasing boiled down to the same idea. Most disappointing to Lucy, however, was the fact that none of the editors had bothered to show up.

"I could have gone to Sam's," she complained, as they boarded the bus that was taking them to the TV studio.

"Shh," cautioned Elizabeth, as the editors began filing onto the bus.

Lucy watched with interest as Phyllis followed Nadine, the beauty editor, carrying her assortment of bags like some sort of native bearer on a safari. She waited until Nadine had taken her place in a window seat and then arranged her bags on the seat beside her before leaving the bus. Phyllis wasn't going to the show, and the other editors Lucy had met were also conspicuously absent. There was no sign of Pablo or the art director, Nancy Glass, or the accessories editor, Deb Shertzer. Instead, Camilla took the front seat, accompanied by a large, almost mannish woman with very short hair wearing a severe gray pantsuit.

Lucy listened to the buzz in the bus. "Who's that?" "Camilla isn't . . . ?" "Oh no, I don't think so." "It would be ironic. . . ." "It would be a hoot!"

Finally, as the bus pulled away from the curb, Camilla stood up and began speaking into a microphone.

"Ladies! Your attention please. As you've probably guessed, we're all going to see the *Norah!* show!" She paused, dramatically holding up her free hand. "As featured guests! You're all going to be on TV and you're all going to meet Norah Hemmings, the fabulous Queen of Daytime TV, in person!"

This was greeted with excitement by the makeover winners, who cheered and applauded. Lucy, however, saw trouble ahead. She hadn't exactly been winning any popularity contests since Camilla noticed her boots and lobster watch at the *before* photo shoot, precipitating the unpopular decision to put them all in absurd regional costumes. To be honest, she certainly wouldn't blame Serena, who didn't share her daughter's enthusiasm for being photographed for a national magazine in a swimsuit, if she never forgave her. Ginny and Amanda had no trouble adopting the glum expressions from the Grant Wood painting; they hadn't appreciated being portrayed as country bumpkins in overalls. Maria and Carmela were enthusiastic sports fans and had enjoyed donning pinstriped New York Yankees uniforms, but Cathy and Tiffany made no attempt to conceal their loathing for the gold-lamé twirler costumes. Lurleen and Faith weren't happy about the Civil War–era hoop skirts they'd had to wear, either.

It wasn't Lucy's fault that Camilla had decided on the demeaning outfits, but she wasn't confident she could convince the others. And now she was pretty sure that the fact that she and Norah were, well, maybe not bosom buddies but definitely more than mere acquaintances, wouldn't sit well with them, either. Norah loved her summer home in Tinker's Cove and made a real effort to get to know the locals; she was sure to mention the fact that she and Lucy were neighbors. Even more awkward was the on-again, off-again romance between Elizabeth and Norah's son Lance. The two had been good friends ever since he spent a year in the Tinker's Cove public school while Norah was involved in a nasty divorce.

"You will all be sitting in the front row," continued Camilla, "so put on your smiles, because if you watch the *Norah!* show you know how often the camera pans the audience, especially the lucky ones in the front. Also, our beauty editor Nadine Nelson will select one mother–daughter team to demonstrate the makeup techniques she used this morning."

Nadine, who was slumped in her seat, apparently dozing, didn't respond.

"Also, our fashion editor, let me introduce Elise Frazier. . . ."

The woman who was sitting next to Camilla lumbered to her feet and gave a curt nod. With her lumpish figure and understated business suit she didn't seem at all what Lucy expected a fashion editor to be like, but then, Lucy reminded herself, she didn't really know anything about fashion magazine editors, except for the handful she had met so far. But from the little she knew, Elise seemed to be the exception to the rule that they were obsessed with fashion and diet. Feeling a nudge from Elizabeth, Lucy turned her attention to Camilla, who was continuing to speak.

"Elise is going to choose one mother–daughter team to model outfits she has specially selected from our upcoming issue," she said, bending down so Elise could whisper in her ear.

Lucy imagined she could hear the wheels turning in the makeover winners' heads as they tried to figure out the best way to be chosen for special treatment.

Elise was scanning the group. "Elise tells me the clothes are size four. Confess, now, who wears size four?"

Carmela and Maria were waving their arms and practically jumping out of their seats.

"I guess we have our models, then," said Camilla. "Now, enjoy the ride. We'll be there in a few minutes."

"Sorry, honey," said Lucy, patting Elizabeth's hand. "I don't think I was ever a size four and I'm certainly not one now."

"I don't think Maria is either," said Elizabeth, as the bus pulled to a stop in front of a tall, gray stone building.

A line of women was behind a row of barriers, waiting to be admitted to the studio, and they watched enviously as the *Jolie* group was ushered ahead of them. Lucy wasn't used to such special treatment and found she enjoyed it, but she also felt a bit uncomfortable, as if she didn't really deserve it.

Sidra Rumford, née Finch and the daughter of Lucy's best friend Sue, was waiting to greet them in the hallway. She was an assistant producer on the show and looked very professional, holding a clipboard and dressed in the New York uniform of a black pantsuit and pink blouse.

"Welcome to the *Norah!* show," she said. "And a special welcome to Lucy and Elizabeth, who are here from my own hometown, Tinker's Cove!"

All eyes were on them as they exchanged hugs and greetings; Lucy could practically feel little darts of jealousy pricking her through her thick plaid coat.

"Back home, we're all so proud of Sidra," she announced to the group in general, as they filed down the hall. "She's a real success story, and so is her husband, Geoff. They've both left our little town and have careers in the big city."

No one replied as they passed through a series of doors and eventually arrived in the studio, where they were seated in the front row, just as Camilla promised. A couple of make-up technicians immediately began touching up their faces with powder while Camilla and Elise consulted with Sidra. Nadine was nowhere to be seen.

After making a few notations on her clipboard, Sidra squared her shoulders and addressed the group. "There's been a change," she said. "Unfortunately, Nadine Nelson, who was going to do a make-up segment for the show, will be unable to appear today because of illness so we're going to have to scratch the beauty and fashion feature to accommodate our substitute guest."

The women groaned, politely, and Sidra held up her hand. "I'm really sorry about this. I know it's disappointing for the moms and daughters who were chosen, but I'm afraid it's unavoidable. You're all still going to be on TV, and Norah herself will introduce you all by name."

This pleased the women, who began patting their hair and checking their reflections in their pocket mirrors. All except for Lurleen and Faith, that is, who apparently didn't carry pocket mirrors and were too disappointed to bother to use them in any case. Maria and Carmela seemed to be taking it better, shrugging and chatting animatedly with each other.

"I wonder what's the matter with Nadine?" asked Cathy, who was seated next to Lucy.

"Probably the flu," said Lucy. "My friend told me there's an outbreak. I've been taking vitamin C."

"That's a good idea," said Cathy. "I'll get some. In fact, I'll get enough for everybody."

"That's a great idea," said Lucy, wishing she'd thought of it. It would have been a good way to rehabilitate her tarnished reputation.

Behind them, the audience members were beginning to file in. Cameramen and other technicians were taking their places and checking their equipment. It was all very casual and seemingly disorganized until suddenly the house lights went down and the familiar theme music came up, and Norah herself appeared, somehow looking larger than life as the audience burst into enthusiastic applause.

"We have a knockout show for you today," began Norah, listing guests including pop singer Beyoncé, sitcom star Trina Hamilton, and "a special segment on kitchen design—I know you're going to be interested in that because we all have to cook, right?"

Norah looked right into the camera and gave her signature moue, and the audience burst into laughter; she had them all in the palm of her hand and she hadn't even announced the free music CDs they'd all be getting.

"But first, I want to introduce our special guests—the winners of the *Jolie* magazine winter makeover for moms and daughters!"

Here we go, thought Lucy, as the hot spotlights hit them. They were so bright that she wanted to squint but reminded herself to smile instead as Norah approached and hugged her.

"I can't believe it!" exclaimed the star, standing between Lucy and Elizabeth and holding them by the hand. "These are my neighbors from Tinker's Cove, in Maine, where I have a summer home. Lucy and Elizabeth Stone."

To Lucy it sounded as if the audience was applauding madly.

"New York is very different from Tinker's Cove, isn't it?"

"It sure is," said Lucy, suddenly finding herself speechless.

"Are you having a good time?"

"We sure are," said Lucy, nodding and smiling for all she was worth.

Norah turned to Elizabeth, who had suddenly gone pale. "Me, too," she managed to squeak, and Norah gave them each a parting hug before moving on. Lucy heard Norah proclaim that Cathy was from Texas, but the rest was a blur as she concentrated on collecting herself. Who would have thought that a brief moment on the small screen would have such an effect? Lucy's head was swimming, her heart was pounding, her mouth was dry as cotton, and her hands were sweaty. She reached over and took Elizabeth's hand; it was ice cold. "Whew," she whispered, hoping they were out of camera range.

"That was intense," said Elizabeth, also whispering.

The show went to commercials after Norah finished introducing the others—at least that's what Lucy assumed was going on as Norah settled herself in a chair and was immediately surrounded by hair and make-up technicians who made minute adjustments to her appearance. Sidra also appeared, escorting a nattily dressed man in his mid-fifties and seating him in the guest chair.

Then, Norah was sitting up straighter and talking into a camera.

"Have I got something amazing for you," she began, introducing a video clip. "Just you watch, you won't believe this."

The audience was directed to a series of video monitors that hung from the ceiling where a model was demonstrating a state-of-the-art kitchen. Norah hadn't overstated the case; the kitchen was equipped with an oven that could hold a dish at refrigerator temperature all day until signaled by telephone to begin cooking and a refrigerator with a digital display that warned when milk and other staples were getting low. When the video was over, Norah introduced her guest, real estate developer Arnold Nelson.

"Now, Arnold, is this stuff for real?" asked Norah. "I mean, I want it, we all want it, don't we?" The audience, including Lucy, responded by clapping enthusiastically. Norah continued, "But where can we get it?"

"Well, Norah, these are the kitchens that we want to put in our new City Gate Towers, which we hope to build right here in New York on Governors Island."

Lucy leaned back, half dozing, as Arnold described the luxury condominiums that were going to be located on an island in New York harbor formerly used as a Coast Guard base.

"You're joshing me! You mean I can actually get a kitchen with all this space-age equipment right now?"

"In a year or two," answered Arnold, "if things go according to schedule. As you know, a citizens' committee is currently considering a variety of proposals for the island, and we're awaiting their recommendations. We certainly hope that City Gate Towers will be part of the final plan."

A second video began to run showing architects' drawings of the towers rising from the green and wooded island. The camera appeared to swoop around the towers, showing them in relation to landmarks including the Verrazzano Bridge, the Statue of Liberty, and the skyscrapers of Wall Street.

"That is a magnificent setting," cooed Norah. "Imagine waking up every morning to that view."

"And freshly prepared hot coffee, too, at the push of a remote button."

Norah's eyes bugged out, and the audience burst into applause.

"Our residents will have the whole city at their feet," continued Arnold, "but they'll also have the charm—and the security—of island living. It's absolutely unparalleled. There's nothing like it anywhere in the world."

"Well, sign me up," gushed Norah. "All that—and remote control coffee. It doesn't get better than that, does it?"

The audience jumped to their feet, clapping, and the cameras turned to pan them in preparation for another commercial break. Seated once again, Lucy found herself wondering about Norah's choice of Arnold as a guest. The segment had been little more than an infomercial for his development, but perhaps he was the best they could find as a last-minute substitute for Nadine.

"Do you believe it?" whispered Cathy.

"Some amazing kitchen," said Lucy, keeping her reservations to herself.

"No, I mean about Arnold."

"What about him?"

"He's Nadine's husband."

Lucy considered the implications of this. "At home, everybody knows everybody, but I didn't expect it to be like that in New York City."

"It isn't," said Cathy, lowering her voice as the house lights went down. "Here it's only everybody who's *anybody.*"

As the show continued, Lucy wondered how the last-minute switch had been arranged. Had Nadine made a quick call from the bus when she realized she was too sick to go on? Lucy hadn't noticed if she had; she only remembered seeing her sleeping. Maybe she'd given a message to Phyllis, while she was helping her get settled on the bus, and she'd made the arrangements from her office. It all seemed less than entirely square to Lucy, who was used to following Ted's strict rules at the *Pennysaver* about keeping advertisements separate from editorial policy. She shrugged mentally. Maybe TV had different standards from newspapers; she really didn't know.

Then Beyoncé was singing, and then the show was suddenly over; everybody was on their feet, applauding madly. Even Lurleen and Faith had forgotten their earlier disappointment and were smiling and clapping.

The high spirits engendered by the show continued as they all boarded the waiting bus for the ride to the hotel, where they would have an hour to rest and change for dinner and a promised Broadway show. Petty jealousies and rivalries were forgotten as Maria treated everyone to a medley of songs about New York, finally getting them all to join in for a rousing chorus of "New York, New York."

A wave of tiredness overcame Lucy as she disembarked from the bus and crossed the hotel lobby, but she was surprised when Elizabeth's steps dragged, too. She was beginning to wonder if she was coming down with the flu when the desk clerk called her name.

The others, who were gathered by the elevator, watched curiously as he presented her with a couple of square, white envelopes. Lurleen, whose eyes were practically popping out of her head, couldn't restrain herself. "What's that?" she demanded. "How come we didn't all get them?"

Lucy examined the envelopes, which were addressed to her and Elizabeth in calligraphic script. "I don't know," she said, turning them over. Seeing the name and address of the sender, she smiled. "It's nothing to do with the magazine," she said. "It's from my friend who lives in New York."

"They look like invitations," said Cathy. "A wedding, maybe?"

"I don't think so. I haven't heard anything about a wedding." Lucy was wondering what was keeping the elevator. She wanted to open the envelopes in private, in her room.

"Goodness, we're all forgetting our manners," said Ginny. "Lucy doesn't need to share her private mail with us."

"I think it's some sort of joke," said Lucy. "Probably one of those funny greeting cards."

The arrow next to the elevator was alight, signaling it was on its way down.

"I could use a joke," said Cathy.

"Oh, all right," said Lucy, slipping her finger under the envelope flap and pulling out an engraved cardboard square. The others were clustered around, craning their necks and reading over her shoulder.

"Oh my," she said, breaking into a big smile. "It is an invitation. To a ball at the Metropolitan Museum of Art. Tomorrow night."

"The AIDS gala," said Cathy, as the doors slid open.

The women crowded aboard, surging ahead of Lucy and Elizabeth, who found themselves outside, looking in at a full car.

"Sorry, no room," chirped Lurleen, as the doors closed.

Lucy and Elizabeth stood in place, looking at each other, then they burst into giggles. "A ball!" exclaimed Elizabeth, jumping up and down with excitement. "There'll be famous people, fabulous dresses . . ."

"Oh dear," said Lucy, her heart sinking as they stepped into an empty elevator. "We don't have a thing to wear!"

Chapter Six

LUXE LOOKS FOR LESS!

W hen the clock radio woke Lucy on Tuesday morning, she doubted there was much chance of getting Elizabeth out of bed. She refused to even open her eyes, instead putting a pillow over her head to block the music and burrowing deeper under the covers.

"You'll miss breakfast," warned Lucy, but there was no answer.

Lucy could barely remember the days when she preferred sleep to food and could only dimly remember the days when a day off meant sleeping until noon. Although, she admitted to herself as she stretched and got out of bed, she could use another hour or two of sleep herself. The magazine was certainly keeping them busy—they hadn't got back to the hotel from the theater until well past eleven the night before.

Stopping at the window to check the weather—gray and cold, what did she expect?—Lucy noticed the invitations to the ball that were perched on the sill. She'd tried to call Sam last night, but all she'd gotten was a busy signal. Her cell phone was also on the sill, charging completed, so she took it with her into the bath-room.

"I'm sorry to call so early," she began, when Sam answered in a groggy voice.

"No, no. I'm up, I'm just not awake yet."

"Same here," said Lucy, chuckling. "I got the invitations. . . ."

"Are you coming? Please! I've been working on it for months, and I know you'll have a great time. All sorts of famous people are coming; there'll be music and dancing and fabulous food. It's going to be *the* social event of the season, at least I hope it is."

"Since when did you become a party planner?" asked Lucy, perching on the edge of the tub.

"Don't ask," groaned Sam. "I got stuck when our fund-raiser left for another job. This isn't the sort of thing I usually do at all, and I don't really like it. I prefer working with clients, making policy, stuff like that. This has been horrible, which is why I really, really want to see some friendly, supportive faces, like yours."

"Oh, believe me, I'd love to come but Elizabeth and I don't have anything to wear."

"No problem," said Sam. "Do what I did. Go to a consignment shop. You can pick up designer duds cheap, and you can even return them the next day."

Lucy was shocked. She couldn't imagine Sam doing anything so tacky as buying a dress for a special occasion only to return it afterward.

"No, it's okay. They don't mind. That's how these consignment shops work. You won't get back as much as you paid, but it's still a good deal."

"The other problem is the makeover. The schedule's brutal, and I'm trying to win this ten-thousand-dollar prize for the best makeover so Elizabeth can go back to college next semester. I can't go sneaking away to a ball."

"*Au contraire,* Lucy. It just so happens that *Jolie* magazine has a table. Camilla Keith's coming, along with several other editors. This is your chance to wow them."

Lucy's mind was spinning. "If they're at the ball, they're not going to be with the makeover winners on the 'round-the-island dinner cruise. . . ."

"So you'll come?"

"Sure," said Lucy. "So where's this consignment shop?"

When Lucy got downstairs there was only a scattering of people, mostly dressed in business attire, in the dining room, but she spotted two familiar faces. Lucy would have preferred to sit by herself but decided it might be viewed as impolite, so after helping herself to fruit salad and yogurt from the buffet she joined Ginny and Serena at their table.

"Where is everybody?" she asked, as the waiter filled her cup with coffee.

"The girls wanted to get an extra hour of sleep," said Ginny.

"Elizabeth, too." Lucy yawned and took a sip of coffee. "Frankly, I could use a bit more sleep myself."

"I know the feeling," agreed Serena. "My biological clock hasn't adjusted to Eastern time. It's seven-thirty for you but it's more like four-thirty for me. I fell asleep during that massage yesterday."

"How was the spa?"

"Very relaxing," said Ginny. "It was the best part so far."

"I'm really looking forward to it," said Lucy. "I don't know how people keep up this pace. Things are a lot slower in Tinker's Cove."

"I could never live in the city."

"Me either," agreed Serena. "Everybody's in such a hurry here. They don't know how to relax and chill."

"And they're so rude," said Ginny.

"I think it's the weather," said Serena. "It's so cold and there's not enough sunshine. It makes people irritable and depressed."

"Have you seen the subway? I'd sure be depressed if I had to face that every day. It's so dirty and nasty. The streets are dirty, too. We wouldn't tolerate it in Omaha."

"I guess it's just a by-product of city life," said Lucy. "So many people and cars in a small space."

"It doesn't seem healthy to me."

"Well, believe it or not, New Yorkers are supposed to be the healthiest people in the country because they're so fit. They walk miles every day. And they also consume less energy. Big cities are actually good for the environment."

From their expressions it was clear that Ginny and Serena didn't believe her.

"It's true," insisted Lucy. "Look at Maria and Carmela—they look fabulous."

"They sure don't hide their figures," said Serena, smoothing her Juicy Couture tangerine hoodie over her ample bosom.

"You'd get arrested if you dressed like that in Omaha," said Ginny, adjusting her turtleneck. "Yesterday you could actually see Carmela's bra. What was she thinking, wearing a black bra under a sheer white blouse?"

"What was her mother thinking, letting her out of the house like that?" Serena's vehemence shocked Lucy, who had yet to see Ocean with her belly covered.

"Not that Maria is much better. I don't know how she gets in and out of those skirts. They're so tight they look like she sprays them on."

"And those nails! They must be two inches long. How can she do anything?"

"Mine break," said Lucy, with a sigh, opening the morning paper. The headline wasn't encouraging: FLU DEATHS RISE.

"I hate stories like this," said Lucy, showing the others. "What are you supposed to do? Stop breathing?"

"Wash your hands," said Ginny.

"Take vitamin C," offered Serena. "And echinacea."

"That's all well and good, but somebody can still sneeze in your face, like Nadine. She was sneezing and coughing all over the place yesterday."

"Do you think she has the flu?" asked Ginny.

"I wouldn't be surprised," said Lucy, spooning up a big chunk of vitamin-C-rich grapefruit.

When Lucy and Elizabeth arrived at the *Jolie* offices, Lucy was relieved to discover they'd been paired with Cathy and Tiffany for wardrobe consultations. She hadn't much liked listening to Serena's and Ginny's complaints about the city and she suspected their comments about Maria and Carmela had more to do with racism than fashion choices. Lurleen and Faith, on the other hand, were sweet and nonjudgmental, but Lucy feared that given half a chance they would try to convert her to their evangelical faith.

Cathy was breezy and cheerful as ever as they made their way to the fashion department, and Lucy suspected her positive attitude was bolstered by the mink coat and five-carat diamond ring she was wearing, not to mention the Hermès Kelly bag she was carrying. Lucy didn't believe you could buy happiness, but she figured a well-padded bank account could smooth a lot of bumps in the rocky road of life.

She was also impressed that Cathy got along so well with her stepdaughter, Tiffany, even though the two were close enough in age to be sisters. At least that was the impression she got from their body language and relaxed banter.

"I wonder what they're planning to dress us in?" mused Lucy as they stepped into the elevator that would take them up several floors to the fashion department. "I didn't see anything at the fashion show that I could possibly wear."

"You better be ready for feathers and see-through net dresses, if that make-up session yesterday was any indication," said Cathy. "That Nadine wanted to put a green stripe across my nose."

"And she wanted to give me blue lipstick," added Tiffany, giggling.

"I think she gave me the flu," said Elizabeth, who looked as if she'd like to go back to bed.

"That reminds me," said Cathy, digging through the fabulous purse as if it were just a plastic number from Wal-Mart, "I've got vitamins for everybody." She finally produced two bottles of vitamin C and gave them to Elizabeth and Lucy as the elevator doors slid open.

Fashion editor Elise Frazier was in the hallway, ready to greet them, dressed again today in a mannish pantsuit. "Welcome, welcome to the fashion department," she said in a flat voice as if she were reciting a tired refrain. "Here we believe we can make every woman look fabulous no matter what her shape or figure flaws."

"So much for all those hours at the gym," joked Cathy.

"Oh, you know what I mean," replied Elise, who was shaped rather like an NFL fullback. "We can all use a little help. I wear heels to make my legs look longer, and I always dress in one color from head to toe because it makes me look slimmer."

"At least that's the theory," muttered Elizabeth, getting a giggle from Tiffany and a sharp look from her mother.

"Oh, here's our accessories editor, Deb Shertzer," trilled Elise. "If you ask me, she's got the best job at the magazine. Shoes, scarves, bags—her office is like Aladdin's cave. You should see the jewelry."

Looking at Elise, Lucy thought her enthusiasm for accessories rang a bit hollow, considering she wasn't wearing a single piece of jewelry and her shoes were simple black pumps with sturdy heels.

"As jobs go, it's not too hard to take," replied Deb, with a sparkle in her eye. Unlike most of the women working at the magazine she was wearing flats, and her black slacks and colorful sweater looked both attractive and comfortable. She turned to Lucy and gave her a big smile. "You're the one with the lobster watch, aren't you?"

Elizabeth looked as if she'd like to disappear.

"It was just a joke present from my husband," said Lucy, sliding up her sleeve to give a better view of the red plastic timepiece. "He got it free at the hardware store."

"Well, I think it's adorable," said Deb. "A lot of designers are coming out with similar ideas for summer. There's one that has a beach umbrella on the face and a smiley yellow sun on the hour hand. I'm going to feature it in the June accessories roundup."

Lucy gave Elizabeth rather a smug look.

"Well, come along and we'll get started," said Elise, leading them into a large room filled with racks of clothes. A cluster of portable screens were arranged at one end to serve as changing rooms, along with a three-sided mirror. "If you ladies don't mind, it would be a lot easier if you'd strip down to your undies, but we have arranged dressing rooms, if you'd prefer."

"Not a problem for me," said Lucy, shrugging out of her coat. "I put on clean underpants this morning."

"Mom," groaned Elizabeth, sinking into a chair.

"It was just a joke," said Lucy, bending down to unlace her duck boots.

"Well, well, I see we don't have to disguise anything," said Elise, looking her up and down. "You have a very trim shape—not a saddlebag in sight." She narrowed her eyes, and Lucy found herself tucking her bottom in and straightening her back. "I think we can try to give you a bit more height; black is good for that."

She turned to Deb, who was sitting on a folding chair with a notebook in her lap. "And heels, of course."

Deb nodded and wrote it down.

Elise turned to Elizabeth, who was slowly divesting herself of her clothing as if it was a painful task. "Such a sweet face," she crooned. "We can give you a bit more sophistication. Something with couture details, and I think black would really set off your lovely pale skin."

Tiffany was next to Elizabeth, slumping a bit to disguise her height. She didn't fool Elise, however. "You're so tall, you could carry a fuller skirt. I have just the thing in black net. We'll top it with a silky turtleneck over a good padded bra."

Tiffany shot her a murderous look but Elise missed it, moving on to Cathy. "Those hours in the gym have certainly paid off for you!" she exclaimed. "Definitely something to show off those toned arms." She stepped back, her hand on her chin. "Though with those boobs we have to be careful—definitely no turtlenecks; they'll make you look like you've got three chins, and we need something fitted at the waist." She clucked her tongue. "I really do think silicone is a bad idea. Those doctors tend to go overboard."

"Hey!" protested Cathy, pointing to her lacey black bra, "this is all me. I didn't have surgery."

Elise looked doubtful. "Right. I'm so sorry. I certainly didn't mean to insult you."

"I'm beginning to feel like a human pincushion," complained Cathy. "First it was Camilla making that crack about trophy wives and now you're knocking my boobs."

Elise drew herself up to her full height, a sight that reminded Lucy of a dragon in some animated Disney film. "I'll thank you not to criticize Camilla. The woman's a genius—and she happens to be one of my best friends."

Glancing at Deb, who was going through a box of scarves, Lucy thought she detected a smirk.

"She may be your friend," said Cathy, "but you have to admit she can be bitchy. Everyone knows that."

Elise was getting quite red in the face, and Lucy was afraid she'd begin breathing fire. "Friendship is a wonderful thing," she said, hoping to defuse the situation. "I think women especially need friends, for a support system. I don't know what I'd do without my friends."

"I met Camilla in college," said Elise, flipping furiously through a rack of clothes. "We were in the same class at Barnard. Nadine, too, and we've been friends ever since."

"Like the Heathers," said Cathy, with a wicked gleam in her eye.

Lucy wished she'd let it drop, but Elise either didn't hear the comment or decided to let it pass. "Now where is that pinstripe pantsuit?" she muttered, marching over to another rack.

The rest of the morning passed without further fireworks between Elise and Cathy, and the women were soon outfitted and accessorized. Lucy had to admit she looked great in the pantsuit and high-heeled boots Elise chose for her, and she was thrilled to learn they would all be able to keep their outfits, even though she couldn't quite imagine what sort of occasion in Tinker's Cove would require such a dressy ensemble.

Cathy, on the other hand, wasn't impressed. "I always wear designer," she said, with a sniff. "I haven't worn anything off the rack since I can't remember when."

"Oh, I can tell you," snapped Elise, unable to resist getting in another dig. "I'll bet it was when you married Mr. Montgomery."

Lucy expected Cathy to answer with a sharp retort but, instead, she smiled at Tiffany. "Mr. Montgomery is a generous husband, and father, isn't he? He always says he's got great-looking girls and he wants us to have pretty clothes."

Hearing this, Elise looked fit to be tied. "If you'll be so kind as to take these things off so I can label them for tomorrow's photo shoot I would appreciate it," she said, speaking to the room in general and avoiding eye contact.

Back in their own clothes, Lucy and Elizabeth made a break for the exit. They had to get dresses for tonight's ball and were planning to use the lunch break to make a quick trip to the designer consignment shop. They were on their way when they encountered Fiona in the elevator.

"Aren't you coming to lunch?' she asked, noticing they were wearing their coats. "They've got a top dermatologist talking about skin care."

"No lunch for us, we're going shopping," said Elizabeth.

"Do you have anyplace particular in mind?"

"Actually, we do," said Lucy. "It's a consignment shop on Sixty-sixth Street."

"Brilliant!" exclaimed Fiona. "Do you mind if I tag along?"

"Please do. We can use your expert advice," said Lucy.

Since time was short Lucy splurged on a cab, and they all piled in together for the ride uptown.

"So how do you like the makeover so far?" asked Fiona.

"It's pretty intense," said Lucy. "Especially with this contest."

"It's exhausting," said Elizabeth.

Lucy quickly added, "But we're loving every minute."

"You don't have to put on a brave face for me," said Fiona. "I'm just the hired help, and if things work out I won't be at *Jolie* much longer."

"Are you looking for another job?" asked Elizabeth.

Fiona was looking out the window. "You could say that."

"I don't blame you," said Lucy. "It must be very stressful working there. It's a very tense atmosphere, at least it seems that way to me. Maybe all fashion magazines are like that."

"Not the ones that are making money," said Fiona.

"Is *Jolie* in trouble?" asked Lucy.

"You bet. And Camilla with it. The publisher gave her an ultimatum that she has to turn a profit in six months or else."

"Or else what?"

"Heads will roll," said Fiona, drawing a finger across her throat. "But I bet it won't be hers."

"Why not?" asked Elizabeth. "She's the boss, after all."

"She's also a survivor. She's very good at rising above the fray. I think she'll fix it so that people she doesn't like, like Pablo and Nancy, will be blamed. The ones who actually have good ideas and work hard will get the ax and she and her Barnard buddies will probably get raises."

"So much cynicism in one so young," said Lucy.

"Listen, I come from the land of Henry VIII and Richard III. Treachery is like mother's milk to me." She looked up as the taxi pulled to a halt in front of the pink-and-white–striped awning of the New to You thrift boutique. "I also love a bargain. Did you ever hear how Henry VIII snagged Hampton Court?"

*   *   *

That night, as she climbed up the steps to the Metropolitan Museum of Art on Fifth Avenue, Lucy could easily imagine that she was attending a royal ball. The museum's classical stone façade was illuminated with floodlights, and strains of music could be heard as they joined the elegantly dressed throng gathered at the door. Once inside, Lucy was overwhelmed by the magnificent great hall, decorated with enormous Christmas trees and floral arrangements; the buzz of voices; and the conflicting scents of perfume.

"Now that we're here, what do we do?" asked Elizabeth. She sounded nervous, despite the fact that she looked lovely in a floaty blue Stella McCartney number.

"Let's cruise around and get something to drink," said Lucy, catching a glimpse of Sam across the room, earnestly engaged in conversation with a photographer. "Maybe we'll run into somebody we know."

"Mom, that's Donald Trump."

"So it is," said Lucy, who had to resist the impulse to gawk.

"And that's Ashton Kutcher."

"Who?" Lucy had spotted a waiter holding a tray of champagne flutes. "Oh my gosh, that's Mikhail Baryshnikov helping himself to champagne."

"Who?"

Lucy was looking for Sam but it was Norah who took them by surprise, engulfing them both in a lavender satin embrace.

"You girls sure clean up nice," she exclaimed. "Isn't this amazing? I bet you've never seen anything like this in Tinker's Cove."

"That's for sure," agreed Lucy.

"If I'm not mistaken, you're wearing Donna Karan. I've got that dress myself."

"It's the first designer dress I've ever worn," confessed Lucy, pleased to have her good taste confirmed. She lowered her voice to a whisper. "I got it at a thrift shop."

"Good for you!"

"Even so, it was awfully expensive. Bill would die if he knew how much I spent."

"Never you mind. You can take it back tomorrow. But tonight, you look like it was made for you."

"Thanks, Norah," said Lucy, stepping aside as Camilla joined their little circle and exchanged air kisses with Norah. She was dressed in a black sheath that emphasized her slimness, with an oversized white ruffle at the neck; Lucy thought it made her look like Cruella De Vil.

"Don't you all look fabulous!" exclaimed Camilla. "I can see my staff has done wonders with, uh, you two girls."

Lucy wasn't about to introduce herself yet again if Camilla couldn't be bothered to remember her name. "What, this?" she said, indicating her dress. "I just pulled it out of my suitcase."

Norah winked and drifted off to chat with another friend.

Camilla watched her go but could hardly run after her. Left with these nobodies, she fingered Elizabeth's dress. "I do so love Stella McCartney. Such a bright talent. Did you get it here or in London?"

"Here," said Elizabeth. "She's my favorite designer."

"I haven't seen you at one of these affairs before," said Camilla, her eyes darting around the room. "Do you get to the city often?"

"To Boston," said Lucy. "Not New York."

"Boston is such a quaint little town. Who do you know there?"

"Lots of people," said Elizabeth, thinking of her friends at Chamberlain College.

Lucy knew that Camilla was probing purposefully, trying to ascertain Lucy's social status, and she was willing to play the game. "Junior Read is a dear friend," she said, referring to the Pioneer Press publisher who had a summer home in Tinker's Cove. It wasn't such a stretch; she'd helped him out of a tight spot a year or two ago.

"Mom, I see Lance," said Elizabeth, suddenly becoming quite perky.

Lucy followed her gaze and saw Norah's son consulting the seating chart. She tended to still think of him as the gangly middle-schooler who had been Elizabeth's first boyfriend and was shocked to see how elegant he looked dressed in a tux. The garish dyed hair he sported as a kid was gone, replaced with a fashionable close buzz cut, and he looked relaxed and confident.

"Run along," said Lucy. "Have a good time."

Elizabeth departed in a flutter of fashionable blue tatters and was embraced enthusiastically by Lance.

"That's Norah's son, isn't it?" asked Camilla.

"They're old friends," said Lucy.

"From school? I believe Lance went to Exeter," said Camilla, naming the prestigious prep school.

"Right, from school," said Lucy, not finding it necessary to mention that they'd met at Tinker's Cove Middle School.

"So what do you do?" asked Camilla, continuing her investigation.

"I'm active in civic affairs," said Lucy, telling herself it wasn't a lie since she covered town events as a reporter for the local newspaper. "And I lunch with friends," she added, thinking of the numerous peanut butter sandwiches she'd enjoyed with Sue and Pam and Rachel. "You know the sort of thing: mostly fund-raising for local charities." Lucy was a mainstay of the Hat and Mitten Fund committee, which provided warm clothing for the little town's less fortunate children.

"We really ought to do a feature on you country ladies," mused Camilla. "We tend to forget that there's life beyond the city."

"Ah, Camilla! Great to see you."

Lucy's eyes widened as she recognized Arnold Nelson, who she'd seen on the *Norah!* show, and waited for Camilla to introduce her.

"Arnold, this is uh, one of our makeover winners."

Lucy took his hand. "I'm Lucy Stone, from Maine."

"Nice to meet you. I hope you'll do me the honor of dancing with me."

"I'd love to," said Lucy, seizing the opportunity to avoid more of Camilla's probing questions. She was irked that the woman couldn't be bothered to remember her name but could easily recall which prep school Lance Hemmings attended. It just showed her priorities.

Her irritation soon vanished, however, as Arnold spun her around the room in an elegant waltz. He was an excellent dancer, and it was a bit like being in a dream, dancing in the arms of this wealthy man who smelled so good, even if he was a bit thick in the middle and had a jowly chin.

"I saw you yesterday, on the TV show," began Lucy, intending to ask him about the City Gate Towers project he hoped to build on Governors Island.

"You know, you don't look at all like someone who needs a makeover," said Arnold, promptly changing the subject. "You look pretty fine as you are."

"Oh, this is after. You should have seen me before," joked Lucy.

"I'd really like to see you after," said Arnold, his voice deepening. "I've got a bottle of champagne on ice at my penthouse and a fresh delivery of caviar from my Russian friend Ivan. Have you ever tasted caviar?"

"I have and I don't like it," said Lucy, wondering if this was a pass.

"Ah, then you've never had really good caviar," said Arnold. "I'd love to introduce you to it. What do you say? A man can get awfully lonely up on the thirty-seventh floor."

Enough was enough, decided Lucy, determined to put an end to Arnold's propositions as the orchestra played the final chords of the waltz.

"How is Nadine?" she asked. "She seemed so miserable yesterday. I thought she might have this flu that's in the news."

"The doctors are puzzled," he said, turning abruptly to follow a willowy blond model Lucy recognized from the fashion show.

Left to her own devices, Lucy decided to check out the buffet of hors d'oeuvres. She figured it would be a deviled-eggs-free zone, and she was right. She was considering trying a piece of sushi, something she'd never had, when she finally spotted Sam. She would have known her anywhere, she realized with amazement. Even in a fancy evening gown Sam was still Sam, with short red hair, oversized eyeglasses and a huge smile. What was surprising, however, was that she was accompanied by two men, one of whom was Geoff Rumford, Sidra's husband.

After hugs, Sam began the introductions. "Lucy, meet my husband, Brad. . . ."

"It's about time," said Lucy, giving him a hug.

"And I understand you know Geoff from home?"

"I sure do. But how do you know him? It seems incredible to me that two of my friends would meet in a big city like New York."

"New York's big, all right, but it's made up of circles of interest. People who are interested in the same things keep on bumping into each other," said Sam.

"Brad and I met when we were both panelists at a community forum about public education," said Geoff.

"This is the last place I ever expected to see you," said Lucy, remembering Geoff as a suntanned lobsterman in Tinker's Cove.

"He's a tagalong, like me," said Brad, wrapping his arms around his wife's waist. "Sam lassoed me into this. She said if she had to organize it there was no way I wasn't going to come."

"And I'm here because Norah needed to fill her table and drafted Sidra."

"Well, a man's gotta do what a man's gotta do," said Lucy.

"This is weird," said Geoff. "By day I'm a mild-mannered high school science teacher; by night, a man about town."

"I'm sure you fill both roles admirably," said Lucy. "How about you, Brad? Do you get to affairs like this very often?"

"Too often," he said, glumly.

"It's not as bad as all that. The food's good," said Sam, punching his arm.

"And there are plenty of pretty girls to look at," said Lucy.

"So long as he only looks," said Sam.

"You don't need to worry there. I have to save my energy. I'm going to be dragging tomorrow morning, and I've got an early morning meeting."

"Governors Island?" asked Geoff. When Brad nodded, he continued, "How's that going? I heard something about a proposal for a maritime trades high school."

Lucy turned to Sam, hoping to catch up with her news while the men talked shop, but she had spotted trouble across the room. "Sorry, Lucy, I've got to get Lady Warburton away from the bar before she disgraces herself. . . . Call me!"

Lucy gave her a little wave and watched as she steered a tottery old woman with an elaborate hairdo over to the buffet, then turned her attention to Brad.

"Everybody's got proposals," he was saying, "but nobody's got funding, except Arnold Nelson. He could break ground tomorrow while everybody else is scrambling, writing grants, and trying to raise money."

"How does he do it?" asked Geoff.

"Glamour," said Brad, nodding sagely. "He works events like this; he uses his wife's contacts at that fashion magazine. Sam tells me the ladies on the ball committee have all invested in Nelco and can hardly talk about anything else."

Lucy found Nelson in the crowd, dancing with a very tall brunette in a short red dress. She had thrown her head back, and her mouth was open in a laugh as if he'd just said something wonderfully clever. "He just looks sleazy to me," she said with a shrug, "but he sure gets around. He was on Norah's show yesterday, pushing that City Gate project."

"Nelco? Is that his outfit?" asked Geoff.

"Yeah. Have you heard something?" asked Brad.

Geoff considered. "Maybe. If it's the same outfit. Could be Felco or Welco—they all sound the same to me."

"Run it by me and I'll check it out," said Brad.

"Well," began Geoff. The band began playing a loud rock tune, and Lucy and Brad stepped closer to hear. "If it's the same outfit, they're building that new biomedical research lab for NYU. It's a Level 4 infectious diseases facility, and it would be one of only a handful in the country. It's desperately needed but I heard there's been all kinds of problems."

"Shoddy construction? Contract disputes?" asked Brad.

"No. Nothing like that. Vandalism. Sand in the gas tanks, brake lines cut, stuff like that. It's really vicious. There have even been death threats. It's got to the point where suppliers and truckers don't want to have anything to do with it."

"It could be neighbors," said Lucy. "They might be afraid of having a germy old lab in the neighborhood."

"I'd put my money on the unions," said Brad. "There's a lot of frustration out there. Even the cops and firefighters are threatening strikes."

"I know there's some concern that Nelco or whoever it is will pull out, which would delay the project, maybe even kill it." Geoff drained his beer. "That would've been a perfect project for Governors Island, you know, instead of Arnold's pricey condos. What happened to the public–private partnership we heard so much about? I thought the private developers were going to fund some of the public projects in exchange for permission to build."

"They all dropped out when the federal government established the national park and started allowing public access. It was the inaccessibility, the exclusivity that had appeal. Now they're saying nobody's going to pay millions for a ritzy address if the hoi polloi can picnic on the lawn. The only one left is Arnold, and he's playing hardball."

"What's the big deal? Access is still very limited, just Saturdays in the summer."

Brad shrugged. "It doesn't bother Arnold, that's for sure. He'll wring a sweet deal out of the city and make a bundle. Subsidized housing for millionaires."

Lucy smiled as Sidra joined their group, looking chic in a shimmering satin column of a dress. "If only your mother could see you now," she said, giving her a hug. "She'd be so proud."

"She wouldn't believe it," said Sidra, laughing. "We used to squabble all the time over my fashion choices." She put her hand on her husband's arm. "I'm sorry, but I have to drag Geoff away. He has to get up early tomorrow, and I promised I wouldn't keep him out too late."

They all said their farewells, then Brad asked Lucy to dance, saying he felt quite neglected by his wife, who was too busy making sure the event ran smoothly to pay any attention to him. He wasn't as good a dancer as Arnold, but Lucy enjoyed herself a lot more. When the orchestra played the final song, "I Could Have Danced All Night," Lucy wished the evening would never end.

Chapter Seven

FAB FASHIONS TO DIE FOR!

Unlike Cinderella, Lucy had both her shoes next morning and her Prince Charming was keeping the home fires burning in Tinker's Cove. Today was the final day of the makeover, and she needed to make the most of it if she was going to have any chance of winning the ten thousand dollars, she thought, hurrying over to the one-hour dry cleaners on Third Avenue with the consignment shop dresses.

She wasn't quite sure when she was going to manage to pick them up and get them back to the shop, but she was determined to try despite today's hectic schedule. This morning all the makeover winners were supposed to get their hair done at one of New York's swankiest salons, Rudolf's, in preparation for the afternoon shoot of the "after" photos. That evening the award dinner was planned, followed by the holiday show at Radio City Music Hall, and the makeover would officially be over. Tomorrow she would return home to tackle the sink full of dirty dishes and the mountain of laundry that she was certain awaited her.

The very thought was depressing, and she let out a big sigh as she laid the dresses on the counter in the dry cleaning shop.

"So the party's over," chuckled the clerk, a black woman with a round face and a big smile.

"You can say that again," said Lucy, a bit surprised at how regretful she sounded. After all, she missed Bill and the kids and even the dog, Libby. She couldn't wait to see them. Really. But experience had taught her that even a brief absence could require some painstaking work repairing relationships. The dog, for example, would wag her tail in glee when they returned, but then she'd refuse to come when called or would scatter her food all over the kitchen floor. The same went for the girls. They would greet her enthusiastically when she arrived, but then the tales of woe would begin: "I couldn't find my long underwear" or "Dad wouldn't let me go to the movies with my friends" or even her all-time favorite, "I think I'm getting leprosy." Bill would make her pay, too, in subtle ways. He'd forget to mail the mortgage payment or would flare up angrily over some trifle or would want to know why she never baked apple pie from scratch anymore.

Truth be told, she wouldn't mind spending a few more days in the city. She'd really enjoyed the hustle and bustle of the streets, where the honking horns of the cabs expressed the impatience everybody seemed to share. She'd also enjoyed the chambermaid service at the hotel, where she didn't even have to make her bed. But best of all, she realized, was the attention she'd received from the magazine's experts. Until now, nobody, herself included, had expressed any concern about the shape of her eyebrows or the condition of her skin. Well, except for Sue, who provided a running critique of her appearance. But Sue was always negative, while the people at the magazine had been a lot more positive. It was "this color becomes you," or "try this lipstick," or "let's bring that hem down an inch and see how it looks," which was a lot easier to take than Sue's constant carping. It had been nice to think of herself for a change.

And, of course, there was the ball. The flowers, the music, the food, the dancing, the clothes . . . it had all been wonderful, a once-in-a-lifetime experience, and she'd never forget it.

"Do you want these dresses in an hour or is one o'clock okay?" asked the clerk, bringing Lucy back to reality.

"One is fine," she said, taking the ticket and hurrying back to the hotel, stopping in a coffee shop to get an enormous bagel and a couple of coffees to go. They were due at Rudolf's in less than an hour and, since there hadn't been any earthquakes this morning, she was prepared to bet money that Elizabeth was still asleep.

So sound asleep, in fact, that she didn't stir when Lucy came into the room.

"Come on, honey. We've got a photo shoot today."

"I'm tired."

"Well, what do you expect when you dance all night and drink a gallon of champagne?"

"Didn't."

"Don't try to pretend you weren't drinking," said Lucy, carefully setting the paper cup of coffee on the tiny nightstand. "I saw you with a glass of champagne. I don't know how they get away with serving underage drinkers, but I didn't see any of the servers asking for ID."

"Mom, I think I'm sick. I ache all over."

"Even a glass or two could give you a hangover because you're not used to it."

"I only had a sip or two."

"Really?" Lucy couldn't help thinking of the headline announcing the flu epidemic's rising death toll.

"Yeah. And I've got this bite on my hand that really hurts." She held out her right hand, which was swollen and had a nasty red bump. "There's no bugs in winter, are there?"

"I don't know. Maybe city bugs are different," said Lucy. "Drink some coffee."

"Maybe some water?"

Lucy went into the bathroom to fill a glass for Elizabeth, and when she returned she discovered the girl had fallen asleep again. She pressed her hand against Elizabeth's forehead and was relieved to find it was cool.

"Come on, honey." Lucy shook her shoulder. "You've got to get up."

The girl's eyes finally opened and she managed to take a sip or two of water. Then, very unsteadily, she made her way to the bathroom.

"Demon rum," muttered Lucy, unaware that she sounded exactly like her great-grandmother, a founding member of the Women's Christian Temperance Union.

* * *

Elizabeth seemed to rally when they arrived at Rudolf's exclusive Fifth Avenue salon, where customers were greeted by a constantly flowing wall of water before being ushered into a luxurious waiting area where they were offered a choice of fresh coffee or herbal tea. Not that they had to wait very long; Lucy had only taken a sip of two of coffee before she was whisked into a private treatment room by a white-coat beautician.

Once Lucy was installed in the chair and covered with a smock, the beautician, an Asian girl with flawless tan skin and long, glossy black hair, began examining Lucy's hair.

"Too dry," was her verdict, "and your color is not flattering."

"Really?"

"You need something warmer, a little red perhaps."

Lucy didn't like the sound of this. "Not red."

"Trust me, you'll see," said the beautician, busily squeezing tubes of color into a plastic dish and stirring enthusiastically.

Soon Lucy's head was slathered with a mudlike substance and tightly covered with a plastic cap. Then she was seated under a hair dryer, next to several other makeover winners. They all looked rather nervous.

"Why are we under the dryer?" asked Lucy, raising her voice to be heard above the noise of the machine.

"Beats me," said Ginny.

"I didn't want any color, I insisted," said Lurleen.

"It's a new process," said Cathy, who was flipping through *Town & Country* magazine. "It sets the color faster."

"I don't have color," said Lurleen. "I specifically said I didn't want it."

"Trust me," said Cathy, nodding sagely. "You got color."

Before Lurleen could protest further, the hood of the dryer was flipped back by a remarkably handsome young man wearing a tight white T-shirt that showed his muscles to advantage. "Ready for your shampoo?" he cooed, leading her away. For once, Lurleen was dumbstruck.

"I hope I get him, too," said Cathy.

"Me, too," piped up Ginny, and they all laughed.

When her turn came Lucy didn't get the young man—she got an enthusiastic girl in a smock who she guessed came from Russia.

"First wash, then intense treatment," she said, shoving Lucy back and hosing off the dye. "I give you head massage, no?"

Lucy felt completely powerless as Olga or whoever she was kneaded and pummeled and pounded her head. Then she was rinsed with scalding water, followed by cold, and slathered with some sort of organic substance that smelled like cow manure.

"What is this stuff?" she asked.

"Good for you; good for hair. I be back in ten minutes."

Soothing music was playing, and Lucy decided she might as well relax. These people were experts, they knew what they were doing. She took a deep breath and closed her eyes.

Next thing she knew she was hit with a blast of freezing water. Reflexively, she jerked to a sitting position and was firmly shoved backward. "Must rinse."

"C-c-cold," sputtered Lucy.

"Good for hair," grunted Olga, apparently ripping Lucy's hair out by the roots. At least that's what it felt like. Only a decade or two later Lucy heard the water stop, a towel was wrapped around her head and screwed tight, and she was propelled upright. "Follow me."

Aware that resistance was futile, Lucy followed the Slavic tyrant down a pink hallway back to her private treatment room. Amazing, she thought, as she seated herself in the chair and studied her reflection in the mirror: there was no trace of the pain she had suffered.

When Lucy's stylist returned and unwrapped the towel, she clucked her tongue appreciatively. "Very good." She proceeded to comb and clip Lucy's hair, working with astonishing speed. Then she was gone and a tall, storklike man wielding a blow dryer appeared. He was completely bald and sported at least twenty silver bangles on each wrist.

"I'm Rudy," he said, whirling her around in the chair so her back was to the mirror.

"Nice to meet you, Rudy," said Lucy, crossing her fingers under the smock. She heard the bracelets jingling as he worked and tried to keep a good thought. It was reassuring to discover Olga hadn't yanked out all her hair; she could feel him brushing and tugging at something. Suddenly the blow dryer's roar was silenced, she was whirled around, and Rudy said, "Voila!"

Lucy was silent, studying her reflection. Her hair was now a subtle auburn, so silky it gleamed. It shimmered and glowed. It looked fantastic. She'd never looked better, and she couldn't understand how a haircut could cause such a dramatic change.

"How did you do that?" she asked.

"Trade secret," he said, and was gone.

When Lucy was escorted back to the waiting area, she discovered all the contest winners were there, congratulating each other on their new hairdos. Everyone except Elizabeth.

Puzzled, and a bit anxious, she turned to her escort. "Where's my daughter?"

"Elizabeth?"

"That's her."

"Don't worry. Just a small delay. She asked if we could stop for a few minutes and let her take a little nap." The girl giggled. "She said she was up late last night, at a ball."

"Can I see her?"

"No. Rudy is finishing her. He doesn't like to be watched when he works."

Lucy seated herself and picked up a magazine.

"Is something wrong?" asked Cathy. "Don't you like your hair? I think it looks fabulous."

"Thanks. Yours, too," said Lucy. "I'm just a little worried about Elizabeth. They say she asked them to let her nap because she was so tired."

Just then Elizabeth appeared and everyone started clapping. The ragged, spiky look had been tamed and her color brightened with buttery blond highlights; she looked radiant, blushing with embarrassment at the group's reaction.

"I hate it," she declared, joking, and everyone laughed.

Fiona was speechless when they arrived at the magazine's beauty department to be made up for the photo.

"Blond! I never would've. . . ."

"Me, either," agreed Elizabeth.

"It looks great."

"Thanks. I wish I'd had it for the ball last night."

"Bummer." Fiona reached for the blush. "Who was there? What were they wearing?"

"Beyoncé is every bit as gorgeous in real life as she is in her videos," gushed Elizabeth. "But Paris Hilton looks even skinnier in real life than she does on TV. Can you imagine?"

"She has great skin, though," said Fiona. "That tan is gorgeous. Fake, sure, but really well done."

"It's actually orange," volunteered Lucy, waiting her turn.

"Elizabeth's a bit peaked today," said Fiona, applying blush liberally with a brush. "Too much champagne?"

"You're starting to sound like my mother," complained Elizabeth.

In the adjacent chair, Lucy suppressed a giggle as Phyllis sponged on foundation.

"Actually, I'm afraid she's coming down with the flu." She paused. "How's Nadine doing?"

"I'm worried," admitted Phyllis. "This isn't like her. She never takes sick days. I can't remember the last time, it was that long ago. She's so devoted to her job."

"Phyllis," said Fiona, leveling her gaze at the assistant beauty editor. "Nadine doesn't even do her job. You do her job."

"Oh, that's not true," protested Phyllis.

"Yes, it is," insisted Fiona. "Think about it. What does she actually do?"

"She's on the phone a lot."

"With her friends."

"She gives assignments."

"So she doesn't have to do them."

"She studies new products."

"Takes them home, you mean. Bags and bags full."

"Well, the manufacturers are developing new products all the time."

"And she scoops them all up. Every single one. When's the last time she offered something to you?"

"It's her prerogative. She's the beauty editor."

"In name only. You do all the work."

"That's nonsense," protested Phyllis, brushing some mascara

on Lucy's lashes. "Nadine's the idea person. I just do what she tells me."

"Admit it," snapped Fiona. "If she never came back you couldn't tell the difference, except we'd all get more free stuff."

"You just want the bottle of Penhaligon perfume," said Phyllis. "Can I take it?"

"Sure." Phyllis giggled. "Just don't tell Nadine."

"Cross my heart," said Fiona, spraying it on liberally.

Lucy was still trying to pin down the fragrance—predominantly floral, but with a hint of something exotic—when they went to the fashion department to try on their new outfits. Lucy had to admit Elise had chosen well: the fitted jacket showed off her figure, and the long, straight pants, with heels underneath, made her legs look longer. Elizabeth's off-the-shoulder top showed off her pale skin beautifully, and the flowing black skirt and boots were a nice change from the jeans she usually wore, yet it still looked fun and casual. They were quite pleased with their made-over selves when they headed for the photo studio.

That satisfaction changed when they saw the other women, all similarly arrayed in varying shades of black. And now that she got a good look at everyone, Lucy realized Rudy had given them all remarkably similar hairdos.

"Oh my gawd," laughed Cathy. "We look like members of the same coven!"

"You shouldn't joke about the devil," said Lurleen.

"That hairdresser was a devil, that's for sure," said Ginny, fingering the shaggy pageboy that was a mirror image of Lucy's and Lurleen's and Serena's styles. "We all have Jennifer Aniston's hairdo."

"But not the rest of her," said Serena, patting her plump bottom, which was now disguised in a black A-line skirt. A scoopnecked blouse with a fitted waist flattered her ample decolletage while vertical stripes slimmed her middle.

"Well, I like the way I look and once I'm back home, away from you guys, I won't look like I was stamped out with a cookie cutter," said Lucy, as Pablo and Nancy arrived.

They both seemed happy enough with the contest winners'

new looks as they wandered from group to group, discussing possible poses.

"Fabulous, fabulous chiaroscuro," murmured Pablo, stroking Elizabeth's shoulder. "I'm thinking Goya, Rembrandt. A play of light and dark, like a classical portrait in a museum. And we'll have a group shot, you know that very big painting of the Spanish royal court?"

"The one with the dwarf?" asked Nancy.

"That's the one," said Pablo, lifting Cathy's face by the chin and turning it from side to side. "But I don't want the dwarf. Maybe a monkey."

"You want a monkey?"

"Yes." Pablo had decided. "I must have a monkey."

"Where am I going to get a monkey? And what if it bites someone. There may be liability issues."

Pablo stamped his foot and tossed his head. "This is what I have to deal with, all the time! How can I be creative when it's always a problem? Just borrow one from the zoo! In Central Park, a few blocks from here, there are plenty of monkeys. I saw them myself."

"Pablo, be reasonable," begged Nancy. "The zoo isn't going to lend us a monkey."

"No?" He hung his head, pouting.

"If you get the pose right you won't need a monkey."

"You're right! Pablo is a genius; I don't need a monkey. The camera is my monkey."

This announcement seemed to satisfy Nancy, but Lucy found it puzzling, as did the others.

"What does that mean? The camera is my monkey?" whispered Lurleen.

"He's an artist," said Lucy, with a shrug.

Before Lurleen could reply, the two women were pulled apart by Pablo's assistant, who was arranging the women according to the photographer's instructions, which he shouted down from his perch on a tall ladder. This familiar routine of being pushed and shoved around and ordered to hold uncomfortable poses for excruciatingly long periods of time was beginning to irritate her. She was also worried about Elizabeth and kept sneaking glances to make sure she was all right, relieved that she was one of the lucky few who'd been posed on a chair. They'd been at it for almost two hours, and Pablo was promising a break when Camilla blew into the studio and planted herself in front of the group, arms akimbo.

"What's going on here?" she demanded.

"This is the after photo," said Nancy, stepping forward. "We're going for a classic look inspired by Goya."

"Goya! Is that why they're all dressed like crows?"

"Actually," said Nancy, "the black looks great."

"It looks like crap."

Nancy shifted uneasily from one foot to another and looked skyward at Pablo, still perched on his ladder. "Pablo says . . ."

"I don't care what Pablo says, I'm the editor here and I say this looks a lot more like *The Stepford Wives* than Goya, despite our little artiste's pretensions, and I DON'T WANT STEPFORD! I want INDIVIDUALITY! I want our readers to think they can buy a new lipstick or get a new dress and it will transform them from ordinary to extraordinary."

Lucy found this exchange fascinating. She had no idea that magazine editors actually uttered the phrases they plastered on the covers. Pablo, however, remained impassive, high above the turmoil below. "Listen," he said, leaning down to speak to her, "this black was not my idea."

"No?" Camilla's back stiffened.

"No! Black is what I got, everyone in black, so I think: What can Pablo do with black? The answer is obvious. Goya. But," he paused and held up a hand, "if it was up to me, I would put each of these lovely ladies in a different color and they would be like a garden of beautiful flowers."

"So who decided to go with black?"

"You know perfectly well," said Nancy, coolly. "Elise chose all the clothes."

Camilla's eyes flashed and there was a collective intake of breath as everyone waited, expecting an explosion. It never came. Instead, Camilla marched over to the intercom and calmly requested that Elise come to the photo studio.

As a reporter, Lucy had learned long ago that bad news travels fast. She figured the photographer's assistant had dropped a word to a friend in the advertising department who had run into someone from the fashion department in the ladies' room. That's how it went, whether you were in a little town like Tinker's Cove or a big city like New York. Still, it was disconcerting when Elise arrived in a flood of tears. Somehow Lucy hadn't pictured her as the emotional type.

"Elise, dear," said Camilla, her voice as sweet as sugar, "do you see anything wrong with this picture?"

"Ohmigod," she wailed, wrapping her arms around Camilla and collapsing into her arms. "I can't believe it."

"Now, now." Camilla was staggering under the larger woman's weight. Fortunately, whether her grief made it impossible for her to support herself or because she realized that Camilla's little bird body was about to snap, Elise slid to her knees, still keeping her arms wrapped around Camilla's tiny waist. Camilla looked extremely put out at the situation. "It's not as bad as that," she snapped, trying to squirm out of Elise's constricting grip. "We'll just get them some different outfits."

Elise lifted her tear-filled eyes to meet Camilla's. "Haven't you heard?"

Camilla's eyes flashed, but she managed to retain control of her voice. "Heard what?"

"Nadine's gone." Elise continued her downward slide to the floor, pulling Camilla down with her. "Nadine's dead."

Chapter Eight

BANISH BLEMISHES:

TIPS FROM TOP DERMATOLOGISTS

Apart from Faith and Lurleen, who immediately fell to their knees and began praying, nobody seemed to know how to react to the news. They all stood awkwardly, watching and waiting.

"Nobody dies from the flu," declared Camilla, struggling to get back on her feet but hampered by her four-inch heels. "Who told you she's dead?"

"Arnold's secretary called," blubbered Elise, as her substantial shoulders shook with sobs and she pounded her fists on the floor. "She said there were complications."

Camilla glared at Nancy and Pablo, who were whispering together in a corner. "Help me up, you idiots!" she screamed.

The two rushed over to the entangled pair. Pablo helped Camilla up while Nancy attempted to console Elise, who was now flat on her stomach with her face buried in her hands.

Back on her pointy little Manolos, Camilla straightened her black-and-white tweed suit and ran her hands through her hair, returning it to its previous perfection. She pointed a crimson-tipped finger at Elise. "Get her up!" she barked to Nancy and Pablo.

Pablo and Nancy's eyes met as they each took one of Elise's elbows and gave the old heave-ho, succeeding only in raising her to her knees. With a second enormous effort they managed to get her somewhat upright.

"Bring her along. I'm going to get to the bottom of this," Camilla declared, stomping out of the studio. Pablo and Nancy followed, struggling to support Elise who was now making pathetic mewing sounds and sniffling noisily.

Everyone seemed to expel a sigh of relief when they were gone, except for Faith and Lurleen, who were absorbed in their prayers.

"Well, I for one am glad this makeover is almost over and I can go home to sunny California," said Serena, giving her daughter a supportive hug. "We don't have flu in California, at least I don't think we do."

"Well, we have it in Omaha," said Ginny, "but otherwise healthy people don't die of it. Did she have some sort of condition like asthma? Some sort of immune deficiency?"

"She always seemed pretty healthy to me," said Cathy. "She never missed any promotions at Neiman Marcus, that's for sure. She'd fly two thousand miles for a free meal."

"You ought to be ashamed," declared Maria, eyes blazing. "It's not a joke. The poor woman is dead, just like we all will be one day." She crossed herself, as did Carmela.

"It sure makes you think," said Cathy, shaking her head. "She had everything. She was married to a millionaire, she had a great job on a magazine, she had it all."

"Were there any kids?" asked Tiffany.

"No. No kids," said Cathy. "At least none that she ever mentioned."

Realizing that her own child had been awfully quiet, Lucy anxiously searched the group for her. She wasn't standing with the others in the anxious little knot they had formed but had retreated to the raised platform, where she was slumped over to one side and fast asleep.

Lucy immediately knew something was very wrong. Elizabeth was a light sleeper and the commotion in the studio would have kept her awake, even if she'd felt tired enough to stretch out on the stage. She also liked her comfort but hadn't even slipped her purse under her head as a pillow. Lucy anxiously remembered how she'd had so much trouble staying awake earlier, and this time, when she felt Elizabeth's forehead, Lucy discovered she was burning with fever. Lucy gave her a shake; her eyelashes fluttered but Lucy couldn't rouse her.

"Is something the matter?" asked Maria. "Should I call an ambulance?"

Lucy shook Elizabeth harder, and her eyes opened.

"Wake up, honey. We need to get you to the doctor. Can you walk?"

"Sure." Elizabeth sat up and Lucy slipped an arm around her waist, pulling her to her feet.

"Thanks, but I think we can manage with a taxi," Lucy told Maria. "Where's the nearest emergency room?"

It didn't matter whether you were at New York Weill Cornell Medical Center or Tinker's Cove Cottage Hospital, all emergency rooms were the same, thought Lucy. She was sitting on one of those standard plastic chairs in the corner of an examining room. Elizabeth was lying on the table, and they were waiting for the doctor. They'd been waiting for what seemed like a long time, and Lucy suspected they'd only been put in the examining room because Elizabeth couldn't sit upright in the waiting room and kept slumping against the other patients. Now she was, once again, sound asleep and the hand with the bite was red and swollen. Lucy didn't like the looks of it one bit.

The door opened and a young man in green hospital scrubs and thick black-rimmed glasses introduced himself as Doctor Altschuler. "What's the problem?" he asked, lifting first one and then the other of Elizabeth's eyelids. Then he slid the stethoscope beneath her sweater and pressed it against her chest, listening intently.

"She's got a fever, she keeps falling asleep, and she's got this nasty bite on her hand," said Lucy. "She's been kind of sluggish for a day or two and I thought she might be coming down with the flu, but we've been very busy, too, and I thought she just might be tired."

"Busy doing what?" asked the doctor, examining Elizabeth's hand.

"We won a magazine contest for a trip to New York and makeovers."

"Where do you live?"

"Tinker's Cove, Maine."

"How long have you been in the city?"

"Since Sunday."

"I assume Tinker's Cove is pretty rural?"

"It's a small town, maybe a couple of thousand people," said Lucy, losing patience. She wanted him to magically make Elizabeth all better. "It's not New York but we have all the modern conveniences."

"Could she have come in contact with a spider?"

"A spider?" Lucy looked at Elizabeth's hand, then at her face. She was a real sleeping beauty.

"In the cellar or something?" prodded the doctor.

"I did have some Christmas presents hidden in the cellar, and she went down to get them," said Lucy, remembering Elizabeth's excited expression as she emerged with the cross-country skis. "I've heard that we do have black widows, but I've never seen one." Lucy grimaced. "I don't know if I'd recognize one, to tell the truth."

"This isn't a black widow bite. I think it's a brown recluse."

Lucy had never heard of such a creature. "Brown recluse?"

"They're called 'recluse' because they're very shy."

Something about the doctor's intensity gave Lucy the idea he had once been a small boy who was very interested in bugs and had probably spent hours at the library learning all he could about them.

"But it's winter," protested Lucy. "Don't they die in winter?"

"They creep into cellars, places like that, where there's enough warmth for them to survive. If they're disturbed, they sometimes bite."

"Is it poisonous?"

"Oh yes."

Lucy's eyes widened. "What's going to happen to Elizabeth? Is there an antidote?"

"No antidote." He shoved his eyeglasses back up his nose and peered reassuringly at her. "Don't worry. They're rarely fatal."

"Rarely! That's not good enough!"

"I'm very confident she'll be fine. She's young and healthy and she'll recover quickly. Of course, we'll keep her here in the hospital and start her on antibiotics as a precaution against secondary infection. We don't have anything to counteract the effects of the bite, but we can treat the symptoms: control the fever, put her on a ventilator if she has trouble breathing, give her medication to control convulsions, that sort of thing."

Lucy was horrified. "Convulsions?"

"Rare, but something we have to watch for."

"Can I stay with her?"

"Absolutely, Mrs. . . . ." He paused to check the chart. "Mrs. Stone. But it's not necessary. This is one of the world's premier medical facilities. We have excellent nurses here and . . ." he checked the chart again, "Elizabeth will get the best of care. I suggest you go down to the cafeteria and get yourself something to eat while we transfer Elizabeth to intensive care."

"Intensive care?"

"One of the nurses can give you directions," he said, on his way out the door.

Shattered, Lucy sat back down in the chair and pulled her cell phone out of her purse with shaking hands.

Bill answered on the third ring. Lucy clung to his hearty voice like a lifeline.

"Elizabeth's sick. Really sick. The doctor says it's a brown recluse spider bite."

"What?"

"In the cellar, maybe when she went down on Christmas Day to get the skis."

"She got bit? How come she never said anything? Is it serious?"

"They're putting her in intensive care." Lucy had trouble with those last two words and started to cry.

"Take it easy, Lucy." Bill's voice was strong. "She'll be fine."

"I'm scared."

"Of course you are. Let me talk to her."

Lucy looked at Elizabeth, who was out like a light.

"She's sleeping. That's all she does."

"Oh." Bill paused, absorbing this information. "Well, it's probably for the best."

Lucy was distracted by the arrival of an orderly.

"They're going to move her now. I better go."

"Keep me posted," said Bill.

Lucy couldn't bring herself to leave Elizabeth and accompanied her on the trip to the intensive care unit. Elizabeth was unaware of the move and slept through it, not even flinching when an IV needle was inserted in her arm.

"You look like you need a break," the nurse told Lucy, as she tucked a blanket around Elizabeth. "There's a cafeteria in the basement."

"I'm fine," insisted Lucy.

"Go. Get something to eat. She'll be here when you get back. I promise."

"I couldn't eat."

The nurse looked at her steadily. "This could be a long haul. You need to keep your strength up. And some food will help with that headache."

"I don't have—" began Lucy, realizing that she did indeed have a headache. A real killer. "Okay."

Lucy felt very small in the elevator, as if worry had somehow shrunk her. She also felt fragile and wished Bill were there to take her in his arms and let her rest her head on his broad chest. He wasn't, though, and the nurse was right, she had to keep up her strength. Maybe eating would help with this hollow feeling, as if a strong breeze could blow her over.

She took a tray and shuffled through the line, taking a tuna sandwich, chips, and a cup of tea. She surprised herself by eating it all and went back for a piece of peach pie and more tea. No wonder she was hungry, she realized with a shock. According to the clock on the wall it was long past lunchtime. She'd already been in the hospital for hours, and it promised to be a long day.

She was on her way to the lobby to see if there was a gift shop where she could buy something to read, something distracting, when she was surprised to recognize Lance coming toward her in the hallway.

"What are you doing here?" she asked, giving him a hug.

"I'm helping a professor of mine with a research project—this place is affiliated with Columbia, you know. What are you doing here?"

"Elizabeth is sick from a spider bite."

Lance cocked his head, looking doubtful. "That's crazy."

"She's in intensive care."

His attitude suddenly vanished. "That's terrible. Can I see her?"

"I'm not sure what the rules are," said Lucy. "There's no point right now. She's sleeping."

"I'll come back tomorrow." His eyebrows met over his classic Roman nose. "Do you know what kind of spider?"

"The doctor said a brown something or other."

"A brown recluse?"

Lucy suspected Lance may have shared the doctor's interest in bugs. "You've heard of it?"

"Sure, I've heard of it." He looked surprised that she hadn't. "But I'll do some research and brush up on the facts. I'll let you know what I find out."

"That would be great," said Lucy, who felt completely at sea. "I'd really appreciate that."

When she returned to the intensive care unit she found Elizabeth was still asleep, but when she pressed her lips to the girl's forehead she discovered her fever had dropped. Reassured, Lucy settled down in a fake leather recliner and opened the latest edition of *Jolie* magazine, which she'd bought in the gift shop.

It was kind of funny, she thought, as she flipped through the pages of ads. Here she'd had this makeover thanks to *Jolie*, but she'd never actually read the magazine. It was Elizabeth who devoured each month's issue and added it to the growing pile in her room. Lucy had never bothered to read it, assuming it was geared to younger women. She didn't read magazines much, anyway, preferring novels and newspapers, and if this particular issue of *Jolie* was representative of the genre, she figured she'd made the right choice. She could hardly believe what she was reading, beginning with a feature article by Nadine defending the use of animals for testing cosmetics.

Lucy's younger girls had spent the last few summers at Friends of Animals day camp so she knew this was a hot issue. Sara particularly enjoyed horrifying her mother with descriptions of rabbits subjected to eye make-up and piglets forced to eat lipstick ingredients. Trying to joke that at least the test animals would look good went over like a lead balloon. "It's torture, Mom," Sara informed her. "Remember, this is the stuff they're testing. It's not safe, like the stuff you buy."

After reading Nadine's article, Lucy found herself agreeing with Sara. Although she argued her case forcefully, Lucy couldn't agree that testing cosmetics was equally important as testing potentially life-saving drugs, for example. She could rationalize the need for the latter, but not the former. No rabbit needed to suffer for longer, thicker lashes.

Depressed, Lucy turned eagerly to the photo spreads. Having seen Pablo at work she was sure they would be visually interesting. Plus, with her newfound interest in fashion she might get some ideas for a new spring outfit. But when she turned to the spring fashion forecast she was shocked to discover it pictured designer cruisewear modeled in a Caribbean shantytown. Gorgeous models with gleaming skin lounged in scanty outfits on tilting porches amidst piles of garbage and debris. A chicken scratched in the foreground of one picture; a stooped, skinny man in an oversized shirt lurked in the background of another. Reading the commentary offended Lucy's soul: the outfits cost thousands of dollars.

Lucy was fuming about the injustice of a culture that afforded some fortunate people thousand-dollar swimsuits while others couldn't afford the necessities of life when she turned the page and saw the filthy, wrinkled face of a homeless woman sporting a diamond tiara and ropes of pearls. She got the concept, all right.

The woman's face expressed human dignity, but the addition of the jewels was demeaning and insulting. Disgusted, Lucy tossed the magazine across the room where it landed with a thud in the wastebasket.

Elizabeth twitched in her bed but didn't wake up, so Lucy reached for the remote to turn on the TV that hung from the ceiling. She was flipping through the channels when the door opened and Nancy Glass appeared, wrapped in a tan Burberry coat. Even Lucy recognized the famous plaid lining.

"How's the patient?" she asked, taking Lucy's hand and squeezing it.

Lucy turned off the TV. "They think she'll be all right."

"I couldn't believe it when they told me she was in intensive care." Nancy's eyes were huge.

"Me, either."

"You poor thing. How are you holding up?"

"I've been better," admitted Lucy. "But at least I know she's getting good care."

"Excellent care. People come here from all over the world. They've developed all kinds of advanced treatments."

"Thanks for telling me that," said Lucy. "I guess they can handle a little spider bite."

"Is that what she has?"

"That's what they say." Lucy was looking around the room for another chair, but there was only the single recliner. "Sit if you want," said Lucy. "I've been sitting for hours."

"No, I'm only here for a minute." Nancy stepped close to the bed and gave Elizabeth's hand a little pat. "You know, maybe we should have her write a first-person account for the magazine. When she gets better, of course. I know Pablo's planning to use some exotic bugs for his next jewelry spread."

"Well, that's a better choice than homeless people." Lucy felt like biting her tongue the minute she said it, but Nancy wasn't offended.

"You didn't like that?" she asked, smiling.

"Not much. I didn't like the shantytown, either."

"I know. Talk about bad taste!" Nancy shrugged. "That's our Camilla. She thinks controversy sells."

Lucy managed a small smile. "That's what my editor at home thinks, too."

"Unfortunately, it doesn't seem to be true, in *Jolie*'s case, anyway." Nancy's eyes had fallen on the crumpled issue in the wastebasket and she grimaced. "A lot of people agree with you—circulation is dropping, and the magazine is losing money."

"I heard that. Not a good time to lose a key editor. How's everybody coping?"

"You mean about Nadine?" Nancy was checking her manicure.

"Everyone must be reeling in shock, no?"

"It could be worse. Nadine was a master at delegating responsibility. Phyllis knows exactly what needs to be done and how to do it."

"That's fortunate."

"Yeah. The magazine will be fine." She was looking at her reflection in the mirror above the sink and tweaking her hairdo. "The one I feel bad for is her husband."

"Arnold?" Lucy remembered his hand on her bottom at the AIDS ball.

"He's a lovely man. So sensitive. I'm sure he's devastated."

"You never know how somebody's going to react to a death in the family," said Lucy, surprised at Nancy's obvious sincerity given her own experience with Arnold. "Grief takes everyone differently."

"Well, I'm going to do everything I can to help him through this difficult time," said Nancy, tightening the belt on her coat.

"Well, thanks for coming by," said Lucy. "I really appreciate it."

"That's me. A regular Miss Goody Two-Shoes," said Nancy, clicking out the door on her stilettos.

Lucy wasn't sure that was exactly the term she'd use to describe Nancy, but you never knew. Just because a woman was glamorous and fashionable and successful didn't mean she wasn't nice underneath. You couldn't tell a book, or a magazine, by its cover. She retrieved *Jolie* from the wastebasket, flipped through a few pages, and shoved it aside. What she needed was something distracting, something silly. Maybe the Three Stooges. At home you could find the Stooges at any hour on some cable channel or other. Lucy knew; the trio had gotten her through many a sleepless night.

But when she switched on the TV there was no sign of Larry, Curly, and Moe. There was, however, a serious young female newscaster in a navy blue suit reporting that the medical examiner was investigating the death of magazine editor Nadine Nelson, now deemed suspicious.

Chapter Nine

EASY SELF-DEFENSE STRATEGIES ANYONE

CAN LEARN

It was supposed to be a vacation but the flight had been terrible. The trouble started at check-in, when the clerk had actually been Moe from the Three Stooges. He was also the pilot, and Larry and Curly were the flight attendants. A couple of passengers got squirted with seltzer water but nobody got drinks, or peanuts, because Larry and Curly were too busy bopping each other on the head and tossing the refreshments around the cabin.

When the plane landed they had to get off by sliding down the emergency chute, and Lucy had to take off her heels, spike heels, before they'd let her slide down. That's why she was running barefoot, trying to catch up with Bill and Elizabeth who were far in the distance on the wide, empty street lined with ramshackle shop fronts. It was eerily quiet, like the set of a cheesy Western movie just before the climactic shoot-out, and people stared at her from the windows and doors but no one spoke.

Suddenly, she was on a beach, a classic Caribbean beach with palm trees, white sand, and turquoise water. She was tired of running so she stretched out in a handy hammock and watched Bill and Elizabeth frolicking in the waves. Then Elizabeth shrieked with delight and plucked something from the water. Waving it, she ran up the beach to show it to Lucy.

It was a shell, a beautiful striated nautilus shell with a pearly lining. But while they were exclaiming over its beauty, something black and evil crawled out of the center. Lucy tried to snatch the shell away from Elizabeth, but before she could grab it the spider hopped onto Elizabeth's hand. Lucy tried to brush it away but paused when she noticed it had a head like a woman. It was a spider with a woman's head, with Camilla's head. She wanted to ask Camilla what had happened, why had she turned into a spider, but before she had a chance, the Camilla spider sank two gleaming white vampire fangs into Elizabeth's hand.

A shriek of protest from the aged recliner chair woke Lucy, and she found herself sitting bolt upright, panting and sweating, in a hospital room. Elizabeth was in the bed, sound asleep.

It was a dream, she realized—only a dream, and there was nothing to be afraid of. She gave her head a shake, clearing her mind of the image of spidery Camilla, and got up to check on Elizabeth. She found the girl was sleeping easily, her forehead was cool, and the bite on her hand was improving: the wound itself was healing and the swelling had gone down.

Reassured that Elizabeth was on the road to recovery, Lucy went out to the nurse's station where she asked for a toothbrush and the nearest ladies' room. When she got back a middle-aged man in pale green scrubs was examining Elizabeth, who was awake and responsive. Lucy gave her a big smile and a thumbs up.

"I'm Dr. Marchetti," he said, shaking Lucy's hand. "I must say I'm quite impressed by your daughter's response to the medication. Antibiotics don't usually have this dramatic an effect on spider bites."

"I'm not convinced it is a spider bite," said Lucy.

The doctor narrowed his eyes. "No? Why not?"

"Well, we live in Maine, for one thing. It's pretty cold there this time of year and you don't see many bugs. Not any, really. Not even fleas on the dog."

"And I don't remember getting bitten," volunteered Elizabeth. "I hate spiders so I'm sure I would have noticed one on my hand."

"Maybe she got bitten here," suggested the doctor as he consulted Elizabeth's file.

"I haven't seen a single bug here, either, but she was exposed to the flu." Lucy remembered the newscast. "Or what I thought was the flu. Considering the way people zip around on airplanes these days, it could be some bizarre jungle thing like monkey pox or malaria. They're investigating."

"Who's investigating what?"

"Nadine Nelson's death," said Lucy, so eager to inform the doctor of this development that she failed to notice Elizabeth's shocked expression. "It was on the TV. They said the medical examiner was investigating."

"And your daughter had contact with this woman? This Nadine Nelson?"

"Oh, yes, we both did. On Monday, at *Jolie* magazine. It was a contest, you see, for mother–daughter winter makeovers. . . ."

Dr. Marchetti wasn't listening. He was out the door.

Elizabeth was white faced. "She died?"

Lucy wished she'd asked to speak to the doctor privately; she'd forgotten that Nadine's death would be shocking news to Elizabeth. "I'm sorry," she said. "I should have realized you couldn't know. You were really out of things."

"Do I have what she had? Am I going to die?"

Lucy gave her a hug. "Do you feel like you're dying?"

"No," admitted Elizabeth. "I feel much better."

"Trust your body," advised Lucy. "They don't know what it is but the medicine is working and you're much improved. You heard the doctor."

"What if I take a turn for the worse?" She flopped her head over, like a rag doll, then sat up. "Actually, I think I might be dying of starvation."

Lucy opened the door and stuck her head in the hallway to see if there was any sign that dinner was imminent. There wasn't.

"I'm hungry, too," she said. "I think I'll go down to the cafeteria and get some provisions."

Remembering hospital protocol she checked at the nurse's station to make sure Elizabeth could eat and, after getting the okay, headed straight for the cafeteria. She was putting two containers of yogurt on her tray when her cell phone rang. It was Lance.

"How's Elizabeth?" he asked, without even saying hello.

"Much improved. She's sitting up and wants something to eat."

"That's great! But I think I should warn you that brown recluse spider bites are very slow to heal. She could be in the hospital for quite a while."

"That's funny," said Lucy, adding a couple of pieces of fruit. "It's already much smaller."

"What?"

"Yeah. The doctor was amazed. Said antibiotics don't usually work like that on spider bites."

Lance didn't reply and Lucy took the silence to mean he was thinking. She took advantage of it to fill two paper cups with coffee, then got in line to pay the cashier.

"You know, my research also pulled up anthrax," he finally said.

"Anthrax?" Lucy gave the cashier a ten-dollar bill and put the change on her tray, which she carried over to an empty table. "Like those postal workers?"

"Yeah."

Lucy remembered the scare, which had dominated the news for weeks. "Didn't a couple of them die?"

"It can be fatal," admitted Lance.

All of a sudden her heart felt like it was in a vise. "But the doctor says Elizabeth is much better."

"There are two kinds," continued Lance. "Inhalation anthrax; that's when you breathe in the germs. It's very serious. But there's also cutaneous anthrax; you get that if you touch the stuff but don't breathe it. And that's not as serious as the other kind."

"You mean Elizabeth's spider bite could really be an anthrax sore?"

"Yeah. And it would respond to antibiotics."

"What's the other kind like? The inhalation kind?" demanded Lucy.

"Like the flu. Like a really bad case of the flu with respiratory problems."

"Really?" Lucy was thinking of Nadine. "And how do people get it? Is it contagious?"

"It's not contagious. You have to be directly exposed to get it."

"It's a germ?"

"A spore, actually, and it's not usually around in the environment, like most germs. It has to be introduced. The post office workers got sick when the anthrax was shaken out of an envelope by a sorting machine. Some nut was sending it to people in the government."

"Right. They had to shut down congressional offices, didn't they? To decontaminate them."

"And that's the other thing," said Lance. "Most germs have a pretty short life span unless they find a host, but not anthrax. It forms spores that can lie dormant for years until they find the right living conditions. That's why it's such a good biological weapon."

"Biological weapon? I think we're getting a little crazy here. You know, Elizabeth never had chicken pox. The others did but she was away at summer camp and missed it. It could be something like that."

"The doctors will figure it out," said Lance. "You think it's okay if I visit her tonight?"

"I think she'd love it," said Lucy. "Right now she's probably wondering what's taking me so long. I'm supposed to be bringing her something to eat."

As she made her way back to Elizabeth's room Lucy tried to remember everything she could about the anthrax scare a few years earlier. It wasn't much, she realized. She didn't even know if they'd ever figured out who had sent the stuff, or why. The only thing she was sure of was that ever since the attack, the discovery of any unspecified white powder was enough to shut down schools and offices until it was positively identified. Some pranksters had even managed to shut down Tinker's Cove High School for an afternoon last fall by spilling some salt on the assistant principal's desk.

"Is that all you got me? Fruit and yogurt?" demanded Elizabeth, when Lucy delivered the tray.

"It's just to tide you over," said Lucy, amazed at Elizabeth's sudden interest in food. Maybe it was true that every cloud had a silver lining. "They're going to bring you a big dinner, eventually. I saw the meal trolley at the end of the hall."

"I don't know how people survive in the hospital," said Elizabeth, digging into the yogurt with a plastic spoon. "You could starve to death."

"Take mine, too," said Lucy, who was too distracted to eat.

"Aren't you hungry?"

She stood up. "I have to make a phone call. I'll be back in a minute."

Standing in the hallway outside Elizabeth's room, Lucy felt a bit like a cartoon character with an angel perched on one shoulder and a devil on the other. The good little angel was telling her that she really ought to alert somebody at *Jolie* magazine about the possibility that the office was contaminated with anthrax, while the bad little devil was telling her it would be a waste of time.

"People's lives are at stake. You must warn them," said the angel.

"How are you going to do that?" scoffed the devil. "Camilla's the one you should call and you can be sure her phone number is unlisted."

"That's just an excuse. You need to find a way," insisted the angel.

"There'll be plenty of time for that later," whispered the devil. "You're exhausted. Frazzled. You deserve some time to take care of yourself."

"You'll never forgive yourself if someone else gets sick because you were too lazy to make a phone call," said the angel.

Lucy checked her watch. It was just after five. That meant the best she could probably do would be to leave a message on Camilla's phone mail. But when she dialed the receptionist answered and put her right through to Camilla.

"I'm so glad I caught you," began Lucy, feeling rather awkward. "There's something I think you should know."

"I heard your daughter's in the hospital. How's she doing?"

"She's going to be fine," said Lucy.

"Well, I'm glad she's recovering. You must excuse me—this is not a good time," she said.

Lucy was suddenly guilt stricken. In her haste to do the right thing she'd completely forgotten that Camilla and Nadine were close friends. The poor woman was probably racked with grief and completely shattered by her loss.

"I'm afraid there's no good time for what I have to tell you," said Lucy, her voice gentle, "but trust me, the sooner you know, the better."

"Well, go on," said Camilla, impatiently.

"Okay," said Lucy. "I think there's a very real risk the *Jolie* office is contaminated with anthrax."

"What?"

"Anthrax. Nadine's death and my daughter's symptoms are consistent with anthrax, at least that's what I've been told."

Camilla's voice was hard. "That's ridiculous."

"Unfortunately, it's not ridiculous at all," insisted Lucy. "And if the offices are contaminated other people are at risk of getting sick. That would be terrible."

Camilla's words were clipped, precise. "The doctors say Elizabeth has anthrax?"

"Well, no," admitted Lucy. "They're still testing. But I did some research and I'm pretty sure. . . ."

Camilla was practically shrieking. "*You* did some research?"

Lucy felt her face warming. "Well, actually it was Lance, Norah's son. He's a student at Columbia and he does research at the hospital with a professor."

"A college kid has some crackpot idea! And you decide to call me?"

Lucy was flabbergasted. Here she'd gone out of her way to do a good deed and Camilla was practically biting her head off. "I thought the sooner you knew the better."

"Oh you did, did you? Well, I'm going to wait for official notification before I go to the expense and trouble of closing the office and having everyone stay home. Furthermore, I don't know who you think you are, spreading ridiculous rumors like this." Camilla paused for breath. "I'm warning you, if you so much as whisper this preposterous idea to anybody I'll slap you with a lawsuit so fast you won't know what hit you."

"Okay," said Lucy, taking a step backward.

"It's been absolutely lovely getting to know you," said Camilla, her sarcastic tone giving the lie to her words, "but I'm sure you know the makeover is officially over tonight. The magazine will no longer assume the cost of your hotel and I hope you have medical insurance because we are certainly not responsible for your daughter's illness and hospitalization." Camilla paused a moment, as if remembering something. "That's right, you were the one who was so very interested in the ten-thousand-dollar prize, weren't you?"

With all the worry over Elizabeth, Lucy had forgotten all about it. The prize, the makeover, it all seemed part of another life. Elizabeth's illness had changed everything. But now that she was recovering, the money would sure come in handy. "Did we win?" she asked.

"Not in your dreams."

Lucy felt as if she'd been slapped, and leaned against the wall. "Well, thanks for telling me," she said, swallowing hard.

"No problem." Camilla's voice was silky and Lucy knew she wasn't finished. "Have a nice day," she purred.

Chapter Ten

SEXY, SEXY: LINGERIE HE'LL LOVE!

L ucy pressed the "end" button on her cell phone and leaned against the wall. Here she'd tried to help Camilla and all she'd gotten was a stinging rebuke. She felt as if she'd been slapped. So that's what you got for trying to do the right thing, she thought. It was true what people said: "No good deed goes unpunished." Her emotions in turmoil, she called home.

"What's going on?" demanded Bill, picking up on the first ring. "How's Elizabeth?"

"Better," she said, quickly. "Much better. She's sitting up, talking, and the wound is already starting to heal. She even asked for some food."

He let out a big sigh of relief. "That's great."

"I know."

"So why don't you sound happy?" he asked. "What's going on?"

"I guess I'm just feeling overwhelmed," said Lucy, hedging. She was terrified by the possibility that Elizabeth might have caught anthrax but she didn't want to alarm Bill unnecessarily. It was a struggle to keep from saying the word. It was right there, on the tip of her tongue, and she had to keep it in while getting other words out. "I don't know how long Elizabeth's going to be in the hospital and I have to find someplace to stay, there's all these expenses, we didn't win the prize. . . ."

"Hey, hey, hey," said Bill. "Calm down. It'll be okay."

"What about the health insurance?"

"I'll take care of it. You take care of Elizabeth, and yourself."

"I'm okay," said Lucy, biting her lip. "But I don't know what I'm going to do after tonight. The magazine is kicking me out of the hotel."

"What?"

"They say the makeover is over and they won't pay for my room any longer. Like I don't have enough to worry about."

"Calm down, Lucy. Give Sam a call. I bet she'd love to have you stay with her."

"I must be going crazy. I can't believe I didn't think of that."

"It's understandable. You're upset. You're away from home and you have a sick child. It's very stressful. But everything's going to be okay."

"I hope so." Something in the hall caught her eye. It was Dr. Marchetti, heading her way in green surgical scrubs and carrying a chart. "I've got to go. The doctor's coming."

"Keep me posted."

"I will," promised Lucy. She closed the phone and turned to meet the doctor.

"Mrs. Stone, I need to have a word with you," he said.

Lucy's heart gave a little jump in her chest.

"We can talk here," he said, leading her to a small waiting area where the scarred coffee table was covered with well-thumbed magazines. He indicated a bright orange sectional sofa. "Have a seat."

"Is everything all right?" she asked, nervously twisting her purse strap.

"Elizabeth's doing very well and I expect she'll make a full recovery. In fact, we're going to move her out of ICU tomorrow, if her progress continues." He paused and leaned forward, resting his elbows on his thighs. The move seemed intimate; the scrubs looked like pajamas to Lucy, and she could see his curly black chest hair sprouting at the V-neck.

She slid back in her seat, away from him. "That's good, right?"

"Right. But the bad news is," he paused, giving her time to prepare herself, "she has anthrax."

It wasn't as if she hadn't been half expecting it, but the news was still devastating. She was suddenly cold and she could barely breathe, she felt as if she had to remind her heart to keep pumping.

Dr. Marchetti took her hand. "Are you all right, Mrs. Stone?"

Lucy struggled to put her thoughts into words. "I knew . . . I mean, I thought it might be anthrax . . ." She shook her head. "I still can't believe it. It's crazy." Suddenly, it occurred to her that tests were often wrong. A false positive they called it. She locked eyes with him. "Are you sure, absolutely sure? Maybe it's something else, like chicken pox."

"We're sure. When you told me about the woman at the magazine, Nadine Nelson, I checked with the medical examiner's office and learned the cause of death was anthrax. We then tested Elizabeth for anthrax and got a positive result. But we caught it early and Elizabeth's prognosis is excellent." He looked down at the file in his hand. "Maybe I misunderstood you. Did you say you thought it might be anthrax?"

"A friend mentioned it. He did some Internet research for me."

He slapped the file down on the coffee table. "And what did this friend tell you?"

"It's a spore . . . there's two kinds . . ." Lucy was aware she was babbling, avoiding her fear. "Is this some sort of terror attack?" she asked. "Are we all going to get sick?"

"It doesn't look like it, at least not yet. But of course there are homeland security concerns and there will be an investigation. The FBI is going to want to talk to you and your daughter."

"The FBI? But we haven't done anything!"

"Of course not. I made that very clear to the investigators. But they do need to track down the source of the anthrax. We've been lucky so far, with only two cases. There doesn't seem to be a widespread outbreak. Still, we have to be concerned. There could possibly be more deaths, if the source of the anthrax isn't discovered."

"But Elizabeth's in the clear, right?"

He leveled his eyes at hers and took both her hands in his. "Listen, I learned long ago not to make promises in this business. There are no guarantees in medicine, too much can go wrong. But having said that, and bearing in mind that complications are always possible, I think it's safe to say she's out of the woods."

"So how much longer will she have to stay in the hospital?"

The doctor studied the chart. "I'm afraid I don't really know. We'll just have to see what happens."

"But you said. . . ."

"I said there are no guarantees. We want to keep an eye on her. She's on some serious medication and there could be side effects." He paused. "Anthrax is very rare, you know, and we're not that familiar with the disease itself. And then, there are some curious anomalies in your daughter's case. . . ."

"Anomalies?"

"Some unusual factors we haven't seen before."

Lucy felt like screaming. "Like what?"

"Nothing for you to be concerned about, honestly. Just variations from the usual course. Frankly, I would have expected her to be sicker."

Relief flooded Lucy. "Oh. That's good then, right?"

"We think so. But we want to be cautious." He got to his feet and handed her a piece of paper. "This is a Cipro prescription for you. You've been exposed so you need to take it as a precautionary measure. Be sure to finish the bottle and take all the pills."

Lucy sat on the couch, staring at the piece of paper in her hand, for a long while after the doctor had left. This was very scary. It wasn't something she was reading about in the newspaper, it wasn't taking place miles away, it wasn't happening to somebody else. It was real life, her life. She folded the prescription and put it in her purse.

When she returned to Elizabeth's room and saw how well she looked, she was reassured. Elizabeth was sitting up in bed eating from her dinner tray. The color had returned to her cheeks and her eyes were sparkling, probably because Lance was perched on the side of the bed. Giddy with relief, Lucy wrapped her arms around her and gave her a big hug.

"Mom! What's the deal?" exclaimed Elizabeth, squirming out her mother's embrace and spearing a chicken nugget.

"You're going to be okay," said Lucy. "I just talked to the doctor. But Lance was right. You have anthrax."

"What's that?" asked Elizabeth, spooning up some applesauce.

"Don't you remember. . . ." began Lance, eager to fill her in.

Lucy stopped him with a glance and a shake of the head. This was no time for a current affairs lesson. "How are you feeling?" she asked Elizabeth.

"Great! When can I leave?"

"I just talked with the doctor and he says you'll probably have to stay for a while."

"Why? I feel much better. Besides, I don't want to spend another minute in this awful johnny!"

Lance laughed. "I think it's kind of cute."

Elizabeth scowled at him. "You would."

Lucy was making a mental note to bring Elizabeth's pajamas when there was a knock on the door and Fiona entered, clutching a bunch of pink and white Oriental lilies.

"I'm not dead," protested Elizabeth, laughing.

"Those are different lilies, I think," said Fiona. "I got these because they smell so nice." She gave them to Elizabeth. "Take a sniff. Heavenly."

"I can smell them from here," said Lucy. "Lovely." She got up. "I'll go see if the nurse has a vase."

When she returned Fiona was also perched on the bed, sitting at the foot, lighting a cigarette.

"You can't smoke in here," said Lucy, horrified. "It's a hospital."

"Really? You Yanks are too much."

"It's not a Yank thing, it's a health thing."

"You know, Americans wouldn't be so fat if they smoked more," said Fiona, putting her cigarettes back in her purse.

"I'll tell the Surgeon General," said Lance.

"It's true," insisted Fiona. "People are much thinner in Europe, much healthier, despite the fact they drink like fish and smoke like chimneys and eat all sorts of fatty foods like fish and chips and foie gras."

"If you like it so much better there, why did you come here?" asked Lance, resentful of the intrusion.

"Oh, I like it here just fine," said Fiona. "And I'd like to stay longer, but I don't think that's going to happen."

"Why not?" asked Lucy, placing the last stem in the vase and setting it on the window sill, where Elizabeth could see them.

"I'm here on a work visa and when the job ends I've got to go." She drummed her fingers nervously. "Is it true what they say? That Nadine had anthrax?"

Lucy stepped close to the bed and took Elizabeth's hand. "You had a close call but you're going to be fine."

"Elizabeth, too?" asked Fiona, her eyes widening.

"That's what the doctor says."

"Well, I'll be gob smacked," said Fiona. "You mean Nadine didn't have the flu, she had anthrax? And everybody at the magazine was exposed?"

"If a lot of people were exposed, they'd already be sick," said Lance. "Of course, they'll close the offices and bring in the hazmat crews and there'll be a big investigation, but it's really just bureaucrats covering their behinds."

"But who would do such a thing?" asked Fiona, staring out the window. "Who would send anthrax to a fashion magazine? Why would they do it?"

They all fell silent, baffled by a new world order in which ideological and religious beliefs were used to justify violence and atrocities against innocent people going about their daily business. These days taking a train or airplane, sitting in a café, or riding a bus to work had suddenly become dangerous.

Lance finally broke the silence. "You know, I don't think this is terrorism," he said.

Fiona snapped her head around to look at him. "What do you mean?"

"Only two people have gotten sick, right?"

Fiona nodded. "Just Nadine and Elizabeth."

"A lot more people would've gotten sick if it was really a terrorist attack on the magazine. And like you said, why would terrorists attack a fashion magazine, anyway? There's lots of better targets, like the subway."

"But if it's not a terror attack, what could it be?" asked Elizabeth.

"Murder," said Lucy.

"Murder!" Elizabeth's eyes were huge. "Who'd want to murder me?"

"Nobody. But I can think of at least one person who wanted Nadine out of the way," said Lucy, remembering Arnold's pass at the AIDS gala.

"So, just for the sake of argument, let's say somebody sent anthrax to Nadine, how could Elizabeth have come in contact with it?" asked Lance.

"However it was delivered, Nadine must have received a lot more than Elizabeth," said Lucy.

"And she must have inhaled it," said Lance. "The inhalation type is a lot more serious. Elizabeth probably only touched it, which is why she got the cutaneous type."

"But what did she touch that Nadine also handled, but that other people didn't?" asked Lucy.

Elizabeth looked thoughtful, going over her actions at the magazine. "The compact!" she exclaimed.

"That's right! Nadine was powdering her face and she dropped the compact and Elizabeth picked it up," said Lucy.

"That would fit," said Lance. "If the anthrax spores were in the powder, they would have been released when she pressed the puff against her face and she would have inhaled them. When Elizabeth picked up the compact, some of the spores must have gotten on her hand."

"Oh, I remember the compact." Fiona's mouth was a round O. "It came a week or two before she got sick. It was lovely, shaped like a pansy with enamel decoration. It just screamed 'spring' and everybody noticed it."

"Where did it come from?" asked Lucy. "Was it a gift? Was there a tag?"

"I doubt it." Fiona shrugged. "Stuff comes in all the time. New products, samples, gifts—there were boxes and boxes arriving every day from cosmetics manufacturers hoping for a mention in the magazine."

"It must have been addressed to Nadine," insisted Lucy. "It

would have been too dangerous otherwise. Anybody could have taken it."

"Believe me, anybody who's messing around with anthrax isn't thinking too carefully about the consequences," said Lance.

"That's not necessarily true," said Fiona. "Nadine was known for grabbing everything that came in."

"Wasn't that her job?"

"Up to a point," said Fiona. "As beauty editor she got to decide what products to feature, whether it's something new and exciting that readers will want to know about or a product that fits in with a story idea, like fresh new scents for spring, that's her decision. But at most magazines extra products are given to the staff. That way, even if the product doesn't get included in the magazine, it's likely that people will use it and talk about it, give it a little boost."

"But not at *Jolie*?"

"Oh no. Nadine hogged it all and everyone knew it. It was kind of a company joke. An industry joke, really. People used to wonder where she kept it all. Her apartment must have been stuffed with it."

"And the murderer took advantage of it to kill her," said Lucy.

"That's cold," said Elizabeth. "I mean, I can't say I liked her. She was kind of weird and she made it pretty clear that she was only interested in herself, but that's not a reason to kill someone, is it?"

"The only reason a murderer needs is a strong desire to get rid of someone," said Lucy.

"I can think of quite a few people who fit that category," said Fiona. "There'll be a lot of gloating at her funeral tomorrow."

"Tomorrow? Isn't that awfully fast?"

Fiona nodded. "It sure is. Phyllis said Nadine was Jewish and they have some religious rule about burying the corpse within twenty-four hours."

"I'm surprised the medical examiner went along," mused Lucy.

"I'm not," said Lance, drily. "Arnold raised a ton of money for the mayor's reelection campaign."

"That's politics for you," said Elizabeth. "Money talks."

"There'll be a lot of talk at that funeral, that's for sure," said Fiona. "Everybody at the magazine will be there. We all got a voice mail message from Camilla pretty much ordering us to go. She's actually having the invitations delivered by messenger tonight."

"You need an invitation?" Lucy had never heard of such a thing.

"Oh, yeah. Otherwise homeless people would come in just to get warm and that wouldn't do at Frank Campbell's. It's terribly toney."

"That's too bad," said Lucy. "I'd love to go."

Fiona's eyes widened. "You would? Why?"

"To pay my respects," said Lucy, sounding as if butter wouldn't melt in her mouth.

Elizabeth wasn't fooled. "You mean you want to snoop around." She turned to Fiona. "At home, Mom's the local Miss Marple."

"Are you really?" asked Fiona.

"Not exactly," said Lucy, "but I am a reporter for the local newspaper."

"She's solved quite a few mysteries in Tinker's Cove," said Lance, speaking to Fiona. "Couldn't she go with you?"

Just then there was a knock at the door and two extremely fit and clean-cut men in dark gray suits walked in. It was obvious to Lucy that the FBI was wasting no time.

"Excuse us for barging in like this," said the taller agent, a black man. "I'm Special Agent Isaac Wood, and this is Special Agent Justin Hall." He indicated his companion, who was shorter and had red hair. "We'd like to ask a few questions."

"We were expecting you," said Lucy. She introduced herself as well as Elizabeth and Lance, but when she turned to Fiona, she discovered that Fiona had slipped away.

"That's all of us," she said, covering the momentary awkwardness with a smile. "Fire away."

"Actually, we're here to interview Elizabeth," said Agent Wood.

"Alone," added Agent Hall, pointedly opening the door and holding it.

Lucy didn't like this one bit. "I don't know," she began.

"It's all right, Mom," said Elizabeth.

Lucy was doubtful. Being interviewed by the FBI was serious business. "I can call Brad," she said. "Remember, he's a lawyer."

"Trust me. That's not necessary."

"Okay," said Lucy. She and Lance left the room reluctantly and the door was shut firmly behind them.

"I hope she knows what she's doing," said Lance, looking worried.

"Me, too," agreed Lucy.

Chapter Eleven

BEST BOUTIQUES: WHERE YOU CAN
FIND YOUR OWN LOOK

It was after ten when Lucy left the hospital. She started to hail a cab, then remembered it was only a few short blocks to her hotel. The walk would do her good. But when she reached the corner, she discovered a welcoming coffee shop that was still open and ducked inside, climbing up on one of the stools and ordering the 24-hour special of two eggs any style, toast, home fries, and choice of bacon or sausage. She ate it all, even the sausage.

Leaving, she passed one of the newsstands that seemed to sit on every corner, noticing that tomorrow's early edition had already been delivered. The proprietor was busy opening the bundles and arranging them. She paused for a moment to check the headlines, amused by the tabloids' preposterous exaggerations about Jen and Brad, Liza and Martha. She also bought a copy of the *New York Times*, curious as to whether the anthrax attack had been reported.

She flipped through it quickly when she got back to the hotel, but all she saw was an obituary. The funeral, she noted, was scheduled for ten in the morning. It was too late to call Sam, so she took a quick shower and then slipped between the crisp, clean sheets, expecting to fall right to sleep. That didn't happen, though. Her mind was too busy with all that had happened and all the things she needed to do. Her top priority was Elizabeth, of course—making sure she got the care she needed to continue getting well.

Now that she knew for sure it was anthrax, with the possibility that the whole city could be at risk, she found Camilla's reaction to her warning simply unbelievable. Why hadn't she taken immediate action? And, come to think of it, why was she still at the office when Lucy called? You'd think she would have been too upset by Nadine's death to stay at work.

Her reaction seemed awfully weird, thought Lucy, reminding herself that you had to make allowances for the bereaved. Grief took everyone differently; some were immediately blown over, others took a while to acknowledge their loss. Furthermore, doctors prescribed all sorts of drugs to help people manage their emotions nowadays, and those drugs often produced odd behavior, like poor Angie Martinelli who had laughed hysterically at her mother-in-law's funeral last month in Tinker's Cove. Though some people said it wasn't the drugs at all, Lucy was willing to give Angie the benefit of the doubt, figuring that if she really had been thrilled at the old woman's death she would have taken pains to hide it. Then again, she had to admit, a lot of folks in Tinker's Cove actually suspected that Angie had something to do with old Mrs. Martinelli's death.

Of course, the fact that Mrs. Martinelli died after eating a cannolli at Angie's house did seem to cast some suspicion on Angie, even though the cause of death was officially a heart attack. Admittedly, Angie was a nurse and she did have access to all sorts of medications and she could have spiked the fatal cannolli, but how could someone like Camilla get access to anthrax? No, Lucy told herself, apart from the lack of outward grief there was absolutely nothing to indicate that Camilla was a murderer, any more than Angie's hysterical laughter proved she had killed her mother-in-law.

After an hour or so of such unproductive thought, Lucy got up and took a Sominex. She finally fell asleep, listening to the constant hum of city traffic, punctuated by sirens.

The wake-up call came promptly at seven, just as she'd requested. Still groggy from sleep, she panicked when she saw Elizabeth's empty bed. Then it all came back to her and she dialed the hospital, learning that Elizabeth had a comfortable night and was continuing to improve. Reassured on that score, she started on the business of dressing and packing. At eight she figured Sam would be awake and called, immediately receiving an invitation to stay at her apartment. Then, after making a quick call to touch base with Bill, she went downstairs for breakfast.

Cathy and Maria were sitting together in the restaurant and waved her over, inviting her to join them. "Tell us all about Elizabeth," said Maria. "How is she?"

"She's much better, thanks," she said, taking a seat.

"That's great news," drawled Cathy, her huge diamond ring flashing as she signaled the waiter to bring coffee. "I was awfully worried about her, considering what happened to Nadine."

"And now they say her death is suspicious," said Maria, her big black eyes bigger than ever. "It was on the news."

"I never heard of such a thing," said Cathy, crossing her silky legs and letting an excruciatingly fashionable stiletto shoe dangle from her toes. "How can they investigate the flu?"

Lucy had to bite her tongue, even though she knew it would be irresponsible to break the news; soon enough all the makeover winners would be contacted by public health officials. She certainly didn't want to start a panic so she changed the subject.

"Are you guys going home today?"

"Tiffany and I are staying a few extra days, but I think everybody else is leaving. I figured that if I was going to come all the way from Dallas I wasn't going to leave without taking in the town. Maria's taking us shopping. She knows all the best places."

"Everything from designer boutiques to sidewalk peddlers," said Maria.

"Which is why we're getting an early start. Tiffany wants people to think she's a fashionista and Carmela's upstairs, helping her decide what to wear. It's a lengthy process." Cathy gave the waiter a big smile. "My friend needs a cup of coffee and we'd like a refill."

"Decaf for me. I'm already feeling wired," said Maria.

"So what happened at the magazine after I left?" asked Lucy, as the waiter set a cup down and filled it.

"It was crazy!"

"All the staffers were running around like chickens with no heads," said Cathy. "We weren't sure what to do; we were all standing around like little lost lemon drops, you know, not part of it really and not sure what to do. Nancy finally remembered us and told us we should leave."

"She was very nice. Very apologetic." Maria's hands were everywhere—she was one of those people who spoke with their hands. "But she said they had to cancel the final dinner party and the holiday show at Radio City Music Hall."

"No Rockettes?"

"I guess they felt it wouldn't have been right, under the circumstances." Cathy stirred her coffee.

"But the girls were disappointed," said Maria.

"We all ate here, at the hotel. It was fine." Cathy furrowed her beautifully arched brows and leaned forward. "Camilla stopped by and presented the ten thousand dollars to Lurleen and Faith. No surprise there."

Maria rolled her eyes. "It was 'hallelujahs' all night." She shrugged. "You can't blame them for being excited but everybody else was pretty down. When you and Elizabeth didn't show we were all worried."

"And, of course, people were upset about Nadine."

"So young!" Maria shook her black curls. "And a woman like her! One who could afford the best care, the best doctors."

"Maybe she had a heart condition," speculated Cathy. "Like those athletes who are fine one minute and drop dead the next."

"But your little girl, well, not-so-little girl, will she be all right? We heard she was in intensive care?"

Lucy suddenly felt guilty. What was she doing sitting around gossiping? She needed to get moving if she was going to check out of the hotel and get her bags moved to Sam's apartment before going back to Elizabeth in the hospital.

"She's feeling much better," she said. "Thanks for asking. Now, if you'll excuse me, I've got to get something to eat."

When she returned with a plate loaded with pancakes and sausage, the conversation continued.

"What are they doing for her?" asked Cathy.

"Just fluids and antibiotics." Lucy took a big bite of syrup-drenched pancake.

"Antibiotics?" Maria's brows shot up. "They don't do anything for the flu."

Lucy suddenly wished she hadn't been so open.

"I know about flu," continued Maria. "I had it last year. I begged for an antibiotic but the doctor wouldn't give it to me. He said it wouldn't do any good. He told me to rest and take chicken soup."

"They actually think it's a reaction to a spider bite," said Lucy, spearing a sausage, "but they're not sure. It's probably not the same thing that Nadine had."

"Spider bite?" Cathy was doubtful. "Now if it were me or Tiffany, I'd say that was a possibility, since we live in the South, but you guys come from Maine. Aren't your spiders hibernating?"

"I would have thought so," said Lucy, licking the last bits of syrup off her fork and placing it carefully on her plate. "I don't really care what caused it, I'm just glad she's on the road to recovery." She stood up. "Now I've really got to go. I don't want to stay away from the hospital too long."

"Have you got a place to stay?" asked Cathy. "I have a suite and we've got plenty of room."

"You could have the couch at my place," added Maria.

Lucy was amazed; she hadn't expected such kindness. "Thanks, that's awfully sweet of you, but an old college friend is letting me stay with her. She's got an apartment on Riverside Drive."

"That's good," said Maria. "In times of trouble, it's good to have a friend."

"Yes, it is," said Lucy, marveling that she'd received three invitations when she'd been worried about finding a place to stay.

Headed uptown in a taxi, Lucy felt lighter, as if sharing her worries with Cathy and Maria had made them less burdensome. Everything was going to be okay. Elizabeth was getting better, she had a place to stay, and she had friends in the city who would help and support her. These were all good things.

She tried to keep that thought as the cab sped through Central Park, but she couldn't quite free herself of the notion that something black and evil had come too close—and it could come back.

The doorman at Sam's building opened the cab door for Lucy and brought the bags inside, but when Lucy explained who she was, he told her no one was home. Sam had left instructions to let her into the apartment but Lucy declined, anxious to get back to Elizabeth in the hospital. She left the bags in his care and, refusing his offer to call a taxi, headed for the subway. It was much cheaper than a cab and faster, too, since the trains didn't have to deal with traffic.

Rush hour was in full swing when she descended the grimy stairs that led to the even grimier station, where the platform was filled with waiting people. Oddly enough, there were free seats on the heavy-duty vandal-proof benches and she sat down, pondering the elements that composed the unique subway aroma. Primarily urine and soot, she decided, with a hint of ozone. She didn't mind the smell; it evoked memories of childhood trips with her mother to see a Broadway show or to shop in now defunct department stores like Altman's and Gimbel's.

Her reverie of days gone by was interrupted when the train rumbled into the station. She got up and joined the mob cramming into the already crowded car, hanging on to a pole for the ride downtown to Times Square, where she took the shuttle over to the East Side and the old Lexington Avenue line. Nowadays the trains had numbers or letters for names but she couldn't be bothered to learn them. The 1 would forever be the Broadway line to her, and the 4, 5, and 6 would be the Lexington Avenue line.

When she exited at Sixty-eighth Street she still had to walk several city blocks to the hospital. No wonder New Yorkers all seemed so trim, she thought, contrasting their way of life with the

rural lifestyle in Tinker's Cove. There, everybody drove everywhere. Nobody walked, even if it was only for a few blocks. It was
a paradox, really. Somehow you'd think people would be healthier in the country, but in truth they got very little exercise unless
they went out specifically looking for it. Taking a walk or going
for a bike ride were recreational activities, not everyday means of
transportation.

As she walked along the sidewalk, which was lined with tall
apartment buildings, she noticed that a lot of people had dogs.
Not just little dogs, either, but Labs and standard poodles and
even a St. Bernard. That surprised her. It seemed a lot harder to
keep a dog in the city, especially considering the requirement that
owners pick up their messes. But everyone seemed to be a good
sport about it; many carried plastic bags at the ready. The dogs
were leashed, of course. They couldn't run free as most dogs did in
Tinker's Cove, where people had big backyards and there wasn't
much traffic.

Lucy was wondering if dogs were really happy in the city when
she arrived at the hospital. A young Lab was waiting outside, tied
to a fire hydrant, and she paused to pet it.

"You look like my puppy," she said, thinking of Libby as she
stroked the Lab's silky ears.

The puppy wagged her tail and gave Lucy a big doggy smile,
and Lucy found herself smiling for the first time that day.

When she got to the ICU, however, she had a scary moment
when she found Elizabeth's bed stripped and empty. Then she remembered Dr. Marchetti had told her she would probably be
moved to a regular room today and went to the nurse's desk to get
directions.

Elizabeth was sleeping when Lucy found her, once again in a
single room. Fiona's flowers had been moved along with her, and
several new arrangements had also arrived, including a large one
from *Jolie* magazine.

Lucy stood for a moment, staring at the card, then checked her
watch. It was nine-thirty. If she left now, she could make the funeral. But what about Elizabeth? Lucy checked her forehead and
discovered it was cool. Even more encouraging, the sore on her

hand was almost entirely healed. She considered her choices: she could either stay at the hospital, watching Elizabeth sleep, or she could go the funeral, and try to figure out who had poisoned Elizabeth and Nadine.

It was no choice at all, really. She checked her cell phone battery and scribbled a note for Elizabeth, leaving it along with some toiletries and fresh pajamas. She wasn't going far and Elizabeth could call if she needed her. She bent down and placed a quick kiss on her forehead, and then she was out the door.

Chapter Twelve

BLACK IS BACK—BUT IT'S
ANYTHING BUT BASIC

Lucy had attended plenty of funerals in Tinker's Cove, but they were nothing like this, she thought as she approached the Frank E. Campbell funeral home on Madison Avenue. Temporary barricades had been set up to contain the inevitable celebrity watchers who had gathered to see exactly who was emerging from the line of limousines that was inching its way along the street. There was a smattering of applause when the mayor arrived and, ever the politician, shook a few hands before recalling he was there as a mourner. Assuming a serious expression he stepped under the maroon canopy and entered the gray stone building. Lucy followed, hot on his heels, but was stopped by a stocky young man in a black suit.

"May I see your invitation?"

Lucy opened her purse and began searching for an imaginary invitation.

"Oh, dear, I must have left it home."

"I'm afraid I can't admit anyone without an invitation."

Lucy feigned a panicked expression. "Oh, please let me in. You see, I work at *Jolie* magazine and everyone's been ordered to go and if I don't show up, well, I'm afraid I'll get in big trouble."

The young man seemed doubtful about Lucy's story but when

Fiona trotted up to the door, calling Lucy by name and waving an invitation, he let them both in.

"Thanks," said Lucy. "You arrived in the nick of."

"No problem," said Fiona, as they handed over their coats to the check room attendant. "He was kind of cute, in a 'Six Feet Under' sort of way." She giggled. "Do you think he got to see Nadine naked?"

"Behave yourself," said Lucy, forgetting for a moment that Fiona wasn't her child. "This is a funeral."

"Righto." Fiona adopted a serious expression. "I'll be good."

Together they followed the stream of mourners proceeding down a plush carpeted hall to the memorial chapel. They could hear the soft strains of classical music and when they entered the chapel, which was filled with white-painted pews like a New England church, they found a string quartet was playing.

Nadine's closed coffin was resting in the front of the room. Arnold was sitting in the first pew, in the seat closest to the coffin. He appeared to be weeping and was being consoled by Nancy Glass, who kept him supplied with fresh tissues. She couldn't seem to keep her hands off him and was constantly patting his shoulder or holding his hand.

Hmm. Not so different from Tinker's Cove, thought Lucy, taking a seat beside Fiona. They were in the back of the chapel, appropriate to their lowly status. The front rows, where name cards were affixed to the pews, were filling up fast with family, colleagues, and celebrities. Lucy spotted Norah, looking very somber and sitting by herself. Anna Wintour from *Vogue* was there, along with Diane Sawyer and Barbara Walters, plus lots of people Lucy didn't recognize but who seemed important—at least to themselves.

Camilla and Elise were the last to arrive. A role reversal had apparently taken place and today Camilla was the one overcome by grief, leaning heavily on her larger friend as they made their halting way down to their front-row seats. Both were clad in black: Camilla in a couture suit with a fitted jacket and a short skirt and Elise in one of the severe pantsuits she favored. This was a very different Camilla from the woman Lucy had seen at the magazine. She seemed unable to support herself and dabbed constantly at her eyes with a lacy handkerchief. Lucy wondered if the realization of her loss had suddenly overtaken her, which she knew it sometimes did at a funeral, when it became impossible to deny the finality of the situation, or if she was simply putting on a show, which she knew people also did because they thought it was expected. Or, thought Lucy, maybe Camilla had finally realized the gravity of the situation now that the investigation had begun. Health officials would soon be closing the *Jolie* offices, if they hadn't done so already, and the workers would be told to seek medical advice; police and FBI agents would be questioning everybody.

There was a considerable fuss as Camilla practically collapsed onto her seat and Elise fanned her with a program. A few rows behind them Lucy noticed accessories editor Deb Shertzer and Nadine's assistant, Phyllis, whispering together. She nudged Fiona and cast a questioning glance in their direction.

"No tears there," said Fiona. "Phyllis has been promoted to replace Nadine."

"Permanently?"

"That's the word."

Lucy was thinking that the promotion had taken place very quickly indeed when the rabbi, dressed in a black robe with velvet trim and a yarmulka, took the podium. "We are here today," he began, "to celebrate the life of Nadine Nelson. Beloved wife of Arnold, dear friend to many, a tireless worker. . . ."

"He didn't know her very well," whispered Fiona, and Lucy had to stifle a giggle.

The rabbi droned on for almost an hour, recounting one or two anecdotes about Nadine but relying heavily on generalities and religious abstractions for his eulogy. He was the only speaker; there were no heartfelt reminiscences from friends and family; no favorite songs, nothing to signify the loss of a unique and much loved individual. Lucy had trouble keeping her mind from wandering and was wondering if there would be refreshments, compulsory in Tinker's Cove, when the string quartet finally played the final chords of Barber's *Adagio* and the service drew to a close. A few people stood and made their way to the front of the room to pay their respects to Arnold, others lingered in their seats, a few dabbing at their eyes, others no doubt taking a few minutes to meditate on the transitory nature of life, or perhaps to plot the rest of their day.

"I have to speak to Camilla," said Fiona, rising. "I want to make sure she knows I'm here."

Lucy remained seated, watching as Norah paid her respects to Arnold. Others were falling into line, including many of the celebrities. Diane Sawyer was taking his hand when a series of flashes went off. It was Pablo, taking pictures.

"What the hell do you think you're doing?" demanded Elise, confronting him.

"Yesterday Camilla told me she wanted funeral photos for the magazine," said Pablo. "A tasteful round-up, that's what she said."

Elise looked at Camilla, who shook her head weakly.

"Liar!" she growled, grabbing for the camera.

"She's the liar," muttered Pablo, nodding towards Camilla and tightening his hold on the camera.

"How can you? At a time like this."

Everyone was silent. A few high profile guests headed discreetly for the door, others stood awkwardly, watching the scene.

"It wasn't my idea," insisted Pablo, shaking his head.

"She was our best friend," hissed Elise, hurrying back to Camilla, who had slipped on a pair of large sunglasses and was sniffling into a handkerchief. She gently led her out of the chapel, guarding her as ferociously as a pit bull.

"Best friend? I don't think so," muttered Pablo, stalking off.

Lucy was tempted to follow him and ask exactly what he meant, but she hesitated, aware that he was in quite a temper. The last thing she wanted was to create a second scene. So she sat, waiting for the crowd around Arnold to thin, and replayed the confrontation in her mind. She didn't doubt for a minute that Camilla had assigned Pablo to take the photos; the magazine always devoted a page to celebrity appearances. Usually it was balls and fund raisers, but Lucy doubted Camilla would think a funeral was any less worthy of exploitation. After all, the level of taste at *Jolie* was remarkably low, if the issue she read was any indication. Anyone who would have homeless people model jewelry wouldn't hesitate to capitalize on her best friend's death. Lucy could picture it: "Norah Hemmings in Prada, Diane Sawyer in Mark Jacobs, and Barbara Walters in Oscar de la Renta console each other at the funeral of *Jolie* beauty editor Nadine Nelson . . . in coffin."

Enough, Lucy told herself. It was time to get moving. Only a few people were standing with Arnold and he was beginning to move towards the door. She'd have a quick word with him and then head for the hospital.

"I'm sorry for your loss," she murmured, approaching him and extending her hand. "My daughter and I enjoyed getting to know Nadine. . . ."

Arnold, however, looked as if he'd seen a ghost. "You!" he snarled, glaring at her. "What are you doing here?"

Lucy's jaw dropped. She certainly hadn't expected this. "I came to express my sympathy," she said, "and I was hoping to have a word with you. Your wife and my daughter are both victims of the same. . . ."

"Not now," he snapped, turning to one of the black-suited attendants. "Get her out of here."

Lucy couldn't believe his reaction. Even worse, two extremely fit young men in black suits were coming her way. "This isn't necessary," she protested. "Please, let me give you my number. I really think we ought to talk."

"We have absolutely nothing to talk about," said Arnold, giving the young men a nod.

Each one grasped her by an elbow and propelled her out of the room, down the hall and through the front door, where they deposited her unceremoniously outside.

"Hey, what about my coat?" she demanded, and one of the young men reappeared in the doorway. Smiling, he tossed it and it landed at her feet, on the gray all-weather carpet tastefully bordered with black.

Chapter Thirteen

CONFUSED BY COLOR? FIND YOUR
PERFECT PALETTE

Lucy snatched the coat and brushed it off, trying to ignore the curious stares of the handful of gawkers still clustered on the sidewalk. It was horribly embarrassing but she put the best face on that she could as she shrugged into the green plaid coat. She wanted to get away quickly and was walking as fast as she could in her high-heeled makeover boots when she was approached by a woman she didn't know.

Only a few days ago Lucy would have summed her up as a rather pleasant-looking thirty-something professional but the makeover had sharpened her eyes. She immediately noticed the cheap haircut, the navy blue pants and trench coat, the imitation leather purse, and the sensible, flat-heeled shoes. She also noticed the black vinyl wallet the woman was holding in her unmanicured hand which contained an FBI identification card.

"Do you mind if we talk for a minute," she said, extending her right hand. "I'm FBI Agent Christine Crandall."

Lucy took the proffered hand. It seemed unfair, somehow, that women in official jobs, like cops and firefighters and even plainclothes FBI agents, never looked quite as good as the men. It was almost as if someone, somewhere, was making sure the dress requirements indicated that these really weren't suitable jobs for women. The mannish clothes that signaled authority didn't flatter them, they needed to carry cumbersome purses, and no matter how much they exercised they couldn't get rid of those stubborn saddlebags. "Actually, couldn't we do it some other time? I'm on my way to the hospital."

"I'm afraid I really have to insist." Agent Christine wasn't taking no for an answer. "There's a coffee shop a few doors down. Shall we go there?"

"I really can't stay too long," muttered Lucy, regretting her decision to leave Elizabeth alone at the hospital. "Coming to the funeral was a mistake."

"I saw you get the bum's rush," said Christine, pulling open the coffee shop door and holding it for Lucy. "How come?"

"I'm not really sure," said Lucy, taking a seat at an empty booth in the back. "It was by invitation only and I wasn't actually invited, but I can't believe that Arnold had the guest list in his head." If anything, she suspected his reaction had been fueled by a guilty conscience.

"Where I come from you don't need an invitation to attend a funeral. Most everybody in town goes and the family takes pride in attracting a crowd. It's almost like a popularity contest—you don't want to have just a handful of mourners, you want everybody to come."

"That's how it is in my town, too," said Lucy, ignoring the menu, which was encased in a sticky plastic sleeve bound with maroon cloth tape. "But I'm beginning to think Tinker's Cove is on a different planet from New York."

Christine laughed. "You could say the same for Chagrin Falls."

Lucy thought it sounded like something from "Rocky and Bullwinkle" but kept that thought to herself. It sure was easy to talk to this FBI agent, though. She hadn't expected her to be so friendly. "And where is Chagrin Falls?"

"Ohio." Christine smiled at the waitress, who was standing with her order pad at the ready. "I'll just have coffee."

"Same for me," said Lucy.

Once that was out of the way Lucy expected Christine to begin questioning her and she was eager to share her thoughts on the case. She was sure the FBI would want to know all about Nadine's compact and her habit of commandeering all the product samples. She could also offer quite a bit of insight into the rivalries at the magazine, and then there was the fact that Arnold had made a pass at her at the gala, which seemed to indicate he was something less than a devoted husband. And, of course, there was Camilla's increasingly strange behavior.

"So how come you and your daughter are in New York?" asked Christine, setting a small tape recorder on the table between them. "You don't mind if I record this, do you?"

The presence of the compact device set off alarm bells in Lucy's head. Maybe all this friendliness was just a trick to get her to let down her guard. "Am I a suspect or something?"

The agent's reply was quick as a whip. "Should you be?"

Lucy felt for a moment as if all the air had been sucked out of the shop. "Oh, no! Not at all."

"Well, then you have nothing to worry about."

"That's what they told Monica Lewinsky," said Lucy. "And Martha Stewart." The waitress set the coffee on the table. "Maybe I should have a lawyer."

Christine ripped a packet of sugar open and poured it into her cup, then peeled open a little plastic bucket of cream and poured it in, stirring smoothly. "That's your right, of course, but I think you're overreacting. Don't you want to help us catch the person who did this to your daughter?"

Lucy lifted her mug and took a sip. "Of course I do. But, frankly, I don't understand why you're questioning me. Agents Hall and Wood were at the hospital last night and they made it very clear that they were only interested in talking to Elizabeth."

"Really? They were there last night?"

Lucy was puzzled. "Didn't you know? Don't you guys talk to each other?"

Christine took a long, long sip of coffee. "Department policy," she said, finally. "We don't like our left hand to know what our right is doing. It corrupts the investigative process."

It sounded reasonable enough to Lucy. She might even be quoting some FBI manual packed with government gobbledygook. "If you say so."

"Okay, then. What brought you and your daughter to New York?"

"Actually, Elizabeth won a contest for mother and daughter makeovers. *Jolie* magazine flew us to the city and put us up at the Melrose Hotel, all expenses paid."

Agent Christine didn't reply and Lucy found herself babbling to fill the silence.

"It meant leaving my husband and the other kids at home during Christmas school vacation but I thought it would be an opportunity to spend some special time with my oldest daughter. After all, who knows where she might go after graduation? It could be my last chance to have her to myself."

"How many other children?"

"Three others, but my oldest son doesn't live with us anymore so it's really just Sara and Zoe. They're fourteen and eight."

Christine stared at her. "And you really thought it was a good idea to fly to New York?"

Lucy's back stiffened. "Why not? She's not a baby anymore and my husband is perfectly capable. . . ."

"Not that. I meant flying. Haven't you heard about 9/11?"

"Of course I've heard about it." Lucy remembered the beautiful sunny weather that day and how she was unable to pull herself away from the TV set as the horror unfolded. "I was just as upset as everyone else. But, hey, aren't you guys supposed to be making flying safer? Aren't we supposed to go about our lives as normally as possible? Not let the terrorists stop us because that would be a victory for them?"

Christine looked at her as if she were crazy. "All it takes is one extremist with a bomb. And it's not just airplanes. They can hit buildings, subways, commuter trains, buses, you name it. The Statue of Liberty, the Empire State Building." Christine was getting rather agitated and there was a gleam in her eye. "Do you know they have nuclear bombs that can fit in a suitcase? And just imagine what a biological agent could do if it were released in the subway."

Lucy was beginning to feel cornered and she didn't like it. Who did this person think she was to make judgments about her choices? "Well, if something like that happens at least I'll know I looked good when I went," she answered, tossing her head. She knew every hair would fall back into place, thanks to her Rudolf haircut.

As a matter of fact, she was beginning to think Agent Christine should spend a little more time worrying about her appearance and a little bit less worrying about doomsday scenarios. Of course, that was her job, admitted Lucy, but she could at least try to look her best while pursuing terrorists and criminals. The poor girl had obviously cut her hair herself or had gone to one of those walk-in places that charge eleven dollars. She didn't bother with make-up, her eyebrows needed shaping, and that navy blue pantsuit she was wearing was all wrong with her pinkish complexion and blond hair. The pantsuit was also much too severe, and that red bow she'd tied around her neck went out in the eighties. Where did she buy her clothes anyway? Goodwill?

"You certainly have a great haircut," said Christine. "I've been admiring it. Who did it?"

"Rudolfo. The magazine sent us to his salon."

"Is he expensive?"

Lucy was surprised by the question. Surely everyone in New York knew about Rudolfo and his five hundred dollar haircuts. "Very expensive, but there are plenty of other good stylists. Ask around."

"That's a good idea."

Encouraged by Christine's reaction, Lucy thought she might offer a bit more advice. "You could also have your eyebrows shaped. It really opens up your face, at least that's what they told us. And if you have it done once professionally you can maintain it yourself with tweezers."

"My sister plucked hers and all she's got left are two tiny arches that look ridiculous."

"That's why you need a professional shaping," said Lucy, aware that she was sounding an awful lot like her friend Sue back in Tinker's Cove. What a change a few days could make. She always resented Sue's unbidden advice, but now she couldn't seem to stop herself from doing the same thing. "You could also get your colors done. They told me I'm a winter and I should wear black, white, and jewel tones. I'm no expert but I think you're a spring and you'd look good in soft pastel colors."

"FBI agents don't wear pink."

"Maybe a sage green suit with a pink blouse? Or a little floral-print scarf, tied cowboy style so it wouldn't get in your way? You can be both professional and feminine." Lucy was beginning to wonder if she'd been possessed by some sort of fashion demon. Indeed, Christine didn't seem to be listening. "But we've gotten off track here," she admitted, swallowing the last of her coffee. "I have some ideas about how the anthrax was delivered. As beauty editor, Nadine got a lot of product samples, including a rather fancy powder compact. She dropped it during our consultation and Elizabeth picked it up, which is probably how she got exposed."

The agent looked at her sharply. "How did you get this information?"

"It's just a theory," said Lucy. "One of Elizabeth's friends did some Internet research and that's what we came up with. It seems to fit the circumstances of the case. Nadine was always powdering her nose. I guess she was known for being vain. And it was also widely known that she didn't like to share the samples and kept them for herself. Putting the anthrax in a fancy compact was a clever touch, though. Whoever sent it to her must have known her well and been confident that she would want to keep such a beautiful trinket for herself. The fact that Elizabeth was exposed was simply bad luck; the anthrax wasn't meant for her. Nadine was the real target, and Elizabeth just happened to be in the wrong place at the wrong time." Lucy tapped her upper lip with her finger. "The big questions, of course, are who sent the anthrax and why did they do it? That's what I'd like to know."

"And is that why you went to the funeral today, even though you weren't invited?"

Lucy's jaw dropped. She was beginning to think she'd underestimated Agent Christine. Just when she was beginning to wonder what her FBI superiors would think if they listened to the tape of their conversation and if she'd get in trouble for discussing hairstyles and fashion tips, it occurred to Lucy that all that small talk might have been a ploy to get her to say more than she otherwise would. If it was, she had certainly fallen for it and right now she felt pretty stupid.

"I simply wanted to pay my respects to a woman who taught me the value of daily moisturizing," said Lucy. She thought about dabbing her eyes with a tissue but decided that would be over-doing it.

"You're an investigative reporter. You want to break this case."

Lucy was stunned. "How do you know what I do? And any-way, that's not important. This is my daughter, you know. Of course I want to find out who poisoned her, but not because I'm going to break a big story. It's because I love her and I want to make sure whoever made her sick doesn't do it to somebody else."

"Which is why you're going to start cooperating and telling the truth," said Christine. "You say Nadine dropped the compact and your daughter picked it up. Why?"

"It practically fell at her feet. It was the polite thing to do."

"Did Nadine throw it at her? Did somebody knock it out of her hand?"

"Nope. She just dropped it."

"How did the others react when she dropped it?"

At this rate, thought Lucy, Agent Christine would be retired before the case was solved. "I don't think anybody noticed. It was all over in a second or two."

"Did anyone else reach for the compact?"

"Not that I noticed. Frankly, I was mostly watching Nadine."

"Why?"

"She was the queen bee, if you know what I mean. Ordering people around, coming up with crazy ideas, and all the time look-ing at herself in the compact mirror. She was completely narcissis-tic. I don't think I ever met anyone like her before. Nobody else mattered to her."

"Yeah, I know what you mean." Christine nodded, then seemed to remember her role. "I mean, you picked all this up in less than half an hour?"

"Well, I've had a lot of time to think about it." Lucy's eyes met the agent's. "Sitting in a hospital room with a sick child does tend to concentrate the mind. I've been over that session in my mind a million times, dredging up every detail."

"Hindsight isn't always accurate," warned Christine. "Your emotions can color your memories."

"I know," admitted Lucy. "But you've probably been talking with lots of people. You're trained to filter out the personal reactions to get to the truth."

"Absolutely."

"So what have you learned so far?"

Christine's unkempt eyebrows shot up and she pursed her mouth. "Any information relevant to this case is strictly confidential and I am not at liberty to divulge it," she said.

There it was again, that darn FBI manual. "Just thought I'd try." Lucy shrugged.

"I don't think I need to keep you any longer," said Christine, crumpling her napkin and tossing it on the table. "But I do think I ought to warn you that obstructing a federal investigation constitutes a felony."

"Felony? That seems kind of harsh. Are you sure it's not a misdemeanor?"

For a brief second Christine seemed confused. "A felony," she snapped, dropping a couple of dollar bills on the table. "Let me make this very clear," she said. "Mind your own business and leave the investigating to the professionals. We don't want you to get hurt."

Having delivered a warning, Agent Christine turned on her heels and sped out of the coffee shop.

Darn, thought Lucy, she hadn't even gotten a chance to share her theory about Arnold or her questions about Camilla.

Chapter Fourteen

ACCESSORIES FORECAST:

BRING ON THE BLING!

Lucy remained at the table after Agent Christine left and pulled her cell phone out of her purse, eager to check on Elizabeth.

"How are you?" she asked.

"Okay."

"Did you find the things I left you?"

"Yeah, thanks, Mom."

"Is there anything else you need? I'm on my way over."

"Right now?" Elizabeth didn't sound eager to see her.

"Yeah," said Lucy. "Is there a problem?"

"Uh, well, Lance is coming. He's bringing me lunch."

"Okay." Lucy sighed. "I'll catch you later."

"No rush, Mom. I'm fine. Really. Come tonight, okay?"

Well, that certainly didn't take long, thought Lucy, ending the call. Already she was a third wheel. She wasn't needed, she was superfluous. That's how it was with college-age kids. One minute you were bailing them out of a crisis and the next you were getting in their hair. She might as well have another cup of coffee. So when the waitress came over with the coffee pot and offered to refill her cup, she accepted and sat, staring into the black liquid, thinking over her conversation with Agent Christine.

The FBI agent was right about one thing. It was ridiculous to think she could identify Nadine's killer. For one thing, she was a fish out of water in the city. Back home in Tinker's Cove she knew her way around, she knew the people. But that certainly wasn't the case here; she'd only been in the city for a few days and hardly knew anyone. And then there was the matter of the murder weapon: anthrax. She hardly knew what it was and didn't have a clue where the killer could have obtained it. It seemed the very last thing that people in Nadine's world of society and fashion could access.

Nevertheless, leaving it to the FBI was like staring at the slick, oily surface of the coffee hoping that a face would magically appear or the steam rising from the cup would take the shape of letters spelling out a name. It was no good. There was no way she could sit around waiting for the official investigation to produce the sicko who had killed Nadine and poisoned Elizabeth. After all, government officials hadn't succeeded in solving the original anthrax attack, and that was years ago. She might not have any better luck, but she had to try.

Investigating was the only thing she knew how to do. She couldn't administer drugs or conduct lab tests to make Elizabeth better; she had to leave that to the doctors and nurses. But as a mother she still wanted, no, *needed*, to help. Even if she only turned up one tiny clue, it would be better than doing nothing.

Besides, if Agent Christine was the best the FBI had to offer, Lucy didn't have a lot of confidence the agency would ever solve the case. She didn't know much about the FBI, but she was aware that its reputation for infallibility had suffered after Oklahoma City and 9/11. Even so, the conversation with Agent Christine had seemed a bit odd. Lucy chewed on her lip. Maybe Agent Christine was new to the job.

Lucy took a sip of coffee and pulled a pen out of her purse. She plucked a paper napkin from the chrome holder on the table and started making a list of names, all possible suspects.

Nadine's husband, Arnold, topped the list. It was a sad but indisputable fact that the husband was always the prime suspect when a wife was murdered, and from what she knew of Arnold he certainly deserved that dubious honor. She clucked her tongue, remembering the pass he made at her at the gala, even while his wife was dying. What a slimeball. She underlined his name and added an exclamation point.

Of course, the fact that he had a roving eye didn't necessarily make him a murderer. Plenty of men felt they had to make a pass at every attractive woman they encountered; it was almost expected, like all men were supposed to love sports. Those who didn't, the guys who'd rather spend Sunday afternoon at the ballet than in front of the TV watching football, were judged as less than manly. Maybe she was placing too much emphasis on one little pass. It had been a clumsy attempt, almost cartoonish, with his talk of champagne and caviar. Maybe he had only been joking and she was such a rube that she didn't get it. Maybe it was some sort of New York compliment.

But that didn't explain his reaction to her at the funeral. You would have thought he suspected *her* of poisoning Nadine, which was patently absurd since Nadine was already sick when they met. Lucy scratched her chin thoughtfully. It could be a smart ploy, however, if he wanted to turn suspicion away from himself. She supposed it could be argued that Elizabeth got sick administering the anthrax to Nadine. It wouldn't hold up for long, of course, but it might give him time to hide evidence or flee to the Bahamas or whatever he might be planning.

And what about Camilla? Lucy wasn't at all convinced that her show of grief at the funeral was genuine. In truth, from what she'd seen of Camilla, it seemed the woman had ice water in her veins. She was essentially interested in only one person—herself. And what had Pablo meant when he'd said Nadine wasn't as good a friend to her as she thought? Had Nadine been angling to get Camilla's job? It was possible; she certainly seemed to have plenty of ideas about how to run the magazine. Everybody knew the magazine was in trouble—did that mean Camilla was in trouble? Camilla was an ambitious woman, and Lucy had no doubt that if she found herself pressured by the publisher on one hand and her old friend on the other, the old friend would have to go. But why not fire her? Did Nadine have some hold on her, some information, that made that option impossible? You didn't need to be a psychiatrist to know that Camilla was driven to succeed. Lucy had

no doubt she would do whatever it took, even murder, to maintain her status as New York's most influential magazine editor.

After Arnold and Camilla, the name that came to mind was
Pablo, the photographer. He must certainly have resented Nadine's influence at the magazine, where Camilla ignored his ideas
in favor of her half-cracked notions. Lucy knew from her own experience how frustrating it was to see her byline on a story she
didn't believe in. An example that came to mind was a puff piece
Ted had insisted she write about the visit of an aspiring pop star
to the outlet mall last summer, even though she had argued that
her time would be better spent on a story about the school budget. He'd overruled her, insisting that the story would appeal to
younger readers. She'd been embarrassed when it appeared, and
she couldn't imagine that Pablo had been very happy about at-
taching his name to a photo spread of homeless people modeling
priceless gems. If he had any artistic integrity at all he must have
been mortified to have his talent employed to mock those unfortunate souls.

Pablo's buddy Nancy was no fan of Nadine's either, thought
Lucy, adding her name to the list. Nancy certainly seemed eager
to comfort Arnold; she'd been all over the man at the funeral. Perhaps she saw herself as the next Mrs. Arnold Nelson and decided
the road to matrimony would be a lot smoother if she got rid of
the first? From her point of view it would be a win–win situation:
even if she failed to snag Arnold, she would have the benefit of
getting Nadine out of the way at work.

Phyllis was another *Jolie* employee who benefited from Nadine's demise: she got her job. Was that reason enough to kill the
woman? After all, Phyllis had seemed devoted to Nadine. If the
woman told her to jump, Phyllis jumped. That was how it appeared anyway, but Lucy knew that appearances could be decep-
tive. Maybe Phyllis resented Nadine every bit as much as Pablo
did but had been better at masking her emotions. Lucy decided
she'd love to know Phyllis's true feelings.

And then there was Elise, the fashion editor who didn't seem
all that interested in fashion. She seemed to be working at the
magazine only because her old college friends Camilla and Nadine were there. It reminded Lucy of a favorite saying of her

mother's: "Three's a crowd." To her mother's way of thinking, people naturally tended to pair off, and not just matrimonially. Two could walk abreast comfortably on a sidewalk, but if there were three someone had to walk alone. Two could sit together at a theater and chat while waiting for the show to start, but not three. Two could ride together in the front seat of a car, but the third had to take the backseat. What if Elise had gotten tired of sitting in the backseat? Would she kill to ride shotgun? Lucy remembered how she had supported Camilla at the funeral, and she added her name to the list, which was growing rather long without even considering the makeover winners.

Most of them could be dismissed, she decided, because they'd had no contact with Nadine before they arrived in New York. There were a couple of exceptions, though. Cathy, for example, had a history of sorts with Camilla and Nadine, having encountered them through her work at Neiman Marcus. And Maria lived in New York. Maybe she'd had some sort of run-in with her. But where would Cathy or Maria, or any of the other people on her list for that matter, get anthrax? And how could they handle it without getting sick themselves?

Lucy reached for her coffee cup and took a sip, but the coffee was cold. She'd been so absorbed in her list of suspects that she'd forgotten to drink it. Coffee had a way of cooling off, and so did investigations, if you let them sit too long. Lucy knew that time was not on her side if she was going to catch the anthrax poisoner, but she didn't know how to begin. Back home she'd simply grab her reporter's notebook and start asking questions, but it wasn't that simple here in New York, especially since she'd been officially warned off by the FBI. She needed to find a way to investigate that wouldn't rouse suspicion: she needed to fly below the radar. But how she was going to do that was anybody's guess. She got up and shrugged into her coat.

Outside, on the sidewalk, it occurred to her that emotion was clouding the issue. As a reporter she'd conducted plenty of investigations in Tinker's Cove and she'd always been more or less personally involved, but not like this. This time it was her daughter who'd been attacked, and she was determined to do everything in her power to bring the poisoner to justice. The hell with justice, she thought, striding along the sidewalk; she'd like to strangle whoever did this to Elizabeth, or even better, she'd like to give this heartless villain a taste of his own medicine. Or hers. She'd like to inject a big fat horse syringe of deadly microbes into his bloodstream and see how he'd feel then.

Walking along the sidewalk in the direction of the hospital, Lucy passed a newsstand and stopped to read the headlines: "Martha Stewart's Jail Décor," "Rosie's New Weight Loss Plan," "What I Saw in Michael's Bedroom," and "Scott Peterson's Girl-friend Talks." Taking a *New York Tattler* off the pile and paying for it, Lucy looked for the story about Nadine's death, but didn't find anything. Tucking it in her bag she came to a decision. There was one surefire way she knew to ignite an investigation, and she was going to do it. She hailed a cab and gave the address of the *Tattler*. After all, what she had to tell them was a lot more sensational than Rosie's latest diet.

The *Tattler* encouraged tips from readers and once Lucy had cleared the metal scanner and her bag had been checked for guns and explosive devices, she was sent straight up to the newsroom to talk to the news editor, Ed Riedel. Her spirits climbed as the elevator chugged upwards; it was such a relief to be doing something positive. She could hardly wait to tell this Ed Riedel the inside story of Nadine Nelson's death.

But when the elevator stopped and the doors ground open, she found she was not the only person in New York who wanted to spill their guts to Ed. She would have to take a number. There wasn't even room on the long bench in the hallway; she would have to stand.

Just as well, decided Lucy, waiting would give her a chance to organize her thoughts. So she unbuttoned her trusty plaid coat and leaned against the wall, alternately shifting her weight from one foot to the other and wishing she'd worn her duck boots. It wasn't long, however, before a seat opened up. The line was moving along briskly. She hoped that was a good sign. Probably none of the others had a story that was as important as hers.

"Seventy-six," called the receptionist, and Lucy hopped to her feet.

"That's me."

The receptionist cocked her head toward a door, and Lucy trotted in to tell Ed Riedel all about it.

He was sitting at a worn, gray steel desk, leaning on one elbow. His chin was resting in one hand; the other hand was busy doodling on a big pad of foolscap. He looked like an old, tired bloodhound, and no wonder, thought Lucy. The things he must have heard.

"Whatcha got?" he asked, getting right to the point.

"Anthrax poison at *Jolie* magazine. Nadine Nelson died of it and my daughter also has it, but she's getting better," said Lucy, making it snappy.

Riedel's bleary eyes suddenly became sharply focused. She felt as if they were lasers, burning right through her.

"Anthrax?"

"That's what the doctors say."

"And Nadine Nelson is . . . ?"

"The beauty editor, wife of real estate developer Arnold Nelson. Her funeral was this morning at Frank Campbell's."

"Rich broad, huh?"

Lucy nodded. "Somebody sent her a powder compact loaded with anthrax. My daughter got some on her skin. She's in the hospital." Ed seemed to be losing his focus so Lucy added, "The FBI is investigating."

"Your daughter works at the magazine?"

"No. We won a mother–daughter makeover."

Ed gave her an appraising once-over but didn't say anything. Lucy didn't much like it and pulled herself up a little straighter. "Listen, this is a big story. I'm a reporter myself, in Maine, and I know news when I see it. I can give you the inside scoop. I saw Nadine when she was sick, I was there when Camilla Keith learned about her death, I've been sitting at my daughter's bedside in the hospital. Just ask me what you want to know."

Ed's gaze had shifted. He was staring off in the distance, drumming his fat fingers against his chin.

"Nope," he said, shaking his head. "I'm not gonna touch this with a ten foot pole."

"Why not?"

"The FBI's involved, and if it really is anthrax like you say, you gotta figure Homeland Security is all over it." He leveled his eyes at her. "You heard of the Patriot Act?"

Lucy suddenly understood why even the *Times* hadn't printed the story. The realization made her sick.

"So nobody's going to print this?"

He scowled and shook his head, then slowly cocked one eyebrow. "Not unless you can tell me who sent the anthrax. Now that would be worth big bucks."

Lucy was definitely interested. "Big bucks?"

"We pay for stories. Why do you think all those people are out there? A story like this could be in the six figures, if you get it right."

"But how am I . . . ?"

He shrugged. "You say you're a reporter."

"But the government couldn't figure out . . ."

He cut her off. "That's why it's worth six figures. Now get out of here."

Lucy got to her feet, feeling slightly woozy. Six figures. "Did you say six figures?"

Ed nodded. "Take my card. Ya never know."

The elevator creaked and groaned ominously as the car descended with Lucy inside. She felt like groaning herself. Maybe even wailing. What was going on? She had a terrific story, she knew it, but even the *New York Tattler* was afraid to print it because of the government. What was the world coming to?

Lucy wanted to give Ed Riedel a piece of her mind. What sort of journalist was he? Wasn't the truth more important than anything? How was a democracy supposed to operate if newspapers were afraid to print the truth? Somebody had poisoned her daughter, somebody had killed Nadine and who knows how many other people, maybe this whole flu epidemic was actually an anthrax attack, and they were going to get away with it.

The little sign on the door said PUSH but Lucy slammed her hand against it, making the door fly open. She wanted to shake some sense into Ed Riedel, into those smug FBI agents, into the whole stupid world.

She marched along the sidewalk, building up a head of steam, when somebody grabbed her arm, saving her from an oncoming car. She hadn't noticed the flashing DON'T WALK sign and she'd almost walked right into traffic. Looking around, she couldn't even tell who had saved her, who she ought to thank. It was time to calm down, she told herself as she waited for the WALK signal. She needed to cool off—she needed a little space, a little distraction. Back home she'd go for a walk on the beach, to get some sea air and clear out the cobwebs, but here she'd have to take a ride on the Staten Island Ferry. She headed for the nearest subway.

When the train pulled into the South Ferry stop, Lucy waited for the doors to slide open so she could get off, but they remained stubbornly closed. In fact, she realized, her car was barely in the station. Belatedly, she noticed a sign warning South Ferry passengers that they must be in the first five cars of the train. Furthermore, passage inside the train to the first five cars was not possible when the train was in the South Ferry station.

So she sat and waited as the train snaked its way around the subterranean loop of track at the bottom of Manhattan Island and exited at Rector Street, the next stop. She was surprised, when she surfaced onto the sidewalk, to find herself in front of a quaint little church, clearly a survivor from colonial times. She paused, peering through the wrought iron bars of the fence, and stared at a stone obelisk marking the grave of Alexander Hamilton. It was a shock to realize he wasn't just a name in the history books but a real flesh-and-blood man who had walked these streets and prayed in this church. Tall office buildings now loomed over it; the lower tip of Manhattan was now home to the stock exchange and brokerage houses. Just beyond the church was Ground Zero, where the Twin Towers had stood before the terrorist attack. Lucy paused at the fence enclosing the enormous empty space, now cleaned up and resembling any other construction site.

On the one hand, she thought, life had to go on. Rebuilding was a way of defying the terrorists. But on the other, it was hard to forget the suffering that had taken place that day. Maybe the site should be left empty as a memorial.

She felt terribly sad leaving the site, but many of the people walking briskly along the sidewalk didn't seem to notice it. Of course, she realized, these people worked nearby and they passed it every day. It was in their consciousness, sure, but they couldn't afford to dwell on the past, or the possibility of a future attack. If they did, they'd go crazy. They certainly wouldn't be able to get on the subway or ride the elevator up to the top of one of the adjacent office towers.

She strolled past the famous statue of the bull, that most American symbol of optimism, and noted that it stood on Bowling Green, now a little park filled with homeless people but once the place where seventeenth-century Dutch settlers had once spent their leisure hours bowling.

George Washington had come here, to nearby Fraunces Tavern, to say farewell to his troops. Walt Whitman had written about New York, and so had Herman Melville. He'd written about the Battery in *Moby Dick*, the same Battery Park she was walking in now, on her way to the ferry terminal. And in much the same way as he'd described, people were still drawn there daily to gaze at the Narrows of New York Harbor, now spanned by the Verrazzano Bridge, and to think of the vast ocean beyond.

The ferry terminal itself was under construction, but renovations to the waiting area were completed, and a small crowd of people had gathered in front of a set of steel and glass doors through which the ferry could be seen approaching. They grew restless as it docked, and they had to wait for the New York–bound passengers to disembark before the doors opened and they could surge forward, down the ramp to the boat. There were plenty of benches to sit on but they were largely ignored by these restless New Yorkers who couldn't imagine sitting down comfortably until the ferry was clear and then strolling aboard in a leisurely fashion. Finally, the crowd thinned, the doors slid open, and the crowd surged forward.

Lucy marched along with the rest down a wide ramp, wondering who all these people were and why they were taking the ferry in the middle of the day. They couldn't be commuters at this hour; maybe they were tourists like her? She glanced about, looking for telltale clues like cameras and shopping bags, and spotted Deb Shertzer walking a few feet from her, wearing her funeral black.

"Hi," said Lucy, with a smile. She was pleasantly surprised to see a familiar face, having grown used to passing hundreds of strangers every day.

"Well, hi yourself," said Deb, falling into step alongside her. "What are you doing down here?"

"I'm just taking a ferry ride to clear my head," said Lucy. "This has all been pretty overwhelming and I need a break."

"No wonder," sympathized Deb, tucking an unruly strand of her short hair behind one ear. "You certainly got more than you bargained for. How's Elizabeth doing?"

Lucy felt that Deb really cared; she wasn't just going through the motions and saying the expected thing. Unlike most of the women at the magazine who took great pains to look smart and fashionable, Deb wouldn't have looked out of place in Tinker's Cove with her boyish haircut, sensible walking shoes, and flower-print cloth tote bag.

"She's much better. Thanks for asking."

A cold blast of air hit them as they stepped aboard the ferry, and Lucy inhaled the familiar scent of gasoline mingled with ozone and salt water and for a moment imagined she was at the fish pier in Tinker's Cove.

"People forget New York is a port city," said Deb, apparently reading her mind. "With all the tall buildings it's easy to forget Manhattan's an island."

"It's not like any island in Maine, that's for sure," said Lucy, peering through the windows in hopes of glimpsing the ranks of skyscrapers clustered around Wall Street. That view was blocked, but she could see a huge tanker passing on the port side, and across the water she could see docks and warehouses lined up on the Brooklyn shore.

"I'd like to stand outside on the deck but I think it's too cold."

"Probably nobody out there today but cuddling couples," said Deb, taking a seat on one of the long benches that filled the ferry's belly. "Believe it or not, a ride on the ferry is a popular cheap date."

Lucy had a sudden panic attack. "I forgot to pay!"

"It's free," said Deb.

"That is a cheap date," said Lucy, taking the seat beside her. "Do you make this commute every day?"

"No. I live in Queens and take the subway to work. My mother lives in Staten Island so I'm taking advantage of a free afternoon to visit her." She looked out the window as the ferry started to pull away from its berth. "The offices are still closed."

"What did you think of the funeral?"

Deb looked at her curiously. "That's right, you were there, weren't you? You saw Elise freak out at Pablo." She shook her head. "That's just like her, you know. I have no doubt Camilla told Pablo to take the photos, then got Elise to take it out on him when she changed her mind."

"Camilla was probably upset," said Lucy. "She and Nadine were friends since college, right?"

"Barnard girls. Elise, too." Her lips curved into a small smile. "Believe me, if I had a daughter, I'd send her anywhere but Barnard."

"I'm sure it's a fine institution," said Lucy. "Has anyone else gotten sick?"

"No . . . but we're all keeping our fingers crossed and taking our Cipro. The offices are closed, of course, so the hazmat crew can do their stuff." Deb sighed. "I'm not looking forward to going back."

"They won't let you in unless it's safe."

"It's still creepy."

"Yeah," agreed Lucy, gazing across the water at a fanciful Victorian structure like a wedding cake sitting on an island. "What's that?"

"Ellis Island. Gateway to America for millions of immigrants."

Lucy hadn't realized it was so close to Manhattan. The immigrants would have been able to see the city as they waited to be admitted. "Can you imagine how heartbreaking it would be to finally get here, after a horrendous sea voyage, with your whole family and everything you owned, only to learn you had tuberculosis or something and they wouldn't let you in?"

"They had quarantine wards; they nursed the sick ones and most of them eventually got in."

"I'd like to think so," said Lucy, gazing at the Statue of Liberty and thinking about those World War II movies that ended with a boatful of refugees, or returning soldiers, gazing at the symbol of freedom. She found herself blinking back a tear. "I bet you're used to seeing her."

"Not really. It's always a bit of a thrill. She's fabulous, even if her accessories are rather unusual and that shade of green doesn't look good on anybody."

Lucy was grateful for the joke. "I agree about the book and torch, but I think those foam crowns would make a good gift for my girls at home."

"A good choice, and affordable, too. Personally, I'd go for something a bit more subdued—I don't really have occasion to wear a tiara."

"I'm glad you approve." Lucy couldn't take her eyes off Lady Liberty and fell silent as the ferry glided by. "Where's Governors Island?" she asked.

"I'm not really sure but it might be that one on the other side." Deb pointed towards a sizeable island with numerous buildings. "It used to be some sort of military base but now it's empty and they're trying to figure out what to do with it."

"Right. Actually, I have a friend who's on that committee." Lucy hadn't realized how close the island was to Wall Street, or how magnificent the views would be. It was also much more built up than she expected, covered with neat brick buildings that could easily be converted to luxury housing. It would be most attractive to the well-heeled investment bankers and lawyers and brokers who worked in the financial district; the island would offer unparalleled security only a short boat ride from their offices. Plus, there was even docking space for their yachts. "I heard Nadine's husband is trying to develop it."

"Could be. I never paid much attention to her private life."

"You got enough of her at work?" asked Lucy.

"You said it, not me." Deb's eyes glittered mischievously.

"I get the sense she wasn't very popular at the magazine," said Lucy, putting out a feeler, "but it's hard to believe that one of her fellow workers would actually poison her."

"Are you kidding? I wouldn't put anything past that crowd," said Deb. "They're all self-centered, shallow, ambitious, and ruthless—it's the fashion industry, after all. The most vital question on all their minds right now is whether purple is really going to be the hot new color this spring. There's a lot riding on it, you know." She looked up as the ferry groaned and slowed in preparation for docking. "This crowd is more likely to skewer you with sarcasm. Where would a fashionista get anthrax? It's not like they sell it at Bloomie's."

"I was wondering the same thing," said Lucy. "I suppose it could have been some sort of terror attack, like before, but it seems funny that only my daughter and Nadine were affected."

"I don't know." Deb shook her head as the ferry shuddered to a halt. "After the World Trade Center attacks, I guess anything is possible." She paused. "If you want to ride back you have to get off and walk through the terminal and get back on. You used to be able to stay on the boat but that's changed."

They walked together until their paths diverged in the terminal; Deb headed for the exit while Lucy followed a shuffling homeless man making his way back to the ferry. She wondered if he actually lived on the boat. It was possible, she guessed; the ride took longer than she remembered. This time she buttoned up her coat and pulled on her gloves, stepping onto the outside deck that wrapped around the boat. The windows were closed, but it was still chillier than the inside sitting area. The wind had died down so she leaned her elbows on the railing and looked across the water at the twinkling outline of the illuminated bridge.

Daylight was fading, Lucy realized, checking her watch. It was nearly four o'clock. She ducked inside and crossed the seating area, coming out on the other outside deck facing the city. The boat began to move, gliding across silky water toward the gleaming skyscrapers, now reflecting the last rays of the winter sun. She sat down on the long bench that wrapped around the outside of the cabin, alone except for one or two other hardy souls, and plunged her hands into her pockets. She heard the thrum of the engine and a boat horn or two, but otherwise it was quiet as the ferry picked up speed. The cloudless indigo sky was deepening, growing darker, though not yet dark enough for stars to appear. In the distance, growing closer, were the illuminated towers of Manhattan, creating their own sparkling constellations in the night sky.

Chapter Fifteen

TAKE OUR TEST AND FIND YOUR

PERSONALITY QUOTIENT

The city was most magical when viewed from a distance. It didn't have nearly the same appeal when you were deep in its bowels, hanging onto a slippery pole in a packed subway car, decided Lucy. The train was empty when she boarded at South Ferry and she'd gotten a seat, but it had filled up rapidly with homeward bound workers. At 59th Street she gave up her seat to a pregnant woman, and by the time she reached 116th Street people were so tightly jammed together that it was difficult to breathe, and she had to battle her way through the crowd to exit. When she finally managed to extricate herself, she stood on the platform and shook herself like a dog, straightening her clothes and catching her breath.

Once outside she found herself in the dark of late afternoon and she savored the experience, strange to her, of walking down a city sidewalk at night. She wasn't the least bit afraid. The stores were still open and plenty of people were about on Broadway, mostly college and high school students with backpacks and businesspeople with briefcases, many pausing to pick up dry cleaning or a quart of milk or a bunch of flowers on their way home.

It occurred to her that it would be nice to bring Sam some flowers, or maybe a cake from a bakery, and she was trying to decide which would be the better choice when she realized she was walking past Barnard College. The realization energized her, making her wonder if fate was taking a hand and pointing the way. This was her chance to see the institution that had earned Deb's disapproval by nurturing Nadine, Camilla, and Elise. Curious, she peered through the bars of the decorative iron fence into an illuminated, treed courtyard. Noting that the gate was open she wandered in, not quite sure what she was looking for. She passed groups of girls walking in twos and threes, bundled up against the cold and clutching piles of books to their chests; some twenty years ago Camilla, Nadine, and Elise would have made a similar group, hurrying back to their dorm after a busy day of classes. She could picture them: Camilla would be the alpha member of the little pack, flanked on either side by her two less self-assured buddies.

Feeling the cold, Lucy stepped into the inviting student center to warm up. She picked up a copy of the student newspaper and sat down on one of the colorful upholstered chairs clustered in the large room, which seemed to be a combination waiting room and hallway. A bookshelf next to her chair held a collection of yearbooks, and she pulled out one from 1982. Leafing through it she discovered that Camilla had been a member of the class of 1984.

Opening that edition she found photos of Camilla Keith and Elise Frazier on adjacent pages. Oddly enough, considering their friendship, she discovered they had virtually nothing in common during their college years. They lived in different dorms, they belonged to different clubs, and they even looked different. Back then Camilla had a certain sophistication that Elise, with very big hair and a pair of oversized eyeglasses, definitely lacked.

Lucy didn't know Nadine's maiden name so she leafed through the pages searching for her first name. There was only one Nadine, Nadine Smoot. Lucy stifled a giggle as she studied the much younger but still recognizable face of the late Nadine. Lucy guessed she might have been strongly influenced by the militant feminism rampant on campuses at the time; there seemed no other explanation for her extremely short, mannish haircut and the plain T-shirt that strained across her braless chest, proclaiming "Sisterhood Is Powerful." Checking the list of undergraduate activities in which Nadine had participated, Lucy learned she had been a founding member of the school's NOW chapter and was also active in the Take Back The Night movement and the women's health initiative.

Weird, thought Lucy, replacing the book. What had brought these three very different women together? What did a campus fashionista, a militant feminist, and an ugly duckling (she mentally apologized to Elise) all have in common? They seemed an extremely unlikely group, especially considering the tendency of college students to clump themselves with similar friends. When she was in college she remembered the wide gulf between the jocks, the sorority girls, the theater kids, and the political activists. Once labeled a member of one of those groups it was practically impossible to breach the gap and make new friends.

Looking down at the newspaper in her lap, Lucy had an idea. She got up and went over to the information desk and asked where she could find old copies.

"How old?" inquired the girl, a perky little brunette with stylish black-rimmed eyeglasses.

"From the eighties."

"You'd need the archives," she said.

Lucy suddenly felt very old. "Where would they be?" she asked.

"Wollman Library." The girl pulled out a map, circled the library, and plotted her route. "Ask for the Lehman Archives."

At the library, the student staff member apologized for the fact that the university newspaper wasn't available online. "You'll have to use the microfiche machine," she said, handing Lucy several spools of film.

"No problem," said Lucy, settling herself in front of the big viewing machine. She didn't mind; she liked the whirring sound the film made as she scanned the pages, she enjoyed viewing the old issues as they actually appeared when printed. She got a kick out of the grainy photos from an earlier era, replete with shoulder pads and Farrah Fawcett hairdos. Did people really go around looking like that? It seemed incredible until she spotted one coed in the same platform shoes she had once worn and groaned out loud.

The student who had given her the films hurried over. "Everything okay?"

Lucy chuckled and pointed at the screen. "I used to have a pair of shoes like that."

"Wow, retro," said the girl, obviously impressed. "They get fifty bucks for those in the vintage clothing stores."

Lucy's jaw dropped. "Really?"

"Yeah. Do you still have them? I'd be interested, if you're a size eight."

"No, I'm a seven and they went to the Salvation Army a long, long time ago."

"Too bad!"

Skimming through the pages, Lucy noticed that Camilla's name and face popped up frequently. She was pictured selling used textbooks at a student council fund-raiser. She was presenting a cash gift to a Head Start program. She had won a *Glamour* magazine contest. And then came the stunning headline: Student Leader Attempts Suicide.

Lucy let out a long breath and leaned closer to read the story.

> *The usual quiet of a weekday evening during midterms, when most students are preparing for exams, was shattered last Tuesday by a scream.*
>
> *"She's going to jump!" shrieked Nadine Smoot, '84, pointing to a small figure clothed in a diaphanous white gown perched on the edge of the Brooks Hall residence roof. She was later identified as Camilla Keith, '84, president of the sophomore class and a member of the student governing council.*
>
> *A crowd immediately gathered in the Arthur Ross Courtyard, but no one seemed to know what to do. Uncertainty reigned as students discussed an appropriate course of action. Some wanted to call campus police and health officials; others maintained such action would be a violation of personal freedom and individual rights. As the controversy raged, Smoot and Elise Frazier, '84, took action, racing up the stairs and joining Keith on the roof.*

The two remonstrated with Keith as students gathered below watched with bated breath. When the sound of approaching sirens was heard, Keith became agitated, stepping closer to the edge. It was then that Smoot lunged at her and brought her safely to the ground in a rugby style lunge, assisted by Frazier.

All three were subsequently transported by ambulance to Columbia Presbyterian Medical Center. Smoot and Frazier were treated for minor abrasions and released. Keith was admitted to the psychiatric unit for evaluation but has since been released. She had no comment, except to thank Smoot and Frazier, whom she said "prevented me from making a very big mistake."

Frazier attributed the happy outcome to Smoot's quick thinking and willingness to take action. "I was terrified." she said, "but Nadine knew what to do."

Smoot said she only did "what any sister would do for another" and went on to point out that women are much more likely to commit suicide than men. "We need to establish suicide-prevention programs here on campus. The administration doesn't want to admit there's a problem but this time they couldn't sweep it under the rug. Camilla was out there in public, showing her pain, and that was very brave."

Personally, Smoot said the incident was an opportunity for her to get to know someone she wouldn't have thought she had much in common with. "Camilla and I are very different; she's more establishment and I consider myself a feminist and a women's rights activist but now I see we're the same under the skin. There's an old Native American saying that if you save someone's life you become responsible for them forever," she said.

Lucy felt chills run up her spine as she finished reading the story. What a creepy thing for Nadine to say. Did she really feel responsible for Camilla's future welfare? Or was she taking advantage of an emotionally vulnerable young woman? And what about Nadine's feminist views? She apparently hadn't hesitated to jettison them when she had an opportunity to join the "establishment" fashion media.

The friendship had certainly benefited Nadine and Elise, who had ridden on Camilla's coattails to assume top positions at *Jolie* magazine. But what about Camilla? Had she grown tired of this everlasting debt? Had Nadine become a serious liability? The magazine was in trouble and her job was in jeopardy, largely because of Nadine's harebrained schemes.

It occurred to Lucy that Camilla might have come to believe there was only one way to rid herself of Nadine. But how would she get her hands on anthrax, wondered Lucy. Designer clothes, sure, she had an unlimited supply. But anthrax? Not usually found in the environs of Seventh Avenue.

Idly, Lucy scrolled the microfilm through a few more issues of the paper, stopping when she came to a photo of Elise, pictured with two beaming professors. She was the 1983 winner of the Jackson-Selfridge prize in biochemistry, awarded for "innovative research with potential agricultural applications."

Ohmigod, thought Lucy. Elise studied biochemistry; she might even have worked as a biochemist before coming to *Jolie*. She might have worked with anthrax herself, or she could have connections, friends who worked with it. As Lucy continued scrolling through the microfilm she thought again of a favorite phrase of her mother's. "Three's a crowd," Mom had always advised, whenever Lucy planned to go shopping or to a movie with a couple of friends. "Two can walk together, two can chat in a theater. If there are four, you can make two couples. But three's a crowd. Someone's always left out."

Lucy didn't usually agree, but this time it seemed that Mom may have been right. Maybe three was a crowd and Nadine was the odd one out.

The idea came to mind again when she and Sam were eating microwave dinners in the kitchen, only this time Lucy was worried she might be the third wheel.

"I hope you don't mind," said Sam apologizing for not providing a home-cooked meal, "but this is what I usually do when Brad's not home for supper."

"Fine with me," said Lucy. "I really appreciate your hospitality. I hope it's not a nuisance having me here."

"A nuisance? Whatever gave you that idea?"

"Well, you and Brad are finally empty-nesters, and now you've got me cluttering up your life."

"Honey, I love the chance to visit with you," said Sam, removing the dinners from the microwave and setting the plastic containers on plates. "Besides, my nights have been pretty lonely these past few months. That Governors Island committee is taking an awful lot of Brad's time."

"What's that all about?" asked Lucy, spearing one of the four small pieces of chicken included with the dinner. "I saw it from the ferry. It seems such a waste. All those buildings and nobody there."

"It's a fabulous piece of real estate but nobody's quite sure what to do with it, so that's why they set up the committee. There's been a fort there since the 1700s, the Army had a base there for years and then the Coast Guard had it for a while. Now about half the island has been preserved as a National Historic District and a national monument but there's plenty of acreage left, most of it old military housing."

"It must have spectacular views," said Lucy. "Arnold Nelson wants to build that City Gate development there, doesn't he?"

"Oh yes he does. But Brad and some of the committee members don't want to see it become a private preserve for the very wealthy. They see it as a resource that should benefit all New Yorkers. Right now it's only open to the public one day a week during the summer, but they'd like to expand so people could enjoy it year round. That demand hasn't been very popular with the developers."

Lucy remembered Brad talking about that at the AIDS ball. "It sounds like he's got quite a fight on his hands," she said, scraping up the last bits of broccoli.

"That he does," agreed Sam, clearing the table. "Brownies for dessert?"

"I thought you'd never ask."

* * *

After enjoying coffee and brownies and watching the evening news with Sam, Lucy headed back out to visit Elizabeth in the hospital. She had checked in by phone several times but hadn't had a chance to visit all day and was feeling guilty about neglecting her daughter. She needn't have worried. When she arrived she found Elizabeth and Fiona watching newlyweds Jessica and Nick and giggling together.

"I can't believe she actually complimented the Secretary of the Interior on the way she decorated the White House," said Elizabeth.

"I heard one that was better than that," said Fiona. "She read that she was pregnant in a tabloid newspaper so she got one of those tests at the drugstore to see if it was true."

Elizabeth couldn't stand it. She was clutching her stomach and pounding her heels against the bed.

"Well, I guess you're feeling better," said Lucy.

"Oh, Mom. Hi."

"I can tell you missed me," said Lucy. "What did you do all day?"

"They kept me busy with tests and food and medicine. Lance was here most of the day and then Fiona came."

"What's new at the magazine?" asked Lucy. "Any developments?"

"Fantastic news, actually," said Fiona. Lucy loved her British accent. "Nobody else has gotten sick, and they've finished testing the office and it came up clean except for a tiny, tiny trace of anthrax, which they've eradicated."

"That's great."

"It has its downside." Fiona was examining her fingernails. "It means I have to go back to work tomorrow."

Lucy was smiling sympathetically when Sidra gave a little tap on the door and came into the room holding a huge bunch of flowers that was almost as big as she was.

"How's the patient?" she asked, bending down to hug Elizabeth. "I wanted to visit right away, but this is the soonest I could manage."

"I feel great. Thanks for coming," said Elizabeth, taking the bouquet and sniffing it appreciatively. "I've never seen such gorgeous flowers."

"I stole them from the set," she said, looking rather guilty. "Believe me, it doesn't matter. They change them every day anyway."

"I'll see about a vase," said Lucy, heading for the door.

"And I guess I'll get moving," said Fiona, with a big yawn. "Got to get up early tomorrow."

"Who was that?" asked Fiona, as they walked down the hall.

"Oh, I can't believe I didn't introduce you. That's Sidra Rumford; she's my best friend's daughter. She lives in the city and works on the *Norah!* TV show."

Fiona's eyes lit up. "Really? TV!"

"Don't tell me you're starstruck," said Lucy. They had reached the elevator and were standing together.

"Sure, a little bit. Who isn't?" Fiona was blushing. "But the truth is, I'm pretty sick of the magazine and I bet they could use a bright young thing like me on the show."

"I'll ask Sidra . . ." began Lucy.

"Oh, you don't have to do that," said Fiona. "Maybe you could just give me her phone number, and her name again. I think I've already forgotten it."

To Lucy's surprise, Fiona had already produced a memo book and a pencil and was waiting expectantly, so she pulled her cell phone from her pocket and gave her the number.

"Thanks," said Fiona, just as the elevator doors slid open. "Cheerio!"

Lucy continued on to the nurse's station where she was given a vase and returned to Elizabeth's room. She found Sidra and Elizabeth deep in conversation.

"What's going on?" she asked, setting the vase in the sink and filling it with water. Lucy wasn't one for arranging flowers so she picked up the bouquet and plunked it into the vase.

"We were just talking," said Sidra, taking the vase and rearranging the flowers. "I was telling Elizabeth about what happened on the show today."

"I missed it. What was it about?"

Sidra's hands, which had been flying about the arrangement, suddenly stopped. "It was about healthy food choices at holiday parties, and Rachael Ray was making a low-fat veggie dip when these two women in the audience got up and started screaming and throwing tomatoes at her and Norah. Rachael took one right in the face, and Norah's cashmere sweater was ruined."

"How terrible!"

"That's awful," chimed Elizabeth.

"Who were they? I thought everybody loved Norah."

"Not these two, that's for sure."

"What were they so mad about?"

"That's the weird thing. You'd think that the reason they disrupted the show was to get publicity for their cause, wouldn't you? I mean, it goes out live on national TV so you'd think they'd at least have a sign or something. But they didn't. Nothing."

"Maybe it was personal," suggested Lucy.

"Norah says she didn't know them. She was really puzzled. Usually there are at least a couple of lawsuits against her, but right now there isn't anything." Sidra carefully added the last flowers to the arrangement and stepped back to study it. "She's furious at the security people. They not only let them get in with their rotten tomatoes, but they didn't hold them for questioning afterward. They just escorted them out."

"How come they didn't call the police?"

"That's what Norah wants to know. Somebody messed up big-time. This time it was only tomatoes, but next time . . . ?" Sidra left the sentence unfinished and carried the arrangement over to the window where she set it on the sill. "There. Now I've got to go."

Sidra was as good as her word, departing in a flurry of air kisses. But after she left, Lucy had a sense of déjà vu. She felt as if she'd been through this before: another close call, another lucky escape. It was the same thing all over again and she didn't like it. After all, no matter how lucky you were, luck eventually ran out.

Chapter Sixteen

WHAT FRENCH GIRLS HAVE THAT YOU DON'T

Even though Lucy knew the *Jolie* offices had been thoroughly tested for anthrax, scrubbed and decontaminated by hazmat experts, she still hesitated when the elevator doors slid open on Friday morning and it took an act of faith to inhale when she stepped onto the freshly cleaned carpet. It smelled clean, sure, but deadly microbes could lurk in tiny crevices and it only took one to make you sick.

The receptionist at the desk opposite the elevator bank didn't seem concerned about her health, however. She seemed happy to be back at work and greeted Lucy cheerily.

"I heard your daughter is doing much better," she said. "That must be a big relief."

"It is," said Lucy, "thanks for asking about her." She launched into the story she'd concocted to explain her visit to the office. "Actually, that's why I'm here. I'm worried about the hospital bill and need to talk to somebody. . . ."

"Of course, all that time in intensive care, the bill must be enormous." The receptionist pursed her lips and furrowed her brow in sympathy. "Don't you have health insurance?"

"We do, but you know how it is. One big claim and they drop you. And I really do think the magazine bears some responsibility."

The receptionist chewed her lip and consulted a staff directory. "Actually, this is the editorial side. I don't know much about the business end of things; they're not even in this building. I guess Camilla would be the logical person to talk to."

She was reaching for the phone when Lucy spoke. "She's got so much on her plate right now, I don't want to bother her." She paused before suggesting the true object of her visit. "What about Elise?"

"I think you're right. Elise would be better." After a quick phone conversation she sent Lucy down the hallway to Elise's office.

The fashion editor met her at the door, and Lucy couldn't help thinking how different she looked now from the photo in the yearbook. The nerdy biochemistry student had transformed herself into a sophisticated businesswoman. The glasses were gone, the frizzy hair had been straightened and highlighted, her tweed suit was beautifully tailored, and her make-up was impeccable. She had also made a remarkable recovery from yesterday's funeral. If she was still grieving for her old college friend Nadine, there was no sign of it. Today she was all business.

"Lucy, this is an unexpected pleasure," she said. "Come right on in." When Lucy had seated herself and declined coffee, Elise took her place on the other side of the desk and tented her hands, displaying a flawless manicure and a gorgeous gold ring with a large blue stone. "What can I do for you?"

Knees together, hands in lap, Lucy took a deep breath and studied the large photograph on the wall behind Elise. It pictured a sculpture of a bare-breasted woman on a chariot accompanied by two smaller women, also bare breasted, on either side of her.

Noticing her interest, Elise enlightened her. "Boadicea," she said. "As queen of the Britons she led a rebellion against the Romans."

"She must have been quite a girl," said Lucy, taking in the spear Boadicea was holding aloft and the scythed wheels of her chariot.

"Oh, she was," said Elise. "But I don't think you've come here to discuss ancient British history."

"No," said Lucy. "This is a tad awkward, you see, but I've been in contact with my health insurance company, and the legal department there seems to think the magazine bears some responsibility for Elizabeth's situation."

Elise raised her eyebrows skeptically. "I've never heard of such a thing."

"Well, me either," said Lucy. "But they seem to feel that since the illness was the result of an intentional poisoning rather than something contagious like the measles that there was a certain degree of negligence. . . ." She was relieved when Elise interrupted her.

"Enough," she said, rolling her eyes. "I have no head for business. You'll have to talk to our legal department."

"And where would that be?"

"Over on Forty-ninth Street." She was writing the information on a slip of paper and handed to Lucy. "I'll call and tell them to expect you."

"Thanks so much," said Lucy, standing. "I hate to be a bother, especially at such a difficult time." She looked down at the floor for a moment, then raised her eyes. "I know you and Nadine were old friends. From college, right?"

"That's right." Elise checked her watch.

"And Camilla, too. Amazing. It's a new world, isn't it, where women have their own old-girl networks?" She managed a chuckle, which she hoped would signal female solidarity to Elise. "And men always say that women are too catty to maintain long-term friendships. You three are, well, *were*, the exception."

"I'm sorry but I have a meeting. . . ." Elise wasn't about to be drawn into a discussion of feminine ethics and was on her feet, heading for the door.

Lucy ignored the cue that it was time to leave and sat in her chair, turning to face Elise. "What's the secret?" she asked quickly. "How did you manage it? To stay friends all these years, I mean? Especially when you all have such different personalities. And Nadine had a husband; that must have changed the dynamics a bit, no?"

"We didn't ask awkward questions," said Elise, opening the door and tapping her foot. "I think that was it."

Lucy slid to the edge of her chair and picked up her bag, but rattled on. "You know, I just have one quick question I'm dying to ask you. I hope you don't mind."

Elise definitely looked as if she did mind, but Lucy didn't give her a chance to object.

"I am so grateful that this makeover gave my daughter the opportunity to come into contact with a successful woman like you. I think you have so much to offer, with your example and your wisdom. . . ."

Elise interrupted. "Would you mind getting to the point?"

"Oh, sorry. I do tend to go on," said Lucy, standing up. "Well, the question is this. You see, Elizabeth's been majoring in chemistry, biochemistry in fact, terrific grades, she's a natural. But she's heard that there's a lot of discrimination against women in graduate programs, and she's not sure if she should continue with it or switch to another field that's more hospitable to women, like communications, for example. I mean, she doesn't want to keep banging her head against that glass ceiling, if you know what I mean."

"I'm afraid I don't have any experience with that."

"Really? I thought I heard somewhere that you were a biochemistry major, that's why I thought you'd be the right person to advise Elizabeth. How did you end up working at a fashion magazine? Do you miss biochemistry?"

Elise was way ahead of her. "No. Mrs. Stone, I haven't been mixing up anthrax in my home lab, if that's what you're getting at. Now I really must ask you to go."

"Oh, I never meant to imply anything of the kind," said Lucy, making her way as slowly as she could manage to the open door, where Elise was standing. "The thought never crossed my mind. I just wondered why you left your field for fashion."

"I think you could say I just fell into it." Elise stepped forward and raised her arm against the door, effectively forcing Lucy toward the hallway.

Lucy countered by leaning closer and whispering in her ear. "I understand. You're probably too good a friend to say anything, but it was because of Camilla, wasn't it? She had some serious emotional problems back then, didn't she? Didn't I hear somewhere that she attempted suicide in college?"

Elise's face was stony. "Where did you hear that?"

"Oh, I don't know. People talk. Maybe I read it somewhere." Lucy lowered her voice. "Of course I don't believe half of what I read. It isn't true, is it?"

"I'm not in the habit of gossiping," snapped Elise, giving the door a push. "You'd have to ask Camilla about that."

"Oh, I wouldn't want to bother her. She certainly seemed awfully fragile at the funeral," said Lucy, blocking the door with her foot. They were now standing toe-to-toe, and Lucy looked Elise straight in the eye. "It was very obvious how much she relies on you, now that Nadine is gone."

Elise stared back, and Lucy realized that even brown eyes could look very cold indeed. "Good day, Mrs. Stone," she said.

Lucy had to step smartly to avoid being hit in the face by the door.

Well, well, well, she muttered to herself, heading down the hallway in the direction of the beauty department. Elise hadn't exactly confessed, but she had been extremely defensive about her relationships with Camilla and Nadine and she'd been awfully quick to deny having anything to do with the anthrax. Lucy felt sure she'd hit a nerve and she intended to keep up the pressure.

Meanwhile, she wanted to get on with phase two of her plan, which was to search Nadine's office. She was pretty sure she could count on Fiona to cooperate, considering the way she and Elizabeth had become such good friends. But when she got to the beauty department it was Phyllis who greeted her.

"Hi, Mrs. Stone. How's our little patient? Would she like some cologne or body lotion? This just came in yesterday—a new scent from Stella McCartney."

Lucy took the box, which was beautifully tied with a purple bow. "Thank you. That's very sweet. I know she'll love it."

Phyllis held up her hands in a gesture of innocence. "No anthrax, I promise. The package is sealed."

"It never crossed my mind. Elizabeth was just in the wrong place at the wrong time." Lucy paused a moment, thinking. She hadn't expected Phyllis to be so friendly, especially after her confrontations with Elise and Camilla. She decided to press her advantage. "Any new developments in the anthrax investigation?"

"Not that I'm aware of," said Phyllis.

"What's the gossip here? What are people saying when they stand around the water cooler?"

The question seemed to fluster Phyllis. "I'd love to talk it over with you but I've got to run. I'm already late for an editorial meeting."

"Oh, I shouldn't keep you. Is Fiona here?"

"No, she's in photo."

"I don't mind waiting here," said Lucy, seeing an opportunity to get into Nadine's office. "I have a message for her from Elizabeth."

Phyllis was fiddling with the doorknob. "Do you believe it? Now we have to lock our offices whenever we leave them. It's a new security directive. It's ridiculous but I can't let you stay here alone."

"Better safe than sorry," said Lucy, who was in reality feeling extremely sorry. Now she wouldn't be able to get a look at Nadine's office unless Fiona was willing to risk her job by violating the new security policy. She decided there was no harm in asking, but there was no sign of Fiona when she arrived at the photo department.

"Fiona? I sent her to get rose petals for the shoot," said Pablo. He was squinting through the camera at an arrangement of beauty products spread on a white drop. "The little one continues to recover, yes?"

"Yes, yes she does."

He clucked his tongue. "Such a shame. Nadine, I won't miss her and her meddling. But for a sweet young girl to suffer, that is very bad."

"Nadine wasn't very popular here, was she?"

Pablo stood up, one hand still on the camera. He was dressed in tight black pants and a striped knit shirt; Lucy couldn't imagine one of the guys in Tinker's Cove wearing an outfit like that, but it sure looked good on him.

"What is the phrase, you can say that again?"

"That's the phrase." Lucy chuckled. "How come?"

"She was stupid, but she had Camilla's ear." He exhaled sharply. "That is no way to run a magazine."

"Do you think Camilla might have figured that out? That she might have wanted to get rid of Nadine?"

Pablo looked at her sideways. "You know what they're saying? Nadine's husband, the billionaire rich guy, when he heard the magazine was in trouble with the publisher, he offered to buy it." He paused. "Only one condition: Camilla would go."

"Who'd be the editor then?"

"Who d'you think? Nadine."

"Nadine?" Lucy was incredulous. "That sounds like a really bad business move."

"He doesn't care. He has lotsa money." Pablo smirked. "He wanted to keep Nadine busy, busy, busy."

Lucy found her heart warming to Pablo. What a guy! He looked good and he loved to gossip. It was almost like talking to one of her girlfriends at home, but better.

"At the funeral, I thought Nancy Glass seemed awfully concerned about Arnold. Do you think he's interested in her?"

Pablo shrugged. "Sure. He's a ladies' man."

This was no surprise to Lucy. "Right. So what does a smart, beautiful woman like Nancy see in him?"

Pablo rubbed his fingers together. "Money."

"Oh."

"You're shocked."

"I guess I think there are easier ways to make a buck than to try to wheedle it out of a fat, ugly rich guy."

Pablo laughed, revealing a mouth full of very white teeth.

"Usually, the husband is the prime suspect when the wife dies, but I guess not in this case," continued Lucy. "Not if he was going to buy a magazine for Nadine."

"It's just a rumor." Pablo's eyes gleamed wickedly. "Maybe he did kill her, but I don't think so. He had a good thing going with her. She liked being the public Mrs. Arnold Nelson, she liked getting good tables in restaurants and getting her picture in the society pages, but I don't think she liked having sex with him." He licked his lips. "I don't think she liked sex at all."

Lucy thought he might be right. Underneath the fashionable clothes and make-up, there was a kind of slovenliness about Nadine. Her clothes didn't fit well, as if she'd recently put on some weight. Her hair color had needed touching up, remembered Lucy, and her nails looked as if she'd just applied polish without bothering to file or shape them. She reminded Lucy of some women she knew in Tinker's Cove who gave up trying to be alluring when they reached a certain age. They cut their hair short and donned elastic-waist pants and devoted themselves to golf or genealogy or anything except their husbands. "But she didn't mind if he had it, as long as he got it from somebody else?"

Pablo nodded approvingly. "In that way, she had a very European attitude."

Lucy was fascinated, but before she could continue the conversation the door flew open and Camilla marched in. Like Elise, she seemed to have recovered remarkably well since the funeral. There was no sign of the grief-stricken woman who had been clinging so pathetically to Elise for support. Today she was clearly in charge.

"Do I have to remind you that we're on deadline?" she snapped at Pablo. Turning to Lucy, she jabbed in her direction with a red-tipped talon. "What the hell do you think you're doing here?"

"Just visiting," said Lucy, all innocence. "I have a message from my daughter for Fiona."

"You can leave it with the receptionist, on your way out."

Lucy suspected security was on the way. "Okay."

"Now."

"Right," said Lucy. "Nice talking to you, Pablo."

She was leaving when she saw Camilla point at the display of cosmetics Pablo was photographing. "Not like this," she said, frowning and waggling her fingers.

Pablo stepped forward, attempting to preserve the carefully designed arrangement, but Camilla stopped him with a glance.

Then, with a sweep of her arm she knocked over the open tubes of lipstick and mascara and eyeliner, sending them rolling every which way and spilling the open bottles of nail lacquer. "Smash them. Break them," she ordered, prying the little cakes of eye color out of their compacts with her nails and tossing them on the table. "Smear them all around. Show the colors. The colors!" She brought her fist down again and again until all that was left was a Jackson Pollock scramble of lurid hues.

Chapter Seventeen

FABULOUS FUN FURS FOR EVERY BUDGET!

Wow, thought Lucy, as she rode the elevator down to the lobby, that was one image she wasn't going to forget anytime soon. If she'd had any doubt that Camilla was crazy, really crazy, the sight of her smashing the cosmetics had convinced her that the editor was no more master of her emotions as an eminently successful fashion journalist than she was when she attempted suicide in college. Worst of all had been her voice, an eerie scream with which she spewed insult after insult at poor Pablo.

The elevator landed with a thud and Lucy exited the building, gratefully inhaling the cold, crisp air. Even loaded with pollutants, it seemed much fresher than the overheated atmosphere in the *Jolie* offices.

Lucy decided that walking the ten or twelve blocks to the hospital would do her good. She'd get some exercise and get rid of some of the tension she'd been building up; plus, she did her best thinking when she was in motion.

And she had plenty to think about, given the rivalries and jealousies she'd discovered at the magazine. Pablo, though he made no attempt to hide his dislike of Nadine, she dismissed as a suspect. It was his sense of humor, which indicated a certain sense of detachment, that argued against him being the killer. He didn't seem to take Nadine or Camilla all that seriously, viewing them as actors in an entertaining soap opera. His talent and standing as a photographer protected him; he could leave anytime he chose, which put him essentially above the fray.

She was also tempted to cross Phyllis off her list of suspects. In theory she had seemed a likely candidate since Nadine's death had meant a big promotion for her. But from what Lucy had seen of her, she didn't seem to be reveling in her new position. If anything, she seemed to approach her new, powerful job as a continuation of her old job. In truth, Nadine's death hadn't meant big changes in the beauty department because Phyllis had really done the lion's share of the work all along. So Phyllis went about her work as she always had, with no sense of self-importance or ego. She'd made a few minor changes, like sharing the samples, but Lucy hadn't sensed any hint of triumphant self-assertion, which she was sure would have been the case if Phyllis had harbored a festering resentment of Nadine and finally decided to take action.

She really couldn't cross off Arnold and Nancy until she knew more about their relationship, but from what Pablo told her it didn't seem as if that was a promising line of investigation. Arnold and Nadine had apparently worked out a relationship that suited them both: he got freedom to exercise his libido and she got money and status.

No, from what she'd learned so far, Camilla was by far the likeliest suspect, especially if what Pablo had told her about Arnold's plan to buy the magazine was true. From what she'd seen of Camilla, Lucy believed she had the most reasons to want Nadine out of her life, permanently, and was just crazy enough to do whatever it took to get rid of her.

Elise, she was sure, would have been happy to do whatever was required to help eliminate her rival for Camilla's friendship. Maybe she didn't cook up the anthrax herself, but she could have had connections who had access to the stuff: an old professor, a fellow student, or perhaps even a colleague. The very fact that she'd jumped to the conclusion that Lucy suspected her of producing the anthrax could indicate a guilty conscience.

Of course, the act of murder usually required a precipitating factor, and Lucy sensed that Arnold's proposed purchase of the magazine was probably the issue that pushed Camilla over the edge. If only she could find out if the sale was really in the works or just a rumor.

Lucy shoved her hands into her pockets and felt the business card Ed Riedel had given her when she visited him at the *Tattler*. Impulsively, she decided to give him a call.

"You probably don't remember me," she began.

"You're the dame from Maine."

Lucy was astonished. "How'd you know?"

"You talk funny."

After living for more than twenty years in Tinker's Cove, Lucy guessed she probably did have a bit of a Maine accent.

"Listen, I've turned up some interesting stuff in the anthrax death at *Jolie* magazine. . . ."

"Who did it?"

"I'm not sure but I've got some promising—"

The editor cut her off. "Call me when you're sure."

Lucy wasn't about to be brushed off so easily. "And I've got some scandalous inside stuff on Camilla Keith. . . ."

"Yeah, and the Pope's Catholic."

Lucy's spirits sank. "I thought I had a scoop."

"You and eight million other people. That woman has ripped into everybody at some point. The whole city's got scars—taxi drivers, florists, interior designers, dog walkers, they all wanna get their story in print."

"I didn't know."

"Keep on trying, kid," he said.

Disappointed at his reaction, Lucy replaced her phone in her purse. By this time she had worked her way over to Lexington Avenue and found herself passing the Melrose, her home for three days, where Cathy was still in residence. As an industry insider, she might have the information about Arnold that Lucy was looking for. Impulsively, she ducked into the lobby where she was greeted warmly by the man at the desk.

"It's nice to see you, Mrs. Stone. How's your daughter doing?"

"Much better," said Lucy, surprised that he remembered her. "Thanks for asking."

"Are you coming back to stay with us?"

"No, I'm staying with a friend, uptown. I am hoping to catch Cathy Montgomery. Do you know if she's still staying here?"

"As far as I know," he said. "I'm not supposed to give out room numbers but you can call her on the house phone."

In a matter of minutes Lucy was connected and heard Cathy invite her up to her suite.

"I didn't really think I'd find you here," said Lucy, when Cathy opened the door. "I was sure you'd be out shopping, if you hadn't already left for Texas."

"Too early for me," said Cathy, waving her hand at the room service table set up by the window. "I like to take my time in the morning. Would you like a cup of coffee? There's plenty and it's hot."

"I would, thanks," said Lucy, seating herself in a comfortable sofa. Cathy's suite was a far cry from the cramped little room she'd shared with Elizabeth; the suite had a spacious living room as well as a large bedroom she could glimpse through an open door. She could hear a shower running, probably Tiffany, getting ready for another day of shopping.

From the large number of boxes and bags scattered around the room it seemed there had been plenty of shopping. Lucy wondered if they'd left anything in the stores for other shoppers to buy. Not that most people would be competing for the same goods—they'd been shopping at places like Prada, Armani, and Ralph Lauren.

"You girls have been busy," said Lucy, accepting a cup of coffee. "Cream? Sugar?"

"Just black."

"It's appalling, isn't it?" said Cathy, crossing her legs and clipping on a pair of pearl and gold earrings. She was dressed for the day in a cream-colored silk blouse and a beautifully tailored pair of mocha slacks. "All I can say in my own defense is that it's mostly stuff for Tiffany. Her mother died quite a few years ago and there hasn't been anyone to help her with clothes and hair and things like that."

"She's lucky. You're more like a fairy godmother than an evil stepmother," said Lucy.

"Don't get me wrong—there are quite a few goodies for me, too." She took a sip of coffee. "You sure can't find stuff like this in

Dallas—there's no place like New York for serious shopping. Except maybe Paris. London's good, too."

"It must be nice," said Lucy, who had never been out of the country and longed to visit places she'd read about. As soon as she'd said it, she wished she hadn't. She hoped there hadn't been any hint of jealousy in her tone.

"Believe me, honey, it is nice and I appreciate every cent I spend. I grew up poor, you know, and I don't intend to set my foot in a Wal-Mart ever again, not if I can help it."

"I don't blame you," said Lucy, completely disarmed by Cathy's frankness.

"I tell you, my first trip to Paris was a real eye-opener: there was no pink polyester anywhere! You can be sure I reported on that fact for the folks at home. And I also told them nobody wore those enormous white athletic shoes you see everywhere here."

"So you traveled for your job?"

"I sure did. I was like a yo-yo, back and forth across the Atlantic, so the folks in Dallas would know what was in fashion." She paused. "Not that I'm complaining. It was great fun, but now that I'm a wife and stepmom my traveling days are pretty much over. We have a full social calendar, and my husband needs me to entertain and to accompany him to events. I'll be running my feet off when I get home—Tiffany's coming out this spring, you know, at the Yellow Rose of Texas Ball and I want her to be the Texas Belle of the Year."

"How lovely," said Lucy, realizing that Cathy's privileged life was work in its way, too. "You know, I was wondering about a few things and I thought you might have the answers."

"Maybe, maybe not," she said with a shrug. "Fire away."

"Well, I heard a rumor that Arnold was planning to buy *Jolie* magazine and make Nadine editor. Do you know anything about that?"

"That rag is for sale, I can tell you that, and I'd bet my six-carat engagement ring that Camilla isn't happy about it because the first thing any buyer is going to do is take a long hard look at the job she's been doing. But I never heard Arnold named as a possible buyer." She studied the ring, which sparkled in the sunlight coming through the window. "If he was thinking of buying it he certainly wouldn't have put Nadine in charge—he's too smart a businessman for that. Nadine would just drive it into the ground. Believe me, I know about men like Arnold. He wants to make money, that's what he's all about, and there's no way he would throw his capital into a sinkhole like *Jolie* magazine."

"Not even as a payoff to Nadine for putting up with his affairs?"

Cathy snorted. "He didn't need to pay her off. If she didn't like it, she could leave, right? And there was no sign she was planning to do that. Besides, from what I've heard, his money's all tied up in his real estate projects. I don't think he could afford *Jolie*."

"I thought he was enormously rich," said Lucy.

"Oh, honey, there's rich and then there's *rich*. These real estate guys are all the same. They've got lots of buildings and stuff, but cash flow is always a problem, which means they've got to borrow and put off payments, stuff like that." Her eyes gleamed wickedly. "But now that Nadine's gone, I imagine his position has improved."

"What do you mean?"

"Insurance, sweetie. I bet he'll pick up a million or two, which should relieve his cash flow problems for a while, anyway."

"At least," said Lucy, mentally kicking herself. Insurance. Why hadn't she thought of that? Rich people had life insurance, too. They could afford lots of it. Arnold suddenly went from the bottom of her list of suspects to the top. You could never ignore the basics, and the husband was always the prime suspect. If only she could talk to Arnold one on one, but how was she going to do that? Considering the way he'd kicked her out of the funeral it was hardly likely that he'd agree to see her.

"I'm ready, let's go." Tiffany was standing in the doorway, dressed in the teen uniform of tight jeans, tiny T, and shrunken blazer.

"Mrs. Stone is here, Tiffany." Cathy's voice was gentle, almost a whisper.

"Oh, I'm sorry." The girl was blushing. "I didn't mean to be rude. Hi, Mrs. Stone. Good morning. Can I get you some coffee?"

"I've got some. Actually, I should be going. I'm on my way to the hospital."

"How is Elizabeth? Say hi to her for me, okay?"

"I will." Lucy stood up and picked her coat off the back of the chair. "She's doing fine. I think we'll be able to go home soon."

"Wait for me, we can all go down together," said Cathy, shoving her foot into a sleek ankle boot and zipping it up. "Get the coats, please, Tiffany."

Tiffany opened a coat closet next to the front door, a feature that Lucy hadn't imagined existed in hotels, and pulled out a white parka for herself and a tawny full-length fur for Cathy. Lucy's jaw dropped at the sight; she'd never seen anything so fabulous. Whatever it was, lynx maybe, it was a lot more glamorous than mink. She had to bite her tongue to keep from asking to try it on. Cathy, however, treated it just like any coat, shrugging into it as they left the suite and patting the pockets to check for her gloves.

While they waited for the elevator Lucy broached her second question. "The other thing I was wondering about has to do with Elise."

"Ah, Elise," said Cathy, raising her eyebrows.

"What do you mean?" asked Lucy.

"That woman is living proof that it's who you know and not what you know that matters," said Cathy. "Camilla pulled her out from nowhere about two years ago and named her fashion editor. It was weird, even for Camilla. I mean, that's the sort of job people usually work into over many years. A good fashion editor knows the designers personally, she has relationships with them. She knows their histories, their muses, their influences."

The elevator came and they all got on.

"Do you know what she did before she joined the magazine?" asked Lucy.

"It wasn't fashion, that's for sure." Cathy snorted. "I don't think Elise could tell a Jean-Paul Gaultier creation from a Calvin Klein."

The elevator doors opened and Cathy sailed into the lobby, turning every head. The bellhops and desk staff all smiled and greeted her, and the doorman stepped smartly to open the door for her. Lucy and Tiffany followed in her wake as, smiling and waving at everyone, she swept through the door onto the sidewalk, where she suddenly stopped.

Lucy watched, horrified, as a motorcycle with two helmeted riders dressed in gleaming black suits suddenly jumped the curb and came directly toward Cathy. She attempted to dodge the machine, and the doorman rushed to help her, but it was too late. She couldn't avoid the bucket of red paint that drenched her beautiful fur coat.

The driver wheeled the motorcycle around, attempting to escape, but the doorman heroically threw himself at the passenger. Lucy caught a glimpse of the driver's shiny imitation leather suit, embellished with numerous zippers, as the motorbike roared off. She rushed to Cathy's side and saw a uniformed cop pounding down the sidewalk to assist the doorman, who was struggling with the attacker he'd dragged off the motorcycle. The cop fumbled, attempting to handcuff the culprit, who took the opportunity to slip out of his grasp and dashed nimbly down the sidewalk and around the corner, leaving the two men bushed and breathing heavily.

"Are you all right?" she asked Cathy, who was standing in the dripping coat, apparently in shock. Next to her, Tiffany was in tears.

"I'm fine," said Cathy. "Just a little stunned."

"Your poor coat," wailed Tiffany.

"I'm afraid it's ruined," said Lucy, who felt like weeping at the loss.

"This old thing? I've had it for years. But why would anyone do something like this?"

"Animal rights," said the doorman, dusting himself off. "They don't approve of wearing fur so they do stuff like this. They even picketed the *Nutcracker* performances this year. My granddaughter was in tears, all upset about the little bunnies that were killed to make fur coats."

"Well, they made a big mistake, then," said Cathy, dropping her coat on the sidewalk. "Because now I'm just going to buy a new coat, and they'll have to kill a whole lot of furry little critters—and they won't be bunnies, I can tell you that."

"What a shame," said Lucy, shaking her head over the coat.

"If you don't mind, I'll need a statement," said the officer, panting as he reached for his notebook.

"Not at all," said Cathy. She turned to go inside, pausing first to say good-bye to Lucy.

Alone on the sidewalk, Lucy started walking in the direction of the hospital. But as she walked, she kept replaying the attack in her mind, like a video: the roar of the motorbike, the riders in their Darth Vader helmets, the arc of thrown paint, and then the splatters that fell like blood. Her steps quickened and she was quite out of breath herself by the time she reached the hospital.

Chapter Eighteen

THE NEW ETIQUETTE:
WHEN IT'S OK TO E-MAIL

The lunch trays had been delivered when Lucy arrived at the hospital but Elizabeth wasn't much interested.

"What exactly is Salisbury steak?" she asked, poking at a lump of mystery meat. It was covered with thick brown gravy and accompanied by an ice cream scoop of mashed potatoes with a puddle of bright orange margarine congealing on top.

"Are you going to eat it?" asked Lucy, who had eaten nothing all day except a bowl of cereal and too much coffee.

"No way. It's disgusting."

"You don't mind if I eat it, then?"

"It's your party," said Elizabeth, grimacing as Lucy took the tray and set it on her lap.

"When are they going to let me out of here?" asked Elizabeth. She was pressing the bed controls and suddenly shot from a reclining position to one that was bolt upright.

"I've been wondering the same thing," said Lucy, her mouth full of potato. "I keep hoping to run into the doctor but he's never here when I am."

"I'm not sick anymore. I feel fine," said Elizabeth, who was now lying on her back and raising her feet.

"Did you tell that to the doctor?"

"Sure. He just says that these things take time and I should be a patient patient." Elizabeth snorted. "It's his version of a joke."

"I wonder if it's something to do with the investigation. Maybe the FBI wants to keep you safe or under observation." Lucy had finished the main course and had moved on to the rubbery rice pudding. "Maybe one of the nurses can tell me something."

"They'll just tell you to talk to the doctor," said Elizabeth, who was now alternately raising her head and her feet.

Finally satisfied, Lucy sat back and took a sip of brown liquid that could have been either coffee or tea. She looked around the room, bright with sunshine and fragrant with flowers. A small flowering bonsai tree in a jade pot caught her eye. "Who gave you that pretty plant?" she asked.

"Brad and Samantha. They were here this morning."

"That was nice of them," said Lucy, giving the plant a closer look. "Did you read the card?"

"I didn't notice it," said Elizabeth. "But I did thank them. Really."

Lucy couldn't help smiling. If there was one thing she'd pounded into her kids' heads it was the importance of saying thank you and writing thank-you notes. That, and not opening someone else's mail. She passed the little envelope to Elizabeth, who opened it and pulled out a white card.

"There's no message. It's just his business card."

"Maybe the florist has a lot of corporate clients," said Lucy, tapping her chin thoughtfully with her finger. It had worked for the Trojans, she thought, why not her? Besides, what was the worst that could happen? She'd get thrown out on her ear. It was a risk she was willing to take, if there was even a slight possibility of talking to Arnold. "You don't need me, do you?" she asked.

Elizabeth's eyebrows shot up. "What do you mean? Where are you going?"

"I have to make a delivery," she said, grabbing her coat and shooting out the door.

It wasn't until Lucy was standing in the lobby of Nelco's famous Millennium Building, holding an overpriced philodendron from a fancy florist in her hand, that she realized her plan needed work. She hadn't realized that most New York office buildings had instituted strict security measures after 9/11 and the Millennium Building was no exception. Access to the elevators was blocked by a security checkpoint complete with a metal detector and several uniformed officers who checked bags. Lucy watched the procedure for a few minutes and was about to turn away when she made a startling realization: they were looking for guns and explosives, but they weren't checking identities. And since she didn't have any guns or explosives, they would let her through.

She soon discovered, however, that the situation was quite different when she reached the top-floor offices of Nelco. There the elevator opened onto a once luxurious lobby that had been converted into something resembling the Berlin Wall's Checkpoint Charlie. The formerly welcoming and spacious reception area had been awkwardly divided with a seemingly impregnable metal and glass wall that limited access to a pair of sturdy sliding metal doors that were activated only after one had cleared a metal scanner. The entire area was under observation from numerous video cameras, and at least twenty armed and uniformed private security guards were on duty; Lucy had never seen anything like it, not even at the airport. She was immediately assigned to one of the two lines of people awaiting entry. The process was slow as each person was questioned and checked against a list before being allowed to pass through the space-age doors.

Lucy quickly decided that a quiet retreat was her best course of action. "Oops," she said while turning to go back to the elevator, "wrong floor."

Her way was immediately blocked by two of the largest men she had ever seen, both clad in matching blue and brown uniforms, with shaved heads and bulging biceps.

"I made a mistake," she said, appalled to discover her voice had become little more than a squeak.

"Just come this way," said one of the guards.

"But I already told you, I made a mistake. This is the wrong floor."

"We have a few questions."

Before she could utter another word, she was hustled across the lobby and through a cleverly disguised doorway she hadn't noticed before. She found herself in a small, bare room where she was immediately divested of her purse, coat, and plant and was thoroughly patted down by one of the guards while the other drew his gun and leveled it at her.

"What do you think you're doing?" she shrieked.

"Routine," said the guard with the gun.

"She's clean," said the other, who had worked his way down to her feet and removed her boots for examination, revealing a tattered pair of knee-highs.

"Give me those back!" she demanded.

Grinning, he handed the boots to her. "What is your business here?"

"I told you," she stammered. "I got off the elevator on the wrong floor."

His eyes were blank, his expression neutral. "What floor did you want?"

"Eighty-four."

"Why?"

"To deliver this plant."

"Who's it for?"

"Andrea Devine," said Lucy, feeling rather clever for coming up with a name so quickly.

"This Andrea Devine is with what firm?"

"Sparkman, Blute, and Blowfish."

As soon as she'd said it Lucy realized she'd made a mistake. She whirled and lunged for the door, and was actually through it, when she ran straight into another guard. He was shoving her back through the door when the elevator binged and the doors slid open revealing Arnold Nelson himself.

"What's going on?" he demanded.

"This woman attempted to gain unauthorized entry," said the guard, who was gripping her firmly by her upper arms.

"Let me go!" shrieked Lucy.

"You again," said Arnold, his eyes narrowing. "What do you want?"

"I want to talk to you about your wife and my daughter and why they both got anthrax," said Lucy. She spoke right up and was gratified to see that the people standing in line and waiting to be admitted were taking notice of the scene and looking on with interest.

"Come with me," said Arnold. His voice was quiet and authoritative.

The guard let go of her arms and Lucy practically fell to the floor in amazement. Catching herself, she trotted after Arnold, like a little page carrying the king's train. Everyone stepped back to let him pass, heads nodded, and people practically bowed and scraped. They eventually reached his office where his secretary's eyes widened in surprise as Lucy was allowed to enter Arnold's inner sanctum.

Arnold lowered himself heavily into a leather chair behind his desk and indicated with a nod that Lucy should seat herself, too. "You're that Stone woman."

"Lucy Stone. My daughter Elizabeth is still in the hospital with anthrax."

Arnold's voice was serious. "Is she getting better?"

"Yes," said Lucy, surprised at his concern.

"So what's the problem?"

"I want to know who did it. Who poisoned your wife and my daughter."

"How would I know?"

Lucy's eyes met his.

Arnold didn't get to be a multimillionaire because he was dumb. He got the point immediately. "You think I did it."

"Uh, of course not," stammered Lucy.

He looked straight at her. "I give you my word. I had nothing to do with it."

Arnold wasn't a handsome man. He was short and fat and flabby. His eyes were too small and his nose was too big, but Lucy understood why he'd been so astonishingly successful. When he looked you in the eye and gave his word, you believed him.

She sat for a minute, looking at the swirling design in the very expensive carpet. Raising her head she looked past Arnold, through the wall of glass behind his desk at the city stretched out far below. The view was magnificent, over the rooftops with their wooden water towers all the way down to the Wall Street skyscrapers and the Narrows beyond. An architect's drawing of the City Gate project was affixed to the window. It was rendered in scale on some clear surface, allowing a viewer in the office to see what the towers would look like if they were built on Governors Island. Other framed drawings of projects were displayed around the office: a shopping mall in New Jersey, apartments in Westchester, dorms for Manhattan College and a lab for New York University. The stylized architect's letters identified it as The Marcus Widmann Institute for the Study of Infectious Diseases. The image reminded her of something Geoff had said at the AIDS gala, that the lab project was in jeopardy.

"You've had threats and you're taking them seriously," said Lucy, turning away from the image of the lab and meeting his eyes. "That's why you have all this security."

Arnold shrugged. "It's part of the business."

"No, this is not your average security setup. There are dozens of guards out there, and that barrier looks pretty serious to me. I bet it's designed to resist sizeable explosions and the whole area can be sealed off in seconds in case of a poison gas attack."

Arnold didn't say a word.

Having gotten this far, Lucy wasn't about to give up. "It's about the lab you're building, right?"

Arnold's eyes widened slightly, but he remained impassive, giving no other clue to his thoughts. "Like I said, I get threats all the time. I don't pay attention. There's no point, because once I've signed a contract, the project is going forward. If I say I'm going to build something, it's going to get built."

"Do you know who's behind these threats?" From somewhere deep in the back of her mind Lucy dredged up a tiny bit of information. "There's even been sabotage, right?"

He shrugged. "Construction is a tough business, and when you're successful you make a few enemies. Competitors, unions, even neighborhood groups. That's how it is."

Lucy couldn't understand his attitude. Why wasn't he angry? Unable to get to him, thanks to his impenetrable security, these saboteurs had sent anthrax to his wife. Why didn't he want to get them? What was she missing here? "Don't you want revenge?" she asked. "Don't you want to make them pay for what they did?"

She thought of Elizabeth, lying unconscious in the emergency room after collapsing at the photo shoot. "I know I do."

Arnold's head was down. He was intently studying his desk's burl-wood pattern. "I have confidence in the FBI," he said. "They have their job and I have mine." He glanced at his watch. "Now, I'm afraid I'm late for a meeting."

"The FBI?" Lucy couldn't believe it. "They still haven't solved the 2001 anthrax attack. Why do you think they're going to do any better this time?"

Behind her, the door opened and one of the guards entered. The message was clear: the meeting was over and one way or another, voluntarily or not, she was going to leave. Lucy got to her feet. "Thanks for your time," she said. "And I'm truly very sorry about your wife."

"Me, too," he said. Much to her surprise, Lucy believed him. He may have been a philanderer, but there was no doubt in her mind that on some level he truly loved Nadine.

One of the security guards was waiting for Lucy in the reception area outside Arnold's office. He helped her on with her coat, then presented her with her purse and the foolish plant, which she refused, before escorting her to the elevator. He accompanied her for the ride downstairs and walked her to the door, where he stood watching to make sure she left the building.

Outside, the cold air was like a slap in the face. Lucy took a deep, invigorating breath. She felt as if she were waking up from a dream. She could remember bits and pieces but she couldn't put it all together so it made sense. It was exactly the same feeling, she thought as she walked along, that she'd had so often upon waking. She would be afraid or confused and would lie in bed trying to remember the dream so she could discover its meaning. The most she could ever do, however, was to recapture a series of disjointed images. Yet always, there was the feeling that there was something more, if she could only remember it.

Heading back to the hospital, she kept thinking about Arnold. What was he really like? There was the obnoxious womanizer she'd encountered at the ball, and then there was the angry Arnold at the funeral who had kicked her out. Today, she'd met the rich and powerful Arnold, secure in his skyscraper fortress high above Manhattan. None of these men seemed to bear any resemblance to Nancy Glass's version of Arnold, the bereft widower in need of her tender loving care, or the suave salesman Arnold she'd seen on the *Norah!* show.

Okay, Lucy admitted to herself, most people were a mix of contradictions, herself included. She loved her family; she loved getting away from them. Nobody was entirely consistent one hundred percent of the time, but Arnold certainly seemed to be an extreme example. Maybe, she thought, he had some mental problem. Split personalities? Schizophrenia? Or maybe he was just a chameleon who adapted to different situations with different responses.

She didn't know the answer, she concluded as she turned the corner by the hospital, but she now suspected that the anthrax attack was designed to send a message to Arnold and he'd gotten it. There had to be a reason for all that security. But who was trying to stop the lab? And were they the same group that was running around town tossing red paint and tomatoes?

When Lucy returned to Elizabeth's room she found Lance sprawled in the chair and clicking through the TV channels with the remote. He seemed quite at home, as if he'd been spending a lot of time there.

"Hi, Lance," she said, setting a couple of chocolate bars she'd picked up in the gift shop downstairs on the bedside table. "It's nice of you to visit Elizabeth but I hope you're not neglecting your studies."

"Nope," he said, turning off the TV. "Classes are over for the day; I studied for a quiz and I've started researching a paper that's due next week. Everything's under control."

"Isn't he amazing?" Elizabeth was beaming at him. "Did you know he's got a 3.9 grade average?"

"Good for you, Lance," said Lucy, watching as Elizabeth picked up one of the bars and began unwrapping it. Lance also had his gaze fixed on Elizabeth, but he wasn't watching to make sure she actually took a bite of chocolate. He looked positively lovesick; it was almost as if he were worshipping at a shrine or something, thought Lucy, feeling like a third wheel.

"I guess I ought to get going," she said, standing.

Elizabeth took another bite of chocolate. "You know, I almost forgot. Brad called. He was looking for you."

"Brad?"

"Yeah. He said he was going out to some island and he thought you might like to go along. Get away from the hospital for a while." She sighed dramatically and rolled her eyes. "Like you're actually here that much, taking care of your poor, sick daughter."

Lucy paid no attention to the sarcasm. "Governors Island?"

"Maybe. He said you'd like it."

"Yeah, it's cool out there," said Lance, his eyes still fixed on Elizabeth.

"Have you been there?" Lucy was surprised; she thought the island was restricted.

"All the time. I've been helping Geoff with a research project. It's real interesting. Because they've cleaned up the water so much, these marine worms have made a big comeback. Problem is, they eat wood, like piers and bulkheads and all that stuff. So Geoff is trying to find a way to protect the wood without hurting the worms."

"Eeew," said Elizabeth. "Do you have to touch them?"

"Actually, no. Geoff handles that stuff. I mostly collect water samples and go exploring." He paused. "There's interesting stuff out there. It's an old military base, you know."

Suddenly, Lucy was convinced she'd found the missing part of her dream, the piece that had been floating around just outside her consciousness. Somehow, she was certain, Governors Island was the key.

"Did they ever do germ warfare research out there?" she asked.

"I don't know. They might have. It makes sense, if you think about it. I mean, if you're going to play around with deadly micro-organisms, it's better to do it on an island than in the middle of a big city."

"Isn't it dangerous, poking around a place like that?" asked Elizabeth. "What if some of the stuff is still around?"

"If anything's left, and I very much doubt there is, it would be harmless. That's the big problem with infectious agents. It's hard to sustain viability over the long term. . . ." He slapped his forehead with his hand. "Except for anthrax. Boy am I dumb! That could be where it came from! It can be viable for forty or fifty years, that's one of its advantages." Lance had pulled a laptop computer out of his book bag and was opening it up.

"Do you think they actually did anthrax research over there?" asked Lucy.

"I know how we can find out," said Lance, clicking away on the keyboard.

"From the computer?" asked Lucy. "That research would probably be classified, and it was all done long before computers, wasn't it?"

"I'm not doing research," he said. "I'm e-mailing Geoff. He says he'll meet us at the marina at three o'clock and take us over there."

Lucy was puzzled. Somehow it had never occurred to her that such a thing as a marina existed on the island of Manhattan. "Geoff has a boat here in the city?"

"Sure. A twenty-two footer. How else could he do the research for the project?"

"Of course." Lucy was still trying to get used to the idea. Somehow New York Harbor, with its ferries and water taxis and tugboats towing barges and container ships and enormous oil tankers, didn't seem like a good place for a little twenty-two-foot boat. Not even for the short crossing to Governors Island. "Is it safe?"

"Sure. We do it all the time."

That was reassuring, kind of, but she didn't think that the makeover outfit she was wearing—a light wool-blend pantsuit with a silk blouse and high-heel boots—would keep her very warm on a small boat in winter. "I'll need to change into some warm clothes. Maybe Sam has some stuff I can borrow."

"Good idea," agreed Lance, reluctantly dragging his eyes away from Elizabeth. "We're also going to need some protective gear like gloves and masks if we're going to be looking for biological toxins. Better safe than sorry."

Lucy couldn't agree more. "And where are we going to get those?"

"This is a hospital, right?" Lance had a naughty gleam in his eye.

"Oh no," cautioned Lucy.

"Don't worry. I know where there's a supply closet." He was out the door before Lucy could protest.

"I better stop him before he gets in trouble," she told Elizabeth, as she shot out the door after him, teetering on her high heels.

Lance was already at the end of the corridor, and Lucy was afraid she'd lose him. She was hampered by those darned boots and she didn't dare run for fear of attracting attention. Lance, on the other hand, was wearing athletic shoes, had awfully long legs, and knew his way around the hospital. She could see him at the end of the hall, rounding a corner, but when she got there found he had vanished into thin air. Lucy's feet hurt and she was out of breath; she was deciding that she might as well go back to Elizabeth's room when she felt a tap on her shoulder. She whirled around and saw an arm extending from behind a door; she quickly stepped inside the supply closet.

"This is stealing. It's not a good idea," she told Lance, who was scanning the shelves of neatly stacked boxes of supplies.

"They'll never miss a few masks and gloves," he said. "Put your weight against that door."

"Oh, great, now I'm an accessory," said Lucy, bracing herself with her feet

"Why are they hiding this stuff?" muttered Lance, peering into box after box.

"Probably because of people like you," said Lucy. She was about to make a joke about the high cost of health insurance when she felt pressure from the opposite side of the door. "Help!" she hissed, throwing her weight against the door. "Somebody's trying to get in."

"Push harder."

"I'm trying," gasped Lucy, pressing with all her might. It was barely enough; she was terrified the door would give.

Lance had joined her and was also pressing against the door. His eyes were round with panic. "What are we going to do?" he whispered.

"Pray," said Lucy, as the pressure on the door continued. She was horrified at the thought of being discovered in the closet. Stealing was bad enough, but even worse was the fact that Lance was a very attractive young man. She couldn't imagine anything more embarrassing than being discovered in a closet with him.

"This door is not supposed to be locked," declared a stern female voice. The knob rattled. "Darn!" They heard footsteps, clicking down the hall, away from the closet.

"That was close," said Lucy, breathing out a huge sigh of relief. She stuck her head out in the hall to make sure the coast was clear while Lance frantically searched the boxes. She was about to abort the mission when he finally found some masks and a second later got the gloves.

"We're out of here," he said, stuffing them in his pockets. But as they strolled ever so casually down the hallway Lucy couldn't help wishing Lance had been a little less impulsive. They were lucky this time, but she was afraid their close escape didn't bode well for the expedition to Governors Island.

Chapter Nineteen

LOOKS THAT GO FROM DAY TO NIGHT!

After trying three times to reach Sam by phone, Lucy finally acknowledged the gruesome truth that she would not only have to stick close to Lance in order to keep an eye on him but also have to borrow his clothing. There was no way she could venture out on the water in her makeover black pantsuit and sleek, black leather city boots. Why oh why had she been so quick to give up her duck boots for these pointy-toed numbers with a three-inch heel? Her feet were killing her, too. How did these women do it?

"Don't worry, I've got plenty of clothes," Lance assured her as they exited the subway a few blocks from his dorm.

"Slow down," she gasped, out of breath from trying to keep up with him. "You're twenty and have long legs. I'm five-two and, well, never you mind how old I am but I am old enough to be your mother."

"Oh, sorry." He looked genuinely abashed. "I didn't think."

"No problem. You don't usually hang out with old fogies like me."

"You're hardly an old fogey, Mrs. Stone. You're actually pretty good looking for somebody your age."

Lucy wasn't sure which was worse: being too old to keep up with his young legs or his condescension. Pretty good looking for her age—ouch!

"My room's on the third floor," he said, full of concern. "Do you think you can make it?" he continued, adding insult to injury. "It's no problem if you can't because there's an elevator, but you're only supposed to use it if you're handicapped."

"I don't think it will be a problem as long as there's oxygen available," she said.

He looked at her oddly. "Oxygen?"

"Just a joke." Lucy was dismayed. What was the matter with kids today? They had no sense of humor and apparently, if Lance was typical, absolutely no ability to focus. While Lucy pointedly checked her lobster watch and tapped her foot, Lance paused in the dorm lobby to check his mail and chat with a friend. Then, when they'd reached the second-floor landing he dashed off, leaving Lucy standing in the stairwell, getting madder by the minute.

"Where did you go?" she demanded when he returned.

"I got these for you." He held out a sturdy pair of well-worn winter boots. "They belong to my friend Julie. Do you think they'll fit?"

"They'll do," said Lucy. Maybe he wasn't such a doofus after all. "Thanks."

They were starting down the hall to his room when Lucy asked where the bathroom was.

"Just around the corner," he said, pointing.

Lucy had a frightening thought. "It's not coed, is it?"

"Nope. The guys' room is on the other side."

What a relief. "I'll meet you in your room."

"Okay." He started down the hall.

"Uh, Lance," she said.

He turned. "Yeah?"

"Your room number?"

"Uh, sorry. It's 306," he said.

But when Lucy emerged, Lance was still in the hallway, leaning against the wall and deep in conversation with another student. "You can borrow my notes, man, no problem, but they won't do you any good 'cause all Philbrick cares about is dates. If you get the years right that's a B, throw in the months and you'll get a B plus and if you get the days you're guaranteed an A."

"Shit. I suck at memorization," moaned the kid, who had shaved his head and was wearing an earring, nose ring, and eyebrow ring. "Uh, sorry," he muttered as Lucy approached. "I didn't know your mom was here."

"She's not my mom."

The kid's eyes widened. "Whoa, cool. Like Ashton Kutcher, huh?"

"Not like that," said Lance, opening the door to his room for Lucy.

"Who is this Ashton Kutcher?" she asked.

"Never mind," he said, showing her in with a flourish. "Welcome to my humble abode."

Lucy knew all about messy rooms and had fought a running battle with her oldest son Toby for years over his habit of dropping clothing on the floor, but she'd never seen anything to compare with Lance's room. It not only smelled like a laundry hamper, it looked like one. In fact, Lucy felt as if she was actually inside one.

"Just take what you want," he said, gesturing generously.

"Aren't there any clean clothes?"

"I don't think so." He opened the closet door so she could see. It was empty except for a lone blue blazer hanging crookedly on a wire hanger.

"Waiting for the laundry fairy?"

He laughed feebly. "If only."

"That's why they invented washing machines." As soon as she said it Lucy realized she was talking like a mother, but she wasn't his mother. He was helping her investigate the anthrax poisoning that had killed Nadine and sickened Elizabeth, and she had no business talking to him like that. Fortunately, he didn't seem to notice.

"This sweatshirt isn't too bad," he said, holding out a thick, hooded number. "And I've got lots of sweatpants and sweaters. I think we better wear dark colors. There's watchmen on the island. . . ."

"Point taken," said Lucy, unbuttoning her jacket.

He pulled a CD out of a wire rack. "Uh, well, you'll probably want some privacy, and I promised to lend this to the girl next door."

"Don't be long," said Lucy. "We've got to meet Geoff in half an hour."

"We've got plenty of time," he told her. "It only takes about ten minutes to get there by subway."

"Right." She didn't believe him for a minute, but she was tired of sounding like a nag.

When he returned ten minutes later Lucy was ready to go, although she felt like the Michelin tire guy in two pairs of sweatpants, a turtleneck, sweatshirt, and sweater topped with a windproof jacket. Everything was much too large, of course, but the boots were only a size or two too big thanks to two pairs of extremely fragrant gym socks, and she had her own gloves and hat. It was a good thing the editors at *Jolie* couldn't see her now, she thought as she clumped down the hall. Or smell her.

Once they were outside the smell didn't matter; the air was filled with noxious gray smoke.

"Is it often like this?" she asked, assuming it was air pollution.

"No," said Lance. "There must be a fire."

As they approached Broadway they saw the street was filled with fire trucks, and hoses were snaking down the steps to the subway station. Cops were busy setting up a barricade and blocking people from the stairs, which were filled with exiting passengers. Some were able to make their own way out; others were carried on stretchers to waiting ambulances with flashing red lights.

"We'll have to go to the next station," said Lance.

"That'll be a waste of time. Trust me. Something like this will shut down the whole line, maybe the whole system," said Lucy. "We better grab a cab."

A lot of other people had the same idea, so they started walking down Broadway in hopes of finding a taxi where it wasn't so crowded. Lucy checked her watch and it was already five minutes before three. They'd never make it in five minutes.

"There's a gypsy, come on." Lance grabbed her hand and pulled her into the street, darting in front of a slow-moving bus and directly into the path of a big black Mercedes, which didn't actually hit them although the driver expressed his deep disappointment at the missed opportunity. Lucy found herself clambering into a beat-up white sedan with a light on top but no official medallion. The driver took off before she'd even closed the door.

"We're going to be late," said Lucy.

"Maybe not," said Lance. "This guy is flying."

It was true. The driver was speeding down Broadway, weaving his way between slower moving vehicles and running all the yellow and some red lights. Lucy held on to the door handle and prayed as an oncoming taxi swerved to avoid them at Seventy-second Street.

"How far do we have to go?"

"South Ferry."

"Lord have mercy."

Lucy wasn't exactly sure how far that actually was, but she knew South Ferry was at the very bottom of the island of Manhattan. They had miles to go, through a maze of city streets crowded with vehicles of every description, all with the potential of causing dreadful bodily harm. The driver careened past taxis, darted in front of delivery trucks, tailgated limousines, braked once for a cement mixer, and cut off bicycle messengers who shook their fists and swore. When they reached West Street, in sight of Battery Park, the driver took the turn too wide and clipped another taxi that was waiting for the light. He would have sped away but was stopped by two other officially licensed cabbies who quickly moved their cars to block the gypsy cab's way.

Lucy put her head in her hands, fearing it was all over. As passengers they were witnesses, maybe even liable in some way. There would be questions to answer, forms to fill out; they'd never make it to the marina before dark.

"Come on." Lance was pulling her out of the cab.

"We can't leave!"

"Oh yes we can." Lance tilted his head toward the cabbies, who were shouting and raising their fists. A crowd was gathering, and it looked like a full-fledged brawl would soon erupt. The only sensible option was to get away as fast as they could.

"How far to the marina?" asked Lucy, as they ran down the street.

"Eight or nine blocks. Can you make it?"

Lucy didn't know, but she was sure going to try. She pounded along the sidewalk, attracting stares, as she followed Lance's lead. It was a little too late to realize it, but she should never have given up jogging. Now she was out of breath and had a stitch in her side and she'd only gone two blocks. One thing Lucy did remember from her jogging days was that if you didn't give up, eventually your body cooperated and it got easier. So instead of collapsing and throwing herself on the ground to catch her breath, she concentrated on making it to the marina without losing sight of Lance. She followed as he pounded past the ferry terminal and made his way along the waterfront, where chain-link fencing and corrugated metal walls barred access to the piers that extended like fingers into the East River. He finally stopped at a gate with a forbidding AUTHORIZED PERSONNEL ONLY sign. Geoff was waiting on the other side.

"I was just about to give up on you guys," he said, opening the gate for them. Dressed in his yellow Grunden fishing pants, he looked just as he had at home in Tinker's Cove where he operated a lobster boat every summer. He led them through a grubby parking area filled with official New York City vehicles to the dock, and Lucy was amazed to see an assortment of small boats bobbing in the water right in the shadow of the big skyscrapers.

"What is this place?" she asked between raspy breaths. Her heart was pounding and she felt as if it was ninety degrees instead of thirty-five.

"It's one of those odd bits that belongs to the city," explained Geoff, leading the way to a rather dilapidated dock. "I got permission to use it because my project is partly funded by the parks department."

The three hopped aboard Geoff's boat, *Downeast Girl*. Lucy was dismayed to discover the cabin was really only a cramped cubby, equipped with a basic toilet and two small bunks filled with an amazing clutter of buckets, rope, books, and cases she assumed contained scientific instruments. They would be making the crossing to Governors Island in what was essentially an open boat.

Geoff quickly got the engine going while Lance untied the lines, but it was already starting to get dark by the time they pulled away from the dock. Lucy sat on the molded fiberglass bench, wrapping her arms around herself and trying not to shiver too violently, lest she upset the boat. It would be bitterly cold out on the water; a sharp breeze was already cutting right through her layers of clothing, now topped by a life jacket. Not that it would be much help if she was unlucky enough to tumble into the water. She'd be dead of hypothermia long before anyone could rescue her.

"Geoff," she began. "Maybe this isn't such a good idea."

"What do you mean?"

"This is too risky."

"There's risks, and then there's risks," he said with a shrug, neatly steering the boat around the end of the dock and heading for open water. "Nadine's dead, Elizabeth had a close call, and now they're threatening Norah."

"Yeah, I heard about the tomatoes."

"Well, it's a lot more serious than throwing a few tomatoes. Sidra got a phone call demanding time on the show for this bunch called OTM. If they don't get it they said Norah would be sorry, just like her friend Nadine."

"You think this group sent the anthrax?"

"I don't know. Maybe they're just making a threat, but I'm inclined to take them at their word. We've got to get to the bottom of it or it won't stop. Who'll be next? Sidra? You? Me?" Geoff was gazing ahead, looking out over the water. "If there's even a slim chance they got the anthrax on the island, it's worth checking it out."

Lucy shivered. "There's an awful lot of traffic on this water."

"We've got lights," said Lance, ever the optimist.

"Lot of good they'll do," muttered Geoff, slowing the boat and waiting for a huge oil tanker to pass. "From the bridge of that thing we're just a little speck. Nope, we've got to watch out for them because chances are they can't see us."

"Ferry's approaching starboard," said Lance, alerting Geoff who was keeping an eye on a tug pushing a barge off the port side.

"Thanks," he said, shifting the rudder and gunning the engine. The boat shot forward and dodged around a sleek, white harbor cruise boat.

"Maybe we ought to turn back," said Lucy. She was beginning to feel very queasy.

"We're halfway there; might as well go on as turn around." Geoff's voice was tight and he was straining to make out the shapes of approaching ships in the fog as he tried to navigate by the sounds of foghorns and the clang of a buoy.

The tension was horrible: at any moment they could be annihilated by one of the huge freighters headed for the docks on the Brooklyn shore.

"What's in those ships?" asked Lucy. "I don't want to die for bananas."

"You name it, they're bringing it in. Cars, computers, air-conditioners, clothing . . . have you heard about the trade deficit?" Geoff's voice was more relaxed. "We're out of the shipping lane now; it should be clear sailing from here."

Now they were alone on the inky water, a large rounded shape looming over them.

"What's that?" asked Lucy.

"Ventilator for the Brooklyn-Battery Tunnel."

"Ohmigosh," said Lucy, who was beginning to picture the waterfront as an illustration in one of the Batman comics Toby used to love so much when he was a kid, filled with massive, threatening structures that seemed to mock the insignificant human inhabitants of the city. Bad thought, bad thought, she chided herself, switching instead to a bright Richard Scarry illustration, where cute animals rode the colorful boats and planes that filled the friendly harbor.

Downeast Girl was suddenly rocked by the wake of a passing tugboat, its powerful engine propelling it swiftly through the water without anything in tow, and Lucy held on to the gunwales for dear life. Coming out here was a really bad idea, she decided. Where was Batman when you needed him?

Chapter Twenty

**ACTIVEWEAR THAT FLATTERS
WHILE YOU GET FIT!**

It was growing dark when they approached the dock, and Lucy braced herself as Geoff slowed the motor and Lance grabbed hold of a ladder and climbed up to make *Downeast Girl* fast. When he'd securely tied the boat to the dock, Lucy hauled herself up the ladder, followed by Geoff. As they stood there on the exposed pier, in the dark and whipped by the wind, the island suddenly seemed very big.

"Where do we begin?" asked Lucy.

"At the old infirmary," said Lance. "Follow me."

There were very few lights on the island, in contrast to the illuminated skyscrapers standing side by side on the much larger island of Manhattan across the water. There was no concern for the price of electricity there, thought Lucy, gazing at the amazing nightly spectacle of the skyline. Even the Brooklyn Bridge and the Manhattan Bridge were outlined in lights, which were reflected in the black water below. Looking in the other direction she could see the glittering and seemingly endless expanse of the Verrazzano Bridge, stretching across the Narrows between Brooklyn and Staten Island. She knew the Statue of Liberty would also be alight, but it was blocked from view by the many buildings on the island.

She was grateful for the darkness as they made their way along winding paths, staying in the shadows and trying to be as quiet as possible to avoid detection by the night watchmen. She felt a little surge of adrenaline; it was exciting to be taking part in a covert nighttime mission.

The island was much larger than it appeared to Lucy from the ferry, and she wished they had some other way of getting around besides their feet. Hers were cold, and the borrowed boots felt heavy and clumsy as she trotted along, doing her best to keep up with the two tall men. Wherever they were going was very far from where they'd docked the boat, and Lucy was beginning to wonder why they couldn't have tied up closer. She was also beginning to think the whole mission was foolish; there were dozens of buildings on the island and they could never search them all. This was worse than searching for a needle in a haystack: how would they know anthrax if they found it? She was tired and out of breath and about to suggest they give up when she realized Geoff and Lance had stopped abruptly at the corner of a building.

She joined them and peeked around the corner where she saw a circle of light.

"Watchman," whispered Geoff, holding his finger to his lips.

"We can't go around, we have to go through," said Lance, anticipating her question.

"Too risky," said Lucy, shaking her head. "Let's go back."

"I'm gonna take a look," said Lance. Before she could stop him he was gone. She and Geoff watched as he crept up to a window and slowly raised his head to peer in. A minute later he was back.

"Coast is clear. Nobody's there."

"If they're not here, they're out on patrol," said Geoff. "We've got to be very careful."

Lucy found herself crouching as she followed the others, although she wasn't quite sure what good it would do. Covert operatives always crouched in the movies and she supposed it was helpful in some way; she hoped it was worth it because it was murder on her back.

They had reached an enormous round fort, towering over them like some sort of ancient Colosseum, when they heard the sound of a car engine.

"Down!" hissed Geoff.

There was no handy bush to hide behind so Lucy dropped flat on her stomach on the grass; it was prickly and stiff with frost and she liked how it felt cool on her chin. She was sweating underneath all the layers of clothing she was wearing; she should have opened her collar and taken off her hat.

They watched as the car proceeded slowly along the road at a steady crawl; occasionally the driver stopped and used a spotlight. The wait was nerve-racking. There was nothing they could do but hope that the light didn't come their way because they would surely be discovered if it did.

It didn't, but they couldn't move until the car was out of sight, and Lucy was frozen stiff by the time it was safe to get up. She was no longer overheated; the cold had penetrated her to the core and she was shivering. Geoff pulled her into the shelter of the fort's tunnel-like entrance. It was dark and dank but at least they were out of the wind.

"Is this it?" she asked, praying that they wouldn't have to go any farther.

"No. There's nothing here."

"Nothing?"

"Just old blankets and stuff." Lance was already moving out. Geoff took her by the elbow and propelled her out of the shelter and back into the cold wind.

"How much farther?" she asked, trying not to whine.

"Your guess is as good as mine," whispered Geoff. "Lance is the one who explored the island. I just poked around the edges, looking for worms."

This side of the island was more crowded and the buildings were closer together with lots of leafless trees and evergreen landscape shrubs; they appeared to be in the section once devoted to housing the military personnel stationed on the island. Lucy could imagine the days when it was a bustling suburban neighborhood, with kids riding bikes and skateboards after school. Now the families were all gone and it was eerily quiet, a ghost town.

"This is it," hissed Lance, pointing to a low, square building with a flat roof. A square metal sign with a red cross hung from a bracket above the door, creaking as it swung in the wind.

Geoff tried the door. "It's locked."

Lance snorted. "What did you expect? We'll have to break in."

Lucy was uncomfortably aware that if they were discovered, the charges would be breaking and entering instead of merely trespassing—quite another kettle of fish. On the other hand, there didn't seem to be any other way to get the evidence they needed.

"Are you game?" asked Geoff.

"Sure." Lucy shrugged. "Anything to get warm."

They stood in the shadow of a holly bush, stamping their feet and rubbing their arms, while Lance worked his way around the building. Their ears were pricked for the least sound, but all they heard was the howling wind and the regular moan of a foghorn. Except for the glittering skyline they could have been back in Tinker's Cove.

"We're in." Lance's whisper startled Lucy and she gave a little jump.

"Man, you sure are quiet," said Geoff.

"I jimmied a window."

Great, thought Lucy. Even though the building was low, the windows were a good five feet up from the ground. She'd need a hoist for sure. This was going to be clumsy and potentially noisy, increasing their chances of discovery.

When Lance stopped at the window Lucy knew she was right. It was even higher than she thought; a small awning window opening outward.

"I can't get up there!"

"Sure you can!" She found herself grabbed around the hips and hoisted upward in one smooth motion. It happened so quickly, however, that she neglected to grab onto the sill and slid back down.

"You were supposed to . . ." gasped Geoff.

"I know. I know. Let's try again."

Geoff was giving her a leg up when the silence was broken by a siren and the dark night was suddenly filled with light. Lucy and Geoff ducked down behind a bush and watched as two police cars screeched to a halt in front of the infirmary and four uniformed watchmen with flashlights ran up to the front door.

"Wha . . ." whispered Lucy, but Geoff firmly placed one hand over her mouth and signaled her to be as still as possible. She crouched lower, heart pounding, as two of the watchmen pounded past their hiding place and made for the back door. Lance was trapped, unless he could find a hiding place.

They waited for what seemed an eternity, listening to the voices of the watchmen as they worked their way through the building. Then came the cry, "Got him!" and it was all over. Lance was hustled out of the building, in handcuffs, and shoved into the back of one of the cars, which immediately took off. The other two watchmen began working their way around the outside of the building, and Geoff signaled to Lucy that they should split up and move away from the open window. Lucy crawled along on hands and knees, her shoulder against the side of the building, until she heard footsteps approaching. Then she froze, afraid to even breathe.

"Must've got in here," said a voice. The bright beam from a powerful flashlight danced around the open window and one of the men shut it. "That'll have to do for now," he said. "Maintenance can reset the alarm in the morning."

"Yeah, let's get back," said the other. "It's colder than a witch's tit out here."

"You can say that again."

Shivering, Lucy agreed with them. She was crouched on the ground, trying to make herself as small as possible, and trying to think warm thoughts so her teeth wouldn't chatter noisily. Feeling a hand on her shoulder she jumped a mile.

"Shh, it's only me," said Geoff.

"What do we do now?"

"Try to think up some story that'll convince them to let Lance go."

"Like what?" asked Lucy, scrambling to keep up with him as he started walking back to the watchman's post.

"I don't know. A fraternity prank?"

"We're kind of old for that, and I'm a girl. What about your science research?"

"I don't think that'll explain breaking and entering."

"How's this?" said Lucy. "We were doing research this afternoon but the boat wouldn't start and it got dark and we were stuck on the island and Lance was looking for shelter for the night?"

"It might work, if they're not too bright," said Geoff. "Maybe we should just tell the truth."

"That's probably best," said Lucy.

They walked along in glum silence. The hulking shadow of the old round fort covered them, wrapping them in darkness. Lucy felt especially low. This whole expedition had been a dumb idea. Lance was in trouble and they would soon join him. She was about to apologize to Geoff for dragging him into this mess when he suddenly stopped and put his gloved finger over her lips. She strained to listen and heard an odd, whirring sound. They dropped to the ground and waited, listening. The sound, although faint, came closer until two dark figures on bicycles whipped past them.

Geoff leaped to his feet and started after them, springing silently across the frosty grass. Lucy followed, doing her best to keep up, relying on instinct rather than sight or sound, and was startled when Geoff stepped out from behind a large tree.

"They went in that building," he said, pointing toward a large brick rectangle punctuated with rows of dark windows. "I'm going to follow them."

"Bad idea. We should tell the watchmen."

"Not yet. We need more information. They'll think we're sending them on a wild goose chase."

He had a point. Nobody would believe they'd seen bicyclists on the island in the middle of the night, in December.

"I'm coming," said Lucy.

"Okay. But let me go first."

Lucy nodded and followed when Geoff opened the door and stepped into the pitch black interior of the building. She couldn't see a thing, and then she saw stars.

Lucy's head hurt and everything was blurry when she opened her eyes. Unbelievably, the image that swam before her was of a gigantic woman with long hair swirling about her face and a bird perched on each shoulder. One arm was raised above her head, holding a flashing sword. Lucy blinked, realizing it was a poster.

"Boadicea?" she asked.

"Good guess, but you're wrong," said a voice. "That's Queen Medb."

Painfully, Lucy lifted her head and turned to see who had spoken. It was Helena Rubinstein. She squeezed her eyes shut and looked again. It wasn't actually Helena Rubinstein; it was Elise wearing oversized black-rimmed glasses and a white lab coat with her hair slicked back from her face. Lucy tried to sit up but couldn't. A thick strap had been fastened across her chest, holding her flat on her back. Her hands were also in some sort of restraint.

"Whuh?" Her voice was thick and hoarse; it was more of a grunt than a question, but Elise was eager to explain.

"She's the heroine of an ancient Celtic legend. A warrior-goddess."

"Ah," said Lucy, dropping her head back on the bed, gurney, whatever it was she was fastened to, and looking around. What she saw didn't encourage her. She guessed she was in some sort of laboratory; there were tables and shelves holding all sorts of beakers and jars and other scientific equipment. More ominously, she noticed, the walls were entirely covered with translucent plastic sheeting; even the door was sealed. She had no way of knowing whether she was ten stories high in the sky or in a sub-sub-basement; there were no windows. Even worse, she was at the mercy of Elise, who was apparently some sort of mad feminist scientist. There was no sign of Geoff.

"Queen Medb is our symbol." The voice was filtered through some sort of sound system and Lucy strained to see where it was coming from. She saw a figure in a white space suit, then realized it was a hazmat suit. Her heart skipped a beat, wondering why the suit was necessary, but she was reassured by the fact that Elise wasn't wearing any sort of protection. If this was some sort of evil scientist's lair, which is what it certainly seemed, she decided they must cook up the microbes in another room.

"Symbol of what?" asked Lucy, trying to make out the face behind the mask

"Operation Terra Mama. We're warriors in the fight to reclaim the earth and restore the proper order of nature. Procreation. Woman power. Matriarchy."

"Sounds good to me," said Lucy. "Can I join?"

"Very funny," scoffed Elise.

"I'm serious," said Lucy. "I believe in all that stuff. Save the planet. Love your Mother. I recycle bottles and newspapers. I even take those awful plastic bags back to the supermarket."

"What we're doing here is a bit more serious."

"I realize that," said Lucy. "But since you're holding me captive I think I deserve some sort of explanation. And where's Geoff?"

"He's fine, just like you," said the robot voice. It sounded eerily familiar and this time, when she peered at the mask, Lucy recognized Fiona.

"Fiona!" she exclaimed, feeling betrayed. "I thought you were Elizabeth's friend!"

"I am. Really I am. She wasn't supposed to get sick. That was a mistake. But she's going to be okay, right?"

"No thanks to you. She could have died, just like Nadine."

"That was unavoidable," said Elise. "We had to show Arnold that we meant what we said."

"He's building this big laboratory for NYU where they're going to do all sorts of tests on animals. We sent letters and faxes and . . ."

"Numerous warnings," interrupted Elise.

"All he had to do was stop the project, stop building the lab."

"Typical man," snorted Elise. "He wouldn't take us seriously."

"So we had to show him."

"And Nadine was hardly blameless herself," said Lucy. Their terrible logic was suddenly clear to her. "She wrote that article for *Jolie* saying how important animal testing is for developing new cosmetics."

"I couldn't believe that!" squeaked Fiona in her robot voice. "That was too much! Rabbits don't want to wear mascara or lipstick, they don't want to be squirted with perfume. It's cruel and unnecessary. Why not use people to test these products? After all, they're the ones who are going to use them. She even wore fur— she gave no thought at all to those poor little creatures who died so she could flaunt her wealth. How many for one coat? Dozens! She deserved to die."

"Cosmetics are a form of submission to male domination," said Elise, her voice oddly flat, as if she was repeating an argument she'd made many times. "Nadine subjected herself to male domination and she encouraged others to do the same thing." Her tone changed, becoming waspish. "Like that Cathy Montgomery, turning herself into a walking advertisement for her husband's wealth with her furs and jewels."

"You certainly showed her," said Lucy, remembering the incident outside the hotel. She was now convinced Fiona was one of the attackers, but who was the other? It certainly wasn't Elise. "I bet she'll think twice before she wears fur again."

"That was a warning," said Elise. "Next time it won't be paint, it will be blood. Her blood."

Lucy shivered, suddenly cold. Until now she'd thought they were mad as hatters, suffering some bizarre obsession or shared mania, but now she realized it was worse than that. They were evil, utterly evil, and would have no pity for anyone who posed a threat to their plans. She had to figure out a way to save herself and Geoff, but all she could think of at the moment was to keep them talking as long as she could. Maybe she could even convince them she was sympathetic to their cause, that she was on their team. Or perhaps convince Fiona to switch sides and help her. "This is quite a setup you've got here. Are we still on the island?"

"It's an old bomb shelter. Elise is so clever, she found it," said Fiona.

Even through the suit Lucy could hear the admiration in her voice. She was one of the faithful, and the job at the magazine was only a cover for her real work: terrorism. She'd do whatever Elise told her to do. And she was very good at it, Lucy realized. Lucy had never guessed. She'd even supplied Sidra's phone number, which Fiona had promptly used to make terrifying threats. If they weren't stopped, Norah would be next. And who else? Sidra? The other workers on the show? The audience? Lucy was convinced they'd stop at nothing. And it looked like she was nothing more than an inconvenient impediment they wouldn't hesitate to remove. Determined not to reveal her fear, she struggled to make it sound as if she were impressed with their ingenuity. "Really! How did you ever find it?" she asked, hoping that Elise's weak spot was flattery.

"I was over here a couple of times with Arnold and Nadine; he was giving tours to investors, that sort of thing. Then I came back in the summer, when they have the ferry and let people visit the island." Elise chuckled; it was a horrible sound. "It wasn't difficult to slip away on my own. If you're a woman of a certain age and you dress in comfortable, practical clothes, you're practically invisible."

Lucy had heard this sentiment before, although it was usually a complaint. She fleetingly wondered about Elise's sexuality and her relationship with Camilla. Had part of her motive for killing Nadine been to eliminate a rival for Camilla's attention, if not her affection? "You really outsmarted them. And you found the anthrax here, too?"

"Anthrax here on the island?"

"I thought the government might have experimented. . . ."

"No! There were never any anthrax experiments here, not that I know of, anyway."

"So where did you get it?"

Elise's eyes were cold. "You can get anything you want if you know the right people and you're willing to pay."

The plastic sheeting rustled and another figure in a shiny white hazmat suit entered the room and announced "Everything's ready" in that spooky electronic voice. Lucy didn't like the sound of this at all. Whatever was ready, she had a feeling wasn't going to be good for her.

"Good," said Elise. "Let's go."

Instinctively, Lucy strained against her bonds, but it was useless. They didn't give an inch, not even a millimeter. Her heart raced as the hooded robot figures came forward, one on either side of the gurney, and began wheeling her through the plastic curtains that shrouded the door and out of the room. As she was rolled along Lucy struggled to identify the second figure, who she guessed must have been the other motorcycle attacker. The light was poor and she couldn't make out the face until she was pushed through more plastic curtains into a brightly lit space where Geoff, still unconscious, was arranged on a similar gurney.

"Agent Christine!" exclaimed Lucy, remembering the supposed FBI agent's dated Goodwill clothes, her plastic wallet, and her confusion about felonies and misdemeanors. "I knew there was something fishy about you."

"Tape her mouth." It was Elise's voice, coming over some sort of intercom system. She hadn't entered this area, and Lucy suspected it was because she wasn't wearing a hazmat suit. There was apparently a greater chance that this area was contaminated. Belatedly, she wished she'd remembered to fill that Cipro prescription Dr. Marchetti gave her at the hospital. It was still in her purse, where she'd tucked it away and promptly forgotten it.

Her thoughts were interrupted when a piece of thick tape was slapped across her face, and she watched mutely as Geoff was wheeled up to a structure that looked like a small garden shed completely covered and sealed with plastic. A flexible metallic tube, like the duct from her clothes dryer, extended from the roof to a glass window through which Elise could be seen moving about. The shed appeared to be some sort of isolation chamber, and Lucy watched in horror as Elise gave a signal, the door was opened, and he was wheeled inside. It was an experiment of some sort and Geoff was a human guinea pig. Angrily, furiously, Lucy wanted to protest their twisted logic. They wouldn't experiment on some stupid mouse—and living in the country, she knew all about mice—but they were willing to sacrifice a human being, a committed teacher, and a loving husband to their crazy plan.

Lucy wanted to give these conscienceless maniacs a piece of her mind, but she couldn't, thanks to the tape. She twisted and thrashed as hard as she could; she couldn't say words but she could produce moans and groans. She tried to make as much noise as she could. She might be at their mercy but she wasn't going to go down without a fight. This was horrible. They were monsters and she knew she was next. Tears came to her eyes as she thought of the kids, of Bill, even the dog. She drew in a big breath through her nose and produced a high-pitched squeal. She made it as loud and as long as she could, again and again, until, to her amazement, the room was suddenly filled with black-clad SWAT team members in gas masks and armed with assault rifles.

One bent over her, peeling off the tape. "Boy, am I glad . . ." began Lucy, only to find herself once again mute as a protective gas mask was placed over her face.

Chapter Twenty-one

THIS NEW YEAR, RESOLVE TO BE
YOUR BEST SELF!

Hours later, after a frantic trip by ambulance and ferry to the hospital where she was thoroughly examined by a masked and robed medical team and intensely questioned by a couple of very serious and utterly genuine government agents, Lucy was finally released. She staggered out of the hospital, clutching a vial of Cipro that this time she was determined to remember to take, and hailed a taxi. Sam and Brad greeted her with hugs when she arrived early in the morning at their apartment.

"Boy, did you give us a scare!" exclaimed Sam. "Where were you?"

Too tired to talk, Lucy gave Brad the papers she'd been given and collapsed on her bed in the guest room. When she finally woke up, around one p.m. on New Year's Eve, she was surprised to find Elizabeth sitting at Sam's kitchen table.

"I've got a clean bill of health. They let me go early this morning."

"It was more like they kicked her out," said Sam. "They must have needed the bed for someone else. I got a phone call to come and pick her up."

'You should have gotten me up," said Lucy. After years of motherhood she wore guilt like an old sweater. "I should have gone."

"It was a pleasure," said Sam. "It's great to see our girl looking so healthy."

It was true. Elizabeth did look good. She'd gained a pound or two in the hospital, and her cheeks were round and rosy.

"It's sure good to be out of there," said Elizabeth. "It makes you appreciate everyday things." She took a long swallow of coffee. "This coffee is so good. And your apartment is so pretty and colorful, after all that hospital beige."

"Is there more coffee?" Lucy asked. "I could sure use some."

Sam was pouring when Brad returned. Lucy looked at him uneasily. "Am I going to jail?" she asked. "And what about Geoff and Lance?"

"Amazingly enough, you're all heroes," said Brad, joining them at the kitchen table. "It seems that the FBI has been watching Elise and company for some time but were never able to find the lab. It was thanks to you that they got the break they needed."

Lucy took a long swallow of coffee. "The FBI was there all the time?"

"Yeah. They'd been concerned about Operation Terra Mama for some time. It's an international feminist ecoterror group. They've been mainly active in England—apparently quite effectively. They managed to indefinitely halt construction of a lab at Oxford University by threatening the contractor and anybody else connected with it. It got so bad that truck drivers wouldn't make deliveries, and taxis wouldn't even go there for fear of retaliation."

"So Fiona brought their tactics over here?"

"Fiona!" Elizabeth's jaw dropped. "She was part of this?"

Lucy nodded and gave her daughter a hug.

"You bet. She's wanted in England on a number of charges, including arson and murder."

"She seemed like such a nice girl," said Sam, who was standing at the counter, making sandwiches.

"It was the accent," said Lucy. "It'll fool you every time."

"Elise was definitely the leader here," continued Brad. "She first got acquainted with OTM when she was doing graduate work at Oxford. She laid low when she returned to the U.S., however, working quietly on building a network of contacts in the science community. She was very patient, getting herself hired at *Jolie* by her old friends and biding her time until an opportunity for action presented itself. Arnold actually took her out to Governors Island several times; he couldn't have been more helpful."

"Where did she get the anthrax in the first place?" asked Sam, setting a platter of sandwiches on the table.

"That's the one thing she won't talk about. She's apparently determined to protect whoever it was. They're checking out all her former colleagues, anyone she might have come into contact with as a scientist. Apparently there's some similarity with the 2001 attack." Brad looked thoughtful. "Maybe this will help them solve that, too. Anyway, at some point she decided to set up her own lab. That's when Fiona—she has a doctorate in microbiology, you know—came over to help."

Lucy and Elizabeth's eyes met over the sandwiches.

"Fiona had a doctorate? I thought she went to beauty school," said Elizabeth. "She sure had me fooled."

Lucy took a bite of tuna salad on whole wheat and chewed thoughtfully. "How did they get back and forth to the island? We had an awful time in that boat."

"They didn't use a boat. This was really clever. They got official transit authority uniforms and used the Brooklyn-Battery Tunnel. Apparently there's some sort of escape hatch in that ventilation tower on the island. They even used an official MTA van, and they had bicycles hidden on the island."

"And the lab?" asked Lucy, talking with her mouth full. "Where exactly was that?"

"It was an old bomb shelter, left over from the cold war. They think Elise must have heard about it somehow and searched until she found it. She made regular weekend trips to the island all last summer on the public ferry."

"This is so weird," said Elizabeth. "Here everybody's worried about Islamic militants but these Terra Mama people were homegrown. I mean, Elise is American and Fiona's British. We're supposed to be allies in the fight against terrorism."

"They were driven by ideology, though," said Sam, "just as much as the Islamists are. They didn't hesitate to kill Nadine."

Lucy shook her head. "I'm not so sure it was all ideology, at least on Elise's part. A lot of it seemed like a grudge against men and women who liked men. I think Fiona was the idealogue. She said she felt badly about Elizabeth getting sick, but it didn't stop her. She thought it was perfectly okay to use me and Geoff as human guinea pigs. It's twisted. Like animals are worth more than people."

"Well, animals are innocent," said Brad. "Only humans cause harm deliberately. It's like those signs in the zoo that identify the most dangerous species in the world."

"Tigers?" guessed Elizabeth.

"Nope. People like us, you and me. The sign has a mirror instead of a picture."

"That's why we have forgiveness," said Sam. "Like the Bible says, faith and hope are important, but charity, love, forgiveness— whatever you call it, it's all the same thing—is the most important. Without love, we have nothing."

They sat silently, pondering this important truth, when Lucy's cell phone began to ring. She expected to hear Bill's voice but instead heard Ed Reidel's gruff New York accent. The *New York Tattler* editor had a proposition for her.

"The FBI's announcing a big arrest in this anthrax case," he said. "You wouldn't know anything about it, would you?"

Lucy perked right up. "Boy, have I got a story for you. I was held captive in an underground anthrax lab by a mad feminist scientist."

She figured he'd laugh it off. After all, she'd lived through it and she still could hardly believe it. But Ed didn't bat an eyelash.

"Cool," he said. "Can you write a first-person account?"

"Sure," said Lucy. "What will you pay?"

There was a pause. Finally, he said, "One hundred."

Lucy's heart sank. So much for the six figures she'd been promised. "This story is worth a lot more than a hundred. Why, even back home I can get at least two from my editor."

"A hundred fifty," he said, with a big sigh. "One hundred fifty thousand, but not a penny more. And it better be worth it."

Lucy's jaw dropped and she swallowed hard. "It will be," she finally said. "I'll get right to work."

She put the phone down and, after taking a few deep breaths, asked Sam if she could use her computer. "The *Tattler* is going to give me one hundred fifty thousand dollars for my story, but I've got to do it right now. He wants it yesterday."

All of a sudden everyone was jumping up and down and hugging her, and Elizabeth was actually crying. "This means I can go back to school, right?"

"Absolutely," said Lucy. "And Sara and Zoe, too. And maybe even Toby, if he wants to try again."

"What about you?" asked Sam. "Don't you want anything for yourself?"

Lucy smiled, considering the possibilities. "Maybe I'll finally get to take that trip to Europe."

"You should."

"We'll see," said Lucy. "First things first. There's no sense counting my chickens until they're hatched. I've got to write the darn thing and see if Ed likes it before I start spending the money."

Elizabeth and Brad exchanged a nervous glance.

"Right now?" asked Sam. "It's New Year's Eve and you're in New York. Don't you want to see the ball drop for real?"

"Yeah, Mom," added Elizabeth. "This might be the only chance I get."

"Well, that's not until midnight. I've got hours, right?"

"People start gathering early, to get the best spots," said Sam. "We usually leave around now."

"You go. I'll work on my story and watch it on TV. Maybe I'll see you."

"No, that's all right," said Sam. "We'll wait for you."

When they left the apartment around ten o'clock by the lobster watch, Lucy still wasn't convinced the expedition was a good idea, given Elizabeth's recent illness. Furthermore, she was worried because she hadn't been able to reach Bill on her cell phone, although she'd called home several times. There was no answer, just the machine, which puzzled her. Where could they all be? Why weren't they home, getting ready to greet the new year?

The subway wasn't very crowded but when they emerged at Times Square they immediately found themselves part of an enormous, boisterous crowd. Everyone was in good spirits, and the weather was perfect: a lovely, clear night with the temperature hovering at a mild forty degrees.

"Where shall we stand? We want a clear view of the ball."

"Let's go over by the TKTS booth up at Forty-seventh Street," suggested Brad, winking at Sam. "That's our favorite spot."

He pointed it out and they began making their way through the throng that packed the entire area, which on an ordinary day would be filled with cars and trucks and taxis. The amazing neon display of colorful lights blinked all around them; enormous bill-boards advertising everything from underwear to the NASDAQ exchange to perennial Broadway shows like *The Phantom of the Opera* and *A Christmas Carol.*

"That's MTV," said Elizabeth, pointing to an upper-story window where a curvaceous girl in a low-cut tank top and a wisp of a skirt was interviewing a rap group of four young men covered head to foot in oversized clothing. The crowd gathered beneath the window was watching raptly, and young girls were screaming in rapture at seeing their idols up close.

"They're broadcasting right now?"

"Yeah."

"Wow. We're really here in the center of things. Everybody, all over the country, is watching and we're right here." Lucy felt as if a veil was being lifted; she just hadn't made the connection. "Wow, this is really cool."

Elizabeth managed not to roll her eyes. "Right, Mom."

It took them a long time to make their way through the crowd to the little island where the TKTS booth stood, and Lucy couldn't quite figure out why it was so important to get to the statue of George M. Cohan, which Brad insisted was their destination. You could clearly see the Times building, with the huge, illuminated ball poised to fall, from anywhere in the entire square. Lucy felt it was a bit rude to keep pushing through the crowd, but people didn't seem to mind. Many were wearing party hats and paper leis, some were holding signs for the TV cameras, and just about everyone had some sort of noisemaker. They laughed and held their breath and joked about resolving to lose weight as their group squeezed past.

Finally, with moments to spare, Lucy felt a strong hand grab her arm and haul her over the curb and onto the TKTS island. She turned to thank the man who'd assisted her and saw Bill's beaming, bearded face. The whole family was ranged around him: Sara, Zoe, Toby, and Molly, too. And Lance. She couldn't believe her eyes. "What are you all doing here?" she stammered.

"We came for New Year's."

"Norah bought us all plane tickets and Lance met us at the airport."

"To surprise you!"

"To make sure you start the year off right." She found herself engulfed in Bill's arms as he bent to kiss her. The crowd roared as the ball began its descent.

"Happy New Year," she whispered. "I have a feeling it's going to be very prosperous."

CHRISTMAS
CAROL
MURDER

Prologue

IVCET

That was easy, thought Jake Marlowe, cackling merrily as he wrote EVICT in the blanks of the word jumble with a small stub of pencil—waste not, want not was his favorite saying, and he was certainly not going to discard a perfectly usable pencil, even if it was a bit hard to grip with his arthritic hands—and applied himself to the riddle: "Santa's favorite meal." Then, doubting his choice, he wondered if the correct answer was really CIVET. But no, then the *I* and *C* wouldn't be in the squares with circles inside indicating the letters needed to solve the riddle, and he needed them for MILK AND COOKIES, which was undoubtedly the correct answer.

He tossed the paper and pencil on the kitchen table, where the dirty breakfast dishes vied for space with a month's worth of morning papers and junk mail and, pressing his hands on the table for support, rose to his feet. He pushed his wire-rimmed glasses back up his beaky nose and adjusted the belt on his black-and-brown–striped terry cloth bathrobe, lifting the collar against the chill. The antique kerosene heater he used rather than the central heating, which guzzled expensive oil, didn't provide much heat. He picked up his empty coffee mug and shuffled over to the counter where the drip coffeepot sat surrounded by old coffee cans, empty milk containers, and assorted bottles. He filled his stained, chipped mug with the *Downeast Mortgage Company* logo and carried it back to the table, sitting down heavily in his captain's chair, and preparing to settle in with the *Wall Street Journal*.

INTEREST RATES HIT RECORD LOW read the headline, causing him to scowl in disapproval. What were the feds thinking? The economy would never recover at this rate, not if investors couldn't reap some positive gains. He snorted and gulped some coffee. What could you expect? People didn't save anymore; they spent more than they had and then they borrowed to make up the difference, and when they got in trouble, which was inevitable, they expected the government to bail them out. He folded the paper with a snap and added it to the stack beside his chair, a stack that was in danger of toppling over.

Jake had saved every issue of the *Portland Press Herald* that he'd ever received, as well as his copies of the *Wall Street Journal*, and since he was well into his sixties that was quite a lot of papers. They covered every surface in his house, were stacked on windowsills and piled on the floor, filling most of the available space and leaving only narrow pathways that wound from room to room.

Jake never threw anything away. He literally had every single item he'd ever owned stashed somewhere in the big old Victorian house. Pantry shelves were filled with empty jelly jars, kitchen drawers were packed to bursting with plastic bags, closets in the numerous bedrooms were stuffed with old clothes and dozens of pairs of old shoes, the leather cracked and the toes curling up. Beds no one ever slept in were covered with boxes of junk, dresser drawers that were never opened contained old advertising flyers, dead batteries, and blown lightbulbs. And everywhere, filling every bit of square footage, were stacks of newspapers. They crawled up the walls, they blocked windows, they turned the house into a maze of narrow, twisting corridors.

When the grandfather clock in the hall chimed nine, time for Jake to get dressed, he shuffled into the next room, once the dining room but now his bedroom, where he slept on an ancient daybed. He sat down heavily, amid the musty sheets and blankets, and began carefully removing the plastic laundry bag from his heavily starched shirt. He was folding up the plastic bag, intending to add it to the sizeable collection he was accumulating beneath his bed, when he heard the neighbor's dog bark.

It was the mail, right on time; he nodded with satisfaction. Jake was one of the first on Wilf Lundgren's route, and the mail was always delivered around nine, barring the occasional storm delay. Fred, the elderly beagle belonging to his neighbor and dentist, Dr. Cyrus Frost, always announced Wilf's arrival, as well as that of the FedEx truck, the garbage truck, and any proselytizing Jehovah's Witnesses.

Jake was expecting his bank statement, which had been delayed a day because of the Thanksgiving holiday, so he decided to collect the mail even though he wasn't dressed. Not that it mattered. He was decent, covered chin to ankles in the long johns he wore all winter; the thick robe was warm and he had fleece-lined slippers. He hurried down the drive, eager to see if the bank statement had come, and as he approached the mailbox he noticed something large and colorful sticking out of it.

Reaching the box, which topped a post next to the street, he examined a padded mailing envelope printed with a red and green Christmas design protruding from the box. A present? He pulled it out, studying the design of candy canes and gingerbread men. It was addressed to him, he saw, and there was a label that warned *Do Not Open Till Christmas*. It was only the day after Thanksgiving, a bit early for a Christmas gift, perhaps, but Thanksgiving was the official beginning of the Christmas season. Not that he had partaken of the annual feast the day before; he and his partner Ben Scribner had gone to the office as usual, but they had agreed to give their secretary, Elsie Morehouse, the day off. They hadn't wanted to, but Elsie had pointed out in no uncertain terms that it was a legal holiday and she was entitled to take it.

Jake pulled the rest of his mail, a couple of plain white envelopes, out of the box. He noted with satisfaction that the bank statement had finally arrived, and looked forward to balancing it. He took pride in the fact that should there be a discrepancy between his calculations and those of the bank, his would undoubtedly be correct and the error would be the bank's. But first things first. He hurried back to the house, hugging the package to his chest, chuckling merrily.

A present. He hadn't received a present in a long time. Who could it be from? He studied the return address, but it didn't make any sense. *Santa Claus,* it read. *North Pole, Alaska.* It must be some sort of joke. Ben Scribner wasn't known for jokes, so he doubted it was from him. Besides, despite their long partnership of over thirty years, they never exchanged presents.

Perhaps it was from a grateful customer, a home owner who had the good sense to appreciate the current low interest rates, sometimes under four percent. That was unlikely, however, thought Jake. Real estate wasn't what it once was—prices were falling and most home owners owed more than their houses were worth.

The economy was bad, no doubt about it. Maybe some tradesman was expressing appreciation for his custom. He did have a faucet replaced this year; maybe it was a thank-you from Earle Plumbing. Ed Earle was probably thankful for one customer who paid on time, cash on the barrelhead. Come to think of it, he'd hired the electrician, too, to fix a busted wall switch. Al Lucier was no doubt appreciative of his prompt payment. Or maybe it was from his insurance agent, who might be sending something more substantial than the usual calendar this year. Only one way to find out, he decided, clutching the package to his chest and hurrying out of the cold and back into the slightly warmer house.

Once inside, with the kitchen door closed behind him, he set the envelopes on the kitchen counter, on top of a stack of empty egg cartons, and carefully examined the package. Only one way to find out what was inside, he decided, and that was to open it. Practically bursting with anticipation, he ripped off the flap.

Chapter One

When the first foreclosure sale of the Great Recession took place in Tinker's Cove, Maine, *Pennysaver* reporter Lucy Stone expected a scene right out of a silent movie. The auctioneer would be a slimy sort of fellow who ran his fingers along his waxed and curled mustache and cackled evilly, the banker would be a chubby chap whose pocket watch dangled from a thick gold chain stretched across his round stomach, and a burly sheriff would be forcibly evicting a noticeably hungry and poorly clad family from their home while his deputies tossed furniture and personal belongings onto the lawn.

The reality, which she discovered when she joined a small group of people gathered in front of a modest three-bedroom ranch, was somewhat different. For one thing, the house was vacant. The home owners had left weeks ago, according to a neighbor. "When Jim lost his job at the car dealership they realized they couldn't keep up the payments on Patty's income—she was a home health aide—so they packed up their stuff and left. Patty's mom has a B and B on Cape Cod, so she's going to help out there, and Jim's got himself enrolled in a nursing program at a community college."

"That sounds like a good plan," Lucy said, feeling rather disappointed as she'd hoped to write an emotion-packed human interest story.

"They're not getting off scot-free," the neighbor said, a young mother with a toddler on her hip. "They'll lose all the money they put in the house—bamboo floors, granite countertops, not to mention all the payments they made—and the foreclosure will be a blot on their credit rating for years. . . ." Her voice trailed off as the auctioneer called for attention and began reading a lot of legalese.

While he spoke, Lucy studied the individuals in the small group, who she assumed were planning to bid on the property in hopes of snagging a bargain. One or two were even holding white envelopes, most likely containing certified checks for the ten thousand dollars down specified in the ad announcing the sale.

But when the auctioneer called for bids, Ben Scribner, a partner in Downeast Mortgage, which held the note, opened with $185,000, the principal amount. That was more than the bargain hunters were prepared to offer, and they began to leave. Seeing no further offers, the auctioneer declared the sale over and the property now owned by the mortgage company.

Ben, who had thick white hair and ruddy cheeks, was dressed in the casual outfit of khaki pants and button-down oxford shirt topped by a barn coat favored by businessmen in the coastal Maine town. He was a prominent citizen who spoke out at town meetings, generally against any measure that would raise taxes. His company, Downeast Mortgage, provided financing for much of the region and there were few people in town who hadn't done business with him and his partner, Jake Marlowe. Marlowe was well known as a cheapskate, living like a solitary razor clam in that ramshackle Victorian mansion, and he was a fixture on the town's Finance Committee where he kept an eagle eye on the town budget.

Since that October day three years ago, there had been many more foreclosures in Tinker's Cove as the economy ground to a standstill. People moved in with relatives, they rented, or they moved on. What they didn't do was launch any sort of protest, at least not until now.

The fax announcing a Black Friday demonstration had come into the *Pennysaver* from a group at Winchester College calling itself the Social Action Committee, or SAC, which claimed to represent "the ninety-nine percent." The group was calling for an immediate end to foreclosures and was planning a demonstration at the Downeast Mortgage office on the Friday after Thanksgiving, which Lucy had been assigned to cover.

When she arrived, a few minutes before the appointed time of nine a.m., there was no sign of any demonstration. But when the clock on the Community Church chimed the hour, a row of marchers suddenly issued from the municipal parking lot situated behind the stores that lined Main Street. They were mostly college students who for one reason or other hadn't gone home for the holiday, as well as a few older people, professors and local residents Lucy recognized. They were bundled up against the November chill in colorful ski jackets, and they were carrying signs and marching to the beat of a Bruce Springsteen song issuing from a boom box. The leader, wearing a camo jacket and waving a megaphone, was a twenty-something guy with a shaved head.

"What do we want?" he yelled, his voice amplified and filling the street.

"Justice!" the crowd yelled back.

"When do we want it?" he cried.

"NOW!" roared the crowd.

Lucy immediately began snapping photos with her camera, and jogged along beside the group. When they stopped in front of Downeast Mortgage, and the leader got up on a milk crate to speak, she pulled out her notebook. "Who is that guy?" she asked the kid next to her.

"Seth Lesinski," the girl replied.

"Do you know how he spells it?"

"I think it's L-E-S-I-N-S-K-I."

"Got it," Lucy said, raising her eyes and noticing a girl who looked an awful lot like her daughter Sara. With blue eyes, blond hair, and a blue crocheted hat she'd seen her pull on that very morning, it was definitely Sara.

"What are you doing here?" she demanded, confronting her college freshman daughter. "I thought you have a poli sci class now."

Sara rolled her eyes. "Mo-om," she growled. "Later, okay?"

"No. You're supposed to be in class. Do you know how much that class costs? I figured it out. It's over a hundred dollars per hour and you're wasting it."

"Well, if you're so concerned about waste, why aren't you worried about all the people losing their homes?" Sara countered.

"Huh?"

"I am concerned," Lucy said.

"Well, you haven't shown it. There hasn't been a word in the paper except for those legal ads announcing the sales."

Lucy realized her daughter had a point. "Well, I'm covering it now," she said.

"So why don't you be quiet and listen to Seth," Sara suggested, causing Lucy's eyes to widen in shock. Sara had never spoken to her like that before, and she was definitely going to have a talk with her. But now, she realized, she was missing Seth's speech.

"Downeast Mortgage is the primary lender in the county and they have foreclosed on dozens of properties, and more foreclosures are scheduled. . . ."

The crowd booed, until Seth held up his hand for silence.

"They'll have you believe that people who miss their payments are deadbeats, failures, lazy, undeserving, irresponsible. . . . You've heard it all, right?"

There was general agreement, and people nodded.

"But the truth is different. These borrowers qualified for mortgages, had jobs that provided enough income to cover the payments, but then the recession came and the jobs were gone. Unemployment in this county is over fourteen percent. That's why people are losing their homes."

Lucy knew there was an element of truth in what Lesinski was saying. She knew that even the town government, until recently the region's most dependable employer, had recently laid off a number of employees and cut the hours of several others. In fact, scanning the crowd, she recognized Lexie Cunningham, who was a clerk in the tax collector's office. A big guy in a plaid jacket and navy blue watch cap was standing beside her, probably her husband. Lucy decided they might be good interview subjects and approached them.

"Hi, Lucy," Lexie said, with a little smile. She looked as if she'd lost weight, thought Lucy, and her hair, which had been dyed blond, was now showing dark roots and was pulled back unattractively into a ponytail. "This is my husband, Zach."

"I'm writing this up for the paper," Lucy began. "Can you tell me why you're here today?"

"'Cause we're gonna lose our house, that's why," Zach growled. "Downeast sent us a notice last week."

"My hours were cut, you know," Lexie said. "Now I don't work enough hours to get the health insurance benefit. Because of that we have to pay the entire premium—it's almost two thousand dollars a month, which is actually more than I now make. We can't pay both the mortgage and the health insurance and we can't drop the health insurance because of Angie—she's got juvenile kidney disease."

"I didn't know," Lucy said, realizing they were faced with an impossible choice.

"We don't qualify for assistance. Zach makes too much and we're over the income limit by a couple hundred dollars. But the health insurance is expensive, more than our mortgage. We were just getting by but then Angie had a crisis and the bills started coming. . . ."

"But you do have health insurance," Lucy said.

"It doesn't cover everything. There are copays and coinsurance and exclusions. . . ."

"Downeast is a local company—have you talked to Marlowe and Scribner? I bet they'd understand. . . ."

Zach started laughing, revealing a missing rear molar. "Understand? All those guys understand is that I agreed to pay them nine hundred and forty-five dollars every month. That's my problem, is what they told me."

"So that's why we're out here, demonstrating," Lexie said, as a sudden huge boom shook the ground under their feet.

"What the . . . ?" Everyone was suddenly silent, shocked by the loud noise and the reverberations.

"Gas?" somebody asked. They could hear a dog barking.

"Fire," said a kid in a North Face jacket, pointing to the column of black smoke that was rising into the sky.

"Parallel Street," Zach said, as sirens wailed and bright red fire trucks went roaring down the street, lights flashing.

A couple of guys immediately took off down the street, running after the fire trucks, and soon the crowd followed. Lucy always felt a little uncomfortably ghoulish at times like this, but she knew it was simply human nature to want to see what was going on. She knew it was the same impulse that caused people to watch CNN and listen to the car radio and even read the *Pennysaver*.

So she joined the crowd, hurrying along beside Sara and her friend Amy, rounding the corner onto Maple Street, where the smell of burning was stronger, and on to Parallel Street, which, as its name suggested, ran parallel to Main Street. Unlike Main Street, which was the town's commercial center, Parallel was a residential street filled with big old houses set on large properties. Most had been built in the nineteenth century by prosperous sea captains, eager to showcase their success. Nowadays, a few were still single family homes owned by members of the town's professional elite, but others had been subdivided into apartments and B and Bs. It was a pleasant street, lined with trees, and the houses were generally well maintained. In the summer, geraniums bloomed in window boxes and the sound of lawn mowers was frequently heard. Now, some houses still displayed pumpkin and gourd decorations for Thanksgiving while others were trimmed for Christmas, with window boxes filled with evergreen boughs and red-ribboned wreaths hung on the front doors. All except for one house, a huge Victorian owned by Jake Marlowe that was generally considered a blight on the neighborhood.

The old house was a marvel of Victorian design, boasting a three-story tower, numerous chimneys, bay windows, a sunroom, and a wraparound porch. Passing it, observing the graying siding that had long since lost its paint and the sagging porch, Lucy always imagined the house as it had once been. Then, she thought, the mansion would have sported a colorful paint job and the porch would have been filled with wicker furniture, where long-skirted ladies once sat and sipped lemonade while they observed the passing scene.

It had always seemed odd to her that a man whose business was financing property would take such poor care of his own, but when she'd interviewed a psychiatrist for a feature story about hoarders she began to understand that Jake Marlowe's cheapness was a sort of pathology. "Hoarders can't let anything go; it makes them unbearably anxious to part with anything," the psychiatrist had explained to her.

Now, standing in front of the burning house, Lucy saw that Jake Marlowe was going to lose everything.

"Wow," she said, turning to Sara and noticing how her daughter's face was glowing, bathed in rosy light from the fire. Everyone's face was like that, she saw, as they watched the orange flames leaping from the windows, running across the tired old porch, and even erupting from the top of the tower. No one could survive such a fire, she thought. It was fortunate it started in the morning, when she assumed Marlowe would be at his Main Street office.

"Back, everybody back," the firemen were saying, pushing the crowd to the opposite side of the street.

They were making no attempt to stop the fire but instead were pouring water on the roofs of neighboring houses, fearing that sparks from the fire would set them alight. More sirens were heard and Lucy realized the call had gone out to neighboring towns for mutual aid.

"What a shame," Lucy said, to nobody in particular, and a few others murmured in agreement.

Not everyone was sympathetic, however. "Serves the mean old bastard right," Zach Cunningham said.

"It's not like he took care of the place," Sara observed.

"He's foreclosed on a lot of people," Lexie Cunningham said. "Now he'll know what it's like to lose his home."

"You said it, man," Seth said, clapping Zach on the shoulder. "What goes around comes around." Realizing the crowd was with him, Seth got up on his milk crate. "Burn, baby, burn!" he yelled, raising his fist.

Lucy was shocked, but the crowd picked up the chant. "Burn, baby, burn!" they yelled back. "Burn, baby, burn."

Disgusted, she tapped Sara on the shoulder, indicating they should leave. Sara, however, shrugged her off and joined the refrain, softly at first but gradually growing louder as she was caught in the excitement of the moment.

Lucy wanted to leave and she wanted Sara to leave, too, but the girl stubbornly ignored her urgings. Finally, realizing she was alone in her sentiments, she shouldered her way through the crowd and headed back to Main Street and the *Pennysaver* office. At the corner, she remembered her job and paused to take a few more pictures for the paper. This would be a front page story, no doubt about it. She was peering through the camera's viewfinder when the tower fell in a shower of sparks and the crowd gave throat to a celebratory cheer.

You would have thought the football team scored a touchdown, she thought, stomping along the sidewalk that tilted this way and that from frost heaves. Nobody cared that a precious bit of the town's heritage was going up in smoke. Nobody but her.

The *Pennysaver* office was empty when she arrived. Phyllis, the receptionist, and Ted, who was publisher, editor, and chief reporter, were most likely at the fire. Good, she thought, he could write the story. She took off her parka and hung it on the coatrack, filled the coffeepot and got it brewing, and then she booted up her computer. She was checking her e-mails when the little bell on the door jangled and Ted entered.

"What are you doing here?" he asked, unwrapping his scarf. "Don't you know Jake Marlowe's house is burning down?" He had removed his Bruins ski cap and was running his fingers through his short, salt-and-pepper hair.

"I was there. I left."

"How come?" His face was squarish and clean-shaven, his brow furrowed in concern. "That's not like you, leaving a big story."

"The crowd freaked me out," she said, wrapping her arms across her chest and hugging herself. "Sara was there—she was part of it, screaming along with the rest."

"You know what they say about a mob. It's only as smart as the dumbest member," Ted said, pouring himself a mug of coffee. "Want a cup?"

"Sure," Lucy replied. When he gave her the mug she wrapped her fingers around it for warmth. "I always liked that old house," she said, taking a sip. "I sometimes imagined it the way it used to be. A painted lady, that's what they call those fancy Victorians."

"Marlowe didn't take care of it. It was a firetrap. Truth be told, it should've been condemned and it would've been if Marlowe wasn't such a big shot in town. But he was on the Finance Committee and the fire chief wasn't about to mess with him, not with Marlowe constantly pushing the committee to cut the department's budget."

"I wonder where Marlowe was," Lucy mused, setting her cup down. "I didn't see him in the crowd. Did you?"

Ted tossed the wooden stirrer into the trash and carried his mug over to his desk, an old rolltop he'd inherited from his grandfather, who was a legendary New England newspaperman. "Nope, he wasn't there."

"Maybe he went away for the holiday," Lucy speculated. "Probably for the best. It would be awful to watch your house burn down."

"Yeah," Ted said, clicking away on his keyboard. "I've got a meeting this afternoon over in Gilead. Do me a favor and follow up with the fire chief before you go home."

Lunch was long past and Ted had gone to his meeting when Lucy noticed the rattling of the old wooden Venetian blinds that covered the plate glass windows, indicating the fire trucks were finally returning to the station down the street. A few minutes later Phyllis came in, wearing a faux leopard skin coat and sporting a streak of soot on her face. "Jake Marlowe's house burned to the ground!" she exclaimed. "What a show. Too bad you missed it."

"I was there for a while," Lucy said. "Your face is dirty."

"Oh, thanks." Phyllis hung up her coat and went into the tiny bathroom, lifting the harlequin reading glasses that hung from a chain around her neck as she went. "Look at that," Lucy heard her saying. "It's soot from the fire. And no wonder—that old house is still smoldering."

"It was some blaze," Lucy said.

Phyllis sat at her desk and applied a liberal glob of hand lotion. "I wonder how it started," she said.

"There was an explosion," Lucy said, suddenly remembering the boom that had disrupted the SAC demonstration.

"Must've been gas—I don't know why people mess around with that stuff. It's awfully dangerous."

"I wonder," Lucy said, reaching for the phone and dialing. In a moment of madness, when he was looking for publicity for a food drive, Chief Buzz Bresnahan had given her his personal cell phone number. Lucy was careful not to abuse the privilege, but today she figured his secretary would be blocking calls.

"Lucy," he barked. "Make it fast."

"Okay. Any idea how the fire started? Was it a gas leak?"

"Not gas. We're not sure. The fire marshal is investigating. It's definitely suspicious."

"Any injuries?"

"No, I'm happy to say," Bresnahan replied. "Gotta go. You better check with the fire marshal's office. I'm pretty sure this is going to turn out to be a case of arson."

"Arson?" Lucy asked, but Buzz had already gone.

Chapter Two

Several firemen and a police patrol remained at the site of the fire through the weekend, watching for flare-ups and keeping thrill seekers and souvenir hunters away from the smoldering pile of rubble. On Monday the fire marshal's team arrived, along with two trained dogs, Blaze and Spark. It didn't take Blaze very long to make a disturbing discovery: the ruins contained a badly burned body, most probably that of the owner, Jake Marlowe.

Lucy finally got confirmation from police chief Jim Kirwan on Wednesday, just before deadline. "Yup, Lucy," he said, "it was definitely murder. Somebody sent Marlowe a mail bomb. It blew up in his face when he opened it."

"Are they sure it was actually Marlowe?" Lucy asked. "I thought there wasn't much left."

"It was definitely Marlowe. His body was in the kitchen. Well, where the kitchen used to be. And Dr. Frost, the dentist who lives next door, recognized some bridgework he did for Marlowe."

"How can they tell it was a mail bomb?" Lucy asked. "Didn't the fire destroy the evidence?"

"I don't know the details; all I know is what the state fire marshal tells me and he says it was a mail bomb. No doubt about it."

"Was it mailed locally?"

"Uh, that he didn't know," Kirwan admitted. "We've got the post office working on it, but the assumption is that it was a local job. Think about it: Marlowe wasn't very popular around town. A lot of people have lost, or are about to lose, their homes to Downeast Mortgage. And Marlowe didn't do himself any favors with that FinCom vote cutting town employees' hours. No, we've got suspects coming out of the woodwork, lots of them." He chuckled. "Which reminds me, Lucy. Who's holding your mortgage?"

Lucy found herself grinning. "Nobody. We paid ours off last year."

"Lucky devils," Jim said. "I wish I hadn't refinanced back in two thousand seven when all the so-called financial experts were saying it was the thing to do. Now I'm underwater, like most everybody else in town. I owe more than the house is worth."

"Just hang on," Lucy advised. "Prices will go back up; they always do."

"I dunno," Kirwan said. "This is one time I kinda feel for the guy who did it. Truth is, I would've liked to do it myself."

"I'm assuming that's off the record," Lucy said.

"Uh, yeah," Kirwan said.

Sitting in Jake's Donut Shop on Thursday morning—this long-time Tinker's Cove institution was named after its owner, Jake Prose—Lucy was staring at the front page photo of Marlowe's burning mansion and mourning the quote she couldn't use. What a bombshell that would have been! Police chief goes rogue! If only she hadn't promised to keep his revealing statement off the record.

"Hey, Lucy." It was her best friend, Sue Finch, and Lucy hopped up to greet her with a hug.

"Some fire," Sue said, glancing at the paper as she took her seat and shrugged out of her shearling coat.

Lucy tapped the head of a small figure standing in the crowd. "That's Sara. She was supposed to be in class but she was out demonstrating with the college's Social Action Committee."

"So Sara's suddenly developed a social conscience?" Sue asked, removing her beret and smoothing her glossy black pageboy with her beautifully manicured hands. "I'm only asking because that leader, Seth, is pretty good looking." She was pointing to the photo of Seth, his fist raised in defiance.

"You think she's interested in him, not the issues?" Lucy asked. She hadn't considered this possibility.

Sue rolled her eyes. "Yes, I do. And by the way, what do I have to do to get a cup of coffee around here?"

Norine, the waitress, was on it. "Sorry, Sue. I got distracted," she said, setting a couple of mugs on the table and filling them. "Ever since the fire I just can't seem to concentrate." She shuddered. "I didn't like Marlowe—nobody did—but that's a terrible way to go."

"You said it," Pam Stillings chimed in, arriving with Rachel Goodman. Pam was married to Lucy's boss, Ted, and she and Rachel completed the group of four friends who met for breakfast every Thursday at Jake's.

"That poor man," Rachel added, lowering her big doe eyes and shaking her head. Rachel was a soft touch, who provided home care for the town's oldest resident, Miss Julia Ward Howe Tilley.

"He wasn't poor," Lucy said, knowing perfectly well that Rachel hadn't been referring to Marlowe's finances. "He was making a bundle off those mortgages and almost everybody in town has one. Chief Kirwan told me he's got more suspects than he can count."

Norine arrived with coffee for Rachel and green tea for Pam, who ate only natural, organic foods. "You girls want the usual?" she asked. Receiving nods all round, she departed, writing on her order pad as she went.

"Let's not talk about the fire," Rachel suggested. "I've got big news."

"Go on," Sue urged. She didn't like dramatic pauses unless she was making them.

"I'm directing the Community Players' holiday production," Rachel announced. "It's Dickens's *A Christmas Carol,* and I want you all to audition."

"Count me out," Sue said, shaking her head. "I couldn't act my way out of a paper bag but I'll be happy to handle the refreshments."

"Great," Rachel said. "But I think you'd make a fabulous Ghost of Christmas Past."

"That's a joke, right?" Sue asked suspiciously.

"Yeah," Rachel admitted. "But I do think Lucy would be great as Mrs. Cratchit. She's so warm and motherly."

"Me?" Lucy didn't recognize herself in that description.

"Actually, yes," Sue said. "You are warm and motherly, even grandmotherly."

Lucy gave her friend a dirty look. "I adore Patrick," she said, naming her son Toby's little boy, "but you have to admit I'm a young grandmother."

"My grandmother wore thick stockings and lace-up oxfords with heels," Pam recalled. "White in the summer and black after Labor Day. I don't think they make them anymore. Her breasts went down to her waist and she wore her gray hair in a bun."

"Fortunately for Lucy they've invented underwire bras and hair dye," Sue remarked.

"And sneakers," Lucy added, naming her favorite footwear as Norine delivered her order of two eggs over easy with corned beef hash and whole wheat toast. Norine passed Rachel her usual Sunshine muffin, gave Pam her yogurt topped with granola, and refilled Sue's cup with coffee.

"Auditions are tonight," Rachel said. "Will you come, Lucy? And how about you, Pam?"

"Ofay," Lucy agreed, her mouth full of buttery toast.

"I'm too busy for rehearsals," Pam said, "but I can do the program for you. I'll get ads and Ted can design it and get it printed."

"That would be great," Rachel said. "Any money we make will go to the Hat and Mitten Fund."

They all nodded in approval. The Hat and Mitten Fund, which provided warm clothing and school supplies for the town's needy children, was a favorite charity.

"Maybe we could give part of the money to the Cunninghams," Lucy suggested. "They're having a hard time right now. Their little girl, Angie, has kidney disease and there are a lot of expenses their health insurance doesn't cover."

"That's a good idea, Lucy," Pam said, a member of the town Finance Committee. "Lexie is one of the town employees whose hours were cut."

"How awful for them," Rachel said. "Just having a sick child is bad enough, but now the Cunninghams have all these financial worries, too."

"They may lose their house," Lucy said.

"Oh," Pam groaned. "I feel so responsible."

"But you voted against those cuts," Sue said.

"The vote was three to two," Pam said. "Frankie and I were the nays—we were outnumbered by the men." She paused. "But now that Marlowe is no longer with us there's a vacancy on the board. Right now we're evenly divided. Taubert and Hawthorne have one goal: keep taxes low. Frankie and I aren't exactly big spenders, but we have a more moderate approach. We need to fill that vacancy with another moderate who understands the value of town services."

"And town employees," Rachel added.

"You're right," Pam said. "Marlowe actually called them parasites who were sucking the taxpayers dry."

"Sounds like a real sweetheart," Sue said sarcastically.

"Not really," Pam said. "So if you can think of anybody who'd be willing to take on a thoroughly thankless task by joining the FinCom, let me know. We want to choose someone at the next meeting."

"Ted did put an announcement in the paper," Lucy said. "Maybe you'll get some volunteers."

"It's a bad time of year to recruit a new member," Pam said. "Everybody's busy with Christmas."

"That's true," Lucy said, remembering that her husband, Bill, had recently expressed a desire to become more active in town affairs. Maybe this was something he'd be interested in doing. She filed that thought for later and turned her attention to her friends.

"Don't forget the auditions tonight," Rachel was saying. "At the Community Church. Can I count on you, Lucy?"

"Okay," Lucy agreed. The audition would make a nice human interest story and she was certain there was no way she was going to get a role. She was no Mrs. Cratchit, for sure.

After leaving Jake's, Lucy spent a few hours at the *Pennysaver,* filing news releases and typing up events for the Things to Do This Week column. As Phyllis had pointed out, there were more listings than usual, because of Christmas. All of the churches were holding bazaars, the Historical Society was having a cookie sale, and the high school was giving a holiday concert. Going beyond Tinker's Cove, the Gilead Artists were having a small works sale, the South Coast Horticultural Society was holding a gala Festival of Trees, and the Coastal Chorale invited one and all to join them in singing Handel's *Messiah*.

"If you did all these things you wouldn't have any time to shop or wrap presents or send Christmas cards," Lucy observed.

"Nobody sends Christmas cards anymore," said Phyllis, who ought to know because her husband, Wilf, was a mail carrier. "They e-mail holiday greetings."

"I never thought of that," Lucy said.

"Well, don't," Phyllis said. "The postal service is having enough problems. They need the business."

"They can count on me," Lucy said. "I always send cards and I like getting them. I put them up around the kitchen door."

She was typing the listing for the preschool story hour when she had an unsettling thought. "Phyllis, did Wilf deliver that postal bomb they think killed Jake Marlowe?"

Phyllis wrapped her fuzzy purple sweater tightly across her ample bosom and blinked behind her pink and black harlequin reading glasses. "I think he must have," she said in a very small voice. "I know the state police have questioned him."

"They don't think . . ." Lucy began.

"I certainly hope not!" Phyllis exclaimed. "He was just doing his job, delivering the mail. He doesn't know what's in the packages—how could he?"

"Of course not," Lucy said. But she was thinking how terrible it would have been if the bomb had exploded early. And seeing Phyllis's bleak expression, Lucy knew her coworker was thinking the very same thing.

When Lucy left the office she checked her list of errands. She needed to cash a check at the bank, the wreaths she'd ordered from the high school cheerleaders were awaiting pickup, and she had to do her weekly grocery shopping. First stop, she decided, was the drive-through at the bank, which was at one end of Main Street. Then she'd zip down Parallel Street to the school, avoiding traffic, and get the wreaths. From there she could sneak into the IGA parking lot from the back, missing the traffic light on Main Street.

She hadn't forgotten about the fire, but she was distracted, making plans for Christmas as she drove along Parallel Street, so it was quite a shock when Marlowe's burned house came into view. She immediately slowed the car, taking in the scorched chimneys, the flame-scarred walls, and the stinking, blackened pile of debris surrounded by a fluttering yellow ribbon of *DO NOT CROSS* tape that was all that remained of the once magnificent house. She'd seen fires before, of course. Fires were big news and she'd had to cover quite a few in her career, but she'd rarely seen one that was so completely destructive. Marlowe's burned-out house was a frightening sight, especially to someone like her, who also happened to live in an antique house.

Batteries, she reminded herself, pressing the accelerator. Don't forget to buy fresh batteries for the smoke alarms.

Not surprisingly, the IGA was out of nine-volt batteries, even the expensive brand-name ones. "We're expecting a shipment on Saturday," said Dot Kirwan, the cashier, who also happened to be police chief Jim Kirwan's mother. Her son, Todd, was also a police officer, and her daughter, Krissy, the town's emergency dispatcher. Dot was well connected and Lucy cultivated her as a prime source of information. "There's been a run on them since the fire. You're supposed to change the batteries when you put your clock back in the spring but it seems that a lot of folks aren't going to wait. They're doing it while it's fresh on their mind."

"Any progress on the fire?" Lucy asked, as she began to unload her cart.

"Not that I've heard," Dot said. She had permed gray hair cut short and wore a bright red smock with her official IGA name tag pinned on her left breast. "They sent some stuff to the crime lab, but I don't think they're going to learn much more than they already know. It was a mail bomb—anybody could've sent it."

"Anybody who knows how to make a mail bomb," Lucy said.

"There's instructions on the Internet," Dot said. "You could make one, if you wanted."

"Well, I don't," Lucy said.

"Me, either." Dot scanned a package of veggie burgers, a mainstay of Sara's diet. "Tell the truth, I kind of miss old Jake. He was a regular customer, came in most days."

"Really?" Lucy was bagging her groceries in the reusable bags that her daughters Sara and Zoe insisted she use.

"Yup. He kept an eye on the dented cans, the day-old bread, even the marked-down meat. He loved a bargain." She paused. "That comes to a hundred thirty-six dollars and seventy-four cents."

Lucy swiped her debit card and punched her code into the keypad. "I guess I'd be rich, too, if I didn't spend all my money on groceries and gas and clothes. . . ."

"That's the secret," said Ike Stoughton, who was buying coffee, sugar, and creamer for his office. "Jake didn't spend much, that's for sure. Never paid more than he had to. I'll miss him, though."

"You're one of the few," Dot said dryly.

Lucy knew Ike, a neighbor, was a highly regarded surveyor. "Did you do much work for Marlowe?" she asked.

"Not too much lately, but a few years ago he took a lot of land by adverse possession and I did the surveying for him." He paused, then cocked an eyebrow. "He didn't pay much, but he was as good as his word and he did pay on time."

Lucy, whose husband, Bill, was a restoration carpenter, knew that all too often clients held back final payments, demanding work they hadn't contracted for, and sometimes paid late or didn't make that final payment until threatened with a lawsuit. "Old time values," Lucy said. "You don't see them so much anymore."

"These days most people can't afford them," Dot said.

"True," Ike agreed, taking his package and nodding toward the big plate glass window at the front of the store. "Looks like snow," he said, and Lucy saw the sky was filling fast with dark clouds.

Chapter Three

A few snowflakes were floating about when Lucy turned off Red Top Road and into her driveway, but they melted as soon as they hit the ground and there was no accumulation. The house was empty, except for Libby the Lab, who gave her a perfunctory greeting before turning to her main interest, which was sniffing at the grocery bags Lucy had set on the floor. She found the one with the chicken in a matter of seconds and Lucy quickly grabbed it and hoisted it on to the kitchen counter.

"Okay," she told the dog. "I know it's hard, all this food and nothing for you."

Libby sat on her haunches and stared at her with her big brown eyes. "I'll play the game if you insist," she seemed to be saying, "even though we both know I'm the boss around here."

Lucy obediently began digging around in the grocery bags until she found the bag of beef jerky treats and gave a couple to Libby, who wolfed them down. "That's all, now," she said, in a firm tone, and the dog slouched off to settle down on her bed. There she set her chin on her paws and watched with interest as Lucy put the groceries away.

That chore done, she popped a chicken and some sweet potatoes in the oven, then began unloading the dishwasher. From time to time she peeked out the window to check on the snow, but it wasn't amounting to much, so the roads would be okay for her returning family members. Zoe was the first to arrive home; now that her friend Amy Whitmore had a driver's license she got a ride with her most days, shunning the school bus.

Bill was next, in his pickup truck. He was a restoration carpenter and had landed a big contract converting an old meetinghouse in nearby Gilead into a walk-in health clinic. He sniffed the air, decided it was chicken roasting, and gave her a peck on the cheek. "Shall I open that chardonnay?" he asked, and receiving a nod, got to work with a corkscrew.

They had just seated themselves at the round oak kitchen table with their glasses of wine when Sara blew in. "Sorry I'm late," she said, unwinding her scarf, striped in the green and white that were Winchester College's colors. "I forgot the time."

"No problem," Lucy said, sipping her wine. "Dinner won't be ready for another fifteen minutes."

"Great." She thundered up the back stairway and slammed the door to her room shut.

"Funny," Bill said. "I thought girls would be quieter than boys."

"Not that I've noticed," Lucy said, laughing.

Promptly at six, what sounded like a herd of elephants but was only Zoe and Sara came pounding down the stairs, looking for dinner. The girls quickly set the dining room table while Lucy dished up the chicken, baked sweet potatoes, green beans, and salad.

"So what's new?" Bill asked, slicing into the chicken with his carving knife.

"The junior class is having a toy drive for Christmas," Zoe said. "I'm in charge of publicity."

"I can help with that," Lucy offered, serving herself salad. "What about you, Sara? Is the college holding a holiday fund-raiser?"

Sara was helping herself to a baked sweet potato. "Charity at Christmas is just a sop, to make people feel good about themselves. The Social Action Committee is working for real economic justice. When we achieve that, charity will be unnecessary—everyone's needs will be met."

"A lofty goal," Bill said.

"And until then, a lot of people right here in Tinker's Cove are in need," Lucy added.

"And the little kids shouldn't have to suffer," Zoe said. "Not at Christmas."

"Christmas is just a day like any other, that's what Seth says. He says Christmas is just a corporate gimmick to get people to spend money they don't have and to distract them from the real problem, which is an economic system that benefits only one percent of the population while the other ninety-nine percent are struggling."

"Who's Seth?" Bill asked, zeroing in on an unfamiliar male name.

"Seth Lesinski. He's amazing, Dad. He's the leader— Well, there are actually no official leaders. . . . He facilitates SAC."

"What's the difference?"

"Oh, he calls the meetings and presents ideas for action, like the protest we had the other day against Downeast Mortgage."

"Sounds like he's the leader," Bill said, helping himself to seconds.

"No, the whole group has to vote."

"Still . . ." Bill began.

"He's very good looking," Lucy interjected. "At least that's what Sue says."

"SAC is not about looks," Sara said, her cheeks flushed with color. "It's not about appearances. It's what we do that's important."

"You've got to admit he cuts quite a dashing figure," Lucy said. "That scarf he wears, and that camo jacket fits like he had it tailored. . . ."

"Don't be ridiculous, Mom."

"Just an observation," Lucy said. "By the way, I'm auditioning tonight. The Community Players are putting on *A Christmas Carol* and Rachel wants me to be Mrs. Cratchit."

"Sentimental Victorian drivel," Sara sniffed.

"Do you really think you can act?" Zoe asked.

"Where are you going to find the time?" Bill asked. "That's if you get the part."

"Not much chance of that," Sara scoffed.

"Rachel thinks I can do it. She asked me specially to audition."

"She's probably just being nice," Zoe said in a consoling voice. "You don't have any acting experience."

"She's right, Mom," Sara said. "You have to have talent to act. Some people can and some people can't. It's genetics."

"You're going to be too busy, anyway, with Christmas and all." Bill ended the discussion by changing the subject. "What's for dessert?"

When Lucy left the house the girls were busy clearing the table and loading the dishwasher, Libby's nose was buried in her dish, and Bill was watching TV. There was about a half inch of wet snow on the ground and she drove cautiously. She'd never auditioned for anything, so she didn't know what to expect, but she thought she might enjoy acting. She was, she admitted to herself, excited at the prospect of trying something new. Wouldn't it be great if she got the part? That would show those naysayers at home!

When she arrived in the basement meeting room at the Community Church she found a handful of people sitting around a couple of tables that had been pushed together. Rachel was there, of course, and so was Bob, her lawyer husband. She recognized a few other people, including Marge Culpepper, and Florence Gallagher, whom she'd recently interviewed for a feature story about the children's books she'd illustrated.

Rachel greeted her with a smile. "Great, you're here, Lucy. I think we can get started. As you can see, I like to keep things very informal. We've got scripts, so we'll read a little bit, and if you have any experience acting, please tell me. Bob, I think we'll start with you. Can you read Scrooge's lines on page five?"

"Is Bob going to be Scrooge?" Lucy couldn't see it. Bob was the sweetest, nicest man she knew. He had a reputation as a bit of a bleeding heart and much of his busy law practice was pro bono.

"Bah! Humbug!" he growled in a very convincing way, and they all laughed.

After he'd read a few lines, complaining to Bob Cratchit about giving him a day off to celebrate Christmas with his family, Rachel thanked him and turned to Lucy.

"Lucy, do you have any acting experience?"

"I do," Lucy said, dredging her memory and coming up with a nugget. "In kindergarten I was Ferdinand the Bull's mother. As I recall, I had a line about how Ferdinand liked to sit quietly and smell the flowers."

"Practically a professional," Rachel said, when the laughter subsided. "I want you to draw on that experience and read Mrs. Cratchit's lines on page thirty-five."

When Lucy finished, Rachel nodded. "Very nice. I think you'll be great."

"You mean I got the part?"

"Absolutely," Rachel said.

After an hour or so Rachel called a break and Lucy struck up a conversation with Marge, who was married to the town's community affairs officer, Barney Culpepper. Marge was going to play the role of Scrooge's housekeeper.

"I wish I'd gotten a more sympathetic role," she said, pouring herself a cup of decaf at the refreshment table. "She pawns his stuff before Scrooge is even buried."

"It's just a foreshadowing, right? It doesn't actually happen," Lucy said. "Just like Tiny Tim doesn't die."

"Oh, now you've wrecked the ending for me," Marge teased.

"Talking about endings, have they made any progress on the fire investigation?"

"Quite a bit of overtime, which comes in handy this time of year. The problem is there are too many suspects. Practically anybody who has a mortgage from Downeast has a motive and that's most everybody in town."

"Not everybody knows how to make a bomb, though," Lucy said.

"There are instructions on the Internet," Marge said, choosing a chocolate frosted donut. "And a lot of folks in town are very handy, used to making do."

"That's true," Lucy said.

Rachel called them back to work, and when they'd all gathered again at the table she made an announcement. "I'm very happy to say that I think we've filled all the parts, and I'm confident we're going to have a terrific show. Some of you are veterans with the Community Players, so you know the drill. Each actor is expected to raise a hundred dollars by selling ads in our program to finance the production."

"You mean we have to pay to play?" Florence asked, raising one beautifully shaped eyebrow. Lucy knew she must be well into her forties, but thanks to moisturizer, hair color, and visits to the gym, she looked much younger.

"That's one I haven't heard before," Rachel said, "but that's about it." She paused. "Is this going to be a problem for anyone?"

"Can we help some other way?" Florence asked. "I could help with the scenery, for example. I hate to ask people for money."

Rachel sighed. "I know things are tight for everyone right now, and I don't want anyone to leave the show because they can't sell a few ads. Let's just leave it that I expect everyone to do their best to come up with the suggested amount." Receiving nods from the cast members, she moved on. "Okay, let's do a read-through and take it from the top."

Friday morning Lucy was crowing about getting the part of Mrs. Cratchit, despite her reservations. She had loved rehearsing, especially enjoying the lively company of the other amateur actors. The evening had been full of laughter and a growing sense of shared purpose.

"Way to go, Mom," Zoe said, giving her a high-five as she ran out the door to catch her ride.

"Break a leg," Sara muttered, offering the traditional advice as she poured herself a cup of coffee and carried it back up to her room where she was working on a paper.

"I guess I won't be seeing much of you," Bill said, poking his egg with a fork and making the yolk run out. "What with rehearsals and all."

"I've put the schedule on the fridge," Lucy said, spreading some marmalade on an English muffin. "Rehearsals are seven to nine most evenings." She took a bite and chewed. "It's not like we even talk to each other much after dinner, anyway. You usually do fantasy football on the computer and I watch TV. It will be good to shake things up a bit."

"I suppose," he said mournfully.

Lucy chuckled. "I think you're the actor in the family."

Bill had the good grace to blush. "I will miss you," he said.

"Come to the rehearsals, then. You could help backstage."

He was quick to come up with a reason to stay home. "Someone should keep an eye on the girls," he said, wiping his plate with his toast.

As Lucy tidied the kitchen she set her mind to considering who might be willing to buy an ad. Most of her friends were watching their pennies with Christmas taking up any spare change. Her old friend Miss Tilley was a possibility, until Lucy remembered that Rachel had probably already asked her. Who, she wondered, as she wiped the counters, was likely to support local theater?

She was rinsing out the sponge when she remembered a series of articles she wrote in September profiling local people with surprising hobbies. The fire chief, Buzz Bresnahan, was a theater buff who traveled to New York City a couple of times a year to see Broadway shows. And his daughter, Alison, was studying theater at Ohio University. Deciding he would be her first target, she dried her hands and reached for her jacket, intending to make her first stop of the day at the fire station.

But when she arrived at the station the ambulance was pulling out of its bay, lights flashing and siren wailing.

She ran inside and caught the dispatcher's eye. "What's up?"

"Medical assistance at Downeast Mortgage," Krissy Kirwan replied, one of Dot's numerous offspring who worked in public safety. "Sounds like a heart attack."

Maybe it was news, maybe it wasn't, Lucy mused. There was only one way to find out, so she got in her car and followed the ambulance down Main Street to the Downeast Mortgage office. The office was in a neat little brick building that had once housed a bank. Stone steps with black wrought iron railings led to a plate glass door, with a window on either side. The ambulance took up most of the small parking lot, so Lucy parked on the street. She hurried to the door, hoping she could slip inside without being noticed, because she knew from previous experience that the rescue team didn't appreciate an audience.

She was just reaching the stone steps when the door flew open and Ben Scribner flew out. From his wailing you would have thought the hounds of hell were pursuing him instead of his faithful secretary Elsie Morehouse.

"You'll freeze out here, Mr. Scribner," she begged him. "Come back inside."

Scribner was standing in the inch or so of snow that was on the ground, shivering in the light sweater he wore over his oxford cloth shirt and khaki pants. His thinning white hair was standing straight up on his head, his eyes were wide with fear, and a line of saliva was dribbling down his chin. "No! No! Get away!"

A couple of EMTs had appeared in the doorway behind Elsie, and a police cruiser was just arriving. "It's just me, Mr. Scribner. Elsie."

Scribner shook his head; he was trembling violently. "Jake Marlowe was here," he said. "I saw him. In the flesh."

Barney Culpepper was getting out of his cruiser and assessing the situation, unobserved by Scribner.

"Now, now." Elsie's voice was soothing. "You know perfectly well that Mr. Marlowe is dead. He died in the fire."

"He did!" Scribner's head was jerking up and down like a bobble-head doll's.

"I know he did. He's dead as a doornail. But he was here! He's come back from the dead."

"That's impossible, Mr. Scribner. You must have imagined it."

"He told me . . ."

"What did he tell you?" Elsie asked, keeping eye contact with Scribner and ignoring Barney's approach, even though she was aware of it.

"He was w-w-warning me."

A female EMT unfolded a red blanket, which she offered to Scribner. "Let me put this around you, warm you up," she said.

"Fire! Fire!" Scribner pointed to the blanket and stepped backward, shivering violently.

The EMT advanced with the blanket and Scribner scuttled backward, right into the officer's waiting arms. Barney had him cuffed and confined to the back of his cruiser in a smooth, practiced sequence of moves. Then they were off, headed to the emergency room. The other rescuers began leaving and Lucy approached Elsie Morehouse.

"Are you all right?" she asked. "That was pretty intense."

"Mr. Scribner's very upset about losing his partner." Elsie had a sweater over her shoulders and her arms were folded defensively across her chest.

"Let's go inside and get you warm," Lucy urged. She fully expected Elsie to tell her to scram, and was surprised when the secretary allowed herself to be led inside. A full coffeepot was sitting on a credenza and Lucy poured a cup, adding a couple of sugars and some milk. "Drink this," she said, and Elsie sat right down like a good little girl and took the mug.

"Did anything in particular set him off?" Lucy asked.

"Mr. Scribner thought he saw Mr. Marlowe's ghost. At first he wasn't afraid, but it seems he didn't like what Mr. Marlowe told him. That's when he got so upset."

"Did he say what Mr. Marlowe told him?" Lucy asked.

Elsie was holding the mug with both hands, and though she was obviously distressed, her makeup and pixie cut hair were perfect. "He was babbling, but I think the gist of it was that if he didn't change his ways the same thing would happen to him. I guess he meant the explosion." She gulped some coffee. "It was all in Mr. Scribner's head, of course. He had some sort of fantasy or hallucination. That's it." She narrowed her eyes. "You're from the paper, aren't you?"

"Uh, yes," Lucy admitted.

"Well, thank you very much for fixing the coffee, but I think you better leave now. And anything you saw here is off the record." She glared at Lucy. "Understood?"

"What you told me is off the record," Lucy said. "But everything that happened outside took place in public and involved town employees. I can and will report it."

"Well, I never," Elsie sniffed, her lips pursed in disapproval. "That's a disgusting way to behave."

"Oh," Lucy responded, her ire rising. "I suppose you think it's perfectly fine to foreclose and make families homeless. That's a nice thing to do?"

Elsie was holding the door for her, indicating she should leave, now. But first she wanted to get in the last word. "You can't let people walk away from their obligations," she said, bristling with righteous indignation. "Think of the moral hazard."

"Moral hazard," Lucy repeated, stepping outside into the frosty morning air. "That's a new one on me."

Chapter Four

"Moral hazard," Lucy repeated, muttering to herself. She'd been hearing that term a lot lately. What on earth did it mean? Could it possibly mean that, if for some reason a borrower couldn't meet his obligations, he would somehow be morally at risk if the creditor adjusted the terms of the loan? That a borrower's morality would be preserved if his family became homeless, rather than if he received a month or two of forbearance?

She thought of Lexie and Zach Cunningham, who were struggling to keep their home and provide medical care for their daughter, and wondered how the theory of moral hazard could possibly apply to them. Their debt would be satisfied if Downeast repossessed their home, but what about their parental obligation to provide shelter for their children? It wasn't Lexie's fault that her hours were cut because of the recession—that was completely out of her control. What were they to do? They had increased expenses because she'd lost her employer-subsidized health care at the same time their income was reduced. That was a simple enough equation to Lucy, but apparently the Ben Scribners and Elsie Morehouses of this world saw it differently. To them the inability to pay all one's bills, a situation commonly known as poverty, was not simply an economic crisis but was a moral one, too.

But what about the lessons she'd learned in Sunday School? She remembered contributing a quarter each week to "help the poor" and had never forgotten that most important Golden Rule: "Do unto others as you would have others do unto you." She was in her car now, driving down the street past several Downeast FOR SALE signs, trying to understand how all these foreclosures could possibly benefit anyone. Families were dislocated, forced to leave their homes and find shelter where they could. The town was losing citizens, sometimes people whose families had made their homes in Tinker's Cove for centuries. And even Ben Scribner must have realized that accumulating a number of properties that nobody could afford to buy was hardly a good business policy.

She found herself wondering about Scribner and Marlowe, and their relationship. It seemed it might have been somewhat strained, considering Scribner's reaction to his dead partner's reappearance. According to Elsie, Marlowe had warned Scribner that he was going to meet a fiery end, just as he did. But from what she'd seen, it seemed that Scribner was actually terrified of his deceased partner. Why should that be? she wondered, turning into the parking area behind the *Pennysaver* office. They'd been partners for decades, the company was a fixture in town, and the two men had always seemed to be of similar minds. Why should Scribner suddenly be afraid of his longtime partner? Lucy could think of only one reason: guilt. If Scribner had a guilty conscience he might well fear the return of a revenge-seeking Jake Marlowe.

Ted and Phyllis were already at work when Lucy arrived. "You're late," Ted said, glancing at the clock. It wasn't a criticism, merely an observation.

"There was an emergency at Downeast Mortgage and I went to see what it was all about," she explained, hanging up her coat.

"Another explosion?" Phyllis asked.

"No, nothing like that. Ben Scribner had a panic attack, that's all."

"Understandable, I guess," Ted said. "He must be feeling kind of paranoid. After all, the fire that killed Marlowe was started by a bomb, disguised as a Christmas package."

Lucy sat down with a thud in her desk chair. "I think that is so mean," she said.

"Yeah," Phyllis agreed, with a nod that shook her double chin. "Sending a bomb is bad enough, but wrapping it up in Christmas paper is . . . Well, I don't know exactly what it is, but it's not nice."

"Really not nice," Lucy said. "It kind of makes you feel bad for poor old Marlowe. He was such a miser, he was probably really excited about getting a present."

"For a minute or two he must have thought somebody actually liked him," Phyllis said.

"Which really wasn't the case," Lucy mused. "He wasn't very popular."

"Truth is, he worked pretty hard to make himself unpopular," Phyllis added.

"Ahem." Ted cleared his throat. "If you ladies don't mind, we have work to do."

They both fell silent and folded their hands in their laps, waiting for instructions.

"Phyllis, this is a list of advertisers who haven't renewed their contracts. I want you to call them, offer them these new reduced rates for our holiday issues." He handed her a couple of sheets of paper, then turned to Lucy. "As for you, Lucy, I want you to check the legal ads for the last year or so and find out how many people have actually lost their homes to Downeast Mortgage. Once you get the properties you'll have to follow up at the Registry of Deeds."

"Sounds like you're planning a big story," Lucy said.

"We'll see," Ted said. "Let's find out the facts first."

This was the sort of assignment Lucy loved. There was nothing better than digging through old papers for nuggets of truth. She loved the big, oversized volumes of bound papers that went back over a hundred years to the days of the old *Courier and Advertiser*. It was unfortunate, in her opinion, that Ted had switched to digitized versions of the more recent papers. She loved leafing through the brown and brittle pages that revealed past times: ads for corsets and transistor radios and cans of Campbell's tomato soup for ten cents. Not that the computer versions didn't have advantages. The computer wasn't dusty, for one thing, and it was a lot easier and faster to find what you were looking for.

By lunchtime, Lucy had made an interesting discovery. Not only had Downeast Mortgage foreclosed on dozens of homes in the county, at least one of those properties was owned by a town employee.

Harbormaster Harry Crawford stood to lose the remaining

hundred and twenty acres of his family's waterfront farm, a property that the Crawfords had held for at least two hundred years. Lucy was willing to bet the amount owed on the mortgage was a mere fraction of what that property was worth. It was prime waterfront, perfect for a resort.

As the afternoon wore on Lucy discovered Crawford wasn't the only town employee to lose a unique piece of property. It seemed that Downeast Mortgage stood to profit handsomely from Marlowe's FinCom vote to reduce town employees' hours. Assistant building inspector Phil Watkins had lost his LEED-certified green home. Lucy remembered writing a story about the house, which had special shingles equipped with solar cells that provided electricity. Watkins had boasted that the house produced so much electricity, in fact, that his meter ran backward and the electric company was paying him. He'd been terribly proud of that fact and Lucy knew he must be heartbroken about losing his energy-efficient home.

Health department secretary Annie Kraus's loss wasn't so remarkable; her home was a simple two-bedroom ranch. Nothing fancy or special about it, except that it was her home. Natural resources officer Nelson Macmillan also lost his property, but it was only a building lot, probably bought as an investment. Or maybe he'd dreamed of building himself the perfect house there one day.

Lucy stared at the list she'd made and sighed. It seemed a sad record of shattered hopes and diminished dreams. She remembered when she and Bill had first moved to Tinker's Cove and settled into the ramshackle handyman's special they'd bought on Red Top Road. The place had a failing furnace, cracked walls and ceilings, peeling wallpaper, and no insulation in the walls except for seaweed and newspaper. She remembered going into baby Toby's nursery one morning and finding him cozy and warm in his footed sleeper, sound asleep in his crib, the covers dusted with snow that had blown through a gap in the wall. They'd worked hard, scraping and painting and repairing, and turned the old house into a cozy, attractive, comfortable home that was now worth many times what they originally paid for it. But it wasn't the thought of profit that had motivated them, it was the desire to make a home for their growing family.

When Lucy finally emerged from the morgue the office was empty and it was dark outside; as often happened when she did research, she'd lost track of the time. It was nearly five according to the regulator clock that hung on the wall above Ted's desk. She had to get a move on if she wasn't going to be late for rehearsal. When she got home she discovered Bill had dinner well in hand and was frying up hamburgers. Even so, the rehearsal was in full swing when she arrived at the Community Church, where some twenty or so cast members were sitting around a table.

"'Are there no workhouses?'" Bob was reading from the script. "'Has the treadmill stopped its useful work?'"

"Ah, Lucy, you're here," Rachel interjected. "Before I forget, I need to measure you for your costume. . . . What did I do with that tape measure? Let's take ten."

While Rachel searched for the tape measure, Lucy got settled, removing her coat and taking the seat at the table indicated by a copy of the script with her name in big block letters. There was also a bottle of water so she took a few sips while she flipped through the pages, looking for the scene they were reading. When she found the line Bob had been reading, she smiled. "Bob, I had no idea you'd be such a terrific Scrooge," she said.

"Isn't he wonderful?" Florence asked, leaning forward in such a way that her blouse fell open, revealing a good bit of lacy black bra. "I had no idea he could be so downright mean!"

There was something in the way she was batting her eyelashes, something in the almost Southern accent that had crept into her voice, that made Lucy wonder if this was *Gone with the Wind* rather than *A Christmas Carol*.

"Bob has hidden talents," Rachel said in a rather snappish voice. "Stand up, Lucy," she ordered, leading her away from the group for a modicum of privacy and slipping the tape around her bust. "I'm beginning to have second thoughts about Florence," she whispered, making a notation of the measurement.

Florence and Bob had their heads together on the opposite side of the table and were chuckling about something; Florence had her hand on Bob's arm.

"She's just friendly," Lucy replied. "Very friendly."

"I'm keeping an eye on her," Rachel whispered, turning to welcome another late comer. "Hi, Al," she said, waving at a middle-aged man who was wearing overalls under a plaid shirt-jacket and was carrying a toolbox. "Everybody, this is Al Roberts. He's going to be building our set."

Al set down his toolbox and gave everyone a wave. "I've got some drawings," he said, pulling some folded papers out of his pocket.

"Great," Rachel enthused. "Let's take a look at 'em."

Al took off his watch cap, revealing a very bald head, and came over to the table, where he spread out the drawings, then pushed his black-framed glasses back up his nose. "The way I see it," he began, "is three flats with different motifs. One is kind of domestic, suggesting paneling and a fireplace, for the interior scenes. Another flat will suggest Scrooge's office, and the third will be a sort of street scene, with a window that opens, for the scene when Scrooge discovers it's Christmas morning. The idea is that we leave them all in place for the entire show but highlight the appropriate backdrop with lighting."

"This is brilliant," Rachel said. "I love that it's so economical."

"You can add props as needed. . . ." Al suggested. "You know, a high desk and a stool for Bob Cratchit, a street lamp for the exterior scenes, a kitchen table for the Cratchit household, a four-poster for Scrooge . . ." He paused. "The only problem is, I'm not much of an artist. I can build the flats but somebody else has got to do the painting."

"Oh, I can do that," Florence volunteered.

"Florence is an artist, you know," Bob said, beaming at her. "She illustrates children's books."

"Great," Rachel said with a curt nod.

"Well, that's fine then." Al rose and gathered up his papers. "I'll get started tomorrow." He turned to Rachel. "Is there any problem getting in here? Do I need a key or anything?"

"It's usually open," she said. "If you're getting the lumber delivered, I think you better set that up with the church office. There are other activities here. The Ladies Aid probably wouldn't want their meeting interrupted."

"They might have tightened things up," Bob suggested. "After the fire, I mean."

The group of actors seated around the table all nodded gravely, and there were murmurs of "terrible" and "shocking."

"People are far too casual about safety," Marge offered. "My Barney's always telling me that folks don't lock their doors—they even leave the keys in the car and then they wonder how it got stolen."

"Locking the door wouldn't have helped Jake Marlowe," Lucy said.

"If you ask me, he got no more than what he deserved," Al said.

"What do you mean?" Florence demanded in a confrontational tone.

"Just that what goes around comes around," Al said. "He treated a lot of people badly, plus he didn't even take care of his own place, that's all. It's not exactly a secret."

Florence nodded. "I know, you're right. I told my uncle, that house was a fire waiting to happen."

"Your uncle?" Lucy asked.

"Ben Scribner. He's my uncle." There was a sort of embarrassed silence and Florence hurried to fill it. "He's scared witless, you know. He won't touch the mail. He's terrified he'll be next."

"I wouldn't be surprised if he was," Al said under his breath, as he put his hat on and pulled his gloves out of his pocket. "Like I said, I'll start on the scenery tomorrow—that's if everything works out with the delivery." He raised his gloves in a salute and turned to go.

"Okay, everyone," Rachel said, clapping her hands. "Back to work. Act one, scene three. Your line, Bob."

Chapter Five

"So how was the rehearsal?" Bill asked on Saturday morning. Lucy was sitting at the round golden oak table in her kitchen, a steaming mug of coffee in front of her, looking out the window. It wasn't an inspiring view on this cloudy morning. The trees were bare and the ground muddy from melting snow. A bright red male cardinal and a couple of chickadees were pecking hopefully at the empty bird feeder, and she made a mental note to fill it.

"It was just a read-through but it went really well. Bob is really talented; he's going to be a great Scrooge. And the guy who's playing Marley's ghost is a real hoot. He moans and wails: 'Mankind was my business. The common welfare was my business.' When he gets those chains rattling he's going to be really terrifying."

"So this is going to be a PG performance, too scary for Patrick," Bill said, filling his mug.

"What's too scary for Patrick?" Sara asked, shuffling across the kitchen floor in her fuzzy slippers and opening the fridge.

"I was just saying that the actor playing Marley's ghost is awfully good," Lucy explained. "And believe me, nothing has changed in the fridge since yesterday, so grab a yogurt and shut the door."

"Why don't you get the good yogurt?" Sara complained, reaching for the orange juice. "The stuff you buy is full of chemicals."

"It's light—it's only got ninety calories," Lucy said.

"You should buy the Greek kind. It's natural."

"It costs twice as much," Lucy said.

Sara slumped down in the chair opposite Lucy's and stared at her glass of juice. Bill pulled the frying pan out of the cupboard, making a clatter, and she covered her ears with her hands. "Do you have to make such a racket?"

Just then Zoe came thumping down the stairs in her boots. "Where's my French book?" she demanded in a loud voice. "Who took my French book?"

"It's where you left it, stupid," Sara growled. "And what do you need it for, anyway? It's Saturday, moron. There's no school, and why are you yelling?"

"Don't call me stupid," Zoe snarled. "I've got a study group meeting to work on a project for French class—Christmas in France—and I wasn't yelling."

"I think it's in the family room, on the coffee table. And, yes, Zoe, you were yelling. And, Sara, there's no need to be insulting." Lucy narrowed her eyes, remembering that when she went to bed last night Sara was still out. "Do you have a hangover?" she asked suspiciously.

"No!" Sara was outraged. "Why do you think that?"

"Just because you're awfully sensitive this morning." Lucy paused, watching as Bill started frying himself a couple of eggs. "You're under age—you shouldn't be drinking."

"I wasn't." Sara wrinkled her nose and stuck out her tongue at Zoe, who was stuffing her French book into her book bag.

Lucy turned her attention to her youngest. "Do you want some breakfast?"

"No. We're meeting at the doughnut shop," she replied, hearing a beep from outside and grabbing her parka. "Gotta go. See you later."

"I wish she'd eat breakfast," Lucy sighed, making sure the door was shut.

"I wish she'd go away," Sara muttered.

"What do you mean by that?" Bill demanded, sitting down at the table and glaring at Sara.

"Oh, nothing. She's just so annoying. So juvenile."

Lucy's and Bill's eyes met for a moment, then Bill dug into his breakfast, poking an egg with his fork and making the bright yellow yolk run out onto his toast. He popped a big piece into his mouth.

"Are you buying free-range eggs, Mom?" Sara asked. "You

should, you know. Those chicken farms are cruel. The hens are kept cooped up in cages, and they never get outside to act like chickens."

"I buy what's on sale," Lucy said. "Which reminds me, Bill. There's an opening on the FinCom now that Marlowe's no longer with us, and Pam was saying she thinks you would be the right person to fill it."

Bill swallowed. "How exactly did a discussion about eggs lead you to the FinCom vacancy?"

"It's obvious," Lucy said, shrugging. "I was thinking about the price of eggs and how expensive things are these days, and I was doing some research yesterday about town employees losing their homes because their hours have been cut by the FinCom. . . ."

"Yeah, rents are really crazy," Sara volunteered. "They've gone sky high."

Lucy and Bill both stared at her. "Rents?" they asked in chorus.

"What do you know about rents?" Bill demanded.

"Are you planning to move out?" Lucy asked.

"Well, sure," Sara admitted. "Of course I want to move out."

"You do?" Lucy asked.

"Why?" asked Bill.

"Because . . . I'm in college. I don't want to be living with my parents. I want to be independent."

"I know, it's tough," Lucy agreed. "But tuition is so high, we can't afford room and board, too. That's why Winchester is perfect. It's right here in town. And they gave you a good deal with that local student scholarship."

"Being a townie is like being in high school," Sara complained. "If I went in with some friends and got a job, a part-time job, I could afford an apartment. At least I thought I could. But the rents have really gone up. Amy and I looked at a place yesterday but it was over seven hundred dollars a month. And it was a dump! The bathroom was all moldy and the kitchen was really icky."

"I don't want you getting a job," Bill said. "Your grades will suffer."

"Most of the businesses around here are laying people off," Lucy added.

"I know," Sara admitted. "I stopped in at Fern's Famous Fudge the other day to see if I could get my old job back, but Dora said she was sorry but she doesn't need any help."

"Jobs are getting scarcer than hen's teeth," Lucy said.

"Now you're back to chickens," Bill said, wiping his plate with his last bit of toast.

"So what about the FinCom?" Lucy asked, pressing the issue.

"I'll think about it," Bill conceded.

"I think they need somebody like you. Right now they're tied. Pam and Frankie think town services are important, but the other two, the men, are budget cutters."

"What do you mean, *somebody like me*? Do you think I'll automatically join the tax-and-spend faction that wants to run the town into bankruptcy?"

"Well, you wouldn't vote to cut things, would you?" Sara demanded. "Not when so many people are suffering."

"Those needy people have to pay taxes, too," Bill replied. "What's the good of, say, keeping town hall open forty hours a week if it means people can't afford to pay their taxes?"

"But those cuts mean a lot of town employees can't keep their homes," Lucy said. "That's not good for the town's economy, either."

"Yeah!" Sara chimed in, glaring at her father. "The one percent is getting rich and the ninety-nine percent are fighting over the scraps, trying to survive."

Bill raised his hands in a sign of surrender. "I'm just saying being on the FinCom is a big responsibility, and if I do it I'm going to make up my own mind. It's a balancing act—I'm very aware of that—and I won't go in with a preconceived agenda."

Lucy was stuffing plates in the dishwasher. "Well, what's the point of doing it if you're not going to change things?"

"Yeah, Dad. Mom's right."

Bill grabbed his jacket off the hook and stared at them, as if he was about to say something. Apparently thinking better of it, he jammed his hat on his head and went out the door, letting it slam behind him.

"I wish you wouldn't upset your father like that," Lucy said, shutting the dishwasher.

"Me?" Sara's voice rose in pitch. "He's not mad at me. He's mad at you." She got up, leaving her empty juice glass on the table. "But don't give up, Mom. Seth says we've got to fight for our rights."

Then she was climbing the stairs to her room and Lucy picked up the glass and put it in the dishwasher. "I'm not your maid," she muttered, thinking, and not for the first time, that there ought to be a labor union for mothers.

In fact, that's what she said to Pam, when she met her later that morning. The two had agreed to spend the day selling ads in the show program to local businesses. Lucy hadn't sold her quota yet and was eager to get it done.

"A labor union for mothers, that's a really good idea," Pam said.

"We'd work to code. We'd have defined duties. No picking up after husbands and children. We'd demand they empty their pockets before putting clothes in the wash. . . ."

"And unroll their socks," Pam added.

"And if they didn't, we'd fine them," Lucy suggested.

"I like that idea," Pam said, smiling.

"You don't think I'm serious," Lucy said.

"Oh, I think you're serious, all right. But I don't think this idea will fly."

"It's a good idea, though," Lucy said, as they went into the liquor store where the clerk, Cliff Sandstrom, greeted them with a smile.

After asking about his family, Pam produced the program for last year's show, open to the full page ad Wine and Dine had taken out then. "The rates are the same—fifty dollars for a full page— and if you throw in another ten, which will go to the Angel Fund, you'll get a little angel printed in the corner."

Cliff seemed doubtful. "Angel Fund?"

"That's for Angie Cunningham. She lives here in town. She's got juvenile polycystic kidney disease and her family's having a rough time coping with medical expenses."

"Oh, right. I know Lexie. She said her hours have been cut."

"She doesn't work enough hours to get health insurance now."

"Doesn't she get COBRA?" he asked.

"Yeah, but she has to pay double what she's used to."

Cliff looked thoughtful. "That's tough," he said. "Look, I'll have to cut down the ad. I can only afford a quarter page this year." He opened the cash drawer and pulled out a couple of bills. "And here's five for the little girl. I wish I could do more."

"Every little bit helps," Lucy said. "Thank you."

"I've got a little girl Angie's age," Cliff said. "I'd go crazy if anything happened to her."

"I know how you feel," Pam said, writing out a receipt. "Thanks again."

The two friends worked their way along the street, but the story was the same everywhere. People wished they could do more, but this year they had to cut back. When Pam and Lucy reached the end of the street Lucy had satisfied her hundred dollar ad quota but had only raised twenty dollars for the Angel Fund. Next up, on the other side, was Downeast Mortgage.

"I don't know if Elsie will even let us talk to Scribner," Lucy said, as they crossed the street. "She's a bit of a pit bull."

"With lipstick?" Pam asked mischievously.

"And eye shadow, too."

But when they stepped inside the mortgage company's office, they found Elsie's desk empty. Apparently even Scribner didn't expect her to work on Saturday—or he was too cheap to pay overtime. He was there, however, working at his desk and keeping an eye on the reception area through the open door.

"What do you want?" he asked in a brusque tone, without looking up.

"Good morning," Lucy said in a cheery voice.

"Season's greetings," Pam added.

"It's not a good morning and I don't observe the season," Scribner said, making a note on the sheaf of papers he was studying. "And I don't have time to waste."

"We won't take much of your time," Lucy said, stepping into the doorway, but not daring to go farther without an invitation to enter his office.

"And we're very sorry about your loss," Pam added, joining her.

"Me, too, and now I've got twice as much work to do." He furrowed his bristly, untamed brows and glared at them through his wire-rimmed glasses. "Now, for the second time, what brings you here?"

"We're from the Community Players," Lucy began. "They're putting on *A Christmas Carol* this year—I'm actually playing Mrs. Cratchit—and we're selling ads in the show program. For fifty dollars . . ."

Scribner turned a page. "Not interested," he said, with a dismissive wave of his hand.

"This year is a little different," Pam said, taking a step forward. "The show is a fund-raiser for Angie Cunningham. She's a little girl who lives here in town and has polycystic kidney disease. Her family is struggling with high medical expenses. It's very difficult in this economy—"

"What business is that of mine?" Scribner demanded.

"Well, they're your neighbors," Lucy said, also taking a baby step forward and standing next to Pam. "They live here in town. And they're customers of yours. Surely it's in your interest to help them."

Scribner folded his hands on his desk and leaned forward. "My interest is charging interest—that's what I do." He laughed. "And I pay plenty in taxes, most of which goes to so-called *entitlements.*" He spit out the last word, as if it left a bad taste in his mouth. "What about Medicaid? And there's that children's health program, CHIP or SHIP or something. They should apply for that."

"I don't know the details," Lucy confessed.

"Those programs are worthy efforts, but they don't cover everything," Pam said. "And there are strict eligibility requirements."

"And so there should be!" Scribner exclaimed, smacking his fist down hard on his desk. "People have to take some responsibility for themselves, don't they? There are far too many freeloaders! Do you know half of the population doesn't even pay income tax? The government actually pays them! Earned Income Credit! How is that right?"

"There's a certain minimum people need to survive," Lucy said. "People who qualify for the Earned Income Credit make very little money indeed."

"Well, they should work harder then!" Scribner thundered. "Make 'em work for their benefits. Put 'em on the roads, picking up trash."

"I take it you're not interested in buying an ad," Pam said.

"You'd be right." Scribner revealed his teeth in something that was more like a grimace than a smile.

"And I presume you don't want to donate to the Angel Fund," Lucy said.

"Exactly right."

"We won't bother you further," Pam said.

"Good." Scribner dismissed them with a curt nod and they left, practically on tiptoes, closing the door quietly behind them.

Back outside, they shivered and pulled on their gloves.

"Wow, what a cheapskate," Lucy said.

"We shouldn't be judgmental," Pam said. She taught yoga and had studied Eastern religions. "He's having a difficult time coping with his loss."

"You'd think that would make him more understanding of others' problems, more compassionate."

"Grief takes everyone differently," Pam said.

"He didn't seem grief stricken to me," Lucy said. "He seemed put out that his partner died and left him with a lot of extra work to do."

"You could be right," Pam admitted, pausing in front of Fern's Famous Fudge. "I hear that all the time, you know. If people are poor it's their own fault—they should just work harder. But there's only so many hours in the day and wages have gone down, not up, in the past few years, and that's if you can even get a job."

"I blame those big box stores," Lucy said.

"You've got a point. They pay minimum wage and they don't give any benefits, and worst of all, they don't give people a full week's worth of hours. They keep them on call, have them come in when they need them, which means they can't get a second job because they don't know when they'll be called to work."

Lucy bit her lip, thinking this sounded a lot like her working conditions at the *Pennysaver*. Pam's husband, Ted, didn't offer health insurance, and she and Phyllis often joked that their wages made them more like volunteers than employees.

"I know," Lucy said. "People used to make a living working in the local stores, but those little businesses can't compete with the national chains."

"Look at the empty storefronts," Pam said, with a wave of her hand. "The Mad Hatter, Chanticleer Chocolates, Mainely Books—they're all gone."

Lucy lowered her voice and nodded toward the pink-and-white–striped curtains that hung in the windows at Fern's Famous. "Sara told me this morning she went in to see if they needed help for the holidays and Dora told her business is so bad she can't use her."

"Tell me about it," Pam moaned. "Ads are down at the *Pennysaver*. Fern's Famous cut their budget, and a lot of businesses aren't advertising at all. Ted's really worried. He doesn't know how much longer he can keep going."

Lucy's heart skipped a beat and her tummy tightened. As much as she complained about her working conditions, she loved her job. She couldn't imagine her life without it. "That's awful," was all she could say.

"Oh, don't worry. He's been drawing on the home equity line to make up the difference." Pam laughed. "We'll be fine as long as this recession doesn't go on too long." She paused, pulling the door open and holding it for Lucy. "And if real estate values recover."

"Hi, ladies," Dora said, greeting them from her spot behind the counter. "What can I do for you?"

Lucy inhaled the warm, seductive scent of chocolate and gazed at the vintage picture that hung on the wall as Pam launched into her spiel. If only life was like that picture, full of sunshine and chocolate and smiling cows and apple-cheeked children. But it looked as if it was going to be a long, hard winter in Tinker's Cove this year.

Chapter Six

When Lucy got to the office on Monday, Phyllis was at her desk but Ted hadn't come in yet. She didn't hesitate to unburden herself of the disturbing knowledge that had bothered her all weekend, following Pam's admission of financial trouble.

"I was out selling ads for the Community Players' program with Pam on Saturday," she began, unwinding her scarf and removing her jacket. "She told me some pretty scary stuff about our jobs."

Phyllis smoothed her sparkly, beaded cardigan over her significant bust and leaned forward, propping her elbows on her desk. "Really? What did she say?"

Lucy went over to the chest-high reception counter that separated Phyllis's work space from the rest of the office. "She said Ted is borrowing against their home equity line to keep the *Pennysaver* going—and she doesn't know how long they can keep doing it."

The thin lines that were all that remained of Phyllis's eyebrows rose above her reading glasses and she nodded, causing her double chins to quiver. "Now that you mention it, I'm not surprised. Ads have been way down." She plucked a copy of the *Pennysaver* from the pile on the counter. "See how thin it is? That's because there's hardly any ads. He's even got a full-page house ad touting lower ad rates."

"I feel really stupid," Lucy admitted. "Here I'm supposed to be a reporter and I never noticed. I've been so wrapped up in Christmas and the show and the kids I didn't notice what was going on right under my nose. Now it turns out I might not have a job—and at Christmas, too."

"That's when the pink slips always come out, which is pretty ironic if you ask me," Phyllis said.

"Right. Just when people's budgets are stretched to the max buying presents and fancy food and all the Christmas stuff. Even the electric bill goes sky high, what with all the lights."

Phyllis's expression was thoughtful as she examined her freshly manicured nails, done in Christmasy red and green stripes. "But if you're realistic, it's not much of a job," she said in a consoling tone. "My pay barely covers my manis and hair appointments."

Lucy scowled, acknowledging that she had a valid point. "If I get some overtime my check might cover the week's groceries and a tank of gas—but it's my job and I like it."

"I know. It's kind of fun. . . ." Phyllis paused, then added, "Some of the time. But face it, I can't remember the last time we got raises. And there's no benefits, none. It's not a real job like Wilf has with health insurance and a pension plan."

"I hate to rain on your parade," Lucy said, "but the postal service is in trouble, too. They're talking about huge layoffs."

"They'll work it out, they always do," Phyllis said, adding a long sigh. "Frankly, I'd be more than happy if he would take early retirement. I've been sick with worry ever since that bomb. He must've delivered it, you know. He handled it. What if it went off? It could've been him who got killed and not mean old Jake Marlowe."

Just then the little bell on the door jangled and Ted marched in, apparently full of vim and vigor. "What's up? How come you're gossiping? Don't you have any work to do?"

"Just keeping our fingers on the pulse of news in Tinker's Cove," Lucy said, hurrying over to her desk.

"And what exactly is so interesting this morning?" Ted asked, stuffing his gloves in the pocket of his parka.

"Cuts in postal service," Lucy said. "I think we ought to interview the postmaster, see what the effect would be. Talk to Country Cousins—they send out all those catalogs."

Ted hung up his coat on the old-fashioned stand that tipped

this way and that with each new addition. "Actually, that's a good idea, Lucy. Why don't you get on it?"

"Righto," Lucy said, booting up her computer. While it clicked and groaned with the effort of turning itself on, she wished she'd kept her mouth shut. Now, in addition to the town committee meetings that she routinely covered, she also had two stories that required a lot of research: foreclosures and postal cuts. Sighing, she reached for the phone, dialing the post office. She was listening to it ring, unanswered, when Wilf Lundgren arrived with the morning mail.

"Hi, sweetie," he greeted his wife, setting the bundle, neatly fastened with a big rubber band, on the counter.

"Hi, yourself," she said, slipping the band off and giving it back to him. "You can use this again."

"Sure will," he said, beaming at her. Wilf had a round face and his cheeks were red from the cold; he was wearing the regulation blue-gray postal uniform. "How's your day been so far?"

"Looking better now that you're here," she replied, with a wink.

"Cut it out, you two," Ted groaned. "You're making me sick."

"Party pooper," Phyllis snapped. She turned to Wilf. "Have you got a date for lunch?"

"Do now," Wilf said, turning to go.

"Hold on," Lucy cried. "Don't go. I need to talk to the postmaster, but nobody's answering the phone."

Wilf adopted a concerned expression. "What for? Do you have a complaint?"

"No, no. I'm just doing a story about these proposed service cuts, that's all."

"I can give you the postmaster's private line, but you've got to promise not to say I gave it to you," he said.

Lucy jotted it down. "Thanks."

Ted was pouring himself a cup of coffee. "How's everybody holding up over there?" he asked, taking a long drink. "Are they worried?"

Wilf shrugged and shifted his heavy bag from one shoulder to the other. "Trying not to," he said. "It's out of our control. There's nothing we can do about it. It's like that bomb that I delivered to

Marlowe. It coulda gone off in my bag—lucky for me it didn't. Maybe we'll get lucky and keep our jobs. Maybe we won't."

"Oh, don't talk about it!" Phyllis exclaimed, with a shudder. "It makes me crazy just to think about that thing going off."

"Yeah," Lucy agreed. "It's scary to think anybody could wrap up an explosive and mail it."

"You said it. It looked like a Christmas present. Even had a *Do Not Open Till Christmas* label." Wilf shoved out his lower lip. "He should've waited; he'd still be alive if he hadn't been such a greedy bastard."

"This isn't the first time there have been mail bombs," Lucy said. "And there was that anthrax scare. People don't realize that being a postal worker is so risky."

"It's the first time we ever had a package bomb here in Tinker's Cove and I sure hope it's the last," Wilf said, glancing at the regulator clock on the wall and heading for the door. "I gotta get going. I'm behind my schedule." He tipped his hat to Phyllis and added a wink. "See you later, babe."

Lucy was laughing; she'd thrown her head back and sent her wheeled desk chair scooting backward. "He's wild about you, Phyllis!" she hooted.

Phyllis pursed her lips primly, but her cheeks had gone quite pink. "Our anniversary's coming up."

"How long is it now?" Ted asked.

"Four years."

"And you're still like newlyweds," Lucy said.

"It's true," Phyllis said, as the fax machine went into action with a whirring sound. "I think it's because we married late. I don't think either one of us ever thought we'd find the right one."

"I guess you were smart to wait," Lucy said, as Phyllis handed her the fax.

"It's from the funeral home. Marlowe's memorial service is Friday afternoon."

"I don't imagine there's much of a body since he was already cremated in the fire," Ted said, causing the two women to groan.

"Who's paying for it?" Lucy wondered. "I don't think Marlowe had any family and I can't imagine Scribner would spend a penny he didn't absolutely have to."

"Unlikely," Ted agreed.

"There won't be much of a spread," Phyllis predicted. "Probably nothing but tea punch and lemon cookies. I don't know if it's worth going. There probably won't be much of a turnout. Marlowe wasn't very popular."

"Maybe not," Lucy said, "but chances are whoever sent that bomb will be there, and I'm going to be there, too."

"I don't think the bomber will be wearing a sign, Lucy, and your week is filling up," Ted said, going through his e-mails. "The state fire marshal's holding a press conference tomorrow morning, in Augusta. I've got that publishers' conference, so you'll have to cover it."

"What time?" Lucy asked, thinking she would need at least an hour to drive to the state's capitol.

"Ten."

"That's not too bad, but it will take most of the morning. I don't think I'll have time for those feature stories."

"Next week, then," Ted said, uncharacteristically accommodating.

On Tuesday, Lucy was on the road by eight-thirty, which turned out to be a very good thing. She made good time on the drive to Augusta, but her GPS completely failed her when she got to the office park where the state fire marshal's office was located. It was a maze of confusing roads and it took her some time before she located the public safety building, where the office was located. Once there, she encountered strict security and had to provide her credentials and allow her bag to be searched; only then was she allowed to pass through the metal detector.

It all seemed to be a lot of fuss about nothing. When she got to the press room she found only a handful of reporters had bothered to show up. The room was clearly set up for an important event: a large video screen stood behind a long table equipped with microphones, and chairs had been set out for at least fifty people. Lucy took a seat next to Bob Mayes, who was a stringer for the *Boston Globe*.

When state fire marshal Sam Carey took his seat, along with three or four others, he was obviously disappointed at the lack of interest. "This has been a remarkably successful investigation, and was conducted in record time," he announced. "I'm a big believer in giving credit where credit is due, and a good deal of credit goes to the Tinker's Cove Fire Department, which provided important evidence." He gave a nod to Buzz Bresnahan, the Tinker's Cove fire chief, who was seated at the end of the table.

Lucy caught Buzz's eye and gave him a little wave as she copied the quote in her long, narrow, spiral-bound reporter's notebook.

"I'm going to pass this over to Phil Simmons, the fire investigator who led the investigation into the fatal Tinker's Cove fire," Carey said, passing the mic to a large, heavy man with curly brown hair and a thick beard.

"Let me begin by saying this investigation was considerably simplified by the fact we knew the fire originated with an explosion. We have the incident records from the TCFD, which responded to a loud explosive blast at precisely oh-nine-one-six hours on November twenty-third. According to this report, the structure at Thirty-five Parallel Street was close to flashover point when the first engine arrived at oh-nine-twenty hours. This is consistent with observed test fire patterns in which a temperature of six hundred degrees was reached between one hundred seventy-three and two hundred fifty-six seconds."

Lucy did a quick computation, discovering that it only took a little more than four minutes for a fire to grow out of control.

"Response was hampered by the fact that the home owner was a hoarder and access to the home was blocked by falling debris. The fire was also fed by this debris, which included a large amount of newspaper. Responders had no choice but to allow the fire to burn and concentrated their efforts on protecting adjacent homes.

"I'll hand this over to Chief Bresnahan now, and he can give you his personal response to the situation."

Buzz Bresnahan was dressed in his official fire chief suit, the one he wore to all the funerals, and all that navy blue and gleaming brass made him look a lot more impressive than the plaid shirt and jeans he usually wore. He squared his shoulders and leaned forward to speak into the mic.

"The heat from the fire was already quite intense when we arrived and flashover occurred before we got any hoses operational. Access to the structure was blocked, but the initial explosion had blown out a couple of windows in the kitchen area, which allowed oxygen to feed the fire. This abnormally high fuel load along with the abundant oxygen made for a very hot fire. Added to this was the heavy load of hoarded materials on the second floor, which caused the second story to collapse." He paused. "I've been criticized for not taking a more aggressive approach to this fire but my first responsibility is to the firefighters and I was not about to endanger their lives. It was only a matter of minutes before that fire reached at least a thousand degrees and it would have been suicide for anyone to attempt to enter the structure."

Lucy wrote it down: *a thousand degrees*. She couldn't imagine such heat. Her oven went to five hundred degrees, tops. A thousand degrees would be twice as hot. No wonder the fire had been so destructive.

"I made the decision to let the fire burn itself out and then to do everything I could to recover what evidence we could for the state crime lab to analyze," he concluded.

"That brings us to the next stage of the investigation," Phil Simmons said. "Jim Cronin is with the Fire Debris Analysis Unit and he'll tell us what they were able to discover."

"People think most of the evidence is destroyed in a fire but that is not necessarily true," said Cronin, a tall, intense man whose hair was thinning. "We used two of our fire dogs, Blaze and Smoky. Blaze is trained to identify human remains and Smoky's specialty is accelerants. They were both successful. Blaze found a badly damaged body, which was identified by dental work as that of Jake Marlowe. Smoky indicated debris containing accelerant, and using chromatography we identified two sources: PETN, a nitroglycerin-style compound that we think created the initial explosion, and kerosene, most likely from a heater, which would explain the rapid ignition that took place."

"Now, as to the cause of death, I'm going to pass this over to Dr. Fred Singh, in the medical examiner's office."

Dr. Singh had a full head of black hair, thick glasses, and was wearing a white lab coat. "This was a very badly damaged body," he began. "I didn't have much to work with. I was able, however, to get a positive identification from the victim's dentist, who recognized bridgework that survived the fire more or less intact. Damage to remaining bone fragments indicate both hands were amputated by the blast. It was also possible to determine that there was considerable damage to the thorax, which leads to the conclusion that death was instantaneous due to the explosive blast, and not a result of the fire."

Amputation, bone fragments, not much to work with . . . the words rattled around in her head and she felt dizzy. *Death was instantaneous. . . .* That was a mercy, at least, but why would anyone intentionally and deliberately wish to inflict such a terrible fate on a fellow human being? It made her feel queasy, sick to her stomach, to imagine such evil.

"So this Marlowe was beyond saving, right?" she heard someone ask. It was Frank Harris, from the *Portland Press Herald,* seated just in front of her. She focused on the back of his neck, dotted with freckles, and the collar of his blue and green plaid shirt, and the nausea passed.

"Correct," Singh said. He looked around. "Any more questions?"

Lucy hoped not. She wanted to get out of there and into the fresh air, but Bob Mayes raised his hand and got a nod. "So this explosion was the result of a package bomb, is that right?"

Sam Carey decided to answer that one. "Yes. The postal service was able to provide us with information that a package was delivered to the house shortly before the explosion, and PETN is consistent with that type of device. The postal worker who delivered the package remembered it because it was wrapped in festive paper, and had a *Do Not Open Till Christmas* label. He said it weighed about a pound, also consistent with the force of the explosion."

Lucy wasn't going to think about it, wasn't going to entertain the possibility that it could have been Wilf, instead of Marlowe, who was killed by the bomb. Not sweet, kind Wilf, who loved Phyllis and was loved back. Not for even one second. She was shaking her head to banish the thought when Bob Mayes followed up with a second question.

"So is there some sort of Ted Kaczynski guy out there, sending mail bombs?" he asked.

"I sure hope not," Carey said, "but only time will tell. I can tell you this: the state police, assisted by my department as well as the local Tinker's Cove PD, are vigorously investigating this crime."

Chapter Seven

On the drive back to Tinker's Cove Lucy found herself rehashing the press conference, despite herself. The details she'd learned were truly horrible. She hadn't really thought about the damage a mail bomb could do to a human body, and now she knew more than she wanted to know. Worst of all, however, was the notion that some insane person might at this very moment be busy building more mail bombs and disguising them as Christmas gifts. It really took the fun out of Christmas, she thought with a shudder, when you were afraid to open the packages that were such a feature of the holiday season. Even worse, she'd done most of her shopping this year on the Internet, which meant a steady stream of packages was already coming to the house.

It was almost lunchtime when she reached Tinker's Cove, so she took a detour through the McDonald's drive-through, but when she studied the menu she had another surge of nausea and ended up driving on without ordering. Phyllis and Ted were both out, so she quickly typed up the press conference story, skipping over the most gruesome details. The *Pennysaver* was a family newspaper, she rationalized, and she didn't want to give anybody nightmares. It was bad enough knowing she'd have trouble sleeping tonight herself.

She had finished the story and was sending it to Ted's file for editing when Phyllis arrived, carrying several large shopping bags with the Country Cousins logo.

"Christmas shopping?" Lucy asked.

"Yeah." Phyllis set down the bags and unbuttoned her coat.

"Ted's at that conference today and I figured I might not get another chance to shop for Wilf. Togetherness is great—but I want his presents to be a surprise. I got him that fancy thermal underwear he's been talking about—and some snazzy pajamas."

"I'm all done, thanks to the Internet," Lucy said, wishing she could go home and take the dog for a walk, anything to clear her head and lift her mood, but that was out of the question so close to deadline. She needed to work on something that would catch her interest, so she decided to tackle the foreclosure story, and called Annie Kraus, who now worked part-time in the health department.

When she identified herself and explained the reason for her call, Annie was reluctant to talk. "I don't know, Lucy," she said. "I don't want everybody in town to know about my troubles."

"I don't have to use your name," Lucy said.

"People will know it's me," Annie objected.

"Well, if they already know, they might as well get the whole story," Lucy replied. "People need to know that low taxes come with a high price."

"That's a good one, Lucy," Annie said.

"Maybe a headline," Lucy said.

"Okay. Well, what happened to me and Larry is pretty much the same thing that happened to a lot of people. We found a cute little house that was just perfect for us. It was the cheapest house in town, but even so it was priced quite high. They were eager to help us over at Downeast, however, and signed us up with an adjustable rate mortgage. It started out at a very low interest rate but then it jumped up after a few years. By that time prices were already falling, the mortgage was for more than the house was worth, but we were managing to make the payments. Just managing. Then my hours were cut and it didn't make any sense for us to sacrifice everything to keep the house. The stress was taking a toll on our relationship, Larry and I weren't really getting along, so we decided to separate and I went back home to live with my parents."

"What about Larry?" Lucy asked, thinking that losing his wife and his home could certainly make a fellow angry. That anger might have motivated him to send the mail bomb.

"Oh, he reenlisted in the coast guard. He's on a high-endurance cutter somewhere in the Caribbean, fighting the war against drugs." She paused. "He's got a leave coming up and I'm hoping we'll get back together."

"I hope it works out for you," Lucy said, thanking Annie and crossing Larry off her list of suspects, feeling rather ashamed of herself for suspecting a man who was serving his country.

The next town employee on her list was Nelson Macmillan, who was now a part-time natural resources officer. When she called him he was more than happy to chat; he said he had a lot of free time on his hands these days.

"It was an investment," he said. "I was caught up in the real estate craze, and it seemed like a no-brainer. My 401(k) wasn't growing like I thought it should, certainly not like real estate, so I cashed out, took the penalty and tax hit, and put it all into a building lot. I had about seventy-five thousand and I financed another seventy-five and thought I'd retire a rich man when I got around to selling it." He chuckled ruefully. "It never occurred to me that I wouldn't be able to keep up the payments. I had seniority, terrific performance evaluations. What could go wrong?"

"The stock market took a dive, too," Lucy said. "Your 401(k) would've lost value, too."

"That's what I keep telling myself," Nelson said. "And I would've been okay, really, if I hadn't had my hours cut."

"So you must be pretty mad at the Finance Committee," Lucy suggested.

"They were faced with a tough situation, too. Tax revenues were down—what could they do? They had to balance the budget. I don't blame them."

Lucy wondered if he was really telling the truth. "You're very philosophical," she said.

"I don't know about that. Truth is, I'm better off than a lot of folks. I own my house free and clear, got enough for groceries and bills. I took a loss, sure, but it was a loss I could afford. The ones I feel sorry for are the folks who are losing their houses—they're the ones who are really hurting. Especially the ones with kids."

"You're right," Lucy said, putting a question mark next to his name. She suspected Nelson Macmillan might be a lot angrier than he was willing to admit.

One more call, she decided, and then she'd make herself a cup of tea. She dialed Frankie La Chance, her neighbor on Prudence Path, who was a real estate agent. Frankie would be able to tell her how the foreclosures were affecting the local real estate market, as well as the increasingly tight rental market.

Frankie answered on the first ring, which rather took Lucy by surprise. "You must be sitting by the phone," she said.

"You know it," Frankie said. "Calls are few and far between and I don't want to miss one."

"That bad?" Lucy asked.

"It's the worst I've ever seen," Frankie said. "Houses that were going for five or six hundred thousand are on the market for two or three, and nobody's buying. Believe me, now's the time to invest. Prices have never been lower, but nobody's got any capital."

"What about rentals?" Lucy asked. "My daughter says rents are going up."

"Is Sara looking for a rental?" Frankie asked, quick to sense a possible opportunity. "I'd be happy to help her find one."

Lucy chuckled, thinking it wasn't very long ago that Frankie spurned rentals, saying they were too much trouble for a small commission. "She'd like to get a place of her own but she doesn't have any money," Lucy said.

"She's not alone, that's for sure," Frankie said. "And she's right—rents are going up a bit, because people have to live somewhere when they lose their homes." She paused. "Is this for the paper?"

"Uh, yeah," Lucy said. "I'm doing a story on foreclosures. Do you mind if I quote you?"

"Oh, no, I'm grateful. Just be sure to mention my company, La Chance and Raymond Real Estate."

"Will do," Lucy said. "Thanks for your time." She added her notes from the call to her developing story, then got up to fill the kettle.

"Put in enough for two," Phyllis said. "I brought in some cocoa mix. With mini marshmallows."

"I better stick to tea," Lucy said, still not trusting her tummy. She unwrapped a tea bag and dropped it in her cup, tore open a packet of cocoa mix, which she poured into Phyllis's mug, then went over to the window to check the sky. Snow had been predicted but you wouldn't know it from the bright blue, cloudless sky. Of course, New England was known for rapid weather changes. If you didn't like the weather, people said, just wait a few minutes. Nevertheless, it seemed a shame to be stuck inside on such a fine day. She'd rather be out in the woods behind her house with Libby, cutting greens to decorate the house and searching for the perfect balsam Christmas tree.

The kettle whistled and Lucy filled the mugs; she was just giving Phyllis her cocoa when the police scanner went off. Lucy didn't recognize the code but she knew the address.

Once again it was Downeast Mortgage.

Abandoning her tea, she grabbed her jacket and headed out the door. The fire trucks were already racing down Main Street, and she followed on foot, figuring the car would only be an encumbrance.

She was out of breath when she joined the small crowd of bystanders that Barney Culpepper was urging to step back. The reason was clear: a gaily wrapped package with a *Do Not Open Till Christmas* label was lying on the sidewalk in front of the Downeast Mortgage office. She stared at it, eyes wide with terror, aware of the terrible damage it could inflict if it was what it seemed to be: a second bomb.

"We don't want a tragedy," he was saying, as a couple of firemen began unrolling a bright yellow *Do Not Cross* tape, creating a spacious perimeter around the package and moving the bystanders some distance down the street. "You don't want to be anywhere near that thing if it goes off."

"How long before the bomb squad gets here?" Lucy asked. The details she'd learned that morning about the bomb that blew up Marlowe's house were all too fresh in her mind and she eyed the package warily.

"Any time now. Lucky for us they were at a training session in Knoxport."

Lucy studied the package, a rectangular shape wrapped in red and green Christmas paper. "How'd it get here? It doesn't look like it was mailed."

"It wasn't," Barney said. "Elsie found it hanging from the knob in a plastic grocery bag—you know how people do, when the door is locked."

Lucy knew. She'd often done the same thing, leaving a requested book or returning a potluck dish, when nobody answered the door. "Do you really think it's a bomb?" she asked. "The bomb that killed Marlowe was sent in the mail."

"We're not taking any chances," Barney said, as the bomb team's special van arrived with a containment trailer in tow. The team, which consisted of four extremely fit-looking young men in blue uniforms and one German shepherd dog, assembled outside the vehicle. Soon one member was dressed in bulky protective padding, and the dog was also togged out in a flak jacket. Lucy snapped photos as the dog and its handler cautiously approached the suspect package.

It was a tense moment and everyone who was watching seemed to be holding their breath. When the dog froze, keeping his eyes fixed on the package, there was a general inhalation followed by a burst of panicked chatter. "It's the real thing," said one woman. "Oh my God," said another, white-faced with tension.

Then the dog and its handler withdrew to the van while another bomb squad member conferred with fire chief Buzz Bresnahan. Moments later the crew opened one of the van's doors and pulled out a metal ramp, allowing a remote-controlled robot to descend. All eyes were on the robot, watching as it approached the package.

Lucy worked her way through the crowd until she was beside Buzz. "That's quite a gadget," she said.

"They call it Andros," he said. "They got it with Homeland Security money. It's got an extendable arm and four video cameras."

Lucy studied the mechanical marvel, which ran on four wheels, had one arm, and a video camera for a head. "It looks like something a kid could make out of Legos," she said.

"No way. This is highly sophisticated machinery. It was just luck that the squad was so close today," Buzz said. "Otherwise we'd have had to wait for them to make the trip from Bangor."

"Pretty lucky." Lucy noticed Ben Scribner and Elsie, standing in a tight group along with other evacuees from nearby businesses. They were all wearing worried expressions and generally looking quite miserable in the cold. Only a few had thought to grab coats or jackets. Scribner was more warmly dressed than most, in a Harris tweed jacket, but he was visibly shivering. Lucy wondered if he was reacting to the chilly weather or actually quaking with fear. Elsie, who seemed capable of handling any challenge, was wearing a fur-trimmed parka and had pulled the hood up so that it covered her face. Maybe she was protecting her complexion from the cold, Lucy thought. Or maybe she wanted to hide her fear? Or perhaps she was concealing a different emotion?

Lucy's attention was diverted by the robot, which was advancing toward the package, moving at a stately pace and emitting a humming noise. When it was within a few feet it stopped and the arm was maneuvered so that it picked up the package. Then Andros rolled backward along the sidewalk until it reached the containment trailer, where the suspect package was deposited. The trailer was sealed, Andros returned to its compartment, and the bomb squad members, including the dog, returned to their van and drove off, leaving the yellow tape fluttering around an empty sidewalk.

Lucy got busy, requesting comments from a few of the bystanders. Dora Fraser, from the nearby fudge shop, was full of praise for the bomb team. "If that thing had gone off," she said, "my store would've been blown to kingdom come." Cliff Sandstrom, who worked at the liquor store across the street, shared his concern about a second package bomb. "I hope this isn't the work of some maniac," he said, furrowing his brow.

Lucy also wanted to get a reaction from Ben Scribner, but there was no sign of him on the street and when she tried the office door she discovered it was locked. She knocked, but nobody answered. Pulling out her cell phone, she called, but her call went to voice mail. She left a message, then walked back to the office, reviewing the photos in her digital camera on the way.

Ted was going to love them, she decided, especially the one with the dog. The handsome German shepherd was clearly focused on the package one hundred percent, performing the lifesaving work he was trained to do. She thought of her own Lab, Libby, who was really only interested in her next meal. If only she could be more like this heroic bomb-sniffing dog. She made a mental note to call the bomb team to get their names, including the dog's. Especially the dog's.

When Lucy got back to the *Pennysaver* office, however, she discovered she didn't need to make the call after all. Buzz Bresnahan had already e-mailed her a press release about the entire incident, with numerous attachments containing information about the bomb team, including the fact that the dog's name was Boomer. She sent a quick reply thanking him, aware that in the current financial climate every Tinker's Cove department head had to become a public relations expert. Buzz was defending his department from budget cuts, and he made it very clear in his press release that the bomb squad was funded by the state, assisted by the federal Department of Homeland Security.

Lucy made sure she included that information in the story, but put it at the end, leading with the human interest angle, the dog, Boomer. She was just winding up the story and thinking about heading home when Ted announced he had received an e-mail from the bomb squad.

Recalling Boomer's immediate response to the suspicious package, she wasn't entirely surprised to learn that it was discovered to be completely innocent of any explosives. It contained an assortment of sausages sent to Scribner from his insurance agent.

"It came prewrapped," said Bill Swift, of Swift and Chase, when she called him for a reaction. "I wanted to express my appreciation to my best customers. I never thought—I mean—I'm so sorry."

Ending that call, Lucy decided to follow up with the bomb squad after all. "What did you do with the sausage?" she asked.

"Oh, we ate it," came the reply, "but we gave most of it to Boomer. That dog really loves sausage."

Chapter Eight

Harriet Sigafoo, the organist, pulled out all the stops for the final hymn, "Just a Closer Walk with Thee," and the mourners gathered for Jake Marlowe's funeral on Friday morning were clearly eager to get moving as soon as they sang that last amen. Jake Marlowe hadn't been very popular in his life and Lucy suspected quite a few people had come simply to make sure the old miser was really and truly dead. Now that they had been assured that this was indeed the case, they were eager to see what was being offered in the collation the minister had invited everyone to partake of in the Fellowship Hall.

As she waited for her pew to empty, Lucy thought of the lines of the hymn: "When my feeble life is o'er / Time for me will be no more. / Guide me gently, safely o'er / To Thy kingdom shore, to Thy shore." Jake Marlowe had run out of time rather sooner than he'd expected, and Lucy wondered if he would have made some different choices if he'd known his end was so close. Perhaps he would have forgiven some debtors, hoping that his own sinful debts would be forgiven. Or perhaps not, she thought, remembering Elsie's warning about moral hazard. Perhaps he thought he was the righteous one and the pearly gates would open wide for him.

Personally, Lucy doubted it. At the very least she expected St. Peter would consign him to a lengthy spell in purgatory, to consider his moral lapses. Jesus said it was easier for a camel to get through the eye of a needle than for a rich man to enter heaven, and Lucy thought that was probably true in Jake Marlowe's case.

She assumed exceptions would be made for rich people who shared their wealth and tried to make the world a better place, people like Bono and Bill Gates. Jake Marlowe hadn't done that. In truth, his single-minded pursuit of wealth had caused a great deal of misery.

Joining the line of people who were filing into the Fellowship Hall, Lucy thought she caught a tantalizing whiff of Fern's Famous Swedish meatballs. Not what she expected, she thought, recalling Phyllis's prediction of tea punch and lemon cookies. But first, she had to negotiate the reception line.

"I'm terribly sorry for your loss," she murmured to Ben Scribner. He seemed quite subdued, she thought, murmuring a barely audible thank you. She suspected he was still quite shaken by the incident with the suspicious package; even though it turned out to be completely harmless it must have been a terrifying experience. He passed her along to his niece, Florence, who greeted her warmly and introduced her to Virginia Irving, Marlowe's ex-wife.

Lucy caught her jaw before it dropped; she never would have guessed that Marlowe was once married, and certainly not to someone as attractive as Virginia. She was an energetic fifty or so, with a fashionable short hairdo. Her skin glowed, her eyes were bright, and any gray hairs were covered with an auburn rinse. She was wearing a subdued greenish gray dress, but instead of the usual black pumps she was sporting a pair of very fashionable high-heeled ankle boots.

"Lucy and I have parts in *A Christmas Carol,*" Florence was saying. "I hope you'll come to the show."

"I'd love to," Virginia said with a warm smile. "It's my favorite Christmas story."

"Mine, too," Lucy said, moving along to check out the buffet table.

"Quite a spread," Marge Culpepper said, getting in line beside her. "I heard that the ex-wife is paying for it."

Lucy surveyed the chafing dishes filled with Swedish meatballs, flounder roll-ups with crab stuffing, chicken Kiev, and beef Stroganoff and concluded Marge was right. The long table seemed to go on and on, offering potatoes au gratin, rice pilaf, buttery noodles, mixed vegetables, a huge bowl of salad, rolls with butter, and then there was a separate dessert table with tea and coffee. "That must be the case," she said. "Ben Scribner would never spend the money for something this lavish."

"You're right about that. Mrs. Irving is the founder of this feast and she's a sweetie," Dora Fraser said, spooning a healthy serving of meatballs onto Lucy's plate. "I don't know what she ever saw in that miserable old codger, but it's thanks to her that we're going to have Christmas after all. Believe me, just last week I was studying my checkbook and figuring we could have either prime rib for Christmas dinner or presents, but not both."

"If Jake Marlowe knew about this he'd be spinning in his grave like a top," Marge said. "I hope they've got him down a good six feet."

"Considering the state of his body, I guess he'd be more like a dust devil," Dora said.

"You're terrible, Dora," Lucy said, adding salad to her plate.

"But you know she's right," Marge said, bursting into giggles.

Looking around, Lucy had to admit there were no sad faces at Jake Marlowe's funeral. She and Marge seated themselves at a table set for four and were soon joined by Pam and Sue. They were a merry group, chatting about their holiday plans. Lucy resisted the temptation to have a second helping of those famous meatballs, and decided to forgo the tempting desserts in favor of a cup of tea. She was just returning to the table when she encountered Virginia and Florence.

"Is everything all right?" Virginia asked. "Is there enough food?"

"Plenty of food and everything is lovely," Lucy said, "and to be honest, quite unexpected. You must have been very fond of Jake Marlowe."

"I was once, many years ago, but we grew apart," Virginia said. "He changed—that's why our marriage ended. But now that he's gone, I want to remember the man he used to be." She gave a sad smile. "My therapist would say it's wishful thinking."

"That's an interesting view," Lucy said, turning to Florence. "How is your uncle taking the loss? And on top of losing his partner, there was the bomb scare. . . ."

"He won't admit it, he's keeping a stiff upper lip, but he's really upset. Losing Jake was like losing part of himself, his right hand or something. They've been partners for thirty-odd years," Florence said. "And now the idea that somebody out there wanted to do Jake harm—that's really shaken him. He feels very vulnerable and that doesn't fit in with his world view. He's the one who's supposed to be in charge."

"It must be quite upsetting," Lucy said, privately thinking it was high time the old cheapskate got a reality check. "Has he had any more panic attacks?"

"No. Doc Ryder gave him some antianxiety medication but I'm not convinced he's taking it." She indicated her uncle, who was sitting by himself in a corner. "As a matter of fact, I think I better go and cheer him up."

"I'll come, too," Virginia said. "It was nice talking to you, Lucy."

Lucy sipped her tea, watching them cross the room. Noticing a photo collage depicting Jake Marlowe's life, she decided to take a look at it. She was curious about him, wondering why he'd become such a miserly hermit, and perhaps the photos would offer an explanation.

The first thing Lucy noticed was that someone had gone to a great deal of trouble to create the display, and she assumed that person was Virginia. The photos were beautifully mounted, in chronological sequence, and had captions written in a lovely calligraphic hand. The photo essay began with a graying photo of an infant tightly grasping a silver rattle, which must have been taken when Jake was only a few months old. That was followed with five or six snapshots, clearly taken together, of a chubby towheaded toddler pulling a little wooden wagon.

Studying the photos, Lucy wondered why Virginia had kept them. She was now Mrs. Irving, so she must have remarried. Once a divorce was final, she imagined most women were eager to get on with their lives and got rid of reminders of their failed marriage, even throwing away their wedding rings. Or maybe that was just in the movies, she thought, examining the pictures that documented Jake's progress through elementary school, prep school (*St. Paul's* read the flowing script), and college (*Dartmouth*).

At St. Paul's he was pictured arm in arm with three other teens, and at Dartmouth he seemed to be quite the life of the party, caught by the camera in company with numerous other glowing youths. The glow, Lucy suspected, came from plenty of alcohol.

But why had Jake changed from the sociable fellow he had been in his youth to the miser he became in later life? It was hard to believe the young man pictured at his first job with longish, curly hair, wearing a once fashionable suit with bell bottom pants, was the same person who lived in that ramshackle house stuffed with old newspapers. There was a clue, perhaps, in the fact that his first job was with a venture capital firm and he was smiling broadly and proudly displaying a fan of hundred-dollar bills in his hand.

There were only a few more photos in the display, and none from Marlowe's later life, confirming Virginia's confession that they had grown apart. Hearing her voice, Lucy looked for a way to get a bit closer to the corner where Virginia and Ben Scribner were sitting. Noticing the memory book set out on a nearby table, she bent over it and began turning the pages.

"Remember when you two met at Fitzhugh Capital?" Virginia was saying. "Old Fitz was a wonderful boss, wasn't he? Remember those fabulous dinners at Locke-Ober's? That Christmas party at the Ritz? The champagne corks were going off like popcorn!" She shook her head, her voice rueful. "When did it all start to go wrong?"

Ben shrugged and shook his head. "Jake was a good partner. I couldn't have asked for better. I'd trust him with my last penny."

"You know," Virginia said, "when I asked for a divorce it was because I thought he was having an affair with another woman, but it wasn't a woman at all. It was money. He fell in love with money."

"He was a good businessman," Ben said. "Nothing wrong with that."

"Oh but there is," Virginia said, placing her hand on Ben's. "There's more to life than business, and I'm afraid you're making the same mistake Jake did. He fell in love with money and it seems you've fallen into that trap, too."

"Nonsense!" Ben said, shaking off her hand and rising unsteadily to his feet. "You're being ridiculous." He waved his hand. "Look at all this! A waste of money!"

Virginia's face was white, and she bit her lip. "No, Ben, not a waste. The waste was Jake's life, hiding himself away in that big old house."

Ben glared at her, but all he was able to come up with in response was a big "Hmph!"

Lucy picked up the pen and wrote her name in the memory book, and when she finished she saw that both Virginia and Ben had left their seats. They weren't the only ones; the room was definitely emptying. Lucy plucked a single cookie from the dessert table and nibbled it, making her way to the coatrack. She was there, buttoning her coat, when Ike Stoughton joined her.

"I didn't expect such a good turnout," he said.

"Funerals are always popular in Tinker's Cove," Lucy said, drawing on long experience.

"Maybe so," Ike admitted. "But I suspect a lot of people wanted to make sure the old bastard was really dead—and the free meal was a bonus."

"There's that, too," Lucy replied, but she was talking to Ike's back. He'd turned, spotting Ben Scribner, and had crossed the small vestibule to approach him, actually cornering him. Ben was looking uncomfortable, but Lucy couldn't hear what Ike was saying, although he did appear to be asking for a favor of some kind. Whatever it was, Scribner wasn't pleased. He was shaking his head and trying to get around Ike.

Suddenly Ike's voice rose. "I tell you, I just need a bit more time. I can pay you next month."

"This is not the place to discuss business," Scribner snarled, glaring at him. "Call my office and make an appointment."

"I'll do that," Ike said. Realizing he was drawing attention to himself, he stepped aside, and Scribner scurried to the coatrack in a sideways move that reminded Lucy of a frightened crab running for cover. Once he'd pulled on his overcoat, he seemed to regain his usual arrogant attitude.

"I don't imagine it will make any difference," Scribner said, pulling his leather gloves from his coat pocket and slapping them against his hand. "A contract is a contract." Then Elsie, his secretary, joined him and the two left the hall, walking in the direction of the Downeast office.

"I bet they're going back to work," Ike said. "He wouldn't even close the business for one day in honor of his partner."

"Oh, that's the last thing Jake Marlowe would have wanted," Lucy said. "He'd expect them to carry on with business as usual."

Ike snorted in disgust. "Unbelievable," he said, shrugging into his bulky down jacket and holding the door for Lucy. They parted when the path met the sidewalk and she headed back to the office, enjoying the opportunity to clear her head in the crisp, cold air.

As she began the short, four-block walk along Main Street to the *Pennysaver* office, Lucy thought that Ike Stoughton was absolutely the last person she would expect to have financial problems. He had a successful surveying business and was known as the man to go to if you had a problem with a property title. Of course, the recession had taken a toll on business, especially real estate. Nevertheless, even foreclosures required accurate surveying, which should have provided at least some work for him.

Probably, she admitted, nothing like what he was doing before the recession, when real estate was booming. These days everybody, it seemed, was making do with less and Ike Stoughton was no exception. Unfortunately for him, Lucy knew, he had high expenses for his daughter, Abby, who had suffered a mental breakdown following the death of her mother.

Lucy paused at a corner, waiting for a car to pass, then crossed the street. When your income dropped you could cut back on some things, but not medical care, especially when your daughter was suicidal. Ike was committed to Abby, and he wanted the best for her, but that didn't come cheap. It was the sort of thing that could make for a motive, Lucy thought. Ike wasn't one to knuckle under to anyone and he might be just angry enough to do something foolish. If he sent the bomb, Lucy was sure he had only meant to scare Jake Marlowe and his partner, Ben Scribner—he wouldn't have meant to kill anybody. Just try telling that to a jury!

When Lucy reached the corner of Main and Sea streets the cackle of an amplified voice caught her attention. Glancing down the hill in the direction of the cove, she noticed a crowd gathered in front of Seamen's Bank and decided to see what it was all about. As she drew closer she recognized the speaker as Seth Lesinski, who was leading Winchester College students in another protest demonstration.

"We all know what the stock market bubble did to workers' savings, don't we?" he asked rhetorically. "It wiped out their retirement savings."

The kids in the crowd all voiced agreement.

"And we know what the housing bubble did to families, don't we? It made them homeless."

Lucy studied the faces of the demonstrators. Most were young, but there were a few older people, too. She recognized several professors from the college, and some of the kids, too, who were Sara's friends. They were clustered together, at Seth Lesinski's feet, and several girls were gazing at him raptly, hanging on every word he uttered. One of them, she realized, was Sara. And Sara, she happened to know, was supposed to be in class. She began worming her way through the crowd, intending to give her daughter a piece of her mind.

"Well, the next bubble is student debt and it's crippling the economy," Lesinski proclaimed. "Student debt is now greater than all the consumer debt combined. Not a problem, you think. What did they tell you and me? That student debt is okay because you'll be able to get a good job and pay it back. Sounds good, doesn't it, if you can get a job. But that's a big *if,* with real unemployment at eighteen percent. So what's going to happen when you and I can't pay back our loans? It's the next big bust and our generation is going to start out bankrupt!"

Now Lucy was behind her daughter and she tapped her on the shoulder. Startled, Sara whirled around. "Mom! What are you doing here?"

"That's what I want to know!" Lucy exclaimed. "What are *you* doing here when you ought to be in class?"

"Mom, what does it matter? We're all gonna be broke. Missing a class or two isn't going to make a bit of difference. It's not like I'm going to be able to get a job, anyway. I might as well give up now, instead of getting thousands of dollars deeper in debt."

Lucy couldn't believe what she was hearing; it went against

everything she'd taught her children. Her kids had to go to college. It was the surest way to a successful career. She'd been so disappointed when Toby dropped out, and so pleased when he'd decided to go back to school and get his degree. There had been times when her oldest daughter, Elizabeth, also wanted to drop out, but Lucy had coaxed and cajoled and convinced her to stick with her studies. She'd graduated from Chamberlain College in Boston with honors and was now in the Cavendish Hotel chain's executive training program.

"Don't be crazy!" she said, yelling over the noise of the crowd. "Look at Elizabeth. She's got a great job."

"Seamen's Bank is ripping you off!" Seth proclaimed, and a number of the kids in the crowd yelled out in agreement. "They're getting rich and you're getting poor!"

"Come on, Sara," Lucy urged. "Let's get out of here."

Sara shook her head. "No, Mom. I'm staying. This is important to me."

Flummoxed, Lucy sucked her teeth. There wasn't anything she could do. She couldn't grab her daughter by the hair and drag her off to class. The only thing she could do was threaten her. "I'm going to tell your father," she said, through a clenched jaw. "Don't think I won't!"

Sara rolled her eyes, then turned her attention to the leader of the protest. "We demand amnesty!" Seth Lesinski yelled, raising his arm and unleashing a wave of shouts. "Amnesty! Amnesty! We demand amnesty!"

Lucy's emotions were in turmoil and her head was ringing from the noise. It was time for her to leave. She slipped through the crowd and began climbing the hill, shaking her head. What was she going to do about Sara? Even worse, what if she was right? Maybe it was crazy to spend tens of thousands of dollars to get her a bachelor's degree when she could spend a few months learning medical billing or massage therapy and have a salable skill. Maybe she should join the coast guard, thought Lucy, recalling a TV commercial and thinking of Annie Kraus's husband.

"Careful!" a voice warned, and Lucy lifted her head, realizing she was about to walk into a lamppost. Embarrassed, she turned and recognized Phil Watkins, the assistant building inspector. He was a friendly guy and they always exchanged pleasantries when she stopped by town hall.

"Thanks," she said with a rueful smile. "I was distracted, wasn't paying attention."

"Happens to all of us," he said, shrugging. "Did I see Sara down there?"

"Oh, yes," Lucy said. "She's become a social activist." She paused. "Were you demonstrating or watching?"

"Demonstrating," Phil said. "Face it, since they cut my hours I've got plenty of time on my hands—and plenty of student loans. If it wasn't for the student loan payments I wouldn't have lost my house." He winced. "Or maybe not. Maybe I'm just kidding myself, but they sure didn't help."

"That house was a labor of love, wasn't it?" Lucy asked. She knew Phil had built his LEED-certified green home himself, banging in every nail.

"Yeah." He nodded. "It's the only LEED house in town. It's energy efficient, built with recycled and sustainable materials."

Lucy knew that; she'd written a story about the project, which was not only kind to the environment but also beautiful and livable. "It's a shame you couldn't work something out with Downeast Mortgage."

Phil scowled. "You know what really sticks in my craw? It's the way Scribner made out like a bandit. That house is worth plenty, even in this depressed market. It's entirely green and a lot of folks, especially rich liberal types, the Prius crowd, are willing to pay for that. I did the work, I had the vision to make it happen, and Scribner's going to make a lot of money off my vision and hard work."

"That's the way it is," Lucy said, with a rueful smile. "The rich get richer and the poor get poorer."

"You said it! I heard that bastard's already sold Macmillan's lot for a fast food restaurant. . . ."

This was news to Lucy. "You mean that building lot of Nelson's?"

"Yeah. Turns out the state is rerouting part of Route 1 and that scrappy bit of pasture has suddenly become prime real estate. Once again, Scribner's going to make a killing." The driver of a green pickup truck honked and Phil looked up, recognizing a friend. He raised his arm in a wave and the truck pulled to the side of the street. "Well, nice talking to you, Lucy. Take care."

Then he hopped into the truck, joining his friend, and the two drove off together. The demonstration was still going strong, so Lucy pulled her camera out of her bag and snapped a few photos before heading back to the office. As she walked, she thought about what Phil Watkins had told her. Downeast Mortgage was certainly profiting from the recession, making a fortune off other people's misfortunes. That wasn't a crime, but that didn't mean it was right. It was no wonder there was a lot of bad feeling toward the company, and its principals, Marlowe and Scribner.

The one person she thought ought to be angry, Nelson Macmillan, had seemed quite philosophical about his loss. Here he'd bought a piece of property that had increased dramatically in value, but he hadn't been able to keep up the payments and he'd lost it. Why wasn't he angry? He stood to make a fortune, if only he'd been able to keep it. And then it hit her. Of course. As the natural resources officer, he would have had inside knowledge of the planned rerouting. His office would have been consulted as a matter of course, to make sure no protected wetlands or endangered species were involved. He'd had inside knowledge that he'd used to buy the neglected acreage, anticipating how it would increase in value.

It was no wonder he seemed so untroubled about his loss. He probably figured it was no more than he deserved, considering how he'd bent the rules in the first place. Or maybe, she thought, he was simply pretending not to be upset. Maybe he was hiding a deep anger, which he'd held close while he plotted his revenge.

Chapter Nine

Phyllis and Ted hadn't returned from the funeral when Lucy got to the office and she figured she knew what was keeping them. Phyllis was probably still gabbing with her friends from the knitting circle and Ted might well be taking advantage of a state senator's appearance at the funeral to discuss some upcoming legislative matters. Considering the senator's reputation, that discussion would most likely be continued in the Irish pub down by the cove and would probably take the rest of the afternoon.

It didn't matter. They weren't needed at the moment. The paper came out on Thursday morning and, except for a few callers with complaints, Friday afternoons were generally quiet. It was too early to start on next week's news cycle, so Lucy usually went through the press releases, looking for story ideas. Phyllis filed the notices by date in a bulky accordion file as they arrived, so Lucy took the file over to her desk and booted up her computer. While she waited for the ancient PC's clicks and grinds to subside, she checked her phone messages, discovering that the postmaster had called, informing Lucy that she would be in her office until 1:30 p.m.

According to the antique clock on the wall it was only twenty-five past, so Lucy quickly made the call. Sheila Finlay wasn't pleased at her timing.

"I was just leaving . . ." she grumbled.

"This won't take long," Lucy promised.

"Oh, all right," Sheila consented, sounding as if she thought she was doing Lucy a big favor.

Of course, the shoe was actually on the other foot: it was Lucy who was doing Sheila a favor. Publicizing the effect of the proposed cuts might well prompt public outcry, which could save the postal workers' jobs.

"What do these cuts mean for Tinker's Cove?" Lucy asked.

"The mail will come a day or two later, I guess," Sheila said. "They're closing the nearest distribution center, so the mail will take longer."

"What about jobs?" Lucy asked.

"Well, we'll lose some, I suppose." She paused. "I'm not at liberty—"

"Can you give me a percentage?" Lucy coaxed.

"I don't think so."

"I've heard some of the smaller post offices will be closed. Is there any danger that we'll lose our post office?" As in most small towns, the Tinker's Cove post office was an important gathering place where people caught up with their neighbors.

"Anything could happen," Sheila said.

Lucy felt like banging her head on the desk. "Do you think it will?" she persisted.

"I don't know." There was a long pause. "I have to go now."

Lucy still had a long list of questions she wanted to ask. "Before you go, what can you tell me about the package bomb . . . ?"

"I don't have anything to say about that."

"Well, thanks for your help," Lucy said, thinking that Sheila hadn't actually been any help at all. Maybe Ted got something from the state senator. Maybe she should call their congressional representative. Maybe she should just write up the inch or two she got from the postmaster and move on to something else.

She began leafing through the press releases, discovering that this Christmas season was going to be much like the last. Every church in the county was holding a Christmas bazaar, the ballet schools were all presenting *The Nutcracker,* and the Historical Society was holding a cookie sale and open house at the Ezekiel Hallett House. And, of course, the Community Players were presenting *A Christmas Carol.* Perhaps there was a story there, if she could come up with a new angle that would convince Ted.

She jotted down an idea or two, then ran out of steam. It was really quite chilly in the office and she was thinking about putting up the heat and debating whether it was worth risking a scolding from Ted, when and if he ever showed up. Maybe she should just make herself a cup of tea and put her coat back on. Maybe she should just get out of there, she decided, shoving her chair back under her desk. She still needed a few more interviews for the foreclosure story and a phone call wasn't nearly as informative as a face-to-face encounter.

Stepping outside, she discovered the sun had disappeared behind clouds and a brisk breeze was blowing off the cove, but Lucy didn't mind. She enjoyed being on the move, working on a story, and she hadn't spoken to Harry Crawford yet. She liked the harbormaster; most everybody did. He was pleasant and affable and generally helpful, unlike some public employees she could mention. He took his job seriously, aware of the dangers faced by those who ventured out to sea. It was one thing to take a pleasant sail on a warm summer day and quite another to chug out past Quissett Point on a dark, cold winter morning to check lobster traps, and Harry did everything he could to make sure that those who went out came back safely to shore.

Nevertheless, she had to admit that Harry had a heck of a motive for killing Jake Marlowe. His family had owned their oceanfront farm for more than two hundred years, raising sheep on the rocky pastures that sloped down to the cove. Now, Downeast Mortgage was selling off that two hundred and twenty acres in a foreclosure auction scheduled a few days after Christmas.

She'd felt sick herself when she saw the ad copy, and it wasn't even her land, so she could imagine how Harry and the other members of his family felt about losing the property. They might well have wanted to send a message, and Harry certainly had the skill to build a bomb. As a farmer and harbormaster he had developed the expertise to keep engines and other equipment working, and knew all about electric circuits. As for explosives, well, that information was all over the Internet.

But knowing Harry as she did, Lucy doubted he would have intended to kill Jake Marlowe. If he had sent the bomb, it would have been a desperate measure designed to frighten Jake, not take his life with a huge explosion and deadly fire.

Reaching Sea Street, Lucy was relieved to see that the demonstration in front of Seamen's Bank was over and the crowd was gone. The steep road that led down to the cove and the town's harbor was clear, only a few cars and trucks parked along the curb. Lucy paused at the top of the hill for a moment, taking in the view she loved from here. The cove hadn't iced over yet and a few lobster boats bobbed at anchor on the blue water. Others had already been taken out and put in storage, shrouded in shiny white shrink wrap and set on jacks in the parking lot.

There was very little activity today, no clanks and hammering, no buzz of engines. Only a little column of smoke rose from the Irish pub, where a cheerful, welcoming fire was kept burning all winter.

Lucy sniffed the pleasant scent of wood smoke as she made her way through the parking lot to the harbormaster's shed. The shed was about the size of a tollbooth, with windows on all sides. It was also empty, closed tight, with a notice on the door announcing the new, reduced hours.

Of course, she thought, feeling rather stupid. She knew Harry's hours had been cut and she should have checked the new schedule on the town's official website before she trudged all the way down here. She was turning to go when somebody called her voice and, shading her eyes with her hand, she noticed Gabe Franco at the fuel dock, pumping gas into his lobster boat.

"Hi, Gabe," she yelled back. "Howzit going?" Gabe's face was deeply tanned, even in winter, and he was wearing yellow oilskin overalls.

"Okay," he said. "Were you looking for Harry?"

"Yeah."

"Well, you know his hours were cut."

"It slipped my mind," Lucy admitted.

"Kind o' crazy, if you ask me. We're having the mildest winter in years and plenty of guys are still lobstering. And there's the oyster farm—they're out there nearly every day, harvesting. There's a big demand this time of year. But I guess they just don't understand at town hall about us folks down here at the harbor." He cocked his head toward Main Street. "There isn't anybody on that Finance Committee that makes a living working the water, not one."

Lucy knew he was right. Pam taught yoga part time, Frankie La Chance was a real estate broker, Jerry Taubert owned an insurance agency, and Gene Hawthorne was an innkeeper. The working people, those who actually worked with their hands, didn't have a representative. "You're right," she said. "Maybe you should offer yourself now that there's a vacancy."

"Not me," Gabe said, glancing at the sky and waving his arm at the wide open space all around him. "I couldn't take being stuck indoors at some meeting when there's all this out here."

"I think you're on to something," Lucy said, with a smile. She gave him a wave and headed back up the hill, listening to the wild calls of the herring gulls wheeling high overhead.

As she climbed up the steep incline she thought about Jake Marlowe's impact on the town, deciding it was extremely negative. Not only had he cut town employees' hours and benefits, reducing their income, but that lost income had hurt local businesses. The cuts also meant reduced services, which working people like Gabe and the other fishermen counted on. Even Bill, she remembered, had been complaining about how long waits for building inspectors were slowing his progress. And that was before you even took the foreclosures into account.

The foreclosures were the greatest source of discontent, however, and the likeliest motive for the package bomb. Phil Watkins, for example, was angry about losing his LEED-certified home and was quite outspoken about it. She wasn't sure if he was angriest about losing the house, or the fact that Downeast Mortgage was profiting handsomely from the foreclosure. Probably both, equally, she decided.

Then there was Nelson Macmillan, who had lost the opportunity of a lifetime. It wasn't every day that a scrappy piece of land littered with cast-off junk became the perfect spot for a fast-food restaurant, and he'd have made a bundle if he'd been able to hold on to it. But now Downeast Mortgage was collecting that bundle and Nelson had lost his retirement savings and was looking at a ruined credit rating. It was enough to make anyone think seriously about taking revenge.

She thought of Ike Stoughton, a proud man who'd humbled himself to beg Ben Scribner for a little more time to pay back his loan. Scribner hadn't been open to the idea; he'd been his usual high-and-mighty self. But Ike was only asking for a bit of time— there was no doubt that he would pay back whatever he borrowed. Everybody was feeling the squeeze, everybody was coping with payments that dribbled in slowly, or partial payments that came with promises to pay the rest "when I can." Lucy had seen the scribbled notes piling up on Bill's desk, IOUs for work he'd done in the last few months.

Bill wasn't taking those chits to small claims court, nor was he asking for liens on his debtors' income or property. Nobody was, except for the big national banks and Downeast Mortgage. Lucy had seen Dot Kirwan at the IGA wave away the offer of a post-dated check, telling a cash-strapped customer to pay when he could. And she'd seen Phil Crawford, Harry's uncle, do the same thing at the Quik-Stop, when a young mother with two little kids strapped into her SUV didn't have quite enough cash to pay for her fill-up.

What difference would it make to Ben Scribner, she wondered, if he worked out new deals with mortgage holders instead of heading straight to court? She thought of Harry Crawford's family farm, going on the block. What good did it do? The Crawfords were losing a source of income, and perhaps more important, family pride. And for what? Ben Scribner certainly didn't need any more money—he had plenty.

Reaching the top of the hill and turning onto Main Street, she noticed a new sign had gone up. The Curl 'n' Cut beauty salon was now for sale, "price negotiable."

Well, thought Lucy, she hoped all these foreclosures were making Ben Scribner happy, since they were certainly causing a lot of misery for everyone else. And then it occurred to her that, of all the people in town, it was Ben Scribner who stood to profit most from his partner's death. Did Ben Scribner send that package bomb to Jake Marlowe? Lucy pressed her lips together, grimly. She wouldn't doubt it, not for a minute.

Chapter Ten

The sky was already darkening when she got to her car, the short winter afternoon almost over before it began. She decided to head home and grab a few minutes for herself, perhaps stretch out on the family room couch with a magazine. She had another rehearsal tonight and had to admit these late evenings were taking a toll. Ordinarily, she'd be joining the rest of the family at the town's annual carol sing, which was scheduled to take place that evening, but she figured the show had to go on, which meant she'd miss it this year.

She was almost home, approaching the corner of Bumps River Road, when she heard a siren. She checked her rearview mirror and saw the town ambulance with lights flashing, coming fast, so she pulled over to let it pass. When it made the turn onto Bumps River Road her heart took a dive. She feared little Angie Cunningham had taken a turn for the worse. She decided to follow and see if she could do anything to help, perhaps give Zach or Lexie a ride, or stay with the younger children.

Her car bounced down the badly paved road, which led to the town dump and was lined with a mix of modest homes and the sort of unsightly businesses that town planners preferred to hide away, out of sight of tourists. There was a rather untidy masonry yard, filled with pallets of bricks and piles of rocks, a transmission service and auto body shop where a number of damaged cars awaited repairs, and a fenced in area boasting a shiny new cell phone tower.

Like the other houses on the road, the Cunninghams' house

was a modest affair, a one-story ranch with an old-fashioned picture window on one side of the center doorway and a couple of smaller windows on the other. It was decorated for Christmas, however, with homemade wreaths on all the windows and a plywood Santa with sleigh and reindeer on the roof. A lighted Christmas tree was in the picture window.

Lucy pulled into the yard and parked next to a stack of lobster pots, taking care not to block the ambulance. She was just getting out of the car when the door to the house opened and the EMTs came out, carrying a stretcher containing a small, blanketed figure. Lexie followed, clutching her unfastened coat around herself and climbing into the ambulance with her daughter. Her face was white with tension, her hair uncombed. She'd probably spent the day anxiously nursing her sick daughter, finally giving in and calling for help.

Lucy blinked back tears, watching this little drama. She was so lucky, she thought, that her children were all healthy and so was her grandson, little Patrick. Oh, they'd had the usual ear infections and colds—Bill broke a leg falling off a ladder, and they'd had a bit of a struggle getting Elizabeth's asthma under control— but for the most part they'd all been remarkably healthy. On the rare occasions when they had been sick or injured, they'd made speedy recoveries. They'd never had to deal with a life-threatening disease such as Angie's kidney disease, and the very idea made Lucy's heart skip a beat. She could only imagine how awful it would be to face the possibility every day that you might lose your child.

The ambulance was leaving and Lucy saw Zach was standing in the doorway, with the two younger children on either side of him. She gave him a yell and hurried across the yard. "Is there anything I can do?" she asked, reaching the front steps. "Do you need anything?"

The ambulance had been silent as it climbed Bumps River Road, but the siren wailed as it made the turn onto the main road and they could hear it as it sped to town and the cottage hospital.

"Oh, hi, Lucy," he said slowly, blinking as if coming out of a coma. Lucy realized he hadn't noticed her until now. "Thanks for stopping."

She repeated her offer of help. "Do you need anything?"

He hadn't shaved this morning, and his plaid flannel shirt and jeans looked as if they could use a wash. "No," he said. "We did a big shopping yesterday."

She could hear loud music punctuated with booms and whizzes coming from the TV inside. "Do you want me to stay with the little ones so you can go to the hospital?"

He shook his head, slowly and carefully, as if he was holding the weight of the world on his shoulders and was afraid of dislodging it. "No, thanks. I'm better here."

"It's no trouble for me to stay," Lucy said.

"Go on." He gave the kids a little shove. "Your show's on TV." They scampered off and he lowered his head. "Truth is, Lucy, I can't take the hospital. Lexie'll call, keep me posted."

"I understand," Lucy said. "Let me know if you change your mind."

"Thanks, I will," he said, closing the door.

Lucy made her way through the yard, past the faded plastic toys and the stacks of lobster pots, past an overturned skiff, and got in her car. As she put the key in the ignition and started the engine it occurred to her that of all the people who lived in Tinker's Cove, the Cunninghams had probably suffered most at the hands of Jake Marlowe and Ben Scribner.

Not only had Lexie lost much-needed income when her hours were cut at town hall, but the Cunninghams also lost their employer-subsidized health insurance because she no longer worked the required number of hours. There were state programs for low-income people, but Lucy knew that these plans had strict eligibility requirements and she also knew that Zach's income from lobstering put them a hair above the income limit. Lucy's own family's health insurance premiums were almost two thousand dollars a month, and they didn't have any preexisting conditions like the Cunninghams. Lucy wasn't quite sure when the new federal law concerning preexisting conditions went into effect, and that, she thought, was part of the problem. The whole health care system was a mess, a confusing jumble of copays and coinsurance and eligibility requirements that kept changing, and now the Cunninghams were at its mercy. Perhaps that was the worst part, she thought, the sense of confusion and uncertainty the system generated. You never knew what amount you were responsible for until you got the form that explained the benefits from the insurance company, and in her experience it was always more than she expected.

If only Lexie had been able to keep her full-time position . . . The family would have the town's gold-plated plan, and they wouldn't have to worry about Angie's medical expenses. When you considered that Downeast was also threatening to foreclose on their little ranch house, the house they'd decorated so gaily for Christmas, it was more than enough to make a person very angry—possibly angry enough to pack a bomb into a holiday mailer and send it off to the person who'd taken away the family's medical plan.

Reaching the end of Bumps River Road, Lucy turned onto the town road and looked back at the Cunninghams' house one last time. Zach was a handy guy; she had no doubt he'd made the plywood Santa on the roof. He'd done a good job, too. Santa was freshly painted, every inch a jolly old soul, and the sleigh and reindeer were finely detailed. She had no doubt that Zach could put a bomb together, but she couldn't quite believe he would. She thought of his resigned expression as he watched the ambulance leave, and his admission that he couldn't cope with the hospital. If anything, she thought, he seemed a beaten man. Events had overtaken him and he could barely keep up with the demands of day-to-day life; he didn't have the time or energy for sinister plots.

When Lucy got to the rehearsal that evening, the church basement was a hive of activity. The cavernous basement room with a stage at one end, which was only occasionally used, had a dusty smell, a scent that Lucy always associated with amateur theatricals. Al Roberts was at the rear of the stage, banging away with a hammer, constructing scenery, and she was pleased to see that two of the three planned panels were already in place. Marjorie Littlejohn and Tamika Shaw were at the piano, working out music for the show. Sue and Pam had set up ironing boards in a rear corner and were pressing costumes and hanging them on rolling garment racks. Lucy greeted them, and asked if they'd found her costume yet, and Pam held up an extremely large blue dress with a lace collar and little black buttons.

"I think it will need to be taken in," Lucy said.

"Not too much," Sue said, casting a critical eye over Lucy's figure. "A dart or two will do it."

"She's terrible," Pam said with a laugh. "This was made for Holly Wigmore, and she's enormous."

"Maybe you can find something else," Lucy suggested. There seemed to be no shortage of costumes; she noticed a number of boxes and trunks piled up in the corner.

"We'll try," Pam said. "Or maybe you've got something that will do."

"All she ever wears is jeans," Sue scoffed.

"They're comfortable," Lucy said, noticing Rachel joining a little group of actors who were clustered on stage. "I better go. I think they're getting started."

"Break a leg," Sue said.

When Lucy joined the group, she discovered they were talking about Angie Cunningham. News traveled fast in Tinker's Cove, where everybody knew somebody on the rescue squad.

"Poor little mite," Marge Culpepper was saying. "What a shame she has to go through all this. She's spent more time in the hospital than at home."

"I can't imagine what her parents are going through," Bob said.

"And now she's been transferred to Portland. It's going to be very difficult for them," Rachel said. "They've got the twins at home, and there's the price of gas, not to mention meals."

"Portland? When did that happen?" Lucy asked.

"Around dinnertime," said Pete Winslow, a nurse at the cottage hospital who was playing Scrooge's nephew Fred. "She needs a kidney transplant and she needs it soon. We can't do it here in Tinker's Cove, so she's got to wait it out at the medical center. The problem is finding a good match."

"What about her parents?" Lucy asked.

"Of course they tried to donate, but neither one is a good match," Pete said.

"Maybe we could have one of those drives," Rachel suggested. "Ask people to volunteer to be screened. I'd be happy to help organize it."

"You've got quite a lot on your plate already with this show," Bob said, placing a hand on her shoulder.

"Donating a kidney seems like an awful lot to ask of a person," Florence said, with a toss of her head. "I mean, it's not like dropping a buck or two in the Salvation Army bucket. How many people would actually volunteer to go through an operation and give up one of their kidneys?"

"You might be surprised," Pete said. "A lot of people want to donate for a loved one, but they're not a good match, so they're setting up these exchanges where the organs are swapped out."

"What do you mean?" Marge asked.

"It's like this," Pete said. "Say your husband needs a kidney, but you're not a good match. Somebody else, say in California, could use your kidney, so you donate your kidney and they fly it out to California. Meanwhile, somebody in Dubuque's brother needs a kidney, and that family member is a match for your husband. So your husband gets the Dubuque kidney, and maybe the California kidney goes to Iowa. I've heard of chains that involved more than twenty kidneys."

"That's amazing," Lucy said.

Florence put her hand on Bob's arm. "There must be quite a lot of complicated legal issues involved in something like that, aren't there?" She licked her lips and leaned toward him, as if hanging on his every word.

Bob cleared his throat. "I don't think so. The whole organ donation thing has become pretty standardized from a legal point of view."

"I've heard of people selling their organs," Florence said, widening her eyes. "Can you imagine?"

Rachel threw a glance in Lucy's direction, then clapped her hands. "Let's get started," she said in a sharp tone. "This is a rehearsal, not a gabfest."

Marge looked at her watch. "Oh, my goodness, is this the time?"

"Seven-thirty," Lucy said.

"The caroling starts at eight, you know," Marge reminded.

Rachel's jaw dropped. "Is it tonight?" The annual carol sing at Country Cousins was a long-standing town tradition and she knew that nobody wanted to miss it.

Marge nodded. "Barney's on special patrol, making sure people can cross the street safely."

"I've been so busy I forgot all about it," Rachel confessed. "No point continuing here. We'll have to reschedule the rehearsal." This announcement was met with approval from the cast, and people started gathering up their coats and hats.

"You're just canceling the rehearsal?" Florence asked, clearly displeased.

"It's the carol sing," Al said. "Everybody goes." He tilted his head toward the door, where most of the cast members were making their departures.

"But there's so much to do for the show," Florence protested, placing her hand on Bob's arm. "Couldn't we at least go through our lines?"

"You've only got one line," Rachel snapped, losing patience. *"Uncle, Fred will be so pleased you've come."*

Bob stepped away, going over to the coatrack and busying himself getting Rachel's coat. Lucy thought he'd made a wise decision.

"Are you sure?" Florence asked. "I thought there was more. I thought Fred's wife was a leading part."

"No, just that one line," Rachel said. "Trust me. Everything will get done. We've got plenty of time."

Almost everyone had left by now. Lucy had joined Bob, who was holding Rachel's coat. Al was standing by the door, where the panel of light switches was located, waiting to turn them off.

Florence wasn't convinced. She was looking at the unpainted flats that Al had erected on the stage. "If you don't mind, I think I'll stay and work out a plan for painting the scenery."

"That's really not necessary," Rachel said.

"I'm not much of a singer," Florence said. "And besides, I won't have time tomorrow. I have to take Virginia to the airport."

"Suit yourself," Rachel said, slipping into her coat and buttoning it.

"Don't forget to turn out the lights," Al said.

The four of them left the hall together, walking the short distance to Country Cousins. There a crowd had already gathered in front of the quaint country store that still sold penny candy, calico by the yard, and cheddar cheese cut from a huge wheel. The porch boasted two benches, one marked *Democrats* and the other *Republicans*, and in fine weather they were filled by old folks who enjoyed debating the issues of the day. The store itself hadn't changed with the times, but the business model had. Country Cousins had grown far beyond the original store and had become a huge catalog and online retailer, with shiny new state-of-the-art headquarters located out on the town line, near the interstate.

Nobody was thinking of that, however, as they greeted Barney and hurried across the road to join friends and neighbors and family gathered around the bonfire that was burning in a steel drum. Lucy spotted Bill and Zoe and squeezed through the crowd to join them. "Where's Sara?" she asked.

"At the college," Bill said.

"SAC meeting," Zoe added.

Then Dick Kershaw blew the first notes of "Deck the Halls" on his cornet and the singing began. It was a fine, clear night, not too cold. Gazing around at the happy faces, Lucy raised her voice in the songs she'd sung every year since she was a child. Some earnest volunteers had printed up booklets with the words to the carols, but nobody needed them, except for the tricky later verses to the "Partridge in a Pear Tree" carol. Then they were all singing the last song, "Silent Night," and almost everyone was gazing skyward, at the bright stars that dotted the sky.

"Oh, darn!" Lucy exclaimed, as the last note ended.

"What is it?" Bill hissed, his voice a mixture of concern and annoyance. "You're spoiling the moment."

"Sorry," she whispered back. "It's just that I left my bag at the church."

"No problem. I parked the truck over there."

"What about you, Zoe?" Lucy asked.

"I'm meeting my friends for hot chocolate at the coffee shop," she said, already on the move. "I've got a ride home."

"Not too late," Lucy said.

"Promise," she called over her shoulder, running to greet her girlfriends. Lucy watched them exchanging hugs and air kisses with all the sophistication of Hollywood starlets.

Bill slipped his arm around Lucy's waist as they made their way back to the church, on the other side of the town green where white lights had been strung in the trees. "That was fun, wasn't it?"

"It's my favorite Christmas thing," Lucy said. Then she added, "Well, except for the presents."

They were laughing together when they reached the church parking lot, where there were only three vehicles: Lucy's SUV, Bill's truck, and Florence's little Civic. Bill got in his truck and started the engine, but promised not to leave until Lucy had retrieved her purse and started her car.

Lucy went inside, calling out Florence's name so she wouldn't be startled. There was no reply, but all the lights were on, except those on the stage and the kitchen, which were dark. Lucy thought Florence must have left, forgetting to turn off the lights, but then she noticed her coat was still on the rack. Lucy spotted her forgotten purse on the table where she'd left it and picked it up, then decided to see if Florence was in the bathroom. A quick check revealed that the ladies room was empty, so Lucy returned to the hall and called Florence's name again. This time she got a reply, a faint moan that came from the stage area.

Lucy immediately ran to the switches and flicked them all on; the kitchen and stage area were now brightly illuminated. The stage was different from before, she realized. The big scenery flats that Al had constructed were no longer standing in place. They'd fallen, and Florence was trapped beneath them.

Chapter Eleven

"I'm coming!" Lucy cried, rushing up the steps to the stage. But when she tried to lift the flats off Florence she found they were too heavy for her to raise by herself.

"Hang on! I have to get help!" she cried, getting a moan in response. Then she was dashing through the hall and out to the parking lot, calling Bill. "I need help!" she yelled. "Call nine-one-one."

"What's the matter?" Bill was out of the truck and running across the parking lot.

"The scenery fell on Florence. She's trapped and I think she's hurt."

Then they were back inside and Bill was hoisting the first of the three flats that had fallen, one on top of the other like huge dominoes. Florence's hand and arm became visible. Then he lifted the second flat and her head and shoulders were revealed. Lucy was calling 9-1-1 and the ambulance was on its way when he got the last piece of scenery off the trapped woman, who had been knocked to the floor, face down.

"Don't move," Lucy warned. "You might have hurt your back."

"Thank God you came," Florence said in a weak voice. "I was afraid I'd be here forever."

Lucy reached for her hand and held it. "It's all right. The rescue squad is on the way."

"I think I'm really okay," Florence said. "It was just that I couldn't get out from under."

"What happened?" Bill asked, examining the flats. Each one was made out of two sheets of plywood nailed to a frame of two-by-fours. "Did you try to move them or something?"

"No," she said, her voice small.

Lucy gave her hand a squeeze. "There'll be time to figure out what happened later." They could hear the ambulance siren coming closer, and then the flashing red and white lights could be seen in the windows. The door opened and the EMTs took charge, slipping a back board beneath Florence and transferring her to a gurney. Then they were off, leaving Bill and Lucy in the empty hall.

"How could that happen?" Lucy asked.

"Beats me," Bill said.

"Maybe they were only set up temporarily, not properly secured," she suggested.

"Seems like a foolish thing to do, what with the rehearsals and people coming and going," Bill said.

"What if I hadn't forgotten my bag? What if we hadn't come back?" she asked, as they reached the doorway.

"It would've been a long, cold night for Florence," Bill said, switching off the lights.

On Saturday morning Lucy phoned Florence to see how she was doing, but her call went unanswered. She tried calling the cottage hospital, fearing that Florence had been admitted, but the operator said there was no Florence Gallagher listed as a patient. Somewhat reassured, she headed out to the grocery store, where it seemed she was spending a lot of time and money lately.

Her grocery bill was always high at Christmastime, she thought, with all of the extra baking supplies she needed. She yanked a cart out of the corral and headed for the produce department, pausing at the holiday display of nuts and candied fruits to grab a bag of pecans and a tub of mixed fruits, wincing at the cost. She picked up a bag of potatoes and, noticing they were "buy one get one free," added a second, then headed for the carrots. She knew that chuck roasts were on sale and was planning to make a pot roast for an old-fashioned Saturday-night dinner, and her recipe required carrots. The problem was whether she could get away with the cheaper conventional carrots, loaded with chemical fertilizer and pesticides, or buy the expensive, organic variety that Sara insisted on. Would Sara even notice? She probably would, Lucy thought, because she often snacked on carrots. Reluctantly, she picked up the two-pound bag of organic carrots, priced at a phenomenal six dollars.

By the time she was ready to check out she was crossing her fingers that she had enough cash in her wallet to pay for the cartload of food, which included fancy Greek yogurt, cage-free eggs, hormone-free milk, gluten-free bread, and organic chicken. Maybe, just maybe, she was thinking, it would be more economical to subsidize Sara's desire to move out.

She was adding a chocolate bar to her cart, telling herself that today of all days she really deserved the jumbo size, when she spotted Florence at the end of the aisle. She was leaning heavily on her cart and was moving slowly, obviously in pain.

"Nothing broken?" Lucy asked, hurrying to her side.

"I was lucky," Florence said, with a tight little smile. "It could have been so much worse. I got off with a few bumps and bruises."

"I wouldn't exactly call it lucky," Lucy said. "It would have been better if it didn't happen at all."

"I was lucky that you guys came and found me. I was afraid I'd be trapped there forever."

"I forgot my bag," Lucy said. "I'm glad we were able to help." She paused. "Do you remember what happened?"

"Not really," Florence admitted. "I was sitting at Bob Cratchit's desk on the stage, sketching out some ideas. Then I heard a slam, like a door or window blowing open, and felt a cool draft, and it seemed to come from backstage. I had that sense you get, you know, that you're not alone, and got up to investigate and . . . well . . . you saw what happened. I was crossing the stage to check the back door and they all just fell on me."

From what Florence was saying, it seemed that an intruder must have entered the hall, perhaps intending to damage the scenery. Or maybe that person had planned to attack Florence. But why would anyone do that? "You have no idea who came in?" Lucy asked.

"I don't even know if somebody was there or not. Maybe it was my imagination," Florence said.

"The church is really old and needs some work," Lucy said. "I bet a window just slipped down—it happens in old buildings."

"You're probably right," Florence said, grimacing with pain. "And stage accidents aren't uncommon. I went on Facebook this morning and quite a few of my actor friends said they'd had similar accidents." She lowered her voice dramatically. "The stage is a dangerous place."

"Life's dangerous," Lucy said, adding that chocolate bar to her cart.

"Chocolate! That reminds me—I need some baking cocoa for my chocolate cheese cake. I always make one for my open house." Her eyes widened. "I do hope you'll come. I have it every year on Christmas Eve and this year I'm inviting the whole cast. It's going to be a blast." She pursed her lips, as if savoring a secret. "Guess what? Uncle Ben actually said he might come, which is amazing since he always flat-out refuses. It would be so good for him. We have lots of food and plenty of wassail and it's just a terrific party if I do say so myself. Will you come?"

"I'll have to check with Bill, but thanks for the invitation," Lucy said. She wasn't sure she wanted to go. . . . Come to think of it, she wasn't really friends with Florence and she really didn't like the way Florence had been behaving toward Bob. And the notion that Ben Scribner might be attending was hardly an inducement. She turned her cart, heading for the checkout. "Take care, now. What do they say? RICE: Rest, ice, compression, and elevation?"

"Something like that." Florence put her hand on Lucy's arm. "You know, I hope you didn't think me uncaring last night, when everybody was talking about Angie Cunningham's need for a kidney."

Actually, Lucy had thought Florence had been rather insensitive but wasn't about to admit it. "Oh, no. It's a very personal sort of thing. Not everyone wants to be an organ donor, not even after they die."

"It's not for me," Florence admitted, "but I do wish the best for that poor little girl. I'm planning to make a donation to the Angel Fund."

"Sooner would be better than later," Lucy advised. "From what I've heard the Cunninghams are really up against it."

"I'll do it today," Florence promised, slowly rolling her cart toward the deli counter.

When she got home, Lucy put the groceries away and began browning the chuck roast. While it sizzled in the casserole, she found herself wondering about Florence's relationship with her uncle, and thought it odd that Florence was so pleased that the old Scrooge might come to her party. It just went to show, she thought, that you never could tell about people. She thought that Scribner and Downeast were a blight on the town, but Florence was hoping to rekindle family connections with him. Lucy gave voice to a little "hmph," doubting that she would be successful.

The scent of browning meat filled the kitchen and Libby had heaved herself off her cushion and was standing next to Lucy, actually leaning her shoulder against Lucy's thigh. "There'll be some for you," Lucy told the dog, wishing that the human family members would show the same appreciation for her cooking. Dinnertime hadn't become a full-fledged war zone, not yet, but Sara was stockpiling arms and wasn't above firing off the occasional warning shot.

That night, predictably, Sara opened fire and sent a missile whizzing into the demilitarized zone. "I found a place to live that's actually affordable," she said, helping herself to mashed potatoes. "It's only two hundred dollars a month—that's probably less than you're spending to feed me, right, Mom?"

Lucy thought of her grocery bill and nodded. "Those carrots are organic," she said, "so you better eat some. They cost almost as much as the roast."

"What does two hundred dollars cover? Does it include food?" Bill asked, holding up the carving knife and fork.

"Yes! Two hundred dollars would be my share of the monthly expenses."

"That doesn't sound very realistic," Lucy said. "Is it an apartment or a house? Where is it?"

"I'm not sure. I'd be going in with a group. It must be a big place 'cause it's a big group."

"Like a hippie commune?" Zoe asked. "That would be cool."

"Who's in the group?" Bill asked.

"Oh, Seth and some others from SAC."

Lucy's eyes met Bill's across the table. Beneath the table, Libby was noisily licking her chops, anticipating her dinner.

"Will you have a room of your own?" Bill demanded.

"What about your studies?" Lucy asked. "I'm afraid you'll spend all your time in meetings, planning demonstrations and making posters."

"Are there going to be a lot of guys?" Zoe asked.

Bill set the carving utensils on the side of the platter. "I think I need to see the place. . . ."

"And we need to know exactly who's living there," Lucy added.

Sara's eyes were filling with tears. "I knew you'd be like this," she said, pushing her chair back and standing up. "You just don't understand! Changing the system is more important than getting good grades! It's not like there's any jobs for grads anyway." She threw her napkin on the table and marched off angrily; they could hear her stamping up the stairs and then slamming her bedroom door.

"She didn't ask to be excused," Zoe said, in her good-girl voice.

Lucy looked at her youngest child, so like an angel with her cheeks like peaches and her big blue eyes. It was just a matter of time, she thought, before she lost her innocence and became a combatant, taking up arms against parental authority just like her sisters and brother before her.

Monday morning found Lucy hard at work at the *Pennysaver* office, pounding away at the keyboard to finish up her story about how Downeast Mortgage profited from Marlowe's Finance Committee vote. This was one story that really ticked her off and her fingers were flying as she recounted how some of the town employees whose hours were cut and who also happened to have mortgages with Downeast were now losing their properties to foreclosure. At the last minute she decided to call Will Carlisle, the mortgage officer at Seamen's Bank, and discovered that his bank's policy was to offer forbearance to struggling mortgage holders.

"The thing is, if they come in before they miss a payment, we'll let them pay interest only for a few months, and that's often all that they need. If the situation continues—say the mortgage holder is facing long-term unemployment—we'll work with them and renegotiate the loan so it's affordable. We're a local bank and we don't see foreclosures as beneficial to the community or to the bank," he said.

"That's terrific," Lucy said. "It's a shame more banks aren't like yours."

"We're small, and the board members are local businessmen. That means we can be a lot more flexible than some too-big-to-fail outfit."

"What did you think of the demonstration the other day—the kids protesting student loans?"

"That's a different kettle of fish," Carlisle said. "Our hands are tied by the feds, but we're trying to figure something out. It's a huge problem. . . . These kids didn't realize what they were getting into. Everybody told them college debt was okay. Personally, I won't let my child take out loans for college. Bella's going to have to live with what we've saved and start at the community college."

"I'm glad to hear you say that," Lucy said, delighted to find her own views reinforced. "We're sending Sara to Winchester. She's got a scholarship and she's living at home, at least for now."

"Smart," Will said.

Lucy thanked him for his time and finished the story, which she sent to Ted for editing. That job done, she busied herself with other stories and didn't think about Downeast again until Wednesday morning when Ted sent the foreclosure story back to her, heavily edited. All the references to Downeast Mortgage had been deleted.

"I can't believe this," she declared. "I worked hard on this, and it's all true. I've got the facts."

"It could be coincidence," Ted said. "Marlowe can't explain himself. We don't know that he had any intention of foreclosing on those town employees."

"Well, what if I call Ben Scribner and ask him? I'll get a comment from him."

"He's hardly going to admit anything of the sort," Ted said.

"That's okay. We'll have him lying on record. It'll be obvious to everyone, because of what's happened. He can say that Downeast never intended to benefit from the FinCom vote, that it was only an effort to control town expenses, but nobody will believe him."

"I don't want you calling him, Lucy." Ted wasn't making a suggestion, he was giving an order.

"Why not?"

"Because it would be harassment. He's just lost his partner, under the most horrible circumstances. . . ."

Lucy thought of all the times Ted had made her call grieving survivors of auto accidents and house fires, insisting that she was only giving them an opportunity to honor their deceased family members. "But, Ted, you always say it helps people through the grieving process if they can talk. . . ."

"No. We're running the story without mentioning Marlowe's vote or Downeast Mortgage. This is a story about how the recession is affecting our town."

"But Seamen's Bank—"

"I know," Ted said. "And I wish to heaven I'd gone to them instead of Downeast when I needed money."

"Oh," Lucy said, suddenly understanding the situation. "I get it."

He shoved his chair back and grabbed his coat, leaving without a word of explanation. Lucy and Phyllis both watched him go.

"It's deadline day," Lucy said.

"He's never done that," Phyllis said. "He's never walked out on deadline."

"Do you think he's coming back?" Lucy asked, her throat tightening.

"I don't think so."

"What are we going to do?"

"You can put it together, Lucy," Phyllis said, sounding like a cheerleader. "You've seen him do it enough times."

"I appreciate your faith in me," Lucy said, "but I don't know where to begin."

"With the first page," Phyllis suggested.

"Okay." Lucy took a deep breath. "What we need is a big photo on the front cover, maybe kids on Santa's knee, something that says Christmas is coming. . . ." she said, thinking aloud as she opened the photo file.

Even as she worked to lay out the paper, clicking and dragging and occasionally swearing in a struggle to arrange ads and stories in what she hoped was an acceptable format, Lucy kept hoping Ted would return. The little bell on the door remained silent, however, and it was nearly two hours past the noon deadline when she finally shipped the file to the printer.

"Good work, Lucy," said Phyllis, who had been watching over her shoulder. "That page-one photo of the little Mini Cooper with a Christmas tree on top is real cute."

"I hope it's okay with Ted," Lucy fretted.

"He's the one who walked out, leaving you holding the bag," Phyllis said with a sniff.

"I'm not sure he's going to see it that way," Lucy said, arching her back and stretching. She felt completely wiped out, her neck and shoulders tight with tension, and she had a low-grade headache. "I'm done here."

Leaving the office, she headed for home where she recruited the dog for a walk. Libby was thrilled at the prospect of running through the woods, and Lucy needed to soothe her frazzled emotions. The sky was milk white, and it seemed as if snow might be coming, but Lucy inhaled the cold, crisp air and marched along, swinging her arms and humming Christmas carols. What was it with that "Little Drummer Boy"? Once you heard it, you were stuck with it. *Rum-pa-pum-pum!*

When she returned home she felt much better. She stretched out on the family room sofa with a magazine and next thing she knew Zoe was asking what she should make for dinner.

Rousing herself, Lucy threw together a meat loaf while Zoe made a salad and set the table. Tonight was the FinCom meeting and Lucy figured she'd fortify Bill with his favorite dinner. After they'd eaten, Lucy and Bill left Zoe in charge of clearing up. Lucy figured she might as well take advantage of Zoe's willingness to cooperate while it lasted.

The meeting took place in the town hall's basement conference room, which was set up rather like a courtroom. The four committee members sat at a long bench equipped with microphones and name plaques. Facing them were several dozen chairs set in neat rows for citizen observers; most of the chairs were empty. At the rear of the room a TV camera was set up, operated by members of the high school CATV Club. As promised, Ted had assigned a freelancer, Hildy Swanson, to cover the meeting since both he and Lucy had conflicts of interest. Hildy wrote the popular Chickadee Chatter bird column.

Lucy and Bill seated themselves in the middle of the room, receiving welcoming smiles from board members Frankie La Chance and Pam Stillings. The other two members, innkeeper Gene Hawthorne and insurance agent Jerry Taubert, ignored them, busy comparing favorite golf courses in Hilton Head. Hawthorne, who was chairman, called the meeting to order promptly at seven o'clock. The first order of business was the reading and approval of the minutes from the last meeting. Once that was done Hawthorne moved on to the first item on the agenda: filling the temporary vacancy left by Jake Marlowe's death. When he asked if there were any volunteers, Bill raised his hand and so did Ben Scribner, whom they hadn't noticed because he had entered late and seated himself behind them.

"Very good," Hawthorne said. "You both understand that this is a temporary position, and that a permanent board member will be chosen at the town election in May?"

Both Bill and Scribner said they understood that was the case. Hawthorne then asked them to each explain why they wanted the job and what they thought the proper role of the Finance Committee should be. He asked Scribner to begin.

"Well," he began, placing both hands on the back of the chair in front of him and getting stiffly to his feet, "I'm volunteering to fill in for my deceased partner, Jake Marlowe. We were partners for a long time and it seems the right thing to do. We agreed on most things and I think he'd want me to take his place."

This was met with nods of agreement from the board members, which Lucy thought was a bad sign for Bill's prospects.

"As you well know, Jake believed that the least government was the best government, and by that he meant the least expensive government. Elected officials have a responsibility to the tax-payers to keep expenses as low as possible, especially in these tough economic times. People are struggling to pay their property taxes as it is, and raising them would create an impossible burden for those who are living on fixed incomes. If I'm appointed, I will be a strong advocate for responsible fiscal policy and I will carefully examine the proposed budget with an eye to cutting wasteful spending."

"Thank you," Hawthorne said. He turned to his fellow committee members. "Any questions?"

They shook their heads, indicating they didn't have any questions. No wonder, thought Lucy, as Scribner's opinions were well known. She wouldn't be surprised if he managed somehow to foreclose on town hall and sell it to the highest bidder.

Hawthorne was busy making a note; when he finished he asked Bill to address the same questions.

"Thanks for giving me this opportunity," he said, by way of beginning. "I've lived here in Tinker's Cove for almost thirty years. We moved here when I quit my job on Wall Street to become a restoration carpenter. I'm self-employed, but I studied business in college and have a strong background in finance."

Lucy thought she heard somebody make a "hmph" sound. It came from behind them and she suspected Scribner was indicating that he found Bill's qualifications unimpressive. Bill was not deterred, however, and continued speaking.

"I have a somewhat more progressive view than Mr. Scribner when it comes to town finances. It seems to me that the recent budget cuts are having a negative effect on the town's economy. Christmas spending generally boosts local businesses, but this year people are struggling to meet their day-to-day expenses and have little left over for the holiday. I made a few phone calls before coming here and learned that the food pantry has seen a twenty-five percent increase in applications and is barely able to meet the need. My daughter has been leading the toy drive at the high school and she says donations are down while requests are up. We've all seen the foreclosure notices, and the for-sale signs that are sprouting up all over town."

Once again, Lucy heard that "hmph," a bit louder this time.

"It seems to me that cutting town employees' income is the very worst thing we can do right now, when we need to give the economy a boost. I understand that the Finance Committee can't solve all these problems, but we don't have to make things worse by laying off town employees." He paused. "Thank you for your time."

When he took his seat Lucy reached for his hand and gave it a squeeze. "That was great," she said with a smile. "Well said."

"We'll see," Bill said, keeping his voice low. "I don't think I convinced Hawthorne and Taubert."

Hawthorne asked if there were any more applicants, and when no one else came forward, called for a vote. Frankie and Pam both voted for Bill, and Taubert voted for Scribner, which was expected. As chairman, Hawthorne had the last vote.

"I'm in a bit of a quandary," he said. "My inclination is to vote for Mr. Scribner, because I agree with him that it's important to keep taxes low, but if I cast my vote for him we'll end up with a tie. That means the decision would go to the Board of Selectmen, and I don't want to cede control of the committee to another branch of town government."

Hawthorne paused here, and Lucy gave Bill's hand another squeeze.

"Furthermore, I've known Bill Stone for a very long time and I know he's a fair and open-minded person who will give serious thought to the matters before the committee."

Lucy was holding her breath; the suspense was killing her.

"So I'm casting my vote for Bill Stone, with certain reservations. Congratulations, Bill."

Bill got to his feet, turned and reached out to shake hands with Scribner, who reluctantly obliged, then left the room. Bill turned back to face the committee members.

"Thanks for your confidence in me. I'll do my very best not to disappoint you."

"That's great, Bill," Hawthorne said. "Genevieve, here, our secretary, has some papers for you to review before our next meeting so you can get up to speed. Keeping that in mind, do I have a motion to adjourn?"

"I so move," Taubert said.

"Second," Pam added.

Hawthorne banged his gavel. "Meeting adjourned."

Bill received congratulations from the handful of concerned citizens who attended the meeting, and hugs from Pam and Frankie. Taubert gave him the briefest of handshakes, and Hawthorne had a few papers for him to sign confirming his appointment. Then he reported to Genevieve, who handed him a banker's box full of documents.

"All this?" Bill asked.

"And those, too," Genevieve said, indicating two more boxes.

"Righto," he said, stacking two of the boxes one on top of the other so he could carry them. "I can't believe you got me into this," he muttered to Lucy.

She picked up the third box and followed him out into the night.

Chapter Twelve

Pam was already at their usual table in Jake's when Lucy arrived on a snowy Thursday morning. Lucy wanted to ask her about Ted's abrupt departure the day before, but Pam wasn't about to give her the opportunity.

"Congratulations!" she chirped, as Lucy sat down and shrugged out of her parka. "Is Bill excited about being on the Finance Committee?"

Maybe, Lucy thought, Pam didn't even know about Ted's hissy fit, when he'd stalked out of the office, leaving her with the job of putting the paper together. Maybe it wasn't the big deal she thought it was. Pam didn't seem the least bit troubled. "Not exactly," Lucy confessed. "He's feeling overwhelmed by those boxes of papers he's supposed to read."

"My advice is to start with the most recent and work backward," Pam said. "He doesn't need to get bogged down in the details. He'll get the picture soon enough."

"You don't know Bill like I do," Lucy said. "He's taking this very seriously. And, by the way," she said, intending to ask if something was bothering Ted, when Rachel joined them.

"What's Bill taking seriously?" Rachel asked. She had several tote bags slung over her arms and had the slightly flustered air of someone who had a long to-do list.

"He got the temporary appointment to the FinCom," Pam said, obviously pleased as punch.

"And he's pulling his hair out, now that he's discovered how much work is involved," Lucy added.

"He'll do a great job," Rachel said, dropping her bags in a pile around her chair. "I can't think of a better person."

"That's the problem," Lucy said. "He really wants to do a good job. He wants to do the right thing. I don't know how he'll handle the criticism. You know, when some member of the Taxpayers' Association accosts him in the post office or gas station and chews him out."

Pam nodded knowingly. "He'll learn soon enough. You have to develop a bit of a thick skin. I listen and nod and sometimes what they say actually makes sense." She paused. "Not often, but sometimes."

Lucy and Rachel laughed as Norine, the waitress, arrived with a fresh pot of coffee. "Where's the black coffee?" Norine asked, referring to Sue's regular order.

"That smells heavenly," Rachel said, wrapping her hands around the mug and inhaling the fragrant brew.

"She must be running late," Pam said, answering Norine's question.

"You look like you're running on empty." Lucy was talking to Rachel, who had rested her elbow on the table and was propping her chin on her hand.

"I've got the show and Miss Tilley and the Angel Fund, and Christmas is almost here and I don't know whether I'm coming or going," she admitted, with a big sigh.

"You've got a lot on your plate," Lucy said, knowing that Rachel spent several hours every day providing home care for the town's oldest resident. "I can help out with Miss Tilley."

"I might take you up on that, Lucy," Rachel said, sipping her coffee.

Pam watched as Norine filled her cup. "Do you think we should order? Sue just has coffee anyway."

"I think so," Rachel said. "I've got a meeting at nine."

"Regulars all 'round?" Norine asked.

They all nodded and she departed, writing in her order pad as she went.

"Who's the meeting with?" Lucy asked.

"Actually, I'm seeing a counselor," Rachel said.

Pam's jaw dropped. "You are?"

Lucy was also shocked. "What's the matter?"

Rachel's face was a portrait of misery, and Lucy noticed her long hair needed a wash, and her nails, usually filed into neat ovals, were ragged and broken. "It's Bob." She sighed. "That's not fair. It's not really Bob. It's me. Things just don't seem to be working."

"Marriage is like that," Pam said. "Every once in a while you hit a rough patch."

"She's right," Lucy said. "Bob adores you."

"Bob takes me for granted," Rachel said. "And I see the way he looks at Florence."

"I think you're imagining things," Lucy said. "I know she's flirtatious, but he doesn't seem the least bit interested. If anything, he tries to avoid Florence."

"When he heard about the accident, he sent flowers," Rachel said with a sniff.

"Who's Florence? What accident?" Pam asked, mystified.

"Florence Gallagher. She's in the show. She's playing Fred's wife," Lucy explained. "I saw her at the supermarket, by the way. She's doing pretty well after the accident. Just a few aches and pains, no broken bones."

"Like I care," Rachel grumbled. "I wish that scenery had squashed her flat."

"What are you talking about?" Pam demanded.

"Some scenery fell on her Friday night. She stayed at the church hall to work on it while we all went to the caroling," Lucy explained. "Bill and I found her trapped under the collapsed sets and called the rescue squad."

"That was lucky for her," Pam said, as Norine set a bowl of granola-topped yogurt in front of her. "Otherwise she might have been stuck there all night."

"Would have served her right," Rachel said.

"Rachel, I really think you're overreacting," Lucy said, taking her plate of hash and eggs. "She's just one of those friendly people. She hardly knows me and she invited me to her Christmas open house."

"I've just got a bad feeling," Rachel said, crumbling her Sunshine muffin. "You know how it is—you just feel that something's not right."

"Have you talked to Bob?" Pam asked.

"Yeah," Rachel said, her eyes filling with tears. "I asked him if he was attracted to Florence and he got mad. He denied it, got all huffy and angry, and that's when I knew."

Lucy stabbed her egg with her fork and watched the yolk ooze out. "He protested too much," she said.

"Yeah." Rachel was fumbling in one of her bags for a tissue and Pam handed her a napkin. She took it and wiped her eyes and blew her nose. "I'm sorry. I didn't mean to upset everybody."

"That's what friends are for," Pam said. "Whatever happens, you know we're here for you."

"That's right," Lucy added, squeezing Rachel's hand.

The three friends were sitting silently, glumly studying their plates, when Sue arrived. "Have you heard already?" she asked, taking the last chair.

"Heard what?" Lucy asked. Sue was as impeccably dressed and made-up as usual, the very picture of country chic in a plaid jacket, corduroy pants, and chunky boots, but even her Chanel foundation couldn't mask the dark circles under her eyes.

"Sidra called last night," she said, naming her daughter, who lived in New York City. "Geoff has kidney disease."

The news hit hard. They all knew Sidra's husband, Geoff Rumford, who was a local boy, as well as his brother, Fred, who was a professor at Winchester College.

"Is it serious?" Rachel asked.

"He's still undergoing tests," Sue said. "But it can't be good, can it? You need your kidneys."

"Yeah, but people have two and you only need one," Lucy said, ever the optimist. "Maybe they can just remove the bad one."

"Sidra's going crazy," Sue said, accepting a cup of black coffee from Norine. "She says she'll donate one of her kidneys."

"What about dialysis?" Pam asked.

"That's what I asked Sidra, but she says they're trying to avoid that. It's pretty miserable. It takes hours and hours and it's painful and has side effects."

"I didn't realize," Pam said.

"Me, either," Lucy said, thinking of little Angie in the hospital in Portland.

"Sidra's having tests, too, to see if she's a good match."

"And there's Geoff's brother," Lucy said, thinking of Fred.

"I know." Sue's expression was serious. "I'm sure it will work out. It's just so worrying right now."

"Of course it is," Rachel said. "We'll keep them in our prayers."

Lucy nodded with the rest, thinking that health really was the most important thing. Suddenly her worries about Sara didn't seem important. She was smart and strong and healthy, and Lucy crossed her fingers, making a wish that she would stay that way.

It was snowing lightly when Lucy left Jake's. She usually took care of a few errands on Thursday morning before going into the office, so she took a turn through the drive-through and cashed a check at the bank, stopped at the drugstore to take advantage of a sale to stock up on toothpaste, and picked up Bill's shirts at the cleaners. None of this took a great deal of mental power, so her mind was free to wander and she found her thoughts settling on Florence Gallagher.

Lucy thought she must be pretty new in town because she only met her for the first time when she'd interviewed her about the children's books she illustrated. Tinker's Cove wasn't very large; there were only a few thousand year-round residents, and you got to know everybody, at least by sight. As she made her way around town, driving carefully because of the snow, Lucy wondered why Florence had chosen to settle in Tinker's Cove. She was, after all, an attractive, single woman, albeit approaching her forties, and it was hard to understand what drew her to the small coastal Maine town. It wasn't as if there were a lot of single people her age. As for employment, well, the prospect was bleak, pretty much limited to low-paying retail jobs. Lucy admired the illustrations she'd seen, but wondered if that produced enough income for Florence to support herself. Perhaps she'd come in hopes of developing her art beyond illustrations; Maine's incomparable beauty did attract a lot of artists. Or perhaps she'd come, thought Lucy, because she wanted to be near her uncle, Ben Scribner. Maybe he was her only relative and she wanted to take care of him in his old age. Maybe he was her richest relative and she wanted to make sure she got mentioned in his will. Maybe, Lucy thought, speculating wildly, Florence wanted to make sure she got all of her uncle's money and got rid of his partner.

That was simply crazy, way out there, Lucy decided, catching sight of the Downeast Mortgage sign and impulsively braking. She was in the neighborhood, she decided, so she might as well pay Ben Scribner a visit and see if the police had made any progress in solving the bombing death of his partner.

She knew she'd have to get past Scribner's secretary, Elsie, and had her line of attack prepared when she entered the reception area, but found she didn't need it after all. Elsie was not at her desk. Instead, Scribner himself was standing there, behind the huge expanse of mahogany, looking through an appointment book.

"Can I help you?" he asked, looking up. It was chilly in the office and Scribner was wearing a thick gray cardigan beneath his Harris tweed jacket.

"I was just passing," Lucy began, "and wondered if there have been any new developments concerning Jake Marlowe's death."

"The police are fools," Scribner said. "They couldn't find a lost cat, not if it wandered in front of them."

Lucy thought he had a point. "They have their ways, procedures and policies and all that. I guess there are good reasons behind it all, but it does seem to slow things down."

Scribner sat down and Lucy thought he looked tired.

"You could hire a private investigator," she said. "Have you thought of that?"

"I have," he admitted, with a sigh.

"Did you hire someone?" Lucy was definitely interested.

He sighed again, a long sigh. "I can't seem to decide." He raised his head and looked at her. "Can you recommend someone?"

"Actually, I can. I do know of a woman in New York. She investigated the Van Vorst mess last summer."

"Sounds expensive." Scribner made the word *expensive* sound rather indecent.

"I would imagine so," Lucy agreed. She thought Scribner looked at least ten years older than he did at the funeral. "It must be hard, losing someone you worked with for all those years."

"They blew him up," Scribner said, with a haunted expression. "It keeps me up at night, thinking about it."

"That's understandable." Lucy paused, debating what to say next, and deciding to go for the obvious. "Maybe you should talk to someone who could help you sort out your emotions."

Scribner snorted. "Now you sound like my niece. She's always fussing over me."

"Florence cares about you," Lucy said.

"She's a nuisance," Scribner declared, with a flash of his former self. "I'm a businessman; I've never really had a family. It's enough for me to understand business. Profit and loss, interest and capital, those are the things I understand, and I don't see what's wrong with that. You can't do anything without money. You can't start a business. You can't buy a house. You can't build a school. People forget all that. Nowadays making money and being successful are viewed as bad things."

"I think it's the lack of money that's got people upset," Lucy said.

"Exactly." Scribner nodded. "It doesn't grow on trees—what do they think? You've got to be prudent, careful. That's what Marlowe was doing. He was trying to balance the town budget." He lifted his fist and banged it down on the desk. "Since when is that a crime?"

For a moment, Lucy was once again eight years old, sitting at her grandfather's big mahogany dining table, and he was banging his fist on the polished surface, making the silverware jump. "The deficit!" he declared, his voice rolling on like thunder, predicting doom. "The deficit will be the ruin of the country!" Only this time, it wasn't her grandfather railing against the government—it was Ben Scribner, defending his partner.

"Do you think he was killed by a disgruntled town employee?" Lucy asked. "Someone who might have thought he engineered the layoffs in order to foreclose on valuable property?"

Scribner's face flushed darkly and Lucy feared he was going to have a stroke or heart attack. "Marlowe would never . . ." he began.

Lucy hurried to placate him. "Of course not. But somebody might have thought that. Maybe Harry Crawford, for example, who's losing his family farm? Or Phil Watkins, who built that energy-efficient house? Did one of them threaten Marlowe, for instance? Or what about . . . ?"

Behind her, Lucy heard the door open and felt a blast of cool air. "Goodness, it's cold out, but the snow has stopped," Elsie declared, hurrying to her desk. "Now what are you up to, Mr. Scribner? Messing about with my papers?"

"Just checking my schedule," Scribner answered, sounding like a schoolboy caught peeking into his teacher's desk drawers.

"And you, Lucy Stone? What can we do for you?" Elsie's expression was challenging, daring Lucy to explain herself.

"I was just checking on the investigation," Lucy said, knowing how lame she sounded.

"Well then, I suggest you go and talk to the police," Elsie said.

Lucy felt the ground slipping away beneath her. "I'll do that . . . Uh, thank you," she said, making what felt like a lucky escape through the door.

Outside, she stopped to collect herself. That woman was scary, she thought, with a little shudder. How did she do it? Talk about assertiveness training—Elsie Morehouse could write the book.

Lucy was opening her car door when she heard a honk and looked up to see Molly had pulled up alongside in her little Civic. Patrick was behind her, in his car seat.

"Hi!" Lucy greeted them.

"We're going to see Santa," Molly said. She was wearing a red Santa Claus hat over her long blond hair. "Want to join us?"

Lucy considered the offer. She had intended to go to the office but there was nothing pressing, nothing she really had to do today. Besides, she was still feeling rather resentful toward Ted. "Sounds good," she said, jumping into the passenger seat beside Molly. As she buckled her seat belt she felt her spirits rise, like a school kid playing hooky.

"I was afraid we wouldn't be able to go because of the snow, but it turned out to be just a squall," Molly said, zipping along Main Street and heading for the highway.

"Ocean effect," Lucy said, calculating that only about a half inch had accumulated on lawns, even less on the road. "Never amounts to much."

"I see blue sky," Molly said. "I bet the sun will be out soon."

Lucy cast her eyes skyward. "My mother used to say you could count on it clearing when 'there's enough blue to make a pair of Dutchman's breeches.'"

"That's a funny one," Molly said.

In the backseat, Patrick was humming a little song to himself.

The trip to the mall passed quickly and they got to Santa's workshop just as it was opening. In the past Patrick had been shy about meeting Santa, but now that he was three and a half he was beginning to be much braver.

"Do you know what you're going to ask Santa to bring you?" Lucy asked.

"Cranky the Crane and Gordon," he replied promptly.

"The rock group?" Lucy inquired.

"No, Thomas the Tank Engine and his many friends," Molly explained. "It's on TV. There are books, videos. . . . It's hard to explain the appeal but somehow it takes over their little brains."

Mother and grandmother watched proudly as the elf opened the gate and Patrick marched right up to Santa and climbed on his lap. "Ho, ho, ho," Santa said. "Have you been a good little boy?"

"Most of the time," Patrick replied with disarming honesty.

"Well, that's pretty good," Santa said. "What do you want for Christmas?"

"Cranky the Crane and Gordon," Patrick repeated.

"We'll see what we can do, young man," Santa said. "Now smile for the camera."

Patrick smiled, the elf snapped the picture, and Lucy found herself forking over ten dollars for a copy. It was worth it, she decided, studying the image of the towheaded, apple-cheeked youngster sitting on the lap of the whiskered, apple-cheeked Santa.

Molly wanted to do a bit of shopping so Lucy offered to take Patrick off her hands for an hour; they would meet for lunch at the sandwich shop. Lucy enjoyed spending time with Patrick, especially now that he was a bit older and they could have a real conversation. They walked along, hand in hand, discussing the displays in the windows.

"Why is that lady flying?" Patrick asked, studying a mannequin suspended on fish line.

"It's to catch your eye," Lucy said. "If she was just standing there it wouldn't be very interesting. Because she's flying, we're looking at her, and we can see her clothes and maybe we'll want to go inside the store and buy them."

"Pink is for girls," Patrick said, commenting on the mannequin's sparkly skirt.

"Mommy might look nice in that," Lucy said.

"Mommy can't fly," Patrick said very seriously.

"No, she can't," Lucy agreed, chuckling to herself.

After doing a complete circuit of the mall, including a stop at the toy store where Lucy bought Patrick a little car, they settled themselves at a booth in the coffee shop to wait for Molly. Patrick was busy coloring his place mat when she joined them, carrying several large shopping bags.

"Looks like you were successful," Lucy said.

"I found some bargains," Molly said, sliding into the opposite seat. "How's your shopping going?"

"I'm almost all done. I did it all online the weekend after Thanksgiving," Lucy admitted. "I didn't feel like dragging around to the stores, and now I'm glad I shopped online because the rehearsals are taking up so much time." She nodded at the shopping bags resting beside her on the banquette. "I couldn't resist a few small things, though, and I still need something for Bill. Something special."

"How's the show going?" Molly asked, opening the plasticized menu and studying it.

"Okay, I guess," Lucy said. "I hope we get a good turnout. If we make any money it will go to the Cunningham family for Angie."

Molly's eyes were big and sad. "I heard she's not doing too well. Zach told Toby they're afraid she won't get a kidney in time." Her glance fell on Patrick's shining blond head, bent over his little yellow car, which he was pushing with chubby fingers. "I can't imagine what Lexie and Zach are going through."

"Me, either," Lucy said, signaling to the waitress.

The western sky was a gorgeous deep red when Lucy got home later that afternoon, and the windows of her old house were aglow in the reflected light. Winter sunsets were gorgeous, with intense color, but they didn't last long, so Lucy made a point of taking a minute before she got out of the car to admire the rosy light, which suffused everything with radiant color, a violin concerto on the car radio providing musical accompaniment to the show. Then, when the light faded to pink and then to gray, she gathered up her purse and shopping bags and went inside.

The answering machine was blinking so she listened while she took off her coat and hat. It was Rachel saying there would be no rehearsal tonight, and Lucy was thoughtful as she unwound her scarf, wondering if Rachel was having some sort of breakdown. She dialed her number but there was no answer, so she left a message, then got busy hiding Christmas presents and cooking dinner. She was scrubbing some potatoes when Sara called to say she was staying at the college to work on a paper and wouldn't be home for dinner, so Lucy put her potato back in the bag. Then, before she returned to the sink, the phone rang again and it was Zoe, saying she was at her friend Jess's house, wrapping presents for the toy drive, and Jess's mom had invited her to stay for dinner.

Her potato went back in the bag, too. Lucy looked at the two remaining Idahos and thought this was going to be her future as an empty nester: two potatoes and two pork chops. It seemed so meager, she thought, used to cooking big meals when there were six of them gathered at the table.

Lucy got the potatoes in the oven and then set two places at the kitchen table, thinking that with just Bill and herself it seemed silly to set the table in the dining room.

As she arranged the place mats and silver, she considered adding a couple of wineglasses. Evenings alone were a rarity and she thought they might as well take advantage of the situation and enjoy a romantic interlude. She recalled Rachel's confession that things weren't going well in her marriage and thought she didn't want to start taking Bill for granted, always putting him off because she was busy. She didn't know if that was the root of Rachel's problems but even Rachel admitted she was doing too much.

"We're dining à deux," she told Bill, when he came home. "Do you want to open a bottle of wine?"

She was terribly disappointed when he declined, saying he wanted to get to work on the FinCom papers. He barely spoke to her when they ate, clearly distracted, and then took his after-dinner coffee up to his office, leaving Lucy alone with her mug of decaf. She cleaned up dinner and settled in the family room to write Christmas cards, trying not to feel hurt that Bill had rejected her.

Chapter Thirteen

Next morning it seemed the old adage about a red sky at night being a sailor's delight was true. The sun was shining brightly in a clear blue sky and the air was as crisp as it could only be on a winter morning in coastal Maine, hypercharged with oxygen and smelling faintly briny. The cold made Lucy's nose tingle as she gassed up the car at the Quik-Stop.

Harry Crawford was doing the same on the other side of the pump, filling his rusty old pickup and complaining about the rising cost of gas. "They say it's gonna go up to five bucks a gallon," he said, glumly watching the numbers scroll by.

"When I pay my bills, I make the check out to *Thrifty Gas Thieves,*" Lucy said. "It makes me feel better but they don't seem to mind. They cash it anyway."

"Thrifty Gas has no shame—if they did they'd change their name," Harry said with a grin. He was wearing the working man's uniform, flannel-lined pants topped with a plaid wool shirt, a thick sweater, thermal hoodie, and a barn jacket. He had well-worn work boots on his feet and a blue knit watch cap on his head. "I gotta say I've got high hopes now that Bill is on the Fin-Com," he said in a serious voice, as he replaced the pump handle. "I need to get my hours back or it's gonna be a real mean winter, that's for sure."

Lucy finished screwing the cap back on her tank, giving it a couple of extra twists, just to be sure it was tight. "He's been working hard, going over all the papers. He's determined to be fair, and wants to look at both sides of the issue."

"Oh, right," Harry said with a knowing wink. "He's a good guy, a working man, not like that Marlowe, who never did an honest day's work in his life."

Lucy pulled her glove back on and shoved her hands in her coat pockets. "Any chance you can keep the farm?" she asked. "Have you been able to work something out with Scribner?"

Harry laughed, a harsh sound, like a bark. "Bastard won't budge an inch. He says he gave me the money when I asked for it, and now that it's my turn to pay, I've got to do it on time or face the consequences. He didn't force me to take out the mortgage. He's held up his side of the bargain and I've got to hold up mine, do what I said I'd do or else I lose the property."

"That's too bad," Lucy said, who remembered Scribner saying pretty much the same thing to Ike Stoughton at Marlowe's funeral.

"Yeah. My granddad held on to the place through the Depression, you know. It wasn't easy, but somehow he did it. I wish he was still around to tell me how, 'cause I sure can't figure out a way."

"Times are different," Lucy said. "If it's any comfort, you're not alone."

"It's not," Harry said. "Crawfords have owned that farm for more than two hundred years and I'm the one who's losing it. It's like I'm not worthy of the name."

"Don't think like that," Lucy admonished, alarmed at his depressed tone of voice. "Like I said, everything's different now."

"I don't know about that. Seems like the same old, same old. 'Socialism for the rich and capitalism for the poor.'"

"That's always been true, for sure," Lucy said. "But I think there's something else going on. Things aren't working the way they're supposed to. Take college, for example. When you get out of college you're supposed to be able to get a job. . . ."

"I don't know about that," Harry said, his expression hardening. "I never had that opportunity."

Lucy wanted to tell him there was no shame in not going to college, that she knew how smart and talented and hardworking he was and that she respected him, but she didn't want to sound patronizing. "Take it easy," she said, reaching for the door handle.

"Don't have any choice," Harry said with a shrug, pulling a single dollar bill out of his pocket. "I'm gonna try my luck on the lottery."

"You can't win if you don't play," Lucy said, repeating the lottery's advertising slogan as she got into her car. "Good luck!"

"I'm gonna need it," Harry said, waving as she drove off.

Lucy was thoughtful as she cruised down Main Street to the *Pennysaver* office. The way she saw it, the lottery was part of the problem, not the solution. It took money from thousands of low-income people, like Harry, and redistributed big chunks of it to a lucky few. Then again, she decided, pulling into a parking space, there wasn't much you could buy with a dollar anymore. You might as well take a chance on winning.

Harry hadn't looked too optimistic about his chances; he'd looked like a desperate man who'd run out of options. She remembered his expression when he'd said he hadn't had the opportunity to go to college and suspected he'd been nursing a grudge for a long time. The question was, she thought as she switched off the engine, whether or not that simmering resentment had driven him to construct a package bomb and mail it to Jake Marlowe. She would never have thought in a million years that Harry Crawford would do such a thing, not until now.

Phyllis was already at her desk, sorting press releases, when Lucy entered the office. "What's happening?" she asked, hanging up her coat.

"More foreclosures," Phyllis said, handing her several sheets of fax paper, all headed with the Downeast Mortgage logo.

"This is not good," Lucy said, speed-reading the legalese and looking for names. She didn't recognize most of them, so she figured they were for second homes owned by summer people. Too bad for them, of course, and not very good for the local economy, but she was relieved that none of her friends or neighbors were losing their homes. None, until she saw Al Roberts's name on the last notice.

"Oh, dear," she said, staring at the paper and checking the address.

"Who is it?" Phyllis asked. "I didn't have a chance to read them."

"Al Roberts."

"Like that family doesn't have enough to worry about, with little Angie waiting for a kidney transplant."

"Are Angie and Al Roberts related?" asked Lucy.

Phyllis's penciled eyebrows rose above her reading glasses. "Of course they are, he's her grandfather."

Lucy remembered how sullen Al had been at the last rehearsal, just before the scenery he had erected had fallen on Florence Gallagher. She wondered if he'd been so distracted with his problems—a desperately ill granddaughter, a daughter struggling to keep her family together with diminished resources, and his own financial troubles—that he'd been careless with the scenery. Or maybe, she wondered, he'd arranged for it to fall on purpose, deliberately striking back at Scribner through his niece.

The jangling bell on the door roused her from her thoughts as Ted entered, bringing a gust of cold air with him. "Glorious day," he said, unwrapping his striped muffler.

Lucy wanted to say something like "Glad you could make it" but bit her tongue. He was the boss, after all, and if he wanted to walk out on deadline day, well, that was his prerogative. Instead she said, "A nice day if you don't count the foreclosures."

Ted glanced at the sheaf of papers she was holding. "Who is it this time?" he asked, unzipping his jacket.

"Al Roberts," she replied. "And a bunch of second homes."

"Let me see." He took the foreclosure notices from her and began perusing, shaking his head as he flipped through them. "A lot of these folks are subscribers," he said. "We send the paper to them all year so they can follow local news. They're good customers, too, according to our advertisers. They order stuff from retailers year round and have it sent, they hire contractors to make repairs, they use heating oil and gas, they pay property managers to keep an eye on their homes." He gave the papers back to her. "It's not good for the town to have all these vacant houses sitting there."

"As if property values aren't low enough," Phyllis said.

"They're going to get lower," Ted predicted gloomily. "We haven't seen the worst of this."

"Isn't there something we can do to pressure Downeast?" Lucy asked. "Get our state rep and other elected officials to put some pressure on Scribner?"

"That's a great idea, Lucy," Phyllis said. "What about the banking commissioner? And the attorney general?"

"We'll start a campaign to save our community," Lucy said.

"Whoa," said Ted, holding up a cautionary hand. "Not a good idea. For one thing, I'm pretty sure everything Marlowe and Scribner did is perfectly legal. And secondly, I can't afford to get Scribner mad at me." He shifted his feet awkwardly. "I can't risk it. He can call my note at any time and there's no way I can meet that payment."

Lucy stared at him. So that was what was behind his strange behavior. "Didn't you read the note before you signed it?"

"Of course I did, and it seemed perfectly okay at the time because it got me a lower interest rate—a full point less than Seamen's Bank was asking." He swiveled his desk chair around so that it faced away from the wall and sat down heavily, making the chair creak. "Those were the days when you walked in a bank and the first thing they did was ask if you wanted any money and they asked how much and said, 'Just sign here.' I never thought I'd have any problem refinancing if he called the note. The value of the house was going up all the time, lenders were tripping over each other to give me money." He snorted. "I thought I was being smart. I never thought the bubble would burst."

"None of us did," Phyllis said.

"We can't just give up," Lucy said. "We have a role to play here. We need to get the facts out and mobilize people to save the town."

"If it's any consolation, there will come a point when even Scribner realizes the folly of foreclosing every time a borrower misses a payment. He's going to end up with a lot of decaying, worthless property," Ted said.

"By then it will be too late," Phyllis said. "Tinker's Cove will be a ghost town."

For a moment Lucy imagined tumbleweeds blowing down Main Street, an image straight out of a Western movie. "Instead of a showdown," she said, "let's try an ambush."

"Somehow I feel as if I've wandered into the Last Chance Saloon," Ted said.

Lucy grinned. "We could do a story about the Social Action Committee at the college, let them take on Downeast."

"That's actually a good idea, pardner," Ted said, brightening. "You could interview their leader—what's his name?"

"Seth, Seth Lesinski," Lucy said, reaching for her phone.

Seth was only too happy to be interviewed and suggested meeting at the coffee shop in the student union later that afternoon. Lucy was seated in a comfy armchair in the attractive space with orange walls and distressed wood floor, planning the questions she wanted to ask, when Seth arrived. He definitely exuded charisma, she decided, as heads turned in his direction. He paused here and there, grinning and exchanging pleasantries, as he made his way toward her, working the room like a pro.

"Thanks for coming," Lucy said, as he seated himself next to her. "Can I get you a coffee or something?"

"No, thanks," he said, shrugging out of his camo Windbreaker but leaving on his black beret and checked Arab-style scarf. She figured it wasn't just for the image of a revolutionary leader he was working so hard to project; his shaved head probably got cold.

"Like I said on the phone, I'm writing this profile for the *Pennysaver* newspaper," Lucy began. "I guess I'd like to begin by asking why you started the Social Action Committee. . . ."

"I didn't start it," Seth said, "and I'm not the president or leader or anything like that. We have no leaders in this movement. Everything is decided by a vote of the members."

Lucy looked at him, wondering if he really believed what he was saying. He was no kid, she realized, noticing the lines around his eyes and a slight graying of the obligatory stubble on his cheeks and chin. No wonder he shaved his head, she thought, suspecting his hair was either graying or balding. "Okay," she said, "but you do seem to be the guy holding the megaphone."

"I know," he admitted, with a rueful shake of his head, "but I'm trying to change that. Nobody besides me seems willing to come forward, but we're holding some public speaking work-shops and I'm hoping to pass the megaphone to others."

Lucy nodded as she wrote this down in her notebook. "Has the group agreed on any goals?" she asked.

"We want foreclosures to stop. We want action on student loans—they've overtaken credit card debt as a national problem. And we want the military budget cut and the troops out of Afghanistan." He paused. "That's especially important to me. I'm here on the GI Bill, you know. I was in the army, saw action in Iraq and Afghanistan." He leaned forward, making intense eye contact. "I saw my friends die and I was lucky to get out alive, and this is not the America we were fighting for. We didn't die and risk our lives so greedy bastards like Marlowe and Scribner could get rich by making people homeless."

Lucy was writing it all down, scribbling as fast as she could and wondering why she'd neglected to bring along her tape recorder. She knew why—she hated the way the machine intruded on an in-terview, making people nervous and stilted. "How many students are in the group?" she finally asked.

"We can draw quite a crowd for a demonstration," he said, looking satisfied with himself.

"But how many go to meetings? How many are actually com-mitted activists?"

"Like your daughter?" he asked, catching her by surprise.

Lucy wasn't about to show he'd rattled her. "Like Sara," she said.

"You know, Sara suggested I contact you and ask to be inter-viewed," he said. "You called me before I got a chance."

This was very unexpected news, considering how irritable Sara had been lately. "Really?" she asked, her voice bright with plea-sure.

"Yeah." He nodded. "She said it would be a good way to pre-sent our ideas to the public. SAC isn't just a college group, you know. We'd like people from the community to join us. We're fighting for them, after all."

"Traditionally there's been a sharp division between town and gown—do you think you can overcome that?"

"I hope so," Seth said. "All we're after is fairness, a level playing field. It's not right for one percent to own forty-two percent of the wealth in this country. It's not right that half the population is living at or below the poverty line. This is the richest country in the world and kids are going hungry, families are losing their homes. It's time that people stood up for themselves and demanded fairness."

"How far should they go?" Lucy asked. "Do you condone violence, like the bombing that killed Marlowe?"

"I would never condone violence; I don't think anybody who's been to war would," he said in a soft voice. His expression was troubled, his eyes were directed at hers but he wasn't seeing her, he was seeing something else, reliving a wartime horror. Then, with a shake of his head, he came back to the present. "If things continue the way they are, I wouldn't be at all surprised to see more violence. That's what happens when people run out of options. They get desperate."

"Let's hope it doesn't come to that," Lucy said.

He smiled, revealing large eyeteeth that gave him a wolfish look. "When hope runs out, that's when there's trouble."

Lucy had a few more questions and the interview continued for a little longer before she was able to wrap it up. When she had no more questions she asked him if she could snap a photo; he was happy to oblige. When she checked the image in her digital camera she thought it reminded her of something, and when she was walking across campus to the parking lot it came to her. He looked like that famous poster of Che Guevara, she decided, not knowing whether to laugh . . . or cry.

Chapter Fourteen

Friday night was pizza night, when the family gathered around the kitchen table instead of eating in the dining room. It was the one night when Lucy used paper plates and paper napkins, and the kids were allowed to drink soda. That had been more of a thrill when they were little, but there was still something special about Friday. Maybe it was just the fact that the work and school week was over, and they could look forward to sleeping in on Saturday.

Bill always picked up the pizza on his way home, and when Lucy saw his headlights in the driveway she called the girls. They came clumping down the back stairs and sat down at the table, waiting for him to set the big box in front of them. Wine was poured, flip tabs on soda cans were popped, and everybody dived in.

"I interviewed Seth Lesinski today," Lucy said, her mouth full of spicy cheesy tomato goodness. "He's a very interesting guy."

"Mmmph," Sara replied.

"He mentioned you. He said you're a 'committed activist.'"

"Sara?" Zoe scoffed. "He should see her getting dressed in the morning, deciding what to wear and fussing with her hair and makeup."

"I sure hope he doesn't see her like that," Bill said, and Lucy wasn't sure if he was joking or not.

"Da-a-ad," Sara protested, blushing. "It's not like that. It's a movement. Seth's interested in making history, not . . . you know, romantic stuff."

"Believe me, Sara, every guy is interested in, uh, romantic stuff." Bill reached for the bottle and refilled his wineglass.

"Why do you always think the worst of people?" Sara demanded, rising from her chair. "Seth is . . . Seth is amazing! He's not immature like the boys on campus. He's got goals and ideas. He fought in Afghanistan. . . . He's a hero!" Then she flung down her crumpled paper napkin and ran upstairs, where she slammed her bedroom door.

"I think she really likes him," Zoe said, finishing off her piece of pizza and reaching for another.

"I think you're right," Lucy said, deciding this could definitely be a problem. "Bill, would you please pass the salad?"

After dinner, Bill buried himself in his attic office with the Fin-Com papers and Lucy got ready to go to rehearsal. Sara didn't answer when she knocked on her door, asking if she wanted a ride anywhere, but Zoe asked to be dropped at her friend Izzy's house.

Lucy was a few minutes late when she got to the church hall, but the rehearsal hadn't started yet. Bob was conferring with Al Roberts on the stage; the scenery hadn't been replaced but was lying on the stage floor in a neat stack. Rachel was seated alone, going over the script, and a chattering group had gathered around Florence, who was holding court at the back of the room.

Lucy took a seat beside Rachel, who cast her eyes in Florence's direction. "You'd think she was the star of the show," she muttered.

"She's just one of those people who's got a big personality," Lucy said. "Bob doesn't even seem to notice her."

"He knows he better not," Rachel growled, causing Lucy to laugh.

"I don't think it's very funny," Rachel said, standing up and clapping her hands. "Places everyone! We're taking it from the top!"

Lucy watched the opening scene, set in Scrooge's office, but when the actor playing Bob Cratchit began stumbling over his lines and had to be coached, she found it tedious and began looking for some distraction. Spotting Marge Culpepper sitting a few rows over, knitting a pair of mittens, she went to join her.

"I hope those are for the Hat and Mitten Fund tree," Lucy

said, referring to a tree in the post office that was decorated with donated hats and mittens.

"You know it," Marge said. "I've made six pairs, and I'm aiming for ten."

"Good for you."

"I like to keep busy at these rehearsals," Marge said.

"Maybe I'll take up knitting, too." Lucy was marveling at Rachel's patience when Bob Cratchit got his lines mixed up for the fourth time. "How's Barney?" she asked.

"Still helping the state cops with the bomb investigation," Marge said. She lowered her voice to a whisper. "They're looking at that college radical, that Seth Lesinski. They think he might have ties to terrorists."

"He's ex-army," Lucy said. "I think he's the last person. . . ."

"You never know," Marge whispered, transferring some stitches onto a stitch holder. "It's hard for vets. Eddie had his troubles," she said, referring to her son, who struggled with drugs as a returning vet. "Sometimes they go a little screwy, get mixed up and start to sympathize with the enemy."

"That seems very unlikely to me," Lucy said, hearing her voice called. "I gotta go—it's my big scene."

"Break a leg," Marge said.

"Not funny," Lucy said, taking her place on stage with Tiny Tim. It was a brief scene, over in a minute or two, and when she exited Lucy found Al Roberts watching in the wings.

"How was I?" she asked.

Her question startled Al, and she realized he'd been lost in his thoughts. "Sorry," he said. "I wasn't watching."

"You must have a lot on your mind," Lucy said sympathetically. "How's Angie doing?"

"Not very good." He looked older than she remembered, and terribly tired.

"I'm so sorry," Lucy said. "Is there anything I can do?"

He shrugged. "They're doing everything they can at the hospital, but Lexie says they haven't got a match for her kidney and every day that goes by . . ."

"I know," Lucy said, biting her lip.

"I want to see her before . . . you know. She might not have very long."

Lucy wondered why he didn't just go. There was nothing keeping him here in Tinker's Cove that couldn't wait. "Why don't you go to Portland?" she asked.

"My truck needs a starter . . . and then the gas. It's pretty old, only gets about eleven miles to the gallon, and what with gas up over four dollars. . . ."

"Take my car," Lucy offered. "I'll catch a ride home with someone. No problem. I'll give you my gas card. Go."

"I couldn't do that," Al said, shaking his head. A number of cast members had gathered around them, waiting for their cues.

"Of course you can," Lucy said. "Let me get the keys for you. Stay here. I'll be back in a minute."

"No, I don't—" Al protested, but Lucy was already down the steps and hurrying to the chair where she'd left her purse. When she got back, Al stubbornly refused to take her keys.

"Please. It's the least I can do." She noticed Florence, who was standing nearby. "Florence will give me a ride home, won't you, Florence?"

"Sure," Florence replied. "Have you got car trouble?"

"No. I'm trying to get Al to take my car so he can visit his granddaughter in the hospital in Portland."

"Doesn't he have his own car?" Florence asked. Others had heard the conversation and were beginning to pay attention.

"Got car trouble, Al?" Bob asked.

"I know a great mechanic," Florence offered.

Al was distinctly uncomfortable with all the attention. His face was turning red and he was fidgeting restlessly, looking for an out. "I've got it under control," he said.

"Listen, if you need gas money, we can pass the hat," Florence suggested. "All for one and one for all—isn't that how it goes?"

"Sure," Marge said. "Angie should see her grandpa."

The group had surrounded Al, whose eyes had taken on a glazed look Lucy had recently seen on an aged lion surrounded by hyenas in a nature film on TV. "The man needs air," Lucy said, trying to give him an exit. Nobody paid attention; they were all digging in their purses and pockets for spare cash.

"Here, I've got five," Florence said, offering Al a neatly folded bill.

"Keep it!" he snarled, and everybody fell still. "I don't want help, not from any of you and especially not from her," he declared, pointing at Florence. Then he turned and stormed out of the hall.

Speechless, they all watched him go.

"What was that all about?" Florence asked.

"Downeast is foreclosing on his house," Lucy said. "I saw the notice today."

"Oh." Florence looked puzzled. "But why does he blame me?"

"Because of your uncle," Lucy suggested.

"Well, that's not her fault," Bob declared, defending Florence. "That's a legal matter between Al and Downeast. It's nothing to do with Florence."

Something brushed Lucy's shoulder, and she realized Rachel was standing beside her, leaning close. "Damn," she whispered, in Lucy's ear.

"I'm sure it's nothing," Lucy said, not sure but hoping it was.

"Oh, I'm not worried about *that,*" Rachel said. "I'm worried about losing Al. The scenery's not finished."

Right, Lucy thought, who didn't believe her for a minute. "I'll ask Bill. He can finish it up if Al doesn't come back."

Rachel squeezed her hand. "Thanks," she said, then clapped her hands smartly. "Places everyone! Act two!"

On Saturday morning Lucy and Molly went to the estate sale at Marlowe's place. The house was gone, the burned wood hauled away and the cellar hole filled in with dirt, but the huge 1866 barn was untouched by the fire and was still standing. It was also full to bursting with stuff, according to the newspaper ad, which promised: *C. 1810 tiger maple Sheraton four-drawer chest, C. 1820 drop-front secretary, empire card table, Civil War-era drum, muffin stand, tilt-top table,* and plenty more. What the ad didn't mention, and what Lucy and Molly soon discovered as they wandered among the pieces of furniture set out on the lawn, was that almost everything was broken and covered with a thick layer of filth.

"I suppose Bill could fix this," said Lucy, standing back to study the muffin stand, which was missing a leg.

"How would you clean it?" Molly asked, her lips pursed in disgust.

"Oh, lemon oil works wonders," said Lucy, who was trying to think where she could put the muffin stand.

"They're asking twenty dollars," Molly said, pointing to the orange sticker. "And it's just the first day of the sale."

"You don't think they're willing to bargain?" Lucy asked.

"Not yet," replied Molly, who'd just heard a woman's offer of thirty dollars for an enamel-topped kitchen table with a broken drawer, which was firmly refused. The table was priced at fifty dollars, which Lucy thought was wildly optimistic.

"Let's keep looking," Lucy said. "The ad promised old tools and I'd like to find something for Bill. Maybe one of those two-man saws, something he could hang up on the wall in his office."

"Maybe you'll find something inside the barn," Molly suggested.

The sale organizers had tried to organize the contents of the barn, but it was a daunting task and most of the stuff was still stacked in piles. Chests of drawers were topped with wooden crates full of junk and topped with three-legged chairs or bushel baskets filled with even more stuff. There were piles of old newspapers and magazines, stacks of moldy books, a child's rusty tricycle, empty picture frames, and cracked mirrors.

Spotting an old photo album, long forgotten in the barn, Molly began turning the pages and studying the pictures. "Look at this," she said, pointing to a pair of women, obviously sisters, dressed in long skirts and hats with enormous brims topped with feathers.

"They must be relations of some sort," Lucy guessed. "Maybe even Marlowe's mother or grandmother."

Molly closed the album. "It makes me feel like a ghoul," she said.

"Don't be silly," said one of the sale workers, a middle-aged woman who had been helping a customer who wanted to take a closer look at a wicker chair. Once the cobwebby chair had been taken down from its lofty perch, she brushed off her hands. "Marlowe sure doesn't need this stuff anymore, and to tell the truth, I don't think he thought much of it when he was alive."

"It doesn't seem so," Lucy agreed, looking at the vast barn. "So much stuff. Why was he keeping it?"

"Couldn't let go of it, that's my guess," the woman said. She was wearing a paper nametag that said *HELLO* in big letters. Her name, Liz, was handwritten in the space beneath. "We see this a lot. You wouldn't believe the stuff people hang on to."

"Such a waste," Lucy mused. "He had all this stuff but I don't think he had any friends. And he had pots of money but he lived in squalor."

"Well, we'll make a bit of money out of this sale so he's doing us some good. His ex-wife—she's the one who hired us—says she's donating her share of the proceeds to charity," Liz said.

"That's Ginny Irving?" Lucy asked.

"Right. She's a real nice lady," Liz said. "Do you know her?"

"I met her at the funeral," Lucy said, wondering if Ginny might be interested in helping the Cunninghams. She was considering how to approach her when somebody carried off a dressing screen, the faded and stained cloth in tatters, and revealed an old carpenter's chest.

"Excuse me," Lucy said, unable to wait to zero in on her find. "It's been nice talking to you," she added, over her shoulder, as she made her way between the piles of furniture. As she went she told herself not to get her hopes up. The chest was probably in dreadful condition and if it wasn't they would undoubtedly want a fortune for it.

When she got closer, however, she discovered the chest was made of mahogany, probably by a ship carpenter. It had rope handles and, once she'd wrestled it free of the milk crate of jelly jars and the potato baskets that were sitting on top of it, she realized the interior shelf with compartments for tools was in pristine condition.

"Those shelves are usually missing," Molly said, "or broken."

"Bill would love this," Lucy said, feeling a sudden, overwhelming need to possess the chest.

"There's no price on it," Molly observed.

"What should I offer?" Lucy asked, somewhat breathless with excitement.

"If it was in a shop, it would be five hundred or more."

"It's not in a shop," Lucy said. "And it's filthy. It's going to take a lot of work to get all this gunk off it."

"What's it worth to you?" Molly asked.

"A lot," Lucy admitted. "But I don't want to pay a lot."

"Ask Liz what they want."

"But what if they want hundreds?"

"I haven't seen anything over a hundred," said Molly, who had been studying the orange stickers. "Offer seventy-five and see what she says."

Lucy's heart was in her throat as she approached Liz, pointing to the chest in what she hoped was a nonchalant sort of way, and asking if she would take seventy-five dollars. To sweeten the deal, Lucy had the cash in her hand, three twenties, a ten, and a five.

Liz was busy counting out cash and making change for a woman who was buying several chests of drawers. She glanced at the ship carpenter's chest, narrowed her eyes, and nodded.

Lucy handed her the cash, restraining herself from crowing as she waited for Liz to write out a sales slip. Then she and Molly each took one of the rope handles and carried the chest to Lucy's SUV, where they stowed it in the way back. It was only when they were driving away that Lucy allowed herself to celebrate. "Can you believe it?" she crowed, banging her hand on the steering wheel and shaking her head. "What a find!"

"Bill will love it," Molly said.

"I know! He'll be so surprised!"

Toby and Patrick were building a snowman when Lucy and Molly arrived at the house on Prudence Path. Lucy and Molly pitched in, and when the snowman was complete asked Toby for help with the chest. He carried it down to the basement and promised to clean it up.

"You don't have to do that," Lucy said. "I can do it."

"I'd like to do it," Toby said. "Let me. It will be my gift to Dad, too."

"Okay," Lucy agreed, relieved to cross that item off her to-do list.

When she went home, she tackled a few more items, including calling Ginny Irving about the Cunninghams.

"Their daughter is terribly sick. She's only ten, and she's in the medical center in Portland. It's difficult for them, what with gas being so expensive and having to buy meals in the cafeteria," Lucy explained. "As it is they're in danger of losing their home. It's a terrible situation and there's no one they can turn to. The grandfather's truck needs repairs and his house is in foreclosure."

"That's terrible. I'm happy to give them the money from the estate sale. I'd like to see it go to somebody who really needs it."

"The Cunninghams really need it," Lucy said. "The Seamen's Bank has set up an account called the Angel Fund."

"Got it," Ginny said. "When I get the check I'll forward it to the fund."

"Thanks, that's very generous."

"Well, let's face it: Jake's life was all about making money and hoarding it. He stopped caring about people. I don't want him to be remembered as a miser. He was once better than that and that's how I'd like him to be remembered, as he was when I first knew him."

"It's very sad," Lucy said.

"I guess I always hoped that he would change, that he'd mellow when he got older," Ginny continued. "People sometimes do, at least that's what I've heard."

"He never really got the chance," Lucy said.

"That's true."

"Have the police made any progress?" Lucy asked.

"They haven't told me, if they did," Ginny said.

"Did he receive threats before the bombing? Anything like that?"

"We weren't close, you know. I didn't have any contact with him after our divorce and during my second marriage. Then after my husband died I had to manage our money, our investments, so I thought of Jake. That was the basis of our relationship. I'd see him about twice a year and he'd report on how the stocks and things were doing. He didn't get personal, except the last time I saw him, he seemed to be growing a bit paranoid. He was nervous and edgy and said something like, 'They're not gonna get me.' I asked who, and he didn't answer, but he said he was keeping a shotgun by his bed."

Lucy was genuinely shocked. "Oh, my goodness," she said.

"Looking back, it seems he wasn't paranoid at all," Ginny said. "It's not paranoia when they're really out to get you."

Chapter Fifteen

When Lucy got to work Monday morning the first thing she did, after flipping the CLOSED sign on the door to OPEN and adjusting the ancient wood venetian blinds to let in some weak winter sunshine, was call the Tinker's Cove Police Department and ask to speak to the chief. Jim Kirwan was polite as always, but Lucy knew it would be a challenge to get any information out of him.

"How are you doing?" he asked.

"Fine," Lucy said.

"And the family?"

"Everybody's fine."

"Is your oldest—the one in Florida, that's Elizabeth, right? Is she coming home for Christmas?" he asked.

"Elizabeth has to work on Christmas, but she's coming home the day after."

"So I suppose you'll be having two Christmases," the chief said.

"I'm really looking forward to seeing her. It's been six months since her last visit," Lucy admitted. "But that's not the reason I called. . . ."

"I didn't suppose it was," the chief said, switching to his official voice.

"I had a little chat with Virginia Irving on Saturday, after the estate sale at Marlowe's place, and she said that Jake Marlowe was extremely paranoid in his last weeks and that he kept a shotgun by his bed. He seemed to think someone was out to get him."

"These old folks tend to be a bit paranoid," the chief said. "I have one old lady who calls me at least once a week, convinced someone has stolen her silver tea service. I send an officer over and it's always in the same place; she just put it away in a closet to keep it safe and forgot where she hid it."

"Well, this is a little different," Lucy said, wondering how stupid the chief thought she was. "Somebody really was out to get Jake Marlowe, and succeeded! It sounds to me as if he'd been receiving threats. He knew he was in danger and he was afraid. So what I'm wondering is whether he reported these threats to your department. Did he?"

"That sort of thing would be confidential," Kirwan said, sounding even more official. "Department policy."

Lucy figured this meant Marlowe had indeed filed a complaint with the department. "I can understand the need for confidentiality when people are alive, but now that he's dead, I don't see how it matters," Lucy said. "Everybody knows that somebody really had it out for Jake Marlowe."

"I'm sorry, Lucy, but policy is policy. I can't start making exceptions—that's a slippery slope."

"How long ago did the threats start?" Lucy asked. "Did he have any idea who was making them?"

"I haven't confirmed or denied any action that Jake Marlowe may or may not have taken in regard to this department," Kirwan said.

"Can I quote you on that?" Lucy asked in a sarcastic tone. She really hated when public officials resorted to speaking in officialese.

"Yes, you may," the chief said. "You can also say that the investigation is continuing and we are cooperating with the state police and the fire marshal's office. And this department is committed to following every lead and will not give up until the person or persons who committed this despicable act are identified. The safety and security of every Tinker's Cove resident is this department's primary concern."

"Is this an exclusive?" Lucy scoffed. "Shall I stop the presses?"

"That would be your decision," the chief said. "Nice talking to you."

"Same here," Lucy said, but her tone of voice made it clear that she didn't really mean it. Not that she'd actually expected to get much out of the chief.

She typed up a few inches, quoting the chief word for word, and sat for a few minutes staring at the computer screen. Then, impulsively shoving her chair back, she hopped to her feet, grabbed her coat, and shoved her hat onto her head and headed over to the Downeast Mortgage office, pulling on her gloves as she went.

Elsie Morehouse wasn't thrilled to see her. "Oh, it's *you,*" she said, adding a sniff that made Lucy wonder if she'd forgotten to use deodorant that morning. "Mr. Scribner is not in."

"I actually wanted to talk to you," Lucy said, grasping at straws.

"I can't imagine why," Elsie said, "unless you wish to apply for a loan." Her tone of voice made it quite clear that she doubted Lucy would qualify.

"Not today, thank you," Lucy said, finding that annoying Elsie was rather enjoyable. "No, I came because I heard a rumor that Mr. Marlowe had received death threats before the bombing. Do you know anything about that?"

"I'm not at liberty to say anything about that," Elsie said, stiffening her back.

"Why ever not?" Lucy asked.

"The police said I wasn't to say anything to anyone about Mr. Marlowe, and especially not to the media."

"I'm not *the media,*" Lucy said. "I'm just the little local paper. The *Pennysaver* is more like a community newsletter, like a nice, chatty note you might get from your aunt, or what your neighbor might say over the fence."

Elsie's face hardened and her permanent curls actually seemed to tighten. "I'm not a fool, Lucy. I know that whatever goes in the *Pennysaver* can be picked up by the Portland and Boston papers, and could even go on TV. And that's why I'm not going to say anything, because I don't want to get in trouble with the police."

"Who's in trouble with the police?" Ben Scribner demanded, entering the office.

"No one's in trouble," Lucy said. "I'm just trying to track down a rumor about Jake Marlowe."

"Marlowe's dead," Scribner said.

"But . . . but . . ." Lucy sputtered, as he walked right past her and into his office, closing the door.

Elsie peered at her over her half glasses. "Now, if you'll excuse me, I have work to do." She managed to give the impression that in her view Lucy was little more than a lazy layabout.

Lucy nodded, staring at the closed door. "Right, well, thanks for your time."

When she got back to the *Pennysaver* office she found Phyllis had arrived and was sitting at her desk behind the reception counter. "Did you have a nice weekend?" she asked, as Lucy hung up her coat.

"Yeah, I got a terrific ship carpenter's chest at the Marlowe estate sale. I'm giving it to Bill for Christmas. What about you?"

"I was there, too. I must've missed you."

"Did you buy anything?"

"I didn't find anything. It was all filthy and terrible. What a way to live, huh? And him so rich. Makes you think."

"It sure does," Lucy said, settling in at her desk and moving on to the Seth Lesinski story. She began the way she usually did, reading through her notes and highlighting a few quotes, organizing her thoughts. She knew it was important to be impartial and not to let her own feelings about the campus organizer color the story; the fact that her daughter seemed to be enamored of him was hardly relevant to the average reader. But she found herself recoiling when she read his prediction about violence, when he said, "I wouldn't be at all surprised to see more violence. That's what happens when people run out of options. They get desperate. When hope runs out, that's when there's trouble."

She sat there, her yellow highlighter pen in her hand, staring at the words. He'd really said them. She remembered the wolfish gleam in his eye and the casual way he'd tossed off the prediction. As if violence was inevitable, even natural to him. And she supposed it would be, after several tours of duty in Iraq and Afghanistan.

Sara saw him as a committed social activist, as someone who wanted changes that would improve people's lives. He said he wanted economic justice for everyone, which was hard to argue against. Lucy herself believed in the Golden Rule: Do unto others as you would have others do unto you. She figured that applied to economics, too, and that in a wealthy, civilized country like the United States everyone ought to have their basic needs met. She didn't want to go hungry and she didn't want other people to, either. She wanted a roof over her head and education for her children—those were things that everyone should have.

She was well aware that some people in Tinker's Cove were struggling financially, and sometimes weren't able to obtain basic necessities for themselves and their families. That's why she and her friends worked hard to raise money for the Hat and Mitten Fund, which provided warm clothes and school supplies for local kids. She wrote sympathetic stories about regional charities in hopes that readers would support them, and she was among the first to write a check for a good cause. She carried her beliefs into the voting booth, too, and voted for candidates whose views were most like her own. She also encouraged her children to volunteer their time to help others who were less fortunate and, she admitted to herself, at heart she was proud of Sara's social activism.

But there was a danger when social activists became frustrated and began to justify violence, which was what Seth Lesinski had done. Protests and demonstrations were one thing, sending a postal bomb was another, and she wondered if Seth Lesinski had confused the two. Had he taken his social activism a step too far? Had he threatened Marlowe, or perhaps even sent the package bomb? It was a disquieting thought, and the fact that Sara was involved with him made it even more disturbing.

Lucy was sitting there, wondering how she could convince Sara that Seth might be a dangerous person, and that it might be wise to step back a bit. She remembered how her earlier attempts had failed and was trying to think of a way to reach her daughter when Ted blew in.

"Writer's block?" he asked, noticing that she wasn't typing.

"Not exactly," Lucy said. "I could write a book on this particular subject, but I don't want to get sued for libel!"

As the day wore on the weak morning sunshine faded and the sky filled with thick, threatening clouds. The streetlights on Main Street had turned on when Lucy left for home around four o'clock, and a light snow was falling, the dancing flakes catching and reflecting the lamplight. She was planning on making spaghetti and meatballs for supper and decided to pick up a bottle of chianti. It was just the sort of night that called for a bottle of red wine.

Bill agreed when he got home and promptly opened the bottle, so they could share a drink while Lucy cooked dinner. It had been a while since they'd really had a chance to talk and Lucy found herself voicing her concerns about Seth Lesinski.

"He's not a kid. He's done several tours in Iraq and Afghanistan," she said, stirring the spaghetti into a pot of boiling water. "I can't imagine what he might have seen and done over there."

Bill was thoughtful, sitting at the round golden oak table and sipping his wine. "Sara sure thinks a lot of him," he said.

"Of course!" The words came out like a small explosion. "He's a man, he's a hero, a warrior, and he makes these eighteen-year-olds who've never been out of Maine look pretty pathetic in comparison. And he has ideals." Lucy sipped her wine. "Ideals are sexy."

"Do you think Sara is involved with him?"

"I don't know," Lucy admitted, "but I do know that she'd like to be!"

Bill stared glumly into his empty wineglass, and reached for the bottle to refill it.

The storm was picking up when they gathered at the candlelit table and they could hear the wind howling outside. "They're forecasting at least a foot," Zoe said, who was studying meteorology in school. "It's a classic nor'easter."

"I wonder if school will be closed tomorrow," Lucy mused. "Classes might even be canceled at Winchester."

"That would be great," Sara said. "I've got a biology quiz tomorrow."

"Better study anyway," Bill advised, "just to be on the safe side."

"It won't be a waste. You'll need to know the material for your final," Lucy said.

Sara rolled her eyes. "It's under control, Mom," she said, helping herself to salad.

Bill, who was well into his third glass of wine, glared at his daughter. "Don't talk to your mother like that," he said.

"I didn't mean anything," Sara muttered.

Zoe was silent, keeping a low profile.

"It's all right," Lucy said, filling Bill's plate with a big pile of pasta. "This is a new meatball recipe. I got it from Lydia Volpe," she added.

"It's really good," Zoe said, eager to keep the peace.

"How are your grades?" Bill demanded. "College isn't like high school. We don't even get to see your grades, even though we're paying a small fortune for you to go."

Sara was shoving a meatball around on her plate with her fork. "They're okay. I'm not failing or anything like that."

"But they're not great?" Bill asked, pressing the issue.

"It's a lot harder than high school," Sara said, her voice rising defensively.

"Maybe you should make an appointment with your advisor," Lucy suggested. "What subject are you having trouble in?"

"Mostly biology," Sara said. "And I don't know why I ever signed up for Chinese—it's impossible."

"Not for millions of Chinese; they manage to speak it," Bill said. "Maybe you need to work harder. You could try studying instead of demonstrating."

Lucy inhaled sharply. This wasn't turning out to be the pleasant, relaxing dinner she'd hoped for. "Let's talk about this later," she urged. "I'm sure we can figure out a way to salvage Sara's first semester."

"I don't know if college is worth it," Sara declared, voicing her frustration. "You can't get a job, even with a degree. I think I'd be better off working for the movement."

"You don't mean that," Lucy said, horrified.

"I do! I don't see the point of all this studying. What good is it? What does it matter if I know what *ontogeny recapitulates phylogeny* means? Who actually cares about some silly, outdated theory?"

"I care," Lucy said, though she hadn't the vaguest idea what Sara was talking about.

"And so do I, dammit," Bill said, banging his fist on the table. "And I'll tell you another thing. You'd be smart to get as far away from those college radicals as you can. That's the sort of thing that can haunt you in later life, especially now when everything is on the Web. Some HR person will Google your name and a photo of you and that Seth Lesinski will pop up and you'll be branded some sort of radical and you won't get the job."

"If that's true, it's too late because I've already been photographed with crazy radicals," Sara said, yanking her napkin off her lap and throwing it on the table.

"Well, you better stop seeing them," Bill yelled. "In fact, as your father, I forbid you to see them."

Sara was on her feet, eyes blazing. "You can't do that."

"Oh, yes I can," Bill insisted. "As long as you're living under my roof you're going to abide by my rules!"

"We'll see about that," Sara said, turning and marching out of the room.

The three of them sat in silence, listening as she climbed the stairs and went to her room. Lucy braced for the slam of the door, but it never came. All she heard was the click of the latch.

It was Zoe who finally spoke. "What's for dessert?" she asked.

Lucy didn't expect to sleep well when she went to bed that night, and she did have trouble falling asleep, but once she drifted off she slept soundly. At one point she thought she heard an engine or motor, and the sound of wheels going back and forth on snow, and decided it must be a town snowplow out on Red Top Road. It was only when morning came that she discovered her mistake.

"Mom!" It was Zoe, and Lucy knew something was very wrong. "Mom!"

She tossed back the covers and ran into the hall, where she found Zoe standing in the doorway to Sara's room.

"Look!" She was pointing at Sara's bed, still neatly made. "She's gone! Sara's gone!"

Lucy ran to the window, where she saw a single line of footsteps through the snow, and tire tracks in the driveway. That wasn't a snowplow she'd heard in the night; it was a car. Sara had called a friend to pick her up. Sara had run away!

Chapter Sixteen

"Bill! Bill! Wake up!" Lucy shook Bill's shoulder and he groaned, shrugging her off and rolling over, pulling a pillow over his head.

"Sara's run away!" Lucy was insistent. This was a family crisis. "You've got to do something!"

Bill swatted the pillow away and rolled onto his back. "Sara's gone?" he asked.

"Yes! She never slept in her bed last night."

This information did not get the reaction Lucy expected. "Well, she couldn't have gotten far in that storm. Is it still snowing?"

"No. There's about nine or ten inches on the ground. Somebody must have picked her up in the night. There's tire tracks in the driveway."

"Must've had four-wheel drive," Bill said.

"Well, that does narrow the field of suspects," Lucy said sarcastically. Most everybody in town had at least one four-wheel drive vehicle.

"She's obviously with a friend. She'll come home when she gets tired of couch surfing," Bill said, yawning. "You know, I could do with some pancakes this morning. Fuel for shoveling."

"Make 'em yourself," Lucy growled, disgusted.

"What? What's the matter?" Bill was truly puzzled.

"Your daughter could be out there in the cold, stuck in a snow-drift, freezing to death, and you want pancakes for breakfast! That's what's the matter!"

"Be realistic, Lucy. She's probably sipping a cappuccino in the college coffee shop, telling her friends all about her horrible parents who don't understand her." Bill was on his feet, yawning and scratching his stomach. "Any chance of those pancakes?"

Lucy glared at him, turned on her heels and marched out of the bedroom. She was down the stairs in a flash, throwing on her coat and hat and scarf and gloves and boots as fast as she could, right over her plaid flannel pajamas. Libby watched anxiously from her dog bed, fearful that all this unusual early morning activity might somehow mean her food dish would remain empty. Then Lucy grabbed the keys to Bill's truck from the hook by the door and marched outside, into the clear, cold morning.

The snow wasn't as deep as she thought, she discovered when she stepped off the porch, and it had drifted somewhat, leaving only a few inches in the driveway. That was no problem for the pickup, and she made it to the road without any trouble. The Tinker's Cove Highway Department had been plowing all night and the road was clear all the way to Winchester College.

Suspecting that Bill might actually be right, she parked in the visitor's lot and went straight to the coffee shop, which was crowded with students and faculty buying take-out cups to carry to their eight o'clock classes. She scanned the faces eagerly but Sara's was not among them. Lucy did spot Fred Rumford, who was a professor, adding cream and sugar to his stainless steel commuter mug of coffee. She greeted him and asked if he'd seen Sara.

"No. I don't think she has any early classes," he said, shoving his glasses back up his nose. "I've never seen her on campus this early, anyway."

"I just thought she might be here," Lucy said, looking around.

"Family crisis?" Fred asked.

"You could say that," Lucy said, suddenly remembering that Fred had a much bigger problem in his family. She'd just learned a few days earlier that his younger brother, Geoff, was ill and needed a kidney transplant. "Oh, forgive me!" she exclaimed. "How is Geoff?"

Fred shrugged and sipped his coffee. "Doing okay, for the time being. They're looking for a match, but no luck so far. I got tested but I'm no good. Apparently nobody in the family is suitable."

"That's too bad," Lucy said. "I suppose there's dialysis."

"They're trying to avoid that. They say he's a really good candidate for a transplant. They just have to find him a kidney. He's on a list, so it's just a matter of time."

"I'll be keeping him in my thoughts," Lucy said. "And if you see Sara, will you give me a call?"

"Do you want me to give her a message?" he asked, looking concerned. "Tell her to call home?"

"Uh, no," Lucy said, imagining how negatively Sara would react to such a request. "I just want to know she's okay."

Fred nodded. "That's probably the best course of action. Give her some room and she'll come to her senses."

"Thanks," Lucy said, wishing she shared Fred's optimism. She was considering her next step when she noticed the coffee shop's enticing smell and decided she might as well have a cup while she considered her options. She got herself a double Colombian and took a seat at the cushioned banquette that ran along the café walls. After a couple of sips of coffee her head seemed to clear and she decided to do the obvious thing, wondering why on earth she hadn't thought to simply call Sara on her cell phone. She rummaged in her big purse and found her phone, took a deep breath and scrolled down her list of contacts until she got to Sara, then hit Send.

She got voice mail, so she left a message. "Hi! It's Mom. Just want to know that you're okay. Give me a call, send me a text. Whatever works for you. Love ya, bye."

Flipping the phone closed, she realized she hadn't felt this low in a really long time. She might as well wallow in it, she decided, staring into her coffee. She'd give herself until she finished the coffee and then she'd pick herself up and get on with her life.

When she drank the last swallow, she'd worked through her emotions, beginning with self-pity (*I'm the world's worst mother.*), gradually transitioning to resentment (*I may not be the world's greatest mother but I don't deserve this.*), and concluding with a surge of anger (*The nerve of that girl!*). She decided to take a quick tour around the quad, just in case she might see Sara, and had reached the science building when she slid on a patch of ice. A kid grabbed her arm, saving her from a nasty spill, and she looked up to thank him, recognizing Abe Goode. He was one of Sara's friends, and he'd even come to the house for dinner a couple of times.

"Mrs. Stone! Are you okay?" he asked. Abe was a big guy, a freckle-faced carrot top, wearing one of those Peruvian knit caps with ear flaps, and he was carrying a pair of cross-country skis over his shoulder.

"I'm fine. Thanks for catching me."

"No problem. This snow's something, isn't it? Fresh powder. I can't wait to get out on the trails."

"What about your classes?" she asked.

"I'll get the notes from somebody," he said. "No problem."

"Say, you haven't seen Sara this morning, have you?" Lucy asked. "I need to talk to her."

"I haven't seen her, but she texted me that she's moved in with that gang on Shore Road."

"Shore Road?"

"Yeah, the social action crowd, Seth Lesinski and his buds. They've got a squat there in a foreclosed house. Some kind of protest." He scratched the stubble on his chin. "It's not my thing. Talk, talk, talk, when you could be skiing."

Lucy smiled. "You've got a point."

Back in the truck, Lucy weighed her options. She finally decided to go to the squat in her role as an investigative reporter. If Sara just happened to be there, it would be a coincidence. She wasn't going there in search of Sara; she was just following up on a tip for her story about Seth Lesinski. And if Sara believed that, she decided, she might just try to sell her the Brooklyn Bridge.

Shore Road, which meandered along a rocky bluff fronting the ocean, was the town's gold coast. It was lined with huge shingled "cottages" built as summer homes in the early 1900s, as well as more modern mansions notable for their numerous bathrooms and ballroom-sized kitchens. One recently constructed vacation home, she'd heard, had eight bedrooms and twelve bathrooms, which made her wonder if the owner had been over-toilet-trained as a child. All the houses, old and new, had amazing ocean views, and most were empty for ten months of the year.

Lucy had no difficulty finding the squat; it was the house with eleven cars in the driveway. She added Bill's truck to the collection and made her way up the snowy path trodden by numerous feet and onto the spacious porch. The door, surprisingly, was ajar on this cold winter day. She stepped inside the enormous hallway, with its curving stairway and gigantic chandelier, and yelled hello, her voice echoing through the cold, empty rooms that had been stripped of furniture and personal effects.

"Hey, welcome," a girl with long blond hair said. Dressed in jeans and several sweaters, she was carrying an armload of firewood.

"Is Seth here?" Lucy asked. "I'm from the local newspaper."

"Cool," the girl said. "Follow me." She led the way into a large living room where a fire was burning in the fireplace, and a collection of air mattresses and cheap plastic lawn furniture was filled with a motley crew of youthful activists. Seth was leading a discussion, pointing to a whiteboard filled with economic terms: national debt, CEO salaries, progressive taxation, redistribution of wealth, economic justice. He paused, greeting her. "Hi, Lucy. Everyone, this is Lucy Stone, from the newspaper."

"Hi, Lucy," they all chorused.

"I don't want to interrupt," Lucy said, scanning the group and looking for Sara. "I just have a follow-up question."

"Right. We'll go in the library." He led the way through the group, and Lucy followed, but she didn't see Sara. Once inside the adjacent room, where the walls were lined with empty bookshelves, he turned to face her. "What did you want to ask me?"

"Well, for one thing, what's going on here?" she asked.

"The house is abandoned, it's in foreclosure, and we want to make the point that people are being forced out of their homes, being made homeless, when there are plenty of empty houses. There's no need for anybody to be homeless. The answer is simple: put the homeless people in empty houses."

"I don't think it's that simple," Lucy said. "Somebody owns this house. It isn't yours."

"A bank owns it. What's the bank going to do with a house? The bank can't move into a house," Seth said.

"What you're doing is illegal," Lucy said. "You're trespassing. What are you going to do when the cops come to evict you all?"

"Nonviolent resistance," Seth said. "I hope you'll cover it, when they come."

"Absolutely." Lucy added as if it were merely an afterthought, "By the way, is my daughter Sara here?"

"I'm not sure," Seth said. "We've got quite a crowd. Some are in the kitchen, making soup for lunch. Maybe she's there." He cocked his head toward the other room, where the group was waiting for him. "I gotta go. We're having a planning meeting."

"Right," Lucy said. "Thanks for your time."

He went back to the meeting and Lucy wandered out into the hall, searching for the kitchen. She found it in the back of the house, flooded with sunlight and featuring ocean views, and she found Sara, too. She was standing at the expansive granite-topped center island, chopping carrots, next to a Coleman camp stove topped with a huge, steaming stockpot.

"Hi," Lucy said.

"What are you doing here?" Sara demanded, her voice bristling with resentment.

"Just checking that you're okay."

"Well, as you can see, I'm fine."

"Great," Lucy said. "I think you should consider coming home."

"Why do you think that? I'm happy here, with my friends. We're doing something important."

"This is illegal. Sooner or later the cops will come and arrest everyone."

"So what?"

"Trust me, you won't like it. Jail's no fun, not even for a few hours, or a night."

"Well, I'm ready to make sacrifices for my beliefs," she said self-righteously, tossing her head.

Lucy sighed. "All right. It's up to you." She went to the door. "Give me a call now and then, okay?"

Sara didn't answer.

Lucy didn't know what to think, or feel, when she got back in the truck and headed home. She was running late, now, and needed to get out of her pajamas before she went to work.

Kids, she thought, shifting into reverse and backing the truck out onto Shore Road. She loved Sara, of course she did, but at this moment she'd cheerfully throttle the ungrateful little witch. She'd been through similar crises before, she remembered, driving the familiar route. Toby had dropped out of college after a single year in which he'd concentrated on partying rather than studying and ended up on academic probation. And there had been numerous flare-ups, especially arguments with his father, that had made his teen years rather difficult.

Elizabeth hadn't exactly been easy, either. She'd insisted on chopping her hair into spikes and wore only black during her senior year of high school, and had developed a surly attitude toward other family members. Her grades had always been good, though, and she continued to succeed academically at Chamberlain College in Boston, although she did have a few unfortunate conflicts with the dean.

Lucy didn't know why she'd expected things to be any different with Sara, but she now knew she'd been lulled into complacency by her third child's easygoing nature. Easygoing until now, she thought, flipping on the signal and turning into her driveway.

The house was empty. Only Libby was home, greeting her with a wagging tail and a big, toothy dog smile. You could always count on your dog, she thought, scratching Libby behind her velvety ears.

There was a note stuck on the fridge with a magnet, from Zoe. It was just a big heart, with a Z in the middle. Lucy smiled when she spotted it, trying hard to ignore the evil little voice that was telling her, "She's a sweetie now, but just wait a few years!"

Minutes later, dressed in her usual jeans and sweater, she added a quick slick of lipstick, tossed the dog a biscuit, and left the house. First stop on Tuesday was always the town hall, where she picked up the meeting schedule for the upcoming week. She always made a point of chatting up the girls in the town clerk's office, often picking up a lead on a story. This week, however, there was an awkward silence when she presented herself at the clerk's window.

"What's up?" she asked, with a bright smile.

"Uh, nothing, Lucy," the clerk's assistant, Andrea, replied. She was a chubby girl in her twenties, with thick brown hair pulled back into a frizzy ponytail.

"It's like somebody died in here," Lucy joked.

"No. We're all fine," Andrea said, handing her the meeting schedule. "Do you need anything else?"

Lucy glanced at the list, which included the usual selectmen's and FinCom meetings, as well as the Planning Committee and Conservation Committee. "Looks like a busy week," she said, hoping to get some sort of conversation going.

"If that's all, I have to get back to work," Andrea said.

"Of course," Lucy said, admitting defeat. Her reporter's nose told her something was definitely going on, something that nobody wanted her to find out about. There were no cheerful greetings, no hellos or good-byes as she passed the various town offices. Instead, heads were quickly turned as soon as she was spotted. She was beginning to wonder if she had the plague or something, when she bumped into Barney Culpepper at the entrance.

"Hey, Lucy!" At least he greeted her warmly.

"Hi, Barney. How's it going?"

"Can't complain," he said, taking off his official blue police winter cap, with the fur-lined ear flaps.

"Do you know what's going on?" she asked. "I got a really odd reception in there this morning."

He pulled her aside, away from the glass doors where they were clearly on view, into a sheltered alcove where a table was loaded with free information booklets on subjects such as preventing forest fires and how to obtain fishing licenses. "Don't say you heard it from me. . . ." he began.

"Of course not."

"The town employees are planning to stage a demonstration at the FinCom meeting Wednesday night. They're going to demand reinstatement of hours and benefits."

"Great," Lucy said. "I'm all for that. Why the attitude?"

"Because of Bill," Barney said. "He's on the committee. . . ."

". . . and I'm his wife," Lucy said, finishing the sentence.

"Yeah. I think they just feel awkward about it."

"Well, they shouldn't," Lucy said. "I'm on their side."

"But nobody knows how Bill's gonna vote," Barney said.

"Not even me," Lucy admitted. "It's going to be an interesting meeting."

"See you there," said Barney, with a wink.

Tuesdays were always busy at the *Pennysaver,* as they all worked to meet the noon Wednesday deadline, and for once Lucy was grateful for the constant pressure that kept her mind from obsessing about Sara. It was only when she left the office that she found herself brooding, worrying about where and with whom Sara would be spending the night.

Dinner was a quiet affair, with just the three of them gathered over tuna casserole at the kitchen table. Lucy was trying to think of a tactful way to warn Bill about the town employee's plans to demonstrate at the FinCom meeting when Zoe broke the silence.

"This is weird," Zoe declared. "I always wished I was an only child but now I don't like it."

"Why don't you like it?" Bill asked, helping himself to salad.

"Nowhere to hide," Zoe said, digging into the casserole. "Besides, I always come out looking pretty good in comparison to the others."

"You're just younger," Lucy said. "You haven't had a chance to get into trouble."

"But now . . ." Zoe began.

"Yes?" Lucy and Bill chorused, swiveling their heads to stare at their daughter.

Her reaction was instantaneous. "See!" she retorted, and they all laughed.

"You can consolidate your favored child status by doing the dishes," Lucy said. "I've got a rehearsal."

"Lucky me," Zoe moaned, but when they'd finished eating she got up and cleared the table without further protest. The leftovers had been wrapped and put away and the dishwasher was humming when Lucy left the house.

The night was cold and crisp and moonlight reflected off the snow that filled the woods and yards alongside the road. The little cluster of houses on Prudence Path were bright with Christmas lights, and the neighborhood looked like a picture on a Christmas card. Farther on, Lucy passed the turn to Shore Road and resolutely drove past, resisting the tug that drew her to Sara.

After rehearsal, Lucy stopped at the IGA to pick up a gallon of milk and some eggs for breakfast. The store was brightly lit but only a few cars were in the parking lot, including the Cunninghams' aged Corolla. Lucy saw them in the cereal aisle as she hurried back to the dairy counter, which was located along the rear wall of the store, and attempted to avoid them by returning through the canned goods. She knew she was being a coward but she was tired. She'd had an emotionally exhausting day and she didn't feel up to coping with their difficult situation.

Her strategy didn't work, however, as she encountered Zach and Lexie at the checkout counter. Dot had added up their order and Lexie was handing over their SNAP benefit card when Lucy got in line behind them.

"Okay," Dot said. "That brings it down to twelve forty-nine, for the pet food."

Zach pulled out his wallet and discovered he only had nine dollars. "What have you got, Lexie?"

Lexie found she had two dollars and twenty-seven cents.

Zach sighed. "I'll take it back and get the smaller bag," he said, picking up the twenty-pound bag of dog chow.

"Don't bother," Lucy said, handing Zach a five-dollar bill. She didn't care if he paid it back but she knew Zach was proud, so she added, "Catch me later, when you've got it."

"Thanks," Zach said, as Dot gave him the change. He turned to Lucy with a serious expression. "I will pay you back."

"I wouldn't hold your breath," a male voice advised, and Lucy turned to see Ben Scribner standing in line behind her, holding a can of store-brand coffee. "Trust me. You can't count on folks who get government handouts and still can't make ends meet."

Suddenly, Lexie whirled around, her face distorted as she struggled with tears. "Who are you to criticize us?" she demanded. "You're a greedy, horrible, nasty, selfish man! You wreck people's lives! You should rot in hell—and I know you will!"

Embarrassed, Zach attempted to quiet his wife. "She doesn't mean it. She's just upset," he said. "Our daughter's in the hospital—she's very sick."

Much to Lucy's amazement, Ben Scribner's features seemed to soften. "Your little girl is sick? How old is she?"

"She's seven, not that you care," Lexie snapped. Her hair, which needed a wash, was pulled back into a ponytail. She wasn't wearing any makeup, not even lipstick on her thin, chapped lips. Her skin was pasty from being indoors too much and stretched so tight over her bones that Lucy thought it might crack.

"Her name's Angie," Zach said.

"And what's the problem?" Scribner asked.

"Juvenile polycystic kidney disease." Lexie hissed out the words.

"And can't the doctors do anything?"

"She needs a kidney transplant, but we're running out of time," Zach said.

"What do you mean?" Scribner asked.

"If she doesn't get it soon," Lexie said in a flat tone, "she's going to die."

Scribner looked astonished, as if the idea that a child could die had never occurred to him.

"So you can take our house if you want. I really don't care, because Angie won't be there. It won't be our home, not without Angie." Lexie turned to Lucy. "Thanks for the loan. We'll pay you back next week," she said.

"Let me know if there's anything else I can do," Lucy said.

Lexie nodded and started to go, then suddenly whirled around and spat in Scribner's face, before running out of the store.

Dot reached under the counter for a roll of paper towels, but Lucy thought she took an awfully long time unrolling a few sheets and handing them to Scribner, so he could wipe the saliva off his face. It was as if she wanted to give him plenty of time to realize what had happened, and to consider what Lexie thought of him.

Chapter Seventeen

The big hand on the clock in the *Pennysaver* office was jerking its way to the twelve on Wednesday morning when Lucy hit the final period and sent Ted her last story, an account of the Planning Committee meeting, when the little bell on the door jangled and Rachel walked in.

"Hi," Lucy said, greeting her with a smile. Phyllis and Ted merely waved, being busy with last minute tasks.

"Is this a bad time?" Rachel asked. She looked frazzled, with dark circles under her eyes. Strands of long dark hair had escaped from her tortoiseshell clip and she kept tucking them behind her ears. When she unbuttoned her coat, Lucy saw she'd topped an unbecoming maroon turtleneck with a ratty old brown sweater, obviously the first things that came to hand.

"No, I'm done, unless Ted finds fault with my five inches on the Planning Committee."

"You're done," Ted said. "I don't think I've got room for it this week."

"I hate it when this happens," Lucy complained. "My precious prose, discarded on the scrap heap of journalism." She was hoping to get a smile from Rachel, but didn't succeed.

"I was just wondering, well, if maybe you could help me this afternoon," Rachel said, sounding as if she didn't really think Lucy would.

Lucy, however, wasn't about to turn her down. She wanted to find out what was causing her friend to be so unhappy. "Absolutely," she said. "What can I do?"

"Miss T and I are going to go over the costumes one last time and we could use another pair of hands. Are you sure you don't mind?" Rachel asked. "I mean, with Christmas and all you must have a lot to do."

"Nothing that can't wait," Lucy said, reaching for her purse.

"It seems an awful lot to ask," Rachel continued in a doubtful tone.

Lucy zipped up her parka and put an arm around Rachel's shoulders. "Look, let's get some coffee and a bite to eat, maybe an early lunch, and we'll take it from there."

At Jake's, Lucy ordered a BLT and a cola. Rachel got a bowl of chowder, which she stirred from time to time with her spoon but didn't eat. "What's going on?" Lucy asked, talking with her mouth full of crunchy toast.

Rachel's expression was bleak. "I don't know. I just can't seem to pull myself together."

"Maybe you've just taken on too much," Lucy said.

"That's what Bob says."

"So things are okay with you and Bob?" Lucy asked.

Rachel suddenly looked anxious. "What have you heard?"

"Nothing," Lucy said, quick to reassure her. "Nothing at all."

Rachel narrowed her eyes. "Sometimes I wish that scenery had done a little more damage to Florence."

Lucy smiled. "Bob's not the sort to be unfaithful."

"Florence doesn't seem to realize that," Rachel said. "She keeps calling and popping up. You've seen how she won't leave him alone at rehearsals."

"I've also seen how Bob brushes her off."

"She's like dog hair. No matter how much you brush her off there's always more."

Lucy laughed, relieved that Rachel hadn't entirely lost her sense of humor.

"The show's going well," Lucy said. "Isn't it?"

"It's coming together," Rachel admitted. "I asked Bill to stop by and check the scenery." She spooned up some chowder. "I hope you don't mind."

"Why would I mind?" Lucy asked, popping the last bit of BLT in her mouth.

"Well, I don't want you to think I'm after your husband or anything."

Lucy coughed and sputtered, choking and reaching for her drink. "Never crossed my mind," she finally said.

Rachel drove them both to Miss Tilley's little Cape house, which was decorated in the spirit of the season with a swag of greens tied with a red ribbon on the front door. Inside, Miss Tilley's small tabletop tree was decorated with antique kugels from Germany, which Lucy happened to know were worth quite a lot of money.

"Your tree is beautiful," Lucy said, examining the handblown ornaments.

"I remember those ornaments from my childhood." Miss Tilley was dressed as usual in a neat twin set and tweed skirt. Her white hair made a curly aureole around her pink-cheeked face. "I wasn't allowed to touch them."

"Is this tree fake?" Lucy asked, touching the plastic needles.

"Much safer for the ornaments," Miss Tilley said, pleased as punch to show that she wasn't stuck in the past. "And you can keep it up as long as you like—it doesn't drop its needles."

"But you don't get the piney scent," Lucy said, as Rachel helped the old woman into her broadcloth coat. She offered her arm to Miss Tilley when they trooped out to Rachel's car, since the walk was a bit slippery, but Miss Tilley refused it in a show of independence. She did the same when they arrived at the church, even sliding a bit on an icy patch as if she were ice skating. Lucy and Rachel exchanged a disapproving glance, as if their aged friend was instead a stubborn toddler.

Once inside, Rachel led them to a corner in the basement hall, where the costumes were hanging on a portable rack. They were stiff and dusty, so they shook them out, and checked that the buttons and zippers were all in working order and added labels identifying each one. A couple of pairs of trousers needed their length adjusted and Lucy busied herself with needle and thread. Miss Tilley brushed the top hats worn by the male characters, and Rachel let out the bodice of Marge Culpepper's costume, which was too tight.

"How are your children, Lucy?" Miss Tilley asked. "Is Elizabeth still working at that hotel in Florida?"

"She is, and she has to work Christmas Day but she's coming the day after."

"Boxing Day," Miss Tilley said. "In Dickens's day rich folk boxed up their old clothes and gave them to their servants on Boxing Day."

"We could use a little more of that spirit these days," Rachel said. "Ticket sales are behind last year's."

"It's the economy," Lucy said. "People are hurting."

"Not everyone is hurting," Miss Tilley sniffed.

"Now you sound like Sara," Lucy said. "She's joined the social action group at Winchester College."

"Good for her," Miss Tilley said. "I like a girl who acts on her convictions."

"I'm not sure whether it's convictions or simple teenage rebellion," Lucy said. "She's left home and is squatting in a foreclosed house on Shore Road."

Rachel paused, seam ripper in hand, a horrified expression on her face. "I'm so sorry, Lucy. Here I was going on about my problems when you must be sick with worry."

"To tell the truth, I'm past worry. Now I'm mostly annoyed."

"But what if she gets arrested?" Rachel asked.

"I hope she does," Lucy declared. "It will teach her a lesson."

"Or confirm her in her beliefs," Miss Tilley said, holding Scrooge's top hat up to the light. "Such a silly fashion," she said. "Isn't it odd what people will wear?"

"Sure is," Bill said. His arrival let in a gust of chilly air. "You wouldn't catch me wearing a hat like that."

"You'd look quite handsome," Miss Tilley said, winking at him.

"Want to try it on?" Lucy teased.

"No way!" Bill hoisted the toolbox he was carrying. "Now what exactly do you want me to do?" he asked Rachel.

"You know how the scenery fell on Florence. I just want to make sure it doesn't happen again. I don't want any more accidents, especially during the performance."

Bill went up on stage, flipping the lights on, and disappeared behind the partly painted flats. He was only gone a moment or two before he returned. "Looks fine to me," he said, with a shrug.

"It's been bolted together and there are braces on the side panels that weren't there before. It's not going to fall."

"Al must have worked on it since the accident," Lucy said.

"Yeah," Bill said. "Those struts weren't there before, and the sections weren't bolted together. It's much safer now."

"But it wasn't safe before?" Lucy asked.

"It wasn't finished," Bill said. "It was a temporary setup."

Lucy was thoughtful. "So you're saying those flats fell because they weren't constructed properly?"

"That's the only way it could've happened," Bill said. "I wouldn't have left them like that but different people do things different ways."

"It does seem terribly careless," Miss Tilley said.

"I'm not sure careless is the word," Lucy said, remembering Florence saying she heard a noise and felt a draft just before the scenery fell, and her sense that she hadn't been alone.

Bill gave her a sharp look. "Anybody can make a mistake," he said, but she knew what he really meant. He was warning her not to poke her nose into matters that didn't concern her.

That evening she found herself accompanying Bill to the Finance Committee meeting. From what Barney had told her about the town employees it was going to be a tense affair and she wanted to give Bill a heads-up. She offered him a little advice as they drove into town.

"I've heard rumors that the town employees are going to show up in force tonight, demanding their old hours and benefits," she said. "You're going to need to keep a cool head and remember it's not about you. You didn't vote to make the cuts."

"I think I can handle whatever happens," Bill said, in a *mind-your-own-business* tone of voice.

I sure hope so, Lucy thought, but didn't say it out loud. She was pretty sure Bill didn't have a clue about the firestorm he was walking into. In fact, the meeting room was packed with town employees and members of the Winchester Social Action Committee when they arrived. Seth Lesinski and his cohorts were seated together on one side of the aisle, while town employees including Harry Crawford, Phil Watkins, and Nelson Macmillan were scattered among the usual concerned citizens on the other.

Lucy took her usual seat near the front of the room and Bill joined the other board members at the long table facing the audience, seating himself behind his shiny new nameplate. At seven o'clock precisely chairman Gene Hawthorne called the meeting to order and, as always, opened the public comment portion of the meeting.

Seth Lesinski immediately jumped to his feet. "I'm here tonight with members—" he began, only to be silenced by Hawthorne.

"It's usual to wait to be recognized by the chair before speaking," he said.

"Sorry," Seth said. "Am I recognized?"

"Go ahead," said Hawthorne, looking annoyed.

"Now that I've been *officially* recognized," Seth began with a smirk, "I'm here to say that I represent the Social Action Committee at Winchester College. Today the committee voted to demand complete and full restitution to the Tinker's Cove town employees' hours, wages, and benefits, and also to demand that town officials immediately demand that Downeast Mortgage cease and desist from foreclosing on delinquent mortgage holders."

This brief speech was well received by most audience members, who clapped and cheered.

Gene Hawthorne once again called for order. "Thank you for your input," he said, when the group finally quieted down. "I would like to point out, however, that tonight's meeting will be limited to discussion and action on the items listed on the previously posted agenda."

This announcement was met with a rumble of disapproval from the audience.

"Well, how do we get on the agenda?" Seth demanded.

"As I mentioned earlier, you need to be recognized by the chair before speaking," said Hawthorne, with a sigh.

Lesinski rolled his eyes and raised his hand.

"Mr. Lesinski," Hawthorne said. "Go ahead."

"I guess this is a point of order," Seth said in a challenging tone of voice. "How exactly does a concerned citizen place an item on the agenda?"

"You contact the committee secretary, Mrs. Mahoney, and she will take it from there. The agenda is posted one week prior to the meeting."

"May I ask another question?" Seth asked. He was bouncing on the balls of his feet.

"You may."

"In effect, that means that at a minimum the committee cannot act on reinstating hours and benefits before next week, which takes us right up to Christmas, right?"

"Actually a bit longer, because we have to vote to include an item on the agenda," Hawthorne said. "And we won't meet again until after Christmas."

"May I speak again?" Seth asked, bouncing a bit faster.

"You may."

"Can you consider taking that vote tonight, at this meeting?"

Hawthorne checked with the other committee members, who indicated they were open to the suggestion.

Jerry Taubert, however, had a cautionary bit of information. "I don't mind voting to include it in a future agenda, but it's really pointless. I'm all for reinstating hours and wages, but the fact is that there simply isn't enough cash on hand in the town account."

"He's right," Bill said. "I've been going over the accounts and there's not much wiggle room, that's for sure. Tax receipts are down and so is state aid."

"And furthermore," Frankie added, "on the other matter, I don't believe the town actually has the authority to tell Downeast Mortgage to stop foreclosures. That's something the town counsel would have to look into."

Hearing this, the crowd became extremely restive. "Well, that's what we pay him for," someone yelled. Harry Crawford and several other men were on their feet, demanding a vote.

"Do I have a motion?" Hawthorne asked, banging his gavel.

Pam raised her hand, moving that Lesinski's demands be placed on the agenda for the next meeting, which was scheduled to take place early in January, after the usual Christmas break. Frankie seconded it and Hawthorne called for discussion, recognizing Jerry Taubert.

"This is a waste of time," he said, getting a smattering of boos.

"Our hands are tied. We don't have the money to reinstate town employees. We'd have to raise taxes and we can't do that without a town meeting vote."

"Hold a special town meeting!" Phil Watkins yelled, eliciting cheers from the citizenry.

"Order! Order!" demanded Hawthorne, banging his gavel. When the crowd quieted down he recognized Bill. Lucy shifted uneasily in her seat.

"As for the demand that the town order Downeast Mortgage to stop foreclosures," said Bill, "I have to point out that there is simply no way we can do that. That is simply a matter of contractual obligations between private parties, and the town has no standing whatsoever in the . . ."

The crowd certainly didn't like hearing this, especially not the SAC kids, who were muttering and booing. Lucy discovered she was holding her breath. She was so tense that her stomach hurt. It was killing her to sit there when she wanted to leap to Bill's defense.

Gene Hawthorne called for order, once again, this time warning that he would have the room cleared unless the crowd observed the proper decorum. Receiving grudging acquiescence, he called for a vote on the motion. "All in favor," he said, and the room fell silent as Frankie and Pam raised their hands.

"Against?" The three men on the committee raised their hands, and the audience immediately erupted with a unified roar.

In a matter of seconds everyone was on their feet. Cardboard coffee cups, balled up wads of paper, even chairs were hurled into the air. The committee members ducked behind their table. Lucy herself adopted a crash position, curling up and placing her arms above her head. Barney Culpepper was blowing his whistle, the meeting room doors were thrown open, and the Tinker's Cove Police Department, all seven officers who had been positioned outside, poured into the room. Seeing the officers in blue, the Winchester group bolted en masse for a side exit. Local folk were more easily subdued, but Harry Crawford did attempt to punch Officer Todd Kirwan. Kirwan avoided the punch and Barney applied the handcuffs, hustling Crawford out of the building.

"Meeting adjourned," Hawthorne declared, wiping his brow with a handkerchief, and the shaken committee members began gathering up their papers and belongings.

Hildy, the freelancer Ted had asked to cover the meeting, was already interviewing Hawthorne. "What's your reaction to tonight's events?" she was asking, as Lucy joined Bill, who was gathering up his papers.

Hawthorne shook his head. "We can't have this sort of thing," he said. "In future, we will have strict security at our meetings. The committee can't work under these conditions, and I want to say that these committee members are struggling with a very difficult fiscal situation and doing their very best to make responsible decisions."

Bill nodded in agreement. "It's very different to be sitting on this side of the table," he said. "We can't be influenced by an unruly mob." Then he took Lucy's arm and they made their way through the overturned chairs and litter to the door.

"Well, don't say I didn't warn you," she said.

"Bunch of hooligans," Bill muttered.

"Those hooligans include your daughter," Lucy said.

"She wasn't here tonight," Bill observed. "At least I didn't see her."

"No, she was probably back at the squat, building bombs."

"Don't joke about it," Bill said sternly, as they climbed into the pickup. "It's not funny."

"I wasn't joking," Lucy said. "There are going to be repercussions, and if I were you, I'd be very careful for the next few days."

"Don't be ridiculous." Bill shifted into reverse and backed out of his parking spot. "Everybody loves me."

"Not anymore," Lucy said.

Chapter Eighteen

Thursday morning, Lucy was lingering in bed with a cup of coffee, watching a morning news show on the old TV that had migrated upstairs when they bought a new flat screen for the family room. The weather reporter was predicting more stormy weather when Bill stomped up the stairs and blew into their bedroom.

"Somebody slashed my tires!" he exclaimed. His tone of voice left no doubt that he was really upset. Also shocked, angry, and indignant. "Can you believe it?"

"Actually, I can," Lucy said, recalling that she had predicted trouble after the contentious FinCom meeting.

He sat on the edge of the bed. "Who would do such a thing?"

"Somebody who's mad at you," Lucy said.

"Because of my vote?"

"Probably." Lucy had a few ideas on the subject. "Or to make a point."

"You know how much this is gonna cost us?" Bill asked. "And not just cash. Time, too. I'm gonna lose an entire day of work, getting new tires."

"You should report it to the police," Lucy said. "It's not just property damage. You're a public official. I'm pretty sure that attempting to intimidate a public official is a crime."

"Somehow I don't think I'm going to get much sympathy from the police department," Bill said. "They're town employees, too."

"True," Lucy said, patting his knee. "And to think, everyone used to love you."

Bill scowled and scratched his beard, now mixed with gray. "At least I know I can count on you not to throw my own words back at me."

"I would never do that," Lucy said, throwing the covers back and getting up. As she stood Bill grabbed her by the hips and pulled her down; she laughed as she rolled back on the bed. "I can't, Bill, I can't. I've got breakfast with the girls in half an hour."

"You're going to be late," Bill said, kissing her and groping for the buttons on her pajamas.

When she was in the car, on her way to Jake's, Lucy suddenly changed her mind about meeting her friends for breakfast. The four friends had agreed early on that their Thursday morning breakfasts were such an important commitment that only serious illness or death counted as legitimate excuses for breaking the date. This morning, however, Lucy found herself calling Sue and begging off. There was something she wanted to do, something that wouldn't wait.

"Well, this is a fine howdy do," Sue said, sounding annoyed. "Rachel's already called and said she's simply got too much to do to make it."

"Oh." Lucy felt a twinge of guilt but brushed it aside. "I hope this isn't a trend."

"Well, it is only a few days till Christmas." Sue sighed. "Pam called last night and said she could only stay for half an hour. She wants to get to an early bird sale at the outlet mall."

Lucy knew that Sue was a dedicated shopper. "Why don't you go with her?" she suggested.

"I think I will," Sue said. "But no excuses next week, right?"

"No excuses," Lucy promised, closing her flip phone and making the turn onto Shore Road.

Glancing out over the ocean, Lucy saw the sky was full of thick gray clouds, hanging low. The water itself was slate gray and choppy. It was the sort of scene that made you fear for anyone out on the sea and, living on the coast, Lucy knew there were plenty of fishermen, coast guardsmen, sailors, and merchant seamen who braved the waves every day. Lucy thought of the plaques on the walls of the Community Church, engraved with the names of those who had gone to sea and never returned: Isaiah Walker, who fell overboard in pursuit of a whale, Ephraim Snodgrass, who contracted yellow fever en route to Manila, and Horace Sanford, USN, whose troop ship was torpedoed by a German U-boat. She shivered, thinking of those poor souls, and the many others who met their fate in the cold depths of the North Atlantic.

Turning into the driveway at the squat, she saw, as before, it was filled with numerous cars. She marched resolutely up to the porch, pushed open the unlocked door, and stepped inside, where she was immediately met by Seth Lesinski.

"Here for a reaction to the FinCom meeting?" he asked, with a wide grin. He was holding a big mug of tea in one hand, a laptop computer in the other, and seemed terribly pleased with himself.

"Not exactly," Lucy said, following him into the library, away from other members of the group who were gathering in the living room.

Seth seated himself at a card table and opened the computer, then leaned back in his chair and took a long drink of tea. "So what can I do for you?" he asked.

"You can stop this campaign of intimidation, that's what you can do," Lucy said, picking up steam.

"I'd call it information, not intimidation," he said.

"My husband's tires were slashed last night," Lucy said in an accusatory tone, "and I think you know all about it."

Seth's eyebrows rose. "I don't."

"I don't believe you," Lucy replied. "And I wouldn't be the least bit surprised to learn you were behind the bombing that killed Jake Marlowe."

"That's crazy," Seth said, looking both shocked and troubled. "How could you ever think I wanted to kill that pathetic old man?"

"I don't think you intended to kill him. I think you meant to frighten him but things went wrong. You're a combat veteran— you know all about guns and explosives—" Lucy said, only to be interrupted.

"Yeah, I know about explosives, but from the wrong end. I've lost good friends, seen them literally ripped apart by IEDs. I would never . . . I'm a patriot, no matter what you might think. I love this country and that's why I'm doing what I'm doing. I'm trying to save it from the greedy bastards who are sucking it dry."

Lucy felt herself falling under his sway. She was almost convinced, actually feeling rather ashamed of her suspicions, when she caught herself. He was clever, she reminded herself, a master manipulator who had seduced her daughter mentally, if not physically. Sara! She suddenly had an urgent, overwhelming need to contact her daughter. Where was Sara?

"Is my daughter here?" she asked in a no-nonsense tone.

"Sara?" he asked.

"Yes, Sara! You know, Sara!"

He shook his head. "I haven't seen her this morning."

And I hope you never see her again, Lucy thought, turning on her heel and heading for the door. Glancing over her shoulder, she caught a glimpse of his computer screen: it pictured a classic comic book bomb, a sinister black globe with a sizzling wick, in front of a waving American flag, and the words *Extremism in the defense of liberty is no vice!*

Her eyes widened and she suddenly felt justified. So much for Seth Lesinski and his protestations of patriotism, his denial of violent tactics! The man was a domestic terrorist and he was seducing decent kids with social consciences to join him. He had to be stopped, she fumed, yanking the car door open and jumping inside. She was going to go straight to the police, she decided. This had gone far enough. It was time for the grown-ups to take charge.

When she marched into Police Chief Jim Kirwan's office, she was surprised to see that Ben Scribner was already there.

"That house belongs to Downeast Mortgage and I demand police action!" he was saying. "Those kids have moved in like they own the place. The utilities are off, you know. No water, no power, no heat. You can only imagine what's going on, the damage they're causing."

"It's worse than that," Lucy said, eager to join the discussion. "They've slashed Bill's tires, and they've got bombs on their computers. . . ."

Both Scribner and Kirwan looked at her. "Bombs?" the chief repeated.

"Bombs!" Lucy declared.

"What's this about tires?"

"All four tires on Bill's truck were slashed this morning," Lucy said. "And you heard Seth Lesinski at the meeting last night, all but predicting violence if their demands weren't met."

"That's not proof," the chief said.

"It's proof enough for me!" Scribner declared. "It's my property and I demand action! I'm a taxpayer, probably the town's biggest taxpayer, and I want those hooligans out of there by the end of the day!"

The chief scowled in concentration, considering his course of action. Finally, he nodded. "Okay," he said, and reached for the phone.

Lucy enjoyed a few moments of self-righteous satisfaction as she made her way to the *Pennysaver* office, congratulating herself that she'd actually managed to help convince the chief to take the correct action. It wasn't until she was walking into the office that it occurred to her to wonder at the strange turn of events that had caused her own interests to align with those of Ben Scribner. That was when she began to doubt she'd done the right thing, but by then it was too late. The police scanner was already buzzing as forces assembled and prepared to raid the squat.

Lucy covered it, of course, standing by the side of the road and snapping photos as uniformed SWAT team members from the state police deployed, accompanied by local officers, and stormed the shingled cottage. The squatters were brought out with their hands fastened behind their backs in plastic snap ties, their coats over their shoulders, and loaded into a school bus. Lucy was clicking away when Sara's face appeared on the digital video screen and she had the sickening realization that her daughter would probably never forgive her.

Once the house was emptied of squatters a team of crime scene investigators went to work, and Lucy also photographed them removing boxes and bags of material. When she asked if they had found evidence of domestic terrorism all she got was a stern "No comment."

Following up at the police station, Kirwan would only say that "the material taken from the squat will be analyzed for evidence of domestic terrorism." For the moment the squatters would be charged with trespassing and the arraignments were under way in Gilead. Lucy raced to the courthouse in the county seat, arriving just in time to produce bail for Sara.

Sara, much to her mother's irritation, did not express gratitude for the hundred dollars in cash that Lucy had extracted from the conveniently located ATM in the courthouse lobby. "I missed a poli sci quiz, 'cause of those cops!" Sara fumed. "And I studied and everything."

"I'm sure you can make it up. Maybe even get extra credit for getting arrested," Lucy said. "You got firsthand experience of the justice system. You should offer to write a paper for extra credit."

Sara narrowed her eyes. "Don't be all snarky, Mom."

"I'm not. I'm serious," Lucy said.

"The judge was horrible. He acted like we were criminals or something."

"You broke the law," Lucy reminded her. "Trespassing is a crime, and after last night's meeting, they're going to suspect the group of doing more than just squatting. You know your father's tires were slashed? Do you know anything about that?"

"No. Of course not. Seth wouldn't have anything to do with violence. He said he saw it firsthand in Iraq and Afghanistan and it's made him a committed pacifist. He believes in passive resistance. When the cops came he told us to go limp and let them arrest us, not to struggle or anything." Sara turned her head and stared out the window of the car, apparently fascinated by the snowy fields and bare trees along the road. "It was you!" she suddenly declared, whirling around to accuse her mother. "You're the one who got the cops to raid the squat!"

"Not really," Lucy said. "I reported the tire-slashing—of course I did. Your dad is a public official and this is intimidation. It's illegal, and it was my duty to report it." She paused, but Sara's expression remained angry and accusatory. "I think it was really Ben Scribner who convinced the chief. He demanded action and he's got friends in high places. I don't think the chief had any alternative, really. It was a question of property rights."

"Private property is theft," Sara declared.

"Well, then I guess you won't mind sharing your Uggs with Zoe and letting her wear them every other day, will you?"

Sara didn't have an answer for that, so she turned her head once again and watched the scenery roll by.

Lucy also was silent, wondering if her suspicions about Seth Lesinski were indeed correct. Sara was young and easily influenced, but she knew that her daughter was really a good person at heart. She wouldn't condone violence—she wouldn't have anything to do with it, of that Lucy was convinced. Maybe Sara was right about Seth Lesinski, and maybe she herself was wrong. But if that was so, who had sent the bomb? And did the same person slash Bill's tires? Were they going to find a brightly wrapped bomb in their mailbox, too?

That night was the dress rehearsal, the final run-through before the weekend performances. Florence had finished painting the scenery, which was still wet, in fact, and Rachel warned everyone to keep clear of it for fear of staining their costumes. Even so, Lucy found the addition of the subtly designed scenery and costumes transformed the show and made it much more believable. Now, Bob wasn't Bob reciting odd, old-fashioned language, he was Scrooge, complete with mutton-chop whiskers, an enormous pocket watch with a massive gold chain and fob, and a high top hat. And she found it easier to believe herself in the role of Mrs. Cratchit, thanks to the long, full-skirted dress and lace-trimmed mobcap.

Lucy knew she was not really much of an actor, but when she played the Christmas Yet to Come scene in which Tiny Tim is predicted to have died, she found tears welling in her eyes. Her voice broke as she gazed at his crutch leaning on the wall, no longer needed, and recalled how Bob Cratchit had found his crippled son "very light indeed" when he carried him on his shoulders.

Rachel gave her a big thumbs-up when she exited the stage, but her thoughts had strayed from Victorian England to the present. It was the possibility that Tiny Tim might die that finally melted Scrooge's hard heart, and Lucy wondered if learning that Angie Cunningham was actually in danger of dying might work in some way to soften Ben Scribner's heart. Or not, she thought, remembering how adamantly he'd insisted that the police clear his property of squatters.

Tragic situations had effects that were hard to predict. She thought of Al Roberts's surprising, angry reaction when the cast members had offered to help him. If he'd been in his right mind, he would have taken her up on her offer and borrowed her car. But his emotions got in the way. Lucy suspected his anger about Angie's situation had grown until it colored everything, including the foreclosure. Did he believe that Scribner was the author of all the family's problems, and had he attempted to get back at Scribner by rigging the scenery to fall on his niece, Florence? Al had walked over to the caroling with her and Bob and Rachel, but he could have left them and gone back to the church hall. She didn't remember seeing him among the crowd gathered around the bonfire, singing carols.

She was pulled back to the present when Rachel announced it was time to run through the curtain call, which she predicted would be a standing ovation, and all thoughts of Ben Scribner and Al Roberts and Angie disappeared in the euphoria of the moment. Rachel was over the top, once everyone was on stage, holding hands and bowing together. She clapped and bravoed and congratulated them all, assuring them that the show would be a terrific success.

Lucy was practically floating as she made her way to the Sunday School classroom that was serving as the women's dressing room, when she passed Bob in the hallway. He was talking on his cell phone, apparently making an appointment with a client who wanted his will written.

"Okay, Al," he was saying. "I can do it tomorrow, but I don't see what the rush is." Then there was silence, while Bob was listening and nodding. "Okay, we'll make it bright and early—nine o'clock suit you?" Then he ended the call, but remained in the hallway, obviously troubled.

"Is something the matter?" Lucy asked.

"Oh, Lucy," he said, looking up and smiling at her. "Great job tonight."

Lucy shook her head. "You're the star of the show; you were

fabulous. I had no idea you had such a mean streak. Who knew that there's a nasty old miser hiding somewhere inside nice generous Bob Goodman?"

Bob chuckled. "It's just acting, I'm happy to say."

"Oh, right," Lucy said, teasing him.

"How's Bill doing?" he asked. "I heard there was quite a kerfuffle at the FinCom meeting last night."

"Not too good," Lucy said. "Somebody slashed the tires on his truck."

Bob's eyebrows rose in shock. "I know the town employees are angry about the cuts, but I didn't think they'd do anything like that."

"Funny," Lucy said. "My first thought was that it was the students, that group led by Seth Lesinski. Kids can be really irresponsible and do crazy stuff."

"Maybe," Bob admitted. "But the town employees have really been hurt by the cuts. Here's just one example. This guy, I'm not gonna mention any names, worked for years and rose through the ranks until he was head of his department. Then he had some health problems and had to take early retirement. He got what probably seemed like a big payout at the time but now isn't so much. He's in real financial trouble. . . ."

Hearing Rachel's voice, calling him for a photo, Bob paused.

"Listen, forget I said that. I shouldn't talk about my clients—" He stopped abruptly. "I'm making it worse, aren't I?"

"Forget it," Lucy said, waving her hand. "I didn't hear a word of it."

Chapter Nineteen

On Friday morning Lucy woke with an odd mixture of dread and excitement—butterflies were definitely fluttering in her tummy. The show was hours away but she knew she was going to be nervously anticipating the opening curtain all day. What if she forgot her lines? What if she suddenly went blank? What then? A million things could go wrong in a stage show, which depended on the perfectly timed efforts of everyone involved, not only the actors but all the behind-the-scenes workers, too. All she could do was keep repeating her lines and hope that everybody else was focused on the show, too.

But first she had a long day to get through. Friday was generally a slow day at the *Pennysaver,* in which she developed a news budget and a list of stories for the next week's edition. She usually started by going through the press releases that had been sent to the paper, looking for possible story ideas. She also checked the town hall calendar of meetings, as well as the docket at the county courthouse. Then, when she'd put together a list of ideas, she checked with Ted, who nixed or approved her ideas and sometimes had a suggestion or two.

There was no rush to get to the office, but Lucy was full of nervous energy and found herself unlocking the door at just a few minutes past eight. Phyllis didn't come in until nine and Ted, being the boss, arrived whenever he felt like it, which was usually around ten-thirty on Fridays, sometimes later. Lucy considered making a pot of coffee and decided against it. Caffeine was the last thing she needed. Her nerves were all ajangle already. Skipping ahead to the next step in her Friday routine, she got the big accordion file of press releases and carried it to her desk, where she began to go through it. It was quite thin this close to Christmas, and nothing caught her interest. Her mind turned to what Bob had told her about one of his clients.

He hadn't given a name, but Lucy remembered writing a story a few years ago when Al Roberts retired, and she was pretty sure that he was the employee whom Bob was talking about. It had been the usual congratulatory fluff piece about an employee who had served the town for many years. In Al's case, he'd been with the highway department for some thirty years, ending his career as superintendent. Even so, thought Lucy, he was a young retiree, not yet sixty. Why, she wondered, had he stopped working at such a relatively young age? As superintendent, he didn't have to perform difficult physical labor. It was an office job, involving meetings and negotiations and scheduling, with occasional site visits to check on work in progress. He had been making good money, too, by local standards. Why did he give it all up? And why had he hired a lawyer?

Lucy suspected two possibilities: Al Roberts had been forced to take early retirement because of either a job performance matter or a health issue. Job performance was an area that nobody in town government liked to talk about, because it made employees and officials vulnerable to criticism from taxpayers. Lucy understood that it was simply unfair for a teacher, for example, to be subject to public scrutiny and criticism for a personal matter, perhaps needing extra sick days to care for an ailing relative. Lucy knew only too well how critical some taxpayers could be of town employees, always eager to claim the privilege because they were ultimately paying the employees' salaries. When it came to health issues and disability claims, especially disability claims, those were even more likely to unleash a torrent of angry outrage.

But as much as Lucy understood the need for town employees' job evaluations to remain confidential, she was often frustrated when she encountered this protective wall of silence. Not everything had to make it into print, but background knowledge was valuable to a reporter in that it gave greater understanding of issues and tensions affecting public policy. It helped to know that the superintendent of schools and the town treasurer absolutely loathed each other. If Lucy needed a comment from the town treasurer on a school budget matter, or vice versa, she knew she was likely to get an unprintable reply.

On the other hand, she admitted ruefully, sometimes she wanted to spice things up a bit. Then a call did the trick, with the addition of a few asterisks and exclamation points because the *Pennysaver* was decidedly a "family-friendly" publication.

This Al Roberts thing was none of her business, she reminded herself, but somehow she couldn't put it out of her mind. It sat there, nibbling away at her thoughts, popping up when she tried to concentrate on the Girl Scout carol sing at the old folks' home or the New Year's Eve party at the VFW. Lucy knew perfectly well that Roger Wilcox, the chairman of the Board of Selectmen, would insist on maintaining the confidentiality of Roberts's records, and Bob Goodman would claim client privilege, but she was also aware of the boxes of town documents that Bill had stashed away in his office. Those boxes were a treasure trove of information, but she was forbidden from looking at them.

They were extremely tempting, but it would be a violation of journalistic ethics to even peek at them. Even worse, a violation of marital ethics, because Bill was entitled to privacy. She wouldn't think of opening a letter addressed to him, except for the bills, which were her responsibility to pay. She would never open a personal letter, like a birthday card or something like that. Never.

She could picture the boxes, however, the image quite clear in her mind. They were beige with a brown stripe, and the words *Documents* was printed on them. They squatted there, in her imagination, and wouldn't leave. It was like that second chocolate bar, a buy-one-get-one-free offer, perhaps. You ate the first and saved the second for later, but you couldn't quite put it out of your mind and you ended up eating it, too.

Lucy checked the clock on the office wall. It was barely nine. Bill would be at his current job, a summer cottage colony renovation, and Ted wasn't due anytime soon. She was only after background information, she told herself, pushing back her chair and reaching for her coat. Deep background, that was all.

Even so, despite her efforts to rationalize away her guilt, she had the uneasy sense that she was doing something wrong when she climbed the narrow stairs to Bill's attic office. Up there, under the sharply angled ceiling, he'd carved out a space for his desk and files. It was his haven, away from the family, and he'd decorated the walls with framed baseball cards from his boyhood collection and New England Patriots posters. Lucy ignored quarterback Tom Brady's rather disapproving gaze as she opened the first box, which contained computer printouts of the town budget from recent years. There was no way she could make head nor tail of that, she decided, replacing the lid.

The second box, however, was more interesting as it contained minutes of the FinCom's meetings, including those of executive sessions. Executive sessions were closed to the public and the press and usually concerned confidential personnel matters such as contract negotiations and disability payments. They had been filed neatly according to date and she soon found records of a discussion concerning Al Roberts's retirement.

According to the minutes, Roberts had requested early retirement on medical grounds, claiming injuries sustained some seventeen years earlier in a roads project. Roberts, who was then foreman of the town's road crew, had set a dynamite charge that exploded too soon and he was injured by flying debris. That injury, he claimed with the support of medical documentation, was now causing moderate to severe back pain that made it impossible for him to continue working as superintendent.

Jake Marlowe had questioned Roberts's claim, pointing out that the town had paid his medical expenses at the time of the accident. He also noted that when Roberts subsequently filed a lawsuit claiming disability, the committee offered him a lump-sum payment that he accepted, rather than taking the case to court. The amount, twenty-five thousand dollars, had probably seemed generous at the time but, Lucy thought, now seemed rather paltry. Marlowe didn't mince words, however, accusing Roberts of attempting to blackmail the committee with this new demand for early retirement. Instead, he suggested, the committee should simply refuse to renew his contract and look for a replacement. In other words, Marlowe had threatened to fire Roberts.

Wow, Lucy thought, sitting back on her heels. She had no idea this was going on. And to think she'd always found FinCom meetings to be boring. Actually, they were. All the exciting stuff took place in executive session.

Reading on, Lucy discovered that cooler heads had prevailed. Jerry Taubert had pointed out that granting early retirement would be far less costly than deciding the matter in court, and he for one thought Roberts had done a very good job as superintendent. Frankie and Pam had also voiced support for Roberts, leaving only Gene Hawthorne to side with Marlowe.

When it came to awarding Roberts's pension, however, Taubert switched sides. Roberts had wanted his pension to be calculated based on the years he would have worked to age sixty-five, but the committee voted to include only the years actually worked, although they did allow him to start collecting immediately.

The actual figures weren't mentioned in the minutes, however, and Lucy had to check those town budgets for the actual payroll figures. She flipped through quite a lot of pages of numbers and finally discovered that Al Roberts was getting $1,257 a month, but Frank Sullivan, the former building inspector who had retired at age sixty-five, was getting $1,979 a month. Lucy did a quick calculation and discovered that was a difference of more than $700 a month.

What did seven hundred dollars a month mean to a man like Al Roberts, Lucy wondered. The answer was clear: it was the difference between keeping up on his mortgage payments or losing his house to foreclosure. She knew he was an angry man and, she realized with a start, he did have some experience with explosives. The question was, she thought, whether he was content to vent his anger through the legal system, or whether he'd taken things further by sending a package bomb to Jake Marlowe. She knew he'd hired Bob, and she hoped that indicated he was content to work within the legal system, but thinking back to Bob's conversation with Roberts, she sensed that Roberts had been growing impatient.

Lucy realized her legs were cramping and she got to her feet, then bent over to stretch out her hamstrings. It wouldn't hurt, she thought, to go and talk to Al. Maybe she could do a feature story about how the recession was forcing many elders to take early retirement, and use Al's case as an example. Perhaps the FinCom would even revisit the issue and take another vote. Perhaps that would be enough to save his house from foreclosure—at the very least it would give him a bit more income with which to find another place to live.

Lucy drove slowly, not sure she was doing the right thing. Al Roberts had a bit of a temper. What if he turned on her? What if he didn't like her nosing around in his affairs? What if he thought she should mind her own business?

Turning down Bumps River Road, Lucy was struck once again by the obvious signs of poverty. Quite a few of the little houses were in disrepair; many sat in yards filled with discarded appliances and wrecked cars. When you were poor, she knew, you hated to let go of anything that might come in useful later. That wrecked car contained parts that could be used to repair another car. And that dryer that no longer ran? It cost money to leave it at the dump and maybe it could be used as a rabbit hutch? Or a food safe, especially in winter, when it could serve as a makeshift freezer. One man's trash was another's treasure, and that was nowhere truer than on Bumps River Road.

Al Roberts's little house, at the corner of Murtry Road, was neater than most and in fine repair. The roof was neatly shingled, and the porch contained only a couple of dark green Adirondack chairs. Lucy knocked on the door, and when there was no answer she cupped her hands around her eyes and peeked through the living room window. There was a plaid couch, a large picture of a stag hung above it, and a coffee table sat in the middle of the room on the braided rug. Squinting to see more clearly, she tried to make out the objects scattered on the coffee table, which appeared to be tools and wire and a broken cell phone.

What was he up to? she wondered, trying the door and finding it unlocked. Pushing it open, she called out a hello, and then his name. Her voice echoed through the empty rooms and, after hesitating a few moments, she stepped inside. Getting a closer look at the coffee table, she felt a rising sense of anxiety. This looked an awful lot like the makings of a bomb. She wasn't sure—maybe he'd just been trying to repair his cell phone, but who did that?

You just took it back to the service provider and got a new one, didn't you? Noticing a neatly folded square of paper, she picked it up, discovering that her hands were shaking. Opening it, she gasped in shock as she read the neat, block-style print.

Sorry, Lexie, but it's better this way. You'll get the insurance money, and maybe there'll be enough left of me to save my kidneys. Love always, Dad.

Suddenly dizzy, Lucy sat down hard in an armchair and immediately began searching for her cell phone, frantically scrabbling through the contents of her handbag. When she finally retrieved it she hit 9-1-1 for the police department.

"What is your emergency?" the dispatcher asked—Dot Kirwan's daughter Krissy.

"A suicide bomber." Lucy's throat was tight; she could barely get the words out.

"Location?"

Lucy went blank. "Oh, golly, I don't know. I found a note." She considered the possibilities. "I bet he's going to Downeast Mortgage. He's going to blow the place up, and himself, too."

"Do you have a victim?"

"Not yet. You've got to hurry. Get there before he does it."

"Who? Who's the bomber?"

"Al Roberts." Lucy couldn't believe this. What was the problem? They had to get a squad car over to Downeast Mortgage, immediately. It was a matter of life and death.

"You think he's going to blow up Downeast Mortgage?" Krissy sounded doubtful.

"And himself. I found a suicide note."

"But no body?"

"No! But I'm pretty sure . . . it says something about insurance money and that he hopes there'll be *enough left* of him to donate his kidneys."

"I don't have an available unit," Krissy said. "They're all out at an accident on the interstate."

"Call mutual aid," Lucy snapped. The town's rescue services had agreements with neighboring towns to provide help in an emergency."

"I can only call mutual aid for an actual emergency," Krissy explained.

"But that will be too late!" Lucy tried not to yell.

"Look, I'll send a unit over to Downeast as soon as one's available. That's the best I can do. I'm sorry, but it's not like anybody's bleeding in the street."

"Not yet," Lucy said, flipping her phone shut and running out to her car. She repeated those words as she sped over the narrow, snow-banked roads to town. "Not yet, Lord, please, not yet. Not yet. Let me get there in time. Please. Not yet."

It was eerily quiet when she pulled up in front of Downeast Mortgage. There had been no explosion, no boom, everything was in place. Normal. Then the door flew open and Elsie Morehouse suddenly bolted down the steps, and it wasn't normal at all. Elsie was standing on the sidewalk, without a coat in ten-degree weather, screaming bloody murder, tears streaming down her face. Lucy grabbed the blanket she kept in the car in case of a breakdown and ran to Elsie, wrapping the blanket around her shoulders. Then she produced her phone and called the police department again.

"Tell them," she ordered, holding the phone.

"He's got a bomb," Elsie sobbed. "He says he's going to blow up Mr. Scribner."

"Move away from the building," Krissy ordered, in a calm, cool, and professional tone of voice. "I've got mutual aid on the way, the bomb squad, too. But the highway's closed due to the accident. . . . Move away from the building."

Lucy closed the phone and dragged Elsie down the street. Her gaze fell on the car, which she had left right in front of the Downeast building. No way, she thought, this isn't going to happen. There was no way she was going to lose her perfectly good but aged car, not when the insurance would only pay book value. Enough was enough, she thought, her blood rising. This had to stop.

She told Elsie to stay put and she ran back up the street to the Downeast building. At the door she paused for a moment, took a deep breath, then pulled it open. She stepped into the reception area where Ben Scribner was sitting behind Elsie's desk, tied to a chair, white as a sheet. Al Roberts was standing behind him, strapping his homemade bomb to Scribner's chest. "I don't want to do this, but you wouldn't get the message," he was saying. "I'd wear it myself, but I don't want my kidneys to get damaged."

"Good thinking," Lucy said, frantically scrolling through the directory on her phone, looking for Lexie's contact info.

"What the hell are you doing here?" Roberts demanded. His eyes were bright, and his chin had a couple of days' worth of stubble.

Lucy held up the phone. "I'm calling your daughter, Lexie, so you can say good-bye." Her fingers were shaking; she'd missed the directory key and the phone was telling her to reset her ring tones.

"Get out of here!" Roberts ordered. "I'm gonna blow this place to kingdom come, and don't think I won't." He paused, then added in a self-satisfied tone, "This bomb is just as big as the one I sent to Marlowe, and you know how that worked out."

Hearing this, Scribner grew even paler, and Lucy could see that his chin was quivering.

Roberts chuckled, a harsh, staccato sound. "You'd think this bastard here would get the idea, but nothing changed. The foreclosures didn't stop. Not even when his precious niece got hurt."

"What?" Scribner blinked, like a blind man who had suddenly recovered his sight. "What's this about Florence?"

"He rigged an accident—the stage scenery fell on her." Lucy couldn't master her voice, which quavered. "She's okay," she added.

"I didn't know," Scribner said.

"You don't know anything, that's the problem," Roberts said. "It's just business to you, not people's homes and lives."

Lucy took a deep breath. "I'm not going anywhere until you talk to Lexie," she said, hoping she sounded a lot braver than she felt. "This will ruin her life, you know."

Roberts was quick to reply. "I'm doing it for her, and Angie."

"You're doing it to get back at Scribner and Marlowe and everybody you think did you wrong," Lucy said. "Lexie will never forgive you."

"She'll get the insurance money."

"They won't pay for suicide," Lucy said, not sure if this was true or not.

"I checked. They will."

"What if the bomb doesn't kill you?" Lucy asked. "What if you survive and then you have to go to jail? There'll be no insurance then."

There was a sudden burst of noise from outside—a siren cut short. It was a mistake, a terrible mistake. The noise alerted Roberts that police had arrived and time was running out.

"You can trust me on this—there'll be no survivors," Roberts said. "Which is why you should get out of here. I'll give you five. . . ."

Scribner's eyes rolled up into his head and his chin dropped forward onto his chest.

"Hold on, what's the rush?" Lucy was backing toward the door.

"You called the cops," Roberts accused. "I'm not bluffing. Get out if you know what's good for you. Four." He paused a long moment, then said, "Three."

Roberts's eyes were glittering, and he was panting, hyperventilating. Lucy was utterly convinced he intended to blow himself, Scribner, and herself, too, into eternity. Heart pounding, Lucy turned and made a dash for the door when she was deafened by an enormously loud bang. Glass shattered. There was smoke and she couldn't breathe. She was coughing and her eyes were filled with tears. Her throat stung and she couldn't swallow. She collapsed, falling to the floor, discovering she was completely helpless and couldn't move. She thought of Bill, of the kids, and then she didn't think of anything at all.

When she came to, she was in an ambulance, and there was an oxygen mask over her face. A medic was leaning over her and she grabbed his arm.

"You're gonna be fine," he said. "Teargas. You had a reaction to the teargas."

"Bomb?" Her throat was raw and her voice came out as a croak.

"Didn't go off," he said. "The bomber's in custody. The other guy's fine—he refused treatment." He glanced up as the ambulance braked to a stop. "Well, here we are," he said, as she was wheeled into the emergency room. "Is there somebody you want me to call?"

Lucy shook her head. Not yet. She wasn't ready to explain to Bill, not yet. Even worse, what was she going to tell Rachel?

Chapter Twenty

It was truly ridiculous, Lucy thought, standing in the wings of the Community Church stage and waiting for her cue, but she felt more nervous about going onstage than she did when she charged into Downeast Mortgage that morning. Then Tiny Tim took his place in front of the toy shop window and she bustled onstage in her numerous petticoats and long, full skirt, carrying an enormous shopping basket. She was no longer Lucy Stone but instead was Mrs. Cratchit, fussing about whether nasty old Scrooge would allow her husband to spend Christmas Day with his family.

She was momentarily knocked out of character when her entrance was met with enthusiastic applause and even a few cheers. Word must have spread about her role in preventing the bombing, she realized as she waited for the audience to quiet down so she could deliver her line. She refused to think about that; in fact, she'd spent most of the day concentrating on not thinking about the entire episode.

"What were you thinking?" Bill had demanded, when she was released from the emergency room.

"I didn't think," Lucy had admitted, her voice a croak because her throat was still sore. "I didn't want the car to get blown up." She paused. "I know it was crazy."

"I'll say," Bill had muttered.

"I hope my voice comes back before tonight," she'd whispered. "I need to stop at the pharmacy and pick up some lozenges and throat spray."

She spent a quiet afternoon watching TV and sucking on lozenges and spraying her throat, and by supper time found her voice was almost normal. The phone rang quite a bit but she ignored it, telling herself she was saving her voice. The truth was she didn't want to talk about the confrontation with Al Roberts, didn't even want to think about it. Most of all, she didn't want to think about what was going to happen to Al, who would most probably spend the rest of his life in jail for sending the mail bomb that killed Jake Marlowe. So instead she flipped through old magazines and ate ice cream for lunch and searched the On Demand menu for old movies. Bill came home early and whipped up a creamy fettuccine Alfredo for dinner, but she didn't have much appetite, due to stage fright.

When she arrived at the church at the appointed time, Rachel greeted her with a hug. "I called and called. . . . I was afraid you couldn't go on tonight."

"Sorry," Lucy said. "I didn't answer the phone because I was saving my voice."

"You're forgiven." Rachel embraced her again. "Break a leg!"

Everyone in the cast was keyed up, and Lucy was afraid their nervousness would get in the way of their performances, but was pleased to discover it had the opposite effect. They were all on the top of their game and outdid themselves, and when Tiny Tim delivered the final line, "God bless us, everyone!" the hall erupted in cheers and stamping and clapping that went on for a very long time. The cast took one curtain call after another until they finally gave up and just stood there, clasping hands and basking in the outpouring of emotion. It was as if actors and audience were joined in one huge explosion of happy Christmas spirit.

Afterward, when Lucy had changed out of her costume, she was met at the dressing room door by Sara, who was holding an enormous bouquet of white carnations and red roses.

"For you, Mom," she said. "You were great."

This was the last thing Lucy expected, and she gave her daughter a big hug. "This is so sweet," she said, tears stinging her eyes. "Thank you."

"I haven't been very sweet lately and I'm sorry," Sara said.

Lucy's shoulders were shaking—she was crying her heart out. After holding herself together all day, she found she couldn't stop sobbing. Bill was there, holding her, and Rachel, too. Sara and Zoe were hugging each other, also crying.

"There, there, it's okay," Bill said, soothing her, and Lucy was trying to apologize for being so foolish, but couldn't seem to stop crying. Until finally, she did.

"You've had a tough day," Rachel said, wiping her own eyes and handing Lucy a wad of tissues.

"Let's go home," Bill urged.

"No," Lucy said, wiping her eyes.

"No?" Bill was surprised.

"I'm starving. Let's get a pizza."

"Great idea!" Bill agreed. "Let's go!"

On Monday morning, Lucy's spirits were still high when she went to work, buoyed by the equally successful performances on Saturday evening and Sunday afternoon. Everyone agreed that *A Christmas Carol* was the Community Players' best production in the group's twenty-year history. Lucy suspected that the group members may have had short memories, as it seemed to her that they always believed their last show was their best. Still, she was smiling when she pushed the door open and set the little bell to jangling.

"Shhh," Phyllis warned, pressing a raised finger to her lips.

"What's going on?" Lucy asked.

"Ted's meeting with Ben Scribner," she said, looking serious. "They've been in the morgue for at least half an hour."

"What's it about?" Lucy asked.

"I don't know, but Scribner was all business when he arrived, demanding an immediate meeting with Ted."

"You don't think he's calling the note, do you?" Lucy asked anxiously.

"That would take some nerve," Phyllis declared, "after what you did."

"Don't think I won't tell him that to his face," Lucy said, raising her voice.

At that moment the door to the morgue popped open and Lucy braced herself for bad news. Which, considering the fact that the two men were smiling and shaking hands, she immediately realized would not be necessary.

"This is excellent," Ted said. "I'm going to put my best reporter on it right away."

"On what?" Lucy asked, furrowing her brows.

"Ben here is developing a plan to sell back all the foreclosed homes to their previous owners at the current, reduced value with new, affordable mortgages," Ted said. "He's also offering refinancing on favorable terms to all mortgagors, including me, who are struggling to keep up with payments due to the recession."

"What's the catch?" Phyllis asked, suspecting a trick.

"No catch!" declared Scribner, who for once looked relaxed and cheerful, actually seeming happy. "It's due to this lady here," he said, with a nod to Lucy. "She risked her life to save my miserable skin and it got me thinking. The truth is, Jake Marlowe and I got carried away. We got greedy. We didn't think about the people we were dealing with, and only thought about the money we were making. But when I was sitting there with that bomb strapped to my chest, I wasn't thinking about how much money I'd made. I was thinking that I'd wasted my life. And then you came, little lady, and gave me a second chance. Believe me, I've done some thinking and I'm not going to waste a single second of the time I've got left."

"That's . . . wonderful." Lucy was not quite sure what to say. It seemed to her that the earth had tilted on its axis and things were suddenly topsy-turvy.

"It's also good business," Scribner added, his blue eyes twinkling shrewdly. "What's the sense of a town where all the houses are empty and decaying? Truth is, I can't sell these properties. I've got too many on my hands and it's costing me money just to keep up with repairs and maintenance. Nope, this'll make our town, our community, stronger, and people will want to live in Tinker's Cove. Prices will start to go up again, and the sooner the better."

"It's too bad you didn't figure this out sooner," Phyllis said, adding a "hmph." "Coulda saved a lot of trouble."

Scribner's face clouded. "I know. I can't help but feel somewhat responsible for Al Roberts. I know there's no excuse for what he did, but Jake and I, well, we certainly contributed to his troubles. I'm going to make sure he gets a good lawyer, and I'm going to help his family any way I can, especially that little girl." He let out a big breath. "The truth is, I owe Roberts a huge debt. Jake Marlowe was a miserable person and now I'm free of him. I'm free to be myself and I'm determined to be a better person."

Hearing this admission, the three *Pennysaver* employees were dumbfounded. Finally, Ted spoke. "Is that for the record?"

"Hell, no!" Scribner said, his face reddening. "And don't think I won't sue!"

Then they were all laughing, laughing until their tummies hurt and they had to sit down, and finally they couldn't laugh anymore.

Word of Scribner's conversion spread through town as everyone was eager to share the story of his remarkable change of heart. Christmas spirit seemed to grow with every telling; people smiled and laughed and greeted each other cheerily as they hurried to complete their preparations for the big day. The people in line at the post office to mail cards and packages shared jokes and stories, people shopping for last minute presents waited patiently for the salesclerks to ring up their purchases, and shoppers at the IGA paused to chat with each other and exchange favorite holiday recipes. In Lucy's memory there had never been such a merry Christmas season in which everyone enjoyed such cheerful fellowship and genuine goodwill.

Lucy almost hated for it to end, but the number of remaining doors on the Advent calendar was down to two. And then there was only one and it was Christmas Eve. The presents were all bought and wrapped, the cookies baked, the tree decorated. The whole family went to church for the candlelight service; Patrick was adorable as a little lamb in the Christmas pageant. Afterward they all went on to Florence Gallagher's open house, bearing covered dishes for the potluck supper.

Florence's house was packed with people, but the jolly crowd was eager to make room for more. The table was loaded with delicious things to eat, carols were playing, everyone was eating and drinking and toasting the holiday. There was a hushed moment when Ben Scribner appeared, carrying a huge cooked turkey from

MacDonalds' farm store, and Florence rushed to greet him with a big hug. Then others joined in the greeting, shaking hands and patting him on the back. Watching, Lucy thought he probably hadn't been greeted so warmly in many years, perhaps never.

She was chatting with Miss Tilley, telling her that the Angel Fund had swelled to over five thousand dollars thanks to a couple of large donations, including one from a secret giver she suspected was actually Ben Scribner, when she noticed Rachel and Bob, kissing under the mistletoe. She gave Miss Tilley a nudge, and the old woman smiled at the sight. "I've been so worried about Rachel," she said. "But now it looks like things are back on track."

"Moving in the right direction, anyway," Lucy said, taking a sip of eggnog.

A few minutes later Sue popped in, saying she couldn't stay long because she was on her way to New York. "Geoff's in surgery," she said. "He's getting a new kidney. He's part of a donation chain, which is actually the longest one they've done so far, with more than twenty exchanges. And guess what? Little Angie's getting a kidney, too! She's actually getting Sidra's kidney." She laughed. "My daughter's kidney is coming home to Tinker's Cove! Imagine!"

"It seems a toast is definitely called for," Miss Tilley said, tapping her glass with a spoon.

Everyone fell silent, waiting expectantly, as Miss Tilley called for all to "charge their glasses," using the old-fashioned phrase. When everyone's glass had been filled, she raised hers: "To friends and family, to Tinker's Cove . . . God bless us, everyone! Merry Christmas!"

With family tensions intensifying in Tinker's Cove, part-time reporter Lucy Stone could really use some time off the grid. But after she RSVPs to an unconventional celebration on remote Holiday Island, Lucy realizes that disconnecting from reality comes at a deadly price. . . .

Lucy doesn't know what to expect as she arrives on a private Maine island owned by eccentric billionaire Scott Newman, only that the exclusive experience should make for a very intriguing feature story. An avid environmentalist, Scott has stripped the isolated property of modern conveniences in favor of an extreme eco-friendly lifestyle. A trip to Holiday Island is like traveling back to the nineteenth Century, and it turns out other residents aren't exactly enthusiastic about living without cell service and electricity. . . .

Before Lucy can get the full scoop on Scott, she is horrified to find one of his daughters dead at the bottom of a seaside cliff. The young woman's tragic end gets pinned as an accident, but a sinister plot unfolds when there's a sudden disappearance. . . .

Stuck on a clammy island with murder suspects aplenty, the simple life isn't so idyllic after all. Now, Lucy must tap into the limited resources around her to outwit a cold-blooded killer—before it's lights out for her next!

Please turn the page for an exciting sneak peek of Leslie Meier's next Lucy Stone mystery

INVITATION ONLY MURDER

coming soon wherever print and e-books are sold!

Chapter One

The little bell on the door to the *Pennysaver* newspaper office in the quaint coastal town of Tinker's Cove, Maine, jangled and Lucy Stone looked up from the story she was writing about the new recycling regulations—paper, glass, and plastic would not be accepted unless clean and separate, no more single stream—to see who had come in, and smiled broadly. It was her oldest and best friend, Sue Finch, looking every bit as stylish and put-together as usual with her dark hair cut in a neat bob and dressed in her usual summer uniform: striped French fisherman's jersey, black Bermudas, espadrilles, and straw sun hat. Skipping a greeting, Sue pulled an envelope from her straw carryall with a perfectly manicured hand and declared, "Guess what came in today's mail? It's an invitation to die for!"

Lucy, who was used to playing second fiddle to Sue, raised an inquisitive eyebrow. She was also dressed in her usual summer uniform: a freebie T-shirt from the lumberyard, a pair of cutoff jeans, and neon orange running shoes. She hadn't bothered to style her hair this sunny June morning, thinking that it looked fine, and had missed a stubborn lock in back that curled up like a drake's tail feather. "Do tell," she said, leaning back in her desk chair.

"Just look at the paper," cooed Sue, pulling a square of sturdy card out of the velvet-smooth lined envelope. "Handmade. And the lettering is hand-pressed. And, oh, the address on the envelope was done by a calligrapher," she continued, handing the envelope to Lucy. "Trust me, something like this doesn't come cheap."

"Is it a wedding invitation?" asked Lucy, admiring the elaborate, swirling script on the front of the envelope. Turning the envelope over and studying the back, she recognized the formally identified senders: Mr. and Mrs. Scott Newman. Everybody in town had heard of the Newmans, who had recently bought an island off the coast and proceeded to hire every contractor in the county to restore the property's long-abandoned buildings, including spending a fortune to save the magnificent barn that was considered an architectural masterpiece.

"No, it's for a 'night to remember,' that's what they're calling it," replied Sue, handing Lucy the invitation. "It's to celebrate the Newman family's donation of the island to the Coastal Maine Land Trust and to thank all the people who worked on the restoration."

"I bet we're invited, too, then," said Lucy, whose husband, Bill, a restoration carpenter, had been the lead contractor for the project. "The invitation's probably in the mailbox at home."

"It's going to be fabulous, if this invitation is any indication," said Sue. "No expense spared and believe me, the Newmans have plenty of expense to spare."

Lucy knew all about Scott Newman; she'd written a profile of the billionaire venture capitalist when rumors started floating that he was interested in acquiring Fletcher's Island for his family's summer vacations. When she interviewed him, she'd been somewhat surprised to learn that he was a keen preservationist who was interested in keeping the island completely off the grid and was refusing to install modern innovations, allowing only the original nineteenth-century technology. He planned to collect rainwater in a cistern, use a primitive electric generation system, and cook on an enormous woodstove, all of which were considered wonderfully advanced when the island was developed by lumber tycoon Edward T. Fletcher. When Lucy asked if this wasn't rather impractical, Newman had replied that it was modern life that was impractical, citing scientific studies linking climate change to human activity. "The old ways were much kinder to the environment, and face it, we've only got one planet, there's no planet B," he declared. "We've got to take care of Earth, or we're all doomed."

Some of the locals hired to work on the restoration project had a good laugh over Newman's proclaimed environmental steward-ship, as restoring the nineteenth-century structures required using thousands of kilowatts of electricity, provided by gas-greedy portable generators. His insistence on using authentic materials such as lath and horsehair plaster rather than sheetrock, and searching out recycled flooring, windows, and doors, not to men-tion hardware, had required lots of workers who had to be ferried to and from the island on power boats that burned gallons of fos-sil fuel. "It's like the cloth versus disposable diapers thing," Bill had told her. "Sure, the disposables fill up the landfill, but wash-ing the cloth diapers uses water and energy. It's kind of six of one and half a dozen of the other when it comes to the environment."

Most controversial was the restoration of the immense barn, which alone was estimated to cost at least two million dollars. The huge number of cedar shingles required for the roof and siding had created an industry shortage that sent the price skyrocketing and shook the commodities market. The *Pennysaver* had received numerous letters to the editor protesting the shingle shortage and arguing that there were better ways to spend so much money. One writer proposed restoring the sprawling local elementary school, for example, which he claimed was a prime example of 1960s ar-chitecture.

Locals had also refused to be bamboozled by Newman's sup-posed generosity in donating the island to the land trust, while re-serving his right to retain it for his own use during his lifetime. It was true that he'd also preserved the rights of the Hopkins family, long-term residents of the island, to remain there, but again, only during his lifetime. And while the agreement set limits on how the island could be used, and was intended to preserve the island's en-vironment in perpetuity, the gift had come with plenty of strings attached and had garnered a large tax deduction for the New-mans, a fact that many writers of letters to the editor had also pointed out.

Despite the controversy, however, the party was eagerly antici-pated by everyone who received an invitation, and that included land trust board members, contractors, local officials, and media, which was pretty much a who's who of the entire town. The question that was on everyone's lips as the big day drew closer was, how were the Newmans going to pull off such a big party while preserving their nineteenth-century lifestyle? Sue Finch wasn't the only one to wonder, "Are we going to have to swim there? And are we all going to be sitting in the dark, huddled around a campfire, toasting wienies on sticks?"

Lucy was pondering that very question when she drove home from work a week or so later and found a rusting and dented old Subaru parked in her driveway. The car was missing a couple of hubcaps, had a crumpled front fender, and the glass on a rear window had been replaced with duct tape and a plastic grocery bag. Continuing her examination with the keen eye of an investigative reporter, she noticed the registration tag was out of date, and so was the required state inspection sticker.

Climbing the porch steps of the antique farmhouse that she and Bill had renovated and entering the kitchen, she was greeted by her aging black Lab, Libby. Arthritis didn't stop Libby from rising stiffly from her comfy dog bed and wagging her tail in welcome, earning her a treat and a pat on the head from Lucy.

Voices could be heard in the adjacent family room and Lucy stuck her head in, curious to learn who owned the Subaru. "Oh, hi, Mom," said her daughter Zoe, quickly disentangling herself from the arms of a shabby-looking fellow with a stubbly, three-day beard. "Mom, this is Mike Snider."

Mike didn't bother to get up from the comfy sectional where he was reclining, or even to lift his head from the throw pillow it was resting on. "Hiya," he said, raising one hand and giving a little flap.

Lucy glared at him, taking in his shaved head, tattooed neck, and torn jeans that clearly needed a wash. Worst of all was the T-shirt with a message that was clearly unprintable for a family newspaper like the *Pennysaver*. "Hiya, yourself," said Lucy, turning on her heel and marching out of the room, leaving no doubt that this was a situation that did not meet with her approval.

Back in the kitchen, Lucy got busy on dinner, noisily pulling pots out of cabinets and slamming them down on the stove. She was filling a pasta pot with water when the couple appeared, holding hands, and were met with a low growl from Libby, who watched Mike through narrowed eyes and flattened ears from her doggy bed. She was clearly considering getting to her feet, painful though it would be, when Mike reached for the knob and pulled the door open. "Catch ya later," he said, before stepping through the doorway. Moments later, Lucy heard the roar of the Subaru's unmuffled engine, which sputtered out a few times before catching and carrying Mike away.

"Who is he? And where did you meet him?" Lucy demanded, turning to face Zoe. Zoe was her youngest, at twenty, and every bit as pretty as her older sisters, Elizabeth and Sara. She shared Elizabeth's dark hair and petite build, but had Sara's peachy skin and pouty lips. Today she was glowing, no doubt the result of her aborted activities on the sectional.

"At school, Mom," she answered, referring to Winchester College, a local liberal arts university where she was a junior, currently majoring in French after trying political science, psychology, and art history. She had hopes of joining Elizabeth in Paris, where her older sister was working as an assistant concierge at the toney Cavendish Hotel. "Mike's a TA in the computer science department. He's really smart. Even Sara says so," she added, bolstering her case with a reference to the family's doubting Thomas, who was a grad student at Winchester.

"He might be smart," admitted Lucy, "but he's certainly not socialized. Libby has better manners, and she's a dog."

"He's a little rough around the edges," said Zoe, beaming, "but Libby only gets up to greet you because she knows you'll give her a treat."

"That was unkind," retorted Lucy, bending over the dog and scratching her behind her ears. "You love me, you really, really love me, don't you?"

The dog yawned and settled her chin on her front paws.

"And that car," said Lucy, reverting to the subject at hand. "The registration's elapsed and so has the inspection, which is understandable since I doubt it would pass. It definitely needs a new muffler."

"Mike's got better things to think about than bother with stuff like that. He's working on a computer game that's going to be revolutionary, that's going to change everything."

"Well, if you ask me, he'd be better off taking a shower and changing into clean clothes."

"Oh, you don't understand anything!" declared Zoe, storming up the stairs to her room, where she slammed the door.

"What was that all about?" asked Bill, stepping into the kitchen and kissing his wife on the cheek, before depositing his empty lunch cooler on the counter. Lucy smiled, noticing that Libby didn't get up for him, but did manage to thump her tail a few times.

"Zoe's got a new boyfriend," explained Lucy. "A real loser."

"She'll learn," said Bill, opening the refrigerator door and extracting a can of beer. "She's got to figure these things out for herself."

"Just you wait until you meet him," said Lucy, tearing up lettuce for salad. "I bet you'll change your tune then."

Bill sat down at the round, golden oak table and popped the tab on his beer. "Whaddya think about this island shindig?" he asked, with a nod at the invitation that was stuck to the refrigerator door with a retro magnet advertising Moxie soda pop. "I'm not gonna have to wear a jacket and tie, am I?"

"No jackets, no ties," said Lucy, repeating the verdict Sue had handed down when Lucy called for advice. "It's resort casual."